note from the author

I really considered **CHECKMATE** to be the end of my storytelling as far as the world of **NOUGHTS & CROSSES** was concerned. But then Tobey Durbridge, a minor character from **CHECKMATE**, played a dirty trick on me. He started whispering in my ear, telling me his story and he wouldn't shut up until I wrote it all down!

Writing **NOUGHTS & CROSSES, KNIFE EDGE** and **CHECKMATE** had already taken up over seven years of my life. I considered that quite enough and was more than ready to move on to other stories. Tobias Durbridge had other ideas.

The idea for **DOUBLE CROSS** entered my head in part as a response to the spate of real-life gun and knife crimes happening to too many of our teenagers. It is very hard, when you are surrounded by that world, not to become a part of it. Tobey tries desperate to stay away from the world of gangs and violence, but he doesn't succeed. **DOUBLE CROSS** is a brutal book, but given the world it is trying to reflect, it had to be.

I wanted **DOUBLE CROSS** to feel more like **NOUGHTS & CROSSES** in tone, but for some progress to have been made in society since the days of Callum and Sephy in the first book of the series. **DOUBLE CROSS** focuses on Tobey's relationship with Callie Rose and this story tells of his deep need for vengeance when something terrible happens to her. This is a story of revenge, retribution and redemption.

I hope you enjoy it.

Will there be another book in the series? Are any of the characters whispering in my ear? Funny you should ask that . . .

malorie blackman

DOUBLE CROSS

www.malorieblackman.co.uk

DOUBLE CROSS

malorie
blackman

CORGI

DOUBLE CROSS
A CORGI BOOK 978 0 552 55960 7

First published in Great Britain by Doubleday,
an imprint of Random House Children's Publishers UK
A Random House Group Company

Doubleday edition published 2008
Corgi edition published 2009
This edition published 2012

1 3 5 7 9 10 8 6 4 2

The Random House Group Limited supports the Forest Stewardship Council
(FSC®), the leading international forest certification organization. Our books
carrying the FSC label are printed on FSC®-certified paper. FSC is the only
forest certification scheme endorsed by the leading environmental organizations,
including Greenpeace. Our paper procurement policy can be found at
www.randomhouse.co.uk/environment.

MIX
Paper from
responsible sources
FSC® C016897

Random House Children's Publishers UK,
61–63 Uxbridge Road, London W5 5SA

www.**randomhousechildrens**.co.uk
www.**totallyrandombooks**.co.uk
www.**randomhouse**.co.uk

Addresses for companies within The Random House Group Limited
can be found at: www.randomhouse.co.uk/offices.htm

THE RANDOM HOUSE GROUP Limited Reg. No. 954009

A CIP catalogue record for this book is available from the British Library.

Printed and bound in Great Britain by CPI Group (UK), Croydon, CR0 4YY

'The latest book in Malorie Blackman's
Noughts and Crosses series,
and potentially the best' ***Independent***

'Blackman "gets" people . . . she "gets"
humanity as a whole, too. Most of all,
she writes a stonking good story'
Guardian

'Few writers can sustain a plot as
well as Malorie Blackman'
Sunday Telegraph

Malorie Blackman is acknowledged as one of today's most imaginative and convincing writers for young readers. *Noughts & Crosses* has won several prizes, including the Red House Children's Book Award and the Fantastic Fiction Award, has been adapted for the stage by the Royal Shakespeare Company, and is soon to be a graphic novel. Malorie has also been shortlisted for the Carnegie Medal.

In 2005 Malorie was honoured with the Eleanor Farjeon Award in recognition of her contribution to the world of children's books, and in 2008 she received an OBE for her services to children's literature. She has been described by *The Times* as 'a bit of a national treasure'.

For Neil and Lizzy,
Mum and Wendy – with love.

And big thanks to Annie and Sue –
what would I do without you?

Lizzy, this is the book you asked me for.
Sort of!

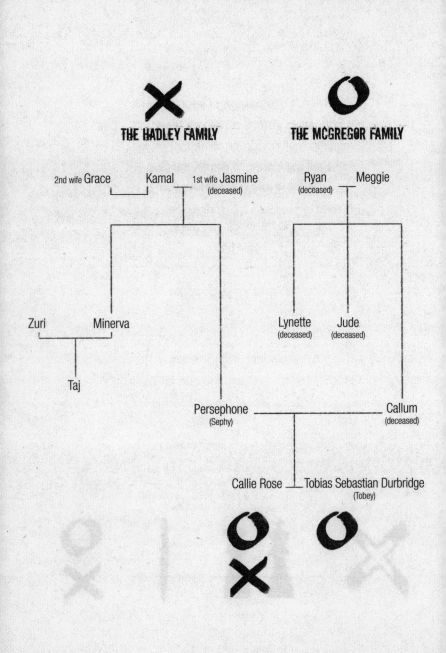

The mere imparting of information is
not education. Above all things, the effort must
result in making a man think for himself . . .
When you control a man's thinking you
do not have to worry about his actions.
You do not have to tell him not to stand
here or go yonder. He will find his
'proper place' and will stay in it.

Carter G. Woodson

. . . What would he do,
Had he the motive and the cue for passion
That I have?

Hamlet – Act II, Scene II

Prologue

The Glock 23 felt heavy and seductively comfortable in my hand. The pearl stock, warmed by my body heat, fitted snugly against my palm. I now held McAuley's custom-made semi automatic.

A real, honest-to-God gun in my hand.

A proper killing machine.

Or was that me? Where did I stop and the gun start? I really couldn't tell any more.

Now what?

McAuley lay on the floor, the previous torrent of blood that had been gushing from his nose now reduced to a trickle. His once crisp, white designer suit and matching designer shirt lay twisted in an ungainly manner around him. The random splashes of red on McAuley's suit resembled an abstract painting. I stared into one particular bloodstain in the middle of McAuley's chest.

'It's more like a Rorschach ink blot than a painting,' I thought inanely.

It reminded me of my own face in skewed profile.

Now what?

McAuley's blond hair hung like day-old spaghetti around his face. It was streaked with random red highlights which occasionally dripped onto his shoulders. Red highlights donated involuntarily by McAuley's last victim. The assorted blood splatters on his jacket alone would fill at least a couple of chapters in a forensic science textbook. I wondered whether the SOCO – scene-of-crime-officer – lucky enough to be assigned to McAuley's body would be an art-lover?

I glanced towards the office door. The heavy, arrhythmic banging on it was beginning to get to me. The noise vibrated straight through my head, making it hard to think. Making a slow fist with my free hand, I dug my short nails as deeply as I could into my palms. I had to resist the temptation to let the frenetic drumming on the door dictate the pace of my thinking.

Think, Tobey. Think.

There had to be a way out of this.

But even as the thought pushed its way into consciousness, I knew I was deluding myself. Turn and face the truth.

Time had run out.

'Durbridge, dig yourself a grave and crawl into it 'cause you are *dead*. D'you hear me?'

I aimed a kick between McAuley's legs and allowed myself a small, satisfied smile as the blood-spattered scumbag howled, curling up like the letter C. Small pleasures. There was nothing and no one in McAuley's office to stop me getting a few kicks in. And if I was going to die . . . The smile faded from my face as I watched McAuley writhe on the floor.

At the sound of their boss's roar of pain, McAuley's men pounded even harder on the office door. Luckily for me, McAuley's paranoia had seen to it that the door was solid, reinforced hardwood. It would hold for a while, but even that door couldn't indefinitely withstand the kind of punishment McAuley's thugs were dishing out. I reckoned I only had a couple of minutes before it gave way completely and then the door wouldn't be the only thing in trouble.

Could I do it? Could I really go through with this?

Hell, yes.

There was a time, less than six weeks and over a lifetime ago, when I'd thought a person could only sink so low. Sooner or later, you went down just as far as you could and after that, the only direction was up. But, just as loving Callie had shown me that Heaven had no roof, hating McAuley and the Dowds had taught me that Hell had no basement.

McAuley started to laugh. Even though his hands were cupped around his groin and he was still curled up, he found this funny. Creepy McAuley, the hard man. My finger stroked at the trigger. White fire blazed through my veins instead of blood, burning away all thought, all feeling. All fear. I had a gun in my hand, like a syringe pumping one hundred per cent pure, unadulterated adrenalin straight into my heart.

The frustrated hammering on the door was growing more insistent.

'You're dead, Durbridge,' McAuley said again, 'and there's nothing you can do about it.'

I pushed the gun barrel against the older man's head, drawing small circles around his temple. McAuley froze.

'Then that makes two of us, you bastard,' I stated softly. 'That makes two of us.'

SIX WEEKS
EARLIER

The Rise . . .

one. Tobey

'Tobey, I was er . . . thinking that maybe you and me could . . . er . . . you know, go to the pictures or go for a . . . er . . . you know, a meal or something this weekend?'

Godsake! Couldn't she get through one sentence, just one sentence, without sticking umpteen 'er's and 'you know's in it first?

'I can't, Misty. I'm already going out.' I turned back to my graphic novel – a humorous fantasy that was better than I had thought it would be when I'd borrowed it from the library.

'Oh? Where're you going?'

'Out.' I frowned, not bothering to look up from my book.

'For the whole weekend?'

'Yes.'

'Out where?'

I turned in my chair to look at her. Misty tossed back her brunette hair with blonde highlights in a peculiarly unnatural move that had obviously been practised to death in front of her bedroom mirror.

'Out where?' Misty asked again.

This girl was stomping on my last nerve now. She'd

been asking me out all term and I'd always found some reason to turn her down. Couldn't she take a hint? Miss I'm-too-sexy-for-myself leaned closer in to me, so close that I had to pull back or she'd've been kissing my neck.

'I'm going out with my family. We're visiting relatives,' I improvised.

I'm too nice, that's my trouble, I thought sourly. Why on earth didn't I just tell her that I wasn't interested in a date or anything else for that matter? For one thing, hugging her would be like trying to cuddle a chopstick. I liked curves. And even if I did fancy her – which I didn't – there was no way I'd ever get it on with an ex-girlfriend of my mate, Dan. That was a definite no.

'Maybe the er . . . erm . . . following Saturday, then? We could maybe . . . er . . . go out then if you'd like?' said Misty.

Rearrange this sentence: hell – freezes – over – when.

The classroom door swung open and Callie Rose strolled into the room. She stopped momentarily when she saw who was sitting in her chair. Scowling, she strode over to Misty.

'D'you mind?' Callie asked.

'I'm talking to Tobey.'

'Not from my chair, you're not,' Callie shot back.

'Er . . . can't you find somewhere else to sit until the lesson starts?' Misty wheedled.

Uh-oh! I held my breath. Callie let her rucksack slip from her hand to the floor as her eyes narrowed. She was one nanosecond away from moving up to Kick-arse Condition 1.

'Misty, you need to get up off my chair,' Callie said softly.

'I'd shift if I were you,' I advised Misty.

Much as I found the thought of a cat-fight over me appealing, I didn't fancy Callie getting into trouble and then giving me grief for what was left of the term.

Misty huffed and stood up. 'Callie, I'm going to remember this.'

'Remember it. Take a photo. Break out your camcorder. I don't give a rat's bum. Just move.' Callie stepped aside so that Misty could squeeze by, before flopping down into her now vacant seat.

'Damn cheek!' Callie carried on muttering under her breath as she dug into her bag for the history books required for our first lesson. She turned to look at Misty, who was now back in her own chair.

'If looks could kill, I'd be seriously ill,' Callie said as she turned to me, annoyance vying with amusement to colour her eyes more hazel than brown. Every time she was upset or angry, her eyes literally turned greener. It was one of the many things about her that got me going. She had the most expressive eyes I'd ever seen. Chameleon-like, they changed colour to reflect her every mood.

'Every time I want to sit down next to you or be within half a kilometre of you, I can't move without tripping over that girl first. What's up with that?'

I sucked in my cheeks in an effort not to chortle. One snicker and Callie would bite my head off. I tried for a nonchalant shrug.

'So what did Miss Foggy want this time?' Callie asked.

'Why d'you insist on calling her Miss Foggy?' I laughed.

I know it was mean, but 'Miss Foggy' really suited Misty.

'That's her name, isn't it? Besides, I'm not the one who chose to name her after a type of weather, and if the shoe fits . . .' Callie said pointedly. 'And you haven't answered my question.'

'She was inviting me out this weekend,' I replied.

I watched keenly for her reaction.

She shook her head. 'Damn! Misty's got it bad.'

'Are you jealous?' I asked hopefully.

Callie's eyebrows shot up so far and so fast, she got an instant face-lift. 'Are you kidding? I just think it's pitiful. She's been chucking herself at you all term and you haven't exactly been rushing to catch her, have you? In fact, most of the time you just fold your arms and let her drop on her face over and over again. You'd think she'd have got the message by now.'

'So you are green-eyed.' I grinned.

'Tobey, I don't know what you're taking, but you need to get yourself to rehab – quick, fast and in a hurry.'

'My girl is jealous.' My grin broadened. 'It's OK, Callie Rose. There'll never be anyone for me but you.'

'Go dip your head,' Callie told me.

'I mean it.' I crossed both my hands over my heart and adopted a ridiculously soppy expression. 'I give my heart . . . to you.' I mimed placing it carefully on the table in front of her. Glowering, Callie picked up her pen and mimed stabbing my heart on the table over and over again.

I burst out laughing, but had to smother it as Mr Lancer, the history teacher, entered the room. Callie started muttering all kinds of dire threats and promises under her breath the way she always did when I got under her skin.

And I loved it. It was music to my ears.

Callie quickly suppressed a laugh as the buzzer sounded for the end of the lesson. I'd spent the last fifty minutes passing her silly notes and making *sotto voce* remarks about Mr Lancer's newly bald head with its deep groove down the middle. It now resembled a certain part of the male anatomy and there was no way I could let that pass without comment. Callie had been in smothered fits of the giggles throughout most of the lesson. I loved making Callie laugh. God knows, she'd done little enough of that since her nana died in the Isis Hotel bomb blast. Callie was reaching for her rucksack on the floor and I'd barely made it to my feet when we had company.

Lucas frickin' Cheshie.

Misty wasn't the only one who couldn't take a hint. OK, so I still wasn't quite sure what to call my friendship with Callie, but I knew what Lucas and Callie weren't – and that was an item. She wasn't Lucas's girlfriend any more, so why did he persist in sniffing around her? Being older than us, he wasn't even in our class. But he must've seen Callie through the classroom window – and now here he was, lingering like an eggy fart. Smarmy git.

Completely ignoring me, Lucas said softly, 'Hi, Callie Rose, how are you?'

Callie's smile faded. She was instantly wary. I was grateful for that, if nothing else.

'I'm fine, Lucas. How are you?'

'Missing you.' Lucas smiled.

Callie searched for something to say, but unable to find

anything, she merely shrugged. I glared at Lucas, but he wasn't going to give me the satisfaction of acknowledging my presence.

'Ignore me all you want, but if you think I'm leaving you alone with Callie . . .' I projected my hostility towards him through narrowed eyes.

'I'm so glad to see you smiling again, Callie Rose. I'm glad you're getting over the bereavement in your family,' said Lucas.

The light in Callie's eyes vanished, as if a great, dark cloud had swept across the face of the sun. Callie's grandmother had died two months before, but Callie wasn't over it. Sometimes I wondered if she'd ever be truly over it.

'And you were so close to your nana Jasmine, weren't you?' Lucas continued.

I glanced at Callie before turning back to Lucas. A Cyclops with a pencil in his eye could see that Callie was getting upset. Lucas would have to be stupid not to see the effect his words were having. And Lucas was a lot of things, but stupid wasn't one of them.

Callie said nothing.

'Callie Rose, if you ever need to talk about your grandmother and how she died or anything, then I'm here for you. OK?' Lucas smiled. 'I just want you to know that I'm your friend. I'll always be your friend. If you need anything from me you only have to ask.'

Dismayed, I turned to Callie again. With a few well-chosen words, Lucas had not only knocked Callie to the ground, but then danced all over her. Her face took on the haunted, hunted look she always wore when thinking about Nana Jasmine. Her eyes glistened green with the tears she desperately tried to hold back. Callie hated for anyone to see her cry. My hands clenched into fists at my side. I had to hold myself rigid to refrain from smacking Lucas a sizeable one.

Lucas put his hand under Callie's chin to slowly raise her head. He was still ignoring me. 'Just think about what I said. I mean every word.' He smiled again, then sauntered off to join the rest of his crew waiting in the doorway for him.

Callie and I were alone in the classroom. I chewed on the inside of my bottom lip. What to say? What to do? I was so useless at this kind of thing.

'Callie . . .' I turned to her in time to see the solitary tear balanced on her lower eyelashes splash onto her cheek.

'Callie, don't listen to him. He was being a git,' I began furiously.

Puzzled, Callie turned to me, her eyes still shimmering. 'He was just trying to be kind.'

'Kind, my arse. He did that deliberately . . .'

'Tobey, what's wrong with you?' Callie whispered. 'You know what, I can't cope with this now.'

'Callie, can't you see what Lucas was up to? He was . . .'

But I was talking to myself. Callie was out the door, leaving me in the classroom.

Alone.

BOMB BLAST VICTIM IDENTIFIED AS JASMINE HADLEY

Jasmine Hadley was yesterday finally identified as one of the victims of the bomb blast at the Isis Hotel. The former wife of Kamal Hadley, ex-MP, was killed five days ago, but it has taken this long to make a positive identification. A source working for the forensic science division of the police force stated, 'The damage to her body was so severe that a combination of dental records and DNA testing had to be used to conclusively identify the victim.' One other unidentified Nought male was also killed in the hotel explosion. The police are making strenuous efforts to establish the identity of this Nought in an effort to ascertain his connection, if any, to the blast. This latest outrage is suspected to be the work of the Liberation Militia, although as yet no one has claimed responsibility. Jasmine Hadley's ex-husband, Kamal Hadley, whose party crashed so ignominiously in the general election held last week, was unavailable for comment.

two. Callie

Try as I might, I just couldn't let go of that newspaper clipping. It was either in my hand or in my head. And it never left my heart. Nana Jasmine's photo shone out alongside the article about her death. I recognized the photo. It was the one with Nana in the middle, my mum and me on her right and Aunt Minerva, Uncle Zuri and cousin Taj on her left. It was at least ten years old and in it Nana looked so happy, so proud. I'd asked Nana about the photo once. I'd only been five or six at the time, so to be honest, I couldn't remember that much about it. And what's more I didn't think the photo was all that, but Nana kept a framed copy on the night table beside her bed, a framed copy on her piano and a smaller version of the same photo in her purse. Taj looked like he'd just finished picking or was just about to pick his nose, Mum appeared a bit fed up and Aunt Minerva was looking at Uncle Zuri instead of straight at the camera. But Nana didn't care.

'I have my whole family beside me,' she told me when I asked her about it. 'That's what makes it so special.' Then she added wistfully, 'The only one missing was your dad, Callum.'

But for the article, they'd chopped off the rest of us,

showing only Nana. The worn, folded seams of the newspaper clipping in my hand had made the paper as fragile as a cobweb, but that didn't stop me from re-reading it. Every day.

Every. Damn. Day.

I tried to imagine what had gone wrong. Had Nana Jasmine tried to return the bomb to Uncle Jude? Is that what happened? Did she go to his hotel to throw it in his face? Did it go off accidentally? Did Uncle Jude detonate it deliberately? Did Nana Jasmine try to run and hide? Was there a struggle? Did they fight over it? If so, then Nana Jasmine wouldn't have stood a chance. She took my bomb and, knowing her as I did, she would've relished handing it back to Uncle Jude. But there's no way she could have known just how dangerous Uncle Jude was. The bomb got him – but it got Nana Jasmine too. How did I even begin to forgive myself for that?

Uncle Jude and Nana Jasmine were dead because of me.

Because of my bomb.

I'd made the thing, put it together with rage and hatred in equal measure. I look back on my life of a few months ago and it's like being a voyeur in someone else's twisted mind. I look into my memories and see the thoughts and actions of a stranger, but a stranger with my face.

'Nana Jasmine, I'm so sorry . . .'

Sorry. Such a ridiculous, inadequate word.

Sorry.

I despised that word.

I buried my face in my hands. I didn't want to see or be seen. At times like this, I just wanted to crawl away and find a place to hide from the world. Hide from myself.

Was there any such place? I would've given everything I owned to find it.

Little moments of forgetfulness. I guess that is all I can hope for now. Tiny fragments of moments when I can forget how my nana died. Sometimes I'll be cooking with Mum and she'll smile at me, or I'll be arguing with Nana Meggie and she'll huff at me, or I'll be doing my homework with Tobey and he'll deliberately wind me up, and in those wonderful, amazing moments, I forget. But such times are few and far apart.

I couldn't even blame Uncle Jude for what had happened. Not really. My uncle was a soldier. A terrorist. A sad, angry, bitter man. Since his death, I'd learned so much about him and the things he'd done. The Internet and my local library had provided all the details I could ever need. I wish I'd taken the time to find out more about him when he was alive. Tobey tried to warn me, so did Lucas, but I wouldn't listen. I thought that Uncle Jude was the only one who understood me, the only one who was honest with me. How could I have got everything so wrong? I'm obviously not very perceptive. And the pitiful thing is that, until Uncle Jude's death, I thought I could tell everything about a person within three glances. God, I was such a fool.

All those lies Uncle Jude told me. All that hatred filling him to overflowing. Hatred that he couldn't wait to pour into me. And I let him. And even though I'd made the bomb at his instigation, that still didn't help when I thought about the way he'd died. Him and my nana . . .

One of the first things this new government did when they came into power a couple of months ago was abolish capital punishment – for good this time, I think. It was abolished over sixty years ago, then brought back five years before I was born after a public referendum indicated that the majority of people in this country wanted Liberation Militia terrorists and those convicted of serious crimes to be executed. This current government claimed that extreme circumstances made for bad laws – like the reintroduction of capital punishment and imprisonment without trial. But part of me just wants to walk into the nearest police station, give myself up and take whatever is coming to me. And if this country still had capital punishment then even better.

'Nana, I wish you could hear me. D'you hate me? You can't hate me any more than I hate myself. I never meant for you to get hurt. I swear that was never my intention. My head was all over the place then. I didn't know who I was or where I belonged. I do now. But I never wanted that knowledge to come at the cost of your life. Mum keeps saying that I mustn't blame myself – it was all down to Jude. But I'm not stupid. Nana, I'm so sorry.'

'Callie Rose, didn't you hear me calling you for dinner?' Mum stood in the doorway, her hands on her hips. 'We're all waiting for you downstairs.'

'Is Nathan here?' I asked, folding up the newspaper article again and placing it in the drawer of my bedside table.

Mum's hands fell to her sides as she walked further into the room. I heard her sigh softly.

'Yes, he is. I invited him for dinner. Callie, d'you . . . d'you mind about Nathan and me? We haven't really had a chance to talk about him since . . . since your Nana died.'

'I don't mind at all, Mum,' I said honestly. 'In fact, I'm glad that you've got someone.'

Mum scrutinized my face, as if trying to gauge how many of my words were true. I met her gaze without flinching or even blinking. I meant every one.

'Something's bothering you about me and Nathan, though,' she said slowly.

I had to smile. Mum was so astute when it came to reading my expressions, far more astute than I had ever given her credit for.

'I was just thinking . . . what about you and Sonny?' I couldn't help asking.

Sonny was Mum's old boyfriend. The only trouble was, he was still in love with her and trying to win her back, even though Mum had told him she was going to marry Nathan.

'Sonny and I were the past. Nathan and I are the present.'

'Does Sonny know that?'

'I've told him often enough over the last few weeks.' Mum sighed again. 'It's time for all of us to move on. I can't live in the past. I won't.'

Was Mum trying to convince me – or herself?

'Mum, are you and Nathan going to get married, or live together or what?'

'I don't know. We talked about getting married, but we might have to put our plans on hold,' Mum admitted. 'Nathan's business isn't doing too well and he's now thinking it might be better to wait.'

'And how d'you feel about that?'

'I think he's right. I . . . we don't want to rush into anything.'

'Mum, Nathan loves you, so why hang about?' I said. 'Life is too short.'

'I guess so,' Mum said faintly.

Was that doubt I heard in Mum's voice? It certainly sounded like it. I wasn't quite sure I got Mum and Nathan's relationship. It seemed to be an affair more of the head than the heart, at least on Mum's part. Sometimes, when she thought no one was watching, a sombre, thoughtful look clouded her eyes, and in those moments, I knew she was thinking about my dad. Once I'd been ashamed that my dad was Callum McGregor, a hanged terrorist. Not any more. And now that I knew just how much Mum and Dad had loved each other, I wasn't surprised that Mum found it hard to give her whole heart to anyone else. It gave me a strange feeling to know that my dad loved Mum and me so much, had sacrificed so much for us, even before I was born. A strange, warm, comforting, sad feeling.

Mum and I both stood in a brooding silence, until Mum opened her arms. I immediately stepped into her embrace. We hugged. Mum stroked my hair. Loving moments turned into peaceful minutes.

On my sixteenth birthday, I was reconciled with my mum. And I lost my nana. It wasn't fair. It just wasn't fair. For a while, after Nana's death, I was so scared that my new relationship with my mum wouldn't last, that things would go back to the way they used to be between us, but thankfully, that hadn't happened. Oh, we'd had the odd hiccup and a couple of shouting matches, but Mum always allowed me to cool off and then she'd come and hug me and tell me that she loved me and my anger would burn away like early morning summer mist. I don't know how I would've coped with Nana Jasmine's death if it hadn't been for Mum. Tobey and Nana Meggie let me know they were there for me, but Mum had never left my side. At Nana Jasmine's funeral she'd held my hand throughout the service to let me know that I wasn't alone. And not once did Mum throw it back in my face that I'd made the bomb that killed Nana Jasmine. Not once. With each smile, each hug, every stroke of my hair she kept trying to tell me that she'd forgiven me. But how could I accept Mum's forgiveness when I knew I'd never forgive myself?

'I love you very much, Callie Rose. You do know that, don't you? And there is nothing on this earth or beyond that could ever change that,' Mum said softly.

I found that so hard to believe, but Mum's face was an open book as she looked at me.

'D'you promise?' I whispered.

Mum smiled. 'Cross my heart.'

'Mum, I love you.'

Mum hugged me harder at that. And I wished . . . I wished so much that Nana Jasmine was still around to see it.

three. Tobey

'Raoul, you blanker, get up!' Dan put his hands to his mouth and yelled so hard, my head started ringing.

'Godsake, Dan! My frickin' eardrums.'

'Sorry,' Dan said with a grin.

I sniffed around his shoulders before recoiling. 'Damn, Dan! Your pits are howling!'

Dan raised his arm to sniff at his armpits. He looked like a bird covering its head with its wing.

'Oh yeah, you're right!' he said, surprised.

I pushed his arm back down before he gassed everyone on the pitch. 'You do know that armpits can be washed, don't you?'

'I forgot to put on some deodorant today.' Dan grinned.

I mean, Godsake!

Our Monday evening football match was well under way. The July evening was still bright and uncomfortably hot. Within minutes of running around, my shirt was sticking to my armpits and my back. Dan and I were on opposing teams, both on the wing, supposedly marking each other. But mostly we were talking. We watched patiently as once again pain stopped play. Raoul was *still* rolling on the ground, clutching his lower leg like he was in a death scene in some bad straight-to-DVD movie.

The Wasteland, where we were playing (or Meadowview Park, as the local authority had it listed on their website), wasn't as busy as usual. Only enough guys had turned up for a seven-a-side football match, hence the reason I was playing. With a full complement of players I was usually relegated to one of the park benches. The Wasteland was a flat patch of rectangular land, with a children's adventure playground at one end and a flower garden enclosed by knee-high blunt railings at the other. Except the flower garden hadn't had any flowers in it for close to two decades, according to my mum. The criss-cross paths of concrete were now used by roller-bladers, skate-boarders and trick cyclists. Anyone using the park for any wheeled activity did so at their own peril – so the numerous signs posted around the place stated. I often wondered if that included pushing baby buggies and pulling shopping trolleys? Closer to the garden than the adventure playground was the football pitch, surrounded on all sides by rusting wire-mesh fencing. It wasn't much, but it was ours. And the football pitch was kept clean of dog crap and clear of litter. All the footballers in the neighbourhood saw to that.

Raoul finally stood up and shook out his leg. About time! The ball was kicked to me and I displayed semi-adequate skills by getting rid of it asap – and to someone on my own side too, which made a change.

'So what d'you reckon?' Dan flashed his new watch about a centimetre away from my nose, twisting his forearm this way and that. It was so close I couldn't see it properly. Was he trying to poke out one of my eyeballs with the thing or what? And eau-de-stinky-pits was repeatedly punching at my nose again.

'The watch?' Dan prompted. 'What d'you think?'

'Does it shoot down low-flying aircraft?' I asked, taking a quick step back.

Dan pursed his lips. 'Not that it says in the manual.'

'Does it contain the nano-technology to drain a subdural haematoma?'

'That's the next model up from this one.'

'Then it tells the time, the same as my cheap effort,' I said.

'Yeah, but mine looks good and cost more than everything you have in your bedroom and then some.'

'Could you lower your arm before you kill me?' I pleaded.

Dan took pity on me and did as I asked.

'Your watch, did you buy it or acquire it?'

'I bought it, you blanker. And I have the receipt and sales certificate to prove it.' Dan frowned. 'You sound just like a Cross copper.'

I held up my hands. 'Hey, it's no skin off my nose where you got it from.'

'Well, I bought it with cash money, made from earning a living rather than dossing at school like some people I could mention.' Dan's frown lessened only slightly.

'And is it accurate?'

'Of course. It's guaranteed to lose only one second every hundred years.'

For the kind of money Dan must've forked out for his watch, it shouldn't lose any time at all – ever. And surely it did more than just turn two strips of arrow-shaped metal through three hundred and sixty degrees periodically?

'So what else does it do?' I asked.

'Nothing else. It's not some digital toy out of a cracker,' said Dan, preening. 'This is pure class.'

'But all it does is tell the time,' I repeated.

'Damn, Tobey. How are we friends? You don't have a clue,' Dan said, exasperated.

'It's a lovely watch, Dan,' I sighed. 'If I ever get married, it'll be to your watch.'

'Feel free to bugger off and die at any time.' Dan scowled.

I grinned. 'Only if you'll bury me with your watch over my heart.'

'Tobey . . .'

'OK, OK. I'll shut up now.'

Dan gave a reluctant smile. He was still annoyed at my lack of open fawning appreciation for his watch, but he'd get over it. I glanced over to the sidelines, wondering which of the girls standing there was Dan's latest girlfriend.

'How's your love life?' I asked.

'Non-existent, thank God!' Dan's reply was heartfelt.

'How's your sex life?'

Dan sighed. 'Non-existent, unfortunately. Talking of sex . . .' His eyes lit up. 'How's Callie Rose?'

Damn! I should've seen that coming. 'Dan, don't start.'

'What?' said Dan, acting the innocent. 'I'm just asking if you two are still an item?'

'We are,' I said firmly.

''Cause if you're not,' Dan continued as if I hadn't spoken, 'I wouldn't mind some of that. She's extra fit – for a Cross.'

'Callie isn't a Cross.'

'She ain't one of us either,' said Dan.

'Then what is she?' I asked, annoyed.

'Extra fit – I already told you.'

We stood in silence for a while. Why had I been so quick to deny that Callie was a Cross? Maybe because I still couldn't quite believe she'd chosen me over Lucas. I couldn't help wondering if she'd wake up one morning and realize . . . realize that she could do better.

'Tobey, chill. I was only messing with your head a bit.'

'I know. Remind me to pay you back for that later,' I replied.

If only I had the money for watches and bracelets and all the things Callie deserved. If only . . . I took hold of Dan's arm to give his watch a proper look.

'That is one cool watch, though,' I admitted.

'You could afford a watch like this too, you know. And more besides,' said Dan.

'You know my job only pays minimum wage.' I shrugged. My Saturday job of almost a year was roughly twenty per cent selling mobile phones and eighty per cent listening to customers whinge. It just about paid for my school stationery and a few textbooks, and that was it. 'So at that rate I should be able to afford a watch like yours in about – what? Five or six years?'

'Selling mobile phones isn't the only game in town,' Dan said pointedly.

'It's the only game I'm interested in playing,' I replied.

'Aren't you tired of having nothing?'

And that was just it. Because I *was* tired of having no money. All the things I could do, all the things I could *be* if I had money kept slipping into my head like mental gate-crashers.

'You could just make deliveries like me,' Dan continued. 'Dropping off a package here, picking up a parcel there.'

For the first time, I started to listen. 'I don't know . . .' I began.

Sensing hesitation like a shark sensing blood, Dan pounced. 'Tobey, it's easy money. Think of all the things you could do if you were holding folding. You could save up to get out of this place for a start.'

'Is that what you're doing?' I couldn't help but ask.

'Nah. If I had your brains, then maybe. But it's this or do something like take food orders and nothing else for the rest of my life. And guess what, that don't appeal. But with your smarts, Tobey, in two years you could be anything you wanted 'cause you'd have the cash to do it.'

Packages . . . deliveries . . . Dan made it sound so innocuous. So very easy.

'Who d'you deliver these packages to?' I asked.

'The people who need them or want them or should have them.'

'And who d'you deliver these packages for?' As if I couldn't guess. 'Cause it sure as hell wasn't the post office.

Dan smiled. 'Does it matter? I pick up the packages and the addresses that each one should be taken to and that's all I know or care about. Tobey, think of the money you could make. I'm tired of having your broke arse trailing behind me all the time.'

Waving the two most eloquent fingers on each hand in his direction, I thought about what he'd said.

If I had money, Callie and me . . .

I cut the thought off at the pockets. I couldn't start thinking that way. I'd go mad if I started thinking that way.

But after all, it was just deliveries.

The odd parcel delivery couldn't hurt.

Unless I got caught . . .

I shook my head, trying to dislodge all visions of cascading money. 'I don't think so, Dan. I just want to go to school and keep my head down.'

'School.' Dan snorted derisively. 'I hope your school isn't going to make you forget who you are.'

Inside, I went very still. 'And what is that exactly?'

'You're a Nought, Tobey. And going to your fancy school isn't going to change that.'

'I wouldn't want school to change that.'

'Some of our friends already think you've sold out. It's up to you to prove that you haven't,' Dan told me.

Sold out? What the——?

'I don't have to prove a damned thing, Dan.'

'Hey.' Dan raised a placating hand. 'I'm only telling you what some of our friends are saying about you.'

Friends? My eyes narrowed as I thought of my so-called friends.

Dan stepped back from the look on my face. 'I'm just saying, you have to be careful that your brain doesn't get smart at the expense of your head getting stupid.'

'Wanting to do something with my life isn't selling out,' I said, banking down my resentment with difficulty. 'Wanting something more than all this isn't selling out.'

'Tell that to Raoul and——'

'No, I'm telling it to you. That crap doesn't even make it to ignorant. Going to school so I can think for myself, so I can make something of myself, is selling out now, is it? We don't need the Crosses to keep us down with that kind of thinking. We'll do it to ourselves.'

Dan took another step back. 'Listen, I was just—'

'The next time Raoul or anyone else starts spouting that bollocks, you send them to me to say it to my face,' I said furiously. 'I'm going to go to school and keep my head down until I can get out of Meadowview and that's all there is to it.'

'Tobey, wake up. That's not even an option,' Dan stated. 'And McAuley can protect you. He's great, almost like a dad to me. Besides which, he's one of us.'

One of us . . .

McAuley was a gangster, pure and not so simple. But his being a Nought was enough mitigation as far as Dan was concerned. McAuley fancied himself as a Nought kingpin. He took his cut of every crooked deal that went down in Meadowview – that's if the Dowd family didn't get in first. The Dowds were the Cross family who ran all the illegal activities in Meadowview that McAuley didn't already have his grubby hands on. Or maybe it was the other way around. Who could tell? They both offered protection to any lowlife who pledged allegiance. Bottom-feeding Noughts tended to join McAuley. Scumbag Crosses joined forces with the Dowds. Criminal fraternity segregation.

A while ago some Nought hooli called Jordy Carson tried to take on the Dowds. He vanished like a fart in the wind. And waiting in the wings to take his place was his second-in-command, Alex McAuley. Everyone said McAuley had learned from his old boss's mistakes. McAuley had no intention of 'disappearing'. So he made sure everyone knew his name and his game. Trouble was, McAuley was even worse than Carson. I guess that for the Dowds and McAuley there was plenty of misery around for everyone to make a profit. Those of us who had to live in Meadowview – the poorer Crosses and us Noughts with a whole heap of not much – saw to that. One of us? Yeah, right.

'The point is, the no-man's-land you want to live on doesn't exist, not for either of us,' Dan continued. 'If you don't pick a side soon, you'll be nowhere.'

'Yeah, but Nowhere looks like a peaceful place to be – especially around here,' I said.

'Nowhere will get you dead,' said Dan. 'On the inside you'll be protected, you'll have back up. McAuley looks after his own. What d'you have at the moment?'

'I have you, Dan.' I smiled.

'Very funny.'

'I know you'll always have my back.'

'Don't rely on that, Tobey,' Dan said quietly.

My smile faded. Dan and I regarded each other.

'Oi, you two! This ain't a chat show,' Liam, the captain of my side, yelled out. 'Kick the damned ball.'

Dan and I both made a show of getting back in the game, but although my body ran around the Wasteland trying to look useful, my head was elsewhere. When pain stopped play again, I stood slightly behind Dan as we both waited for the game to restart and the ball to head our way.

I couldn't help thinking about what he had said.

I felt like I'd been asleep and had just been kicked awake. I'd always assumed that Dan would have my back and vice versa. But Dan running errands for McAuley had evidently changed all that. I'd blinked and missed it. Hell, I'd blinked and my world was suddenly a lot more complicated.

Years ago, I thought that getting into Heathcroft High School was it, the be-all and end-all of my existence. I'd thought that all I needed to do was keep my head down and my grades up to make it through. After school, I'd go to university and at the end of all that, I'd be something big in the financial markets. I had it all figured out. I wanted a job that'd make me tons of money. But that was stuff for the future. I'd forgotten that I still needed to make it through the here and now first. The present was filled to overflowing with McAuley and the Dowds and needing to belong to a gang just to be able to walk the streets. The present was all about friends who had your back and turning away from those who didn't. The present was hard work, not to mention dangerous.

I realized Dan had been right about one thing.

The no-man's-land I was clinging to wasn't firm ground at all, but quicksand.

four. Tobey

At school the next day, Dan's words kept ringing in my head. I walked home alone because Callie had a singing lesson after school, and I still couldn't forget what Dan had said. I'd barely shut the front door before my sister Jessica emerged from the living room. She was wearing faded jeans and a long-sleeved red T-shirt that was now more faded pink than any other colour. Her light-brown hair shot out in gelled spikes around her head. Her lips were already pinned back into a mocking smile. My heart sank. I knew what that look meant. I took off my school jacket and tossed it over the banister.

'How come you're not at work?' I frowned.

'It's my day off,' Jessica replied. 'What's with that face?'

'I'm having a bad day, Jessica. So back off.'

'How about we meditate together?' my sister suggested.

And the sad thing was, she was serious. She's into all that hippy-dippy, transcendental, rental-mental bollocks. Or at least, she was this fortnight. A month ago kick boxing had been the way to cure all of society's ills. And the month before that it'd been colour therapy. Apparently the reason I was so permanently irritable was because I wore too much blue and ate too much red and brown.

I walked past her towards the kitchen. 'Jess, I'm not in the mood for your nonsense this evening, I'm really not.'

'Tobey, what you need to do is submerge yourself in Lake You,' said Jess, following me. 'Get to know your true self . . .'

Lake You . . . Godsake!

'Jessica, get away from me,' I said.

'What's the matter, Tobey? Girlfriend giving you trouble?'

'Feel free to drop dead at any time.'

'Ooh! Sounds like you didn't get any under or over the clothes action today,' Jessica laughed.

I glared at her, but from the huge, moronic grin on my sister's face, she still didn't get the message. It took a lot to bring Jess down.

'Just how far have you two gone anyway?' she asked.

I went over to the fridge. If I ignored her, maybe she'd take the unsubtle hint and bog off.

'Come on, Tobey. Tell all. Inquiring minds want to know,' Jessica teased.

I opened the fridge door. 'Jess, what can I get you? Orange juice? Lemonade? Your own business?'

'Your business *is* my business,' Jessica informed me.

I grabbed a can of ginger beer and pushed past her.

'Tetchy!' Jessica called after me. 'Someone isn't getting any.'

Godsake! This was all I needed. First Dan. Now my sister.

'Jessica, go away,' I told her.

'Definitely not getting any,' Jessica called after me.

I headed out into the hall just as the front doorbell sounded. Being closest, I opened the door.

'Hi, Tobey. Ready to work on our history project?'

I frowned, moving out of Callie's way as she swept past me. I sniffed silently. Callie was wearing the cinnamon-spice perfume I'd given her last Crossmas. She never wore anything else now. Damn, but I loved the way she smelled.

'I thought you didn't want to do it until tomorrow.' I frowned. 'And what happened to your singing lesson?'

'Mr Seacole is ill today so my lesson was cancelled. I tried to find you at lunch time to tell you, but you were wearing your cloak of invisibility.' Callie graced me with an accusatory stare. 'I just got home and Nathan is round *again*, and he and Mum are making cow eyes at each other, so it was stay at home and be sick down my blouse or come and see you.'

'I take it I only just won?'

'It *was* close,' Callie agreed with a smile.

Callie wore her dark-brown hair tied back in her usual plaited ponytail. She'd changed out of her school uniform and into denim jeans and a light-pink, tight pink, long-sleeved T-shirt. A figure-hugging, curve-clinging, light-pink, tight pink, long-sleeved T-shirt. Dark-blue sandals showed off her unpainted toenails. She was five feet seven and most of it seemed to consist of legs. Legs and boobs. I forced myself to focus on Callie's face before she decked me. She started up the stairs to my bedroom.

'You got our history notes?' she asked, turning back to me.

I dug out my memory stick from my trouser pocket and waved it at her. I didn't go anywhere without it. 'It's all on here.'

'Hi, Callie. You OK?'

'I'm fine thanks, Jessica.' Callie smiled at my sister. 'Tobey and I are doing our history project together.'

'Enjoy,' said Jessica. 'Just remember to keep the bedroom door open and at least one foot on the floor at all times.'

'Ha frickin' ha,' I called out as I followed Callie up the stairs.

Jessica cracked up laughing. She really thought she was funny. My sister was older than me by only eighteen months and although she worked part-time as a hairdresser, she still lived at home. On her wages, she'd be at home until she was a pensioner. I wasn't going to settle for that. No way.

There'd come a day when I'd have money dripping out of cupboards. I'd promised myself that from the time I started at Heathcroft. Success was all a matter of mental attitude. And I had the right stuff. I was going to be rich – by any means necessary. Any legal means, of course. No way was I going to make my money with the shadow of prison hanging over my head. At least the shadow of the noose had now been permanently removed. And about time too.

Callie turned at the top of the stairs to grin at me. I was well aware of how much me and my sister amused her. But Jessica knew exactly what to say to wind me up. Especially when she teased me about Callie. Actually, now I come to think about it, only when she teased me about Callie.

Once we reached my bedroom, I must admit, I closed my bedroom door a little louder than was absolutely necessary. I was more than a little annoyed at my sister's dense comments. What if Jessica's teasing put Callie off coming to my room at all?

'Tobey, should I strip off and lie on the bed?' Callie asked. 'That'd really give your sister something to tease you about!'

'Yes, please.' I grinned. If only.

'You wish,' Callie scoffed.

Yeah, I did actually.

'I can dream, can't I?' I gave a mock sigh.

I took off my school shirt and put on a clean white T-shirt pulled out of my wardrobe. Thanks, Mum! I decided to leave my school trousers where they were, on my body. I wasn't in the mood to listen to Callie tease me about my 'skinny uncooked chicken legs', as she kept calling them. I sat at my tiny desk, connecting my memory stick to the family computer, which stayed in my room as I used it the most.

'Tobey, all joking aside, why don't you tell your sister we're just friends?' Callie stated.

I glanced away so that Callie couldn't see my face. 'I've tried, but she didn't believe me.'

'I've told Jess more than once that you don't think of me as anything but a pain in the neck, but she didn't believe me either. I wonder why?' Callie frowned, sitting down on my bed. She glanced at her watch. 'How long d'you reckon today?'

'I give her three minutes.' I sighed, for real this time. 'And counting.'

'Nah. I reckon seven minutes, fifteen seconds,' said Callie. 'Your sister will want to wait until she thinks we're really into something before she bursts through the door.'

'You're wrong. Two or three minutes at the most. Any longer and she'll be afraid she's missing something.'

'What has she heard about you that I haven't?' Callie frowned. 'Bit of a fast lover, are you?'

Careful, Tobey . . .

'I've never had any complaints,' I replied.

Callie regarded me, a strange expression on her face before she turned away to trace the lightning-fork pattern on my duvet. 'Well, we're not all as easily pleased as Misty.'

Misty? What on earth did this have to do with Misty? More to the point, what did it take to please Callie? Had Lucas already given her some idea about that? Our conversation was spiralling away from me dangerously. Nothing I said now would come out right, so better to say nothing.

Callie stood up and headed for my desk. 'Let's see all this cool stuff you've come up with for our project then.'

I tried to access the files on the memory stick, but the computer didn't even recognize that a memory stick was connected. After trying twice more, I tried to access it directly via the operating system. Weird symbols and hieroglyphics scrolled across my screen.

'Tobey, where are my files?' Callie's voice was low, her question rhetorical. She could see as well as I could what had happened to her files.

'This isn't my fault,' I said quickly. 'I only bought this thing last month. It's supposed to be state of the art.'

'State of the another-word-beginning-with-A more like,' Callie said in disgust. 'Tobey, I really don't want to have to do all my sections again.'

'Didn't you take a backup of your notes?' I said.

'Not the latest version, no. I changed some stuff at school before loading it onto your memory stick, then I deleted the files afterwards. And what about all the film clips you added and the other stuff you said you did at school? Are they gone too?'

I nodded. 'I'll just have to do it all again. Don't worry, it'll only take me a couple of hours.' I tried to reassure Callie, knowing full well I'd lost a lot more than two days' work. It would take ages to add all the graphics and re-edit all the film clips I'd included in our presentation. Godsake!

'What happened to your memory key? Did you microwave it or something?'

'Or something.' I pulled the wretched thing out of the USB port and scowled down at it.

'Take it back to the shop you bought it from and get a refund,' said Callie.

I nodded, not holding out much hope. I had no idea where I'd put the receipt. I returned the memory stick to my pocket, mightily cheesed off. Maybe the shop would exchange it without the receipt as I didn't want my money back.

Callie headed back to my bed. 'Well, we can still carry on with the rest of our report. And I'll update my sections when I get back home.' She glanced at her watch as she sat down. 'If your sister is about to burst in on us, you'd better come over here and sit next to me. After all, you wouldn't want to disappoint her.'

I did as requested. I sat so close that our arms and thighs were squashed against each other. I could feel Callie's body heat warming me through my clothes.

'What d'you smell of?' I asked, sniffing at her neck.

'Why? Is it minging?' Callie sniffed at her wrist doubtfully. I suppose she had the same perfume I'd given her on her wrists as well. And of course she didn't reek. She smelled lovely.

'You smell of biscuits,' I told her.

Callie's eyebrows shot up. 'Thanks.'

'That's a compliment.'

Looking deeply unimpressed, Callie said, 'Tobey, a few words of advice. Don't tell Misty or any of your other girlfriends that they smell of biscuits. Tell them they smell of flowers, that they smell sexy, erotic, exotic, good enough to eat even, but not that they smell of biscuits.'

'But I like biscuits,' I protested.

'Is this another of your wind ups?' Callie said suspiciously.

I grinned at her, deciding that no answer would be the best answer in this case. I really did love the way Callie smelled and she smelled of biscuits, but I suspected if I pressed the issue, she'd go home and flush the rest of my Crossmas present to her down the loo.

Callie sighed and lay back on her elbows. I wished she wouldn't do that. It made her boobs stick out even more. Once again I had to force myself to concentrate on the area above Callie's shoulders.

'Fancy watching a film once we've finished our homework?' Callie asked.

I was instantly on my guard. 'What kind of film?'

'*Angie's Mystery* is on at nine o'clock,' Callie suggested.

'What's that?'

'It's a contemporary social drama set in—'

'Never mind where it's set. No.' The words 'social drama' were all I needed to hear to make up my mind on that one.

'Or there's *Lovelorn* on at the same time on Channel—'

'Hell, no! If it's got "love" in the title, I'm gone,' I told her straight. 'Can't we watch an action or a horror film?'

'What if I told you *Lovelorn* is an action musical.'

An action musical? Yeah, right.

'Nice try!'

Callie sighed. 'What's wrong with a romantic drama?'

'Callie, I'm not watching some drippy film that's all angst and sickly sweet sentimentality so you can sit there sighing and sniffing next to me,' I said. 'No way.'

'There's nothing wrong with the odd cathartic cry,' Callie informed me. 'I learned that when Nana Jasmine died.'

'Well, I wouldn't know,' I replied.

Callie tilted her head as she regarded me. 'No, you wouldn't,' she agreed. 'Didn't you cry when your dad left?'

'Nope.' I wasn't going to cry over that. It wasn't like he hadn't run out on us before. And if he ever came back, he was bound to do a runner again. Crying over him would be like crying because the sun rose each morning.

'When was the last time you cried?' Callie asked with a frown.

'Years and years ago,' I said truthfully.

'There's nothing wrong with crying. Sometimes it's the only thing that makes things better.'

'I'm not even sure I know how any more.' Crying wasn't me. 'Can we change the subject please?'

Callie sighed, but did as I asked. 'So what d'you reckon your sister's excuse for bursting in on us will be this time?'

I shrugged. 'Who knows? Getting back one of her magazines?'

'Hunting down her college homework?' said Callie.

Like I'd keep any of her wigs or hairdressing stuff in my room. Jess went to hairdressing college just one day a week, but the stuff she brought home was pushing me and Mum out of the house.

'How about checking up on Cuddles, my pet snake . . . ?' I suggested.

'Despite the fact that Cuddles died over five years ago,' Callie pointed out wryly.

'Ah, but Jessica can commune with friendly spirits,' I reminded her. 'Snakes included.'

'Your sister is a woman of many talents.'

'If only that included minding her own—'

The door was flung open, its hinges protesting with a severe creak.

'I hope I'm not disturbing you two. Did you call me, Callie?' said Jessica. 'I thought I heard you call me.'

Callie and I exchanged a look. I didn't even have to glance down at my watch.

'I win,' I said softly.

'I did call you actually,' said Callie. 'I'm just about to make mad, passionate love to your brother and I wondered if you'd like to watch?'

'Ugh! Callie, I thought you had better taste.' Jessica's face contorted at the thought.

'Nope. I love the way Tobey and I get down and dirty. Watch us, Jessica. You might learn something.'

Callie pulled at the back of my T-shirt, almost strangling me in the process. I fell backwards before my Adam's apple was cut in two. Callie pounced. That's the only word for it. She pounced. Before I could blink, her lips were on mine and her tongue was darting into my mouth. And damn, it felt good. I wrapped my arms around her and pulled her closer.

'That is so gross.' Jessica's voice barely registered. 'I'm outta here. You two have moved beyond sad into pitiful.'

I was vaguely aware of my bedroom door being slammed shut, but I didn't care. I pulled Callie closer still. Blood was rushing round my body, then to one particular part of my body. Callie smelled good, tasted great and felt even better. It took a few seconds to realize that Callie was trying to push away from me. I reluctantly let her go.

'We can stop now,' Callie told me, her warm breath fanning over my face. 'Your sister has gone.'

Sod my sister.

'Let's hope that cures her of her nosiness. For some reason Jessica didn't fancy the idea of watching you get your leg over.' Callie laughed.

'Godsake, Callie. Even I'm grossed out by that idea.' My lips twisted at the thought.

Callie sat up abruptly. Her smile had vanished. 'Making love with me would gross you out? Thanks a lot.'

I stared at her, then sat up myself. 'I meant . . . that's not what I meant. I meant about my sister being present.'

Callie's head tilted to one side. 'It's OK, Tobey. I get it. I'm not Misty.'

Was she nuts?

'I don't want you to be Misty. God forbid.'

Callie shrugged. She dug into her school rucksack and took out a couple of books. I sighed inwardly. She didn't believe me. Or was she winding me up as payback for earlier? Because if so, she was doing a first-class job. Usually I was streets ahead of her when it came to teasing, but over the last few months, the scales had been tipping in the other direction. She got to me like no one else.

'Callie, there's nothing going on between me and Misty,' I said.

'If you say so.' Callie still didn't look me in the eye.

'I do. And it means a lot to me that you believe that.'

'Why?'

'It just does,' I said, trying and failing to keep the impatience out of my voice. 'OK?'

'OK,' replied Callie. 'Ready to work on our school project now?'

Well, if she wanted to concentrate on homework, then I could too. Two could play that game.

'Now, about the Second World War – what point of view d'you want to write our newspaper article from? The POV of us winners or the losers?' Callie asked.

'I don't mind,' I said. 'You choose.'

'Which is what you always say whenever I ask you to make a decision,' said Callie, the faintest trace of irritation creeping into her voice. 'If you made an actual decision for yourself, would you get a nosebleed, or maybe a brain aneurysm?'

'What's wrong now?' I asked, exasperated.

Callie contemplated me, her head tilting to one side again. 'Tobey, what are we? Apart from uncomplicated?'

'We're friends,' I replied at once. 'We're good friends. Aren't we?' What was Callie getting at?

Callie nodded. 'I guess so.'

'Don't you know?'

'I'm waiting for you to figure it out, so you can tell me,' said Callie.

'What does that mean?'

'I'm waiting for you to figure that one out as well.' Callie smiled. 'Let's get on with our homework.'

Sometimes I don't understand Callie. At all.

I'm a reasonably smart guy, but I just don't get her.

Damn, but she's complicated.

five. Callie

Sometimes I don't understand Tobey. At all.

He's the smartest guy I know, but he just doesn't get it.

Damn, but he's dense.

six. Tobey

'Tobey, you still haven't told me about your careers meeting. How did it go?' asked Mum.

'Fine.' I grinned, putting down my glass of orange juice. 'Mrs Paxton was really encouraging. She reckons any university in the country will take me with the grades I can achieve if I don't let my work slip. And she's personally going to write my university reference.'

Mum smiled faintly at my enthusiasm, but I couldn't help it. Both Mrs Paxton, our head, and Mr Brooking, the school careers advisor, had basically told me that the world was mine, as long as I was prepared to keep working for it. It didn't matter what Dan and some of my friends outside of school said: I was going to go to university. Every time I thought of my future, it made me smile. And nothing and no one was going to hold me back or even break my stride.

My family were all sitting down having breakfast together, which was kind of rare as Mum's a nurse at Mercy Community Hospital, so she worked shifts. Jessica was still half asleep and picking at her fried egg and bacon. My plate was almost empty and I was eyeing Jessica's egg. If she wasn't going to eat it then I had room left in my stomach, as long as the egg wasn't cold. But if I took too much interest in Jess's breakfast, she'd gobble it up and swallow it down just to spite me.

'Mum, it's actually going to happen.' My smile widened.

'Hopefully,' said Mum.

'Not hopefully. It's gonna happen,' I amended. 'I'm going to university.'

Mum just shrugged.

'To do what?' asked Jessica.

'Something that'll make me a lot of money like an Economics or a Maths degree or maybe Business Studies with Information Technology,' I replied.

'That'll make you money?' Jessica said sceptically.

'Working with money makes money,' I said. 'Everyone knows that.'

'Don't you want to do a degree because you're interested in the subject rather than for the money you'll make at the end of it?' asked Jess.

'I'm being practical.'

'What would you do if you didn't have to worry about a job at the end of it?' my sister asked.

'I dunno.' I'd never really thought about that as it wasn't going to happen. 'Maybe Politics or Law. Something like that.'

'Tobey, don't set your heart on university,' Mum said gently. 'I can't afford three or four years' worth of fees, not on top of what I have to fork out to Jessica's college. I just don't have the money.'

'I know, Mum. Don't worry, I've got it all worked out. I'll take out a student loan to cover the tuition fees. And I'll start saving the money I earn from every holiday job I have from now on.'

'It's not just tuition fees,' Mum warned. 'You'll have to pay rent and bills and buy books and food.'

'University is for the rich or those prepared to be in debt until they're middle-aged. It's just another way of keeping us Noughts down,' Jess added.

'Isn't it more of a poor-versus-rich thing?' I frowned.

'Please,' Mum groaned. 'No politics at the breakfast table. It's too early.'

Going to university had always struck me as more of a social class thing than a race thing. As long as I wasn't going to one of those snooty, snotty 'historical' universities where they interviewed you first to ascertain your family's bank balance and social standing, what was the problem? If I got good grades in my end-of-school exams and I paid the tuition fees, surely that was enough for most universities and they wouldn't care that I was white? Mrs Paxton reckoned I had the right stuff to get into any university in the country. So, enough. I wasn't going to give voice to my doubts or argue the point. I was in too much of a good mood.

'Jess has a point, though,' said Mum. 'I mean, is that what you really want? To be in debt until your hair turns grey?'

'That's why, after university, I'm going to get a job that makes a lot of money so I can pay off the loan faster,' I said.

My good mood was rapidly evaporating. Mum and Jessica were only trying to make sure that I knew what I was letting myself in for, but they were both beginning to jump up and down on my nerves.

'Why d'you want to go to university anyway?' Jessica sniffed.

'Because I can,' I snapped. 'Because less than twenty years ago, a Nought going to university was unheard of, unless they were super rich. Because that door is open and all I have to do is walk through it.'

'For all the good it'll do you,' Jessica muttered.

'And that right there is why you'll be doing the same job in the same place for the same wage in thirty years' time.' I glared at her. 'Your attitude is why you'll always fail.'

'Thanks a lot,' Jess said indignantly.

'Does the truth hurt?' I asked with just a modicum of spite.

'Tobey, that's enough,' Mum admonished me.

'She started it,' I said childishly.

I sipped at my coffee, glaring at my sister. She gave as good as she got.

'So, Jess, how's college?' Mum asked, trying to draw her attention.

'Too much writing,' said Jess. 'Why on earth do I have to write essays on hair textures and nutrition and the structure of hair follicles? I want to cut and style hair, not lecture on it.'

'You do get to cut hair as well though, don't you?' Mum sounded worried.

Jessica wasn't keen on writing. Never had been.

'Yeah, but not enough,' my sister sighed. 'The four essays we had to do this year plus my exam next week count for sixty per cent of the total end-of-year mark.' Her eyes clouded over. Something was wrong . . .

'How d'you get the other forty per cent?' I asked.

'Practical work at my work placement and one practical assignment in front of my tutor,' said Jess.

'What's the pass mark for this year then?' I frowned.

'Seventy per cent.'

'And what happens if you fail?' I asked.

'She leaves college and gets a full-time job,' Mum answered before Jessica had the chance.

'They let you redo the year again as long as you pay the fees,' Jessica said, studying the peeling and chipped veneer on our table.

'No, Jess. If you fail this year, no more college,' said Mum sternly.

'How many of this year's essays have you done?' I asked.

'What is this? Some kind of inquisition?' Jessica exploded. 'I've done my essays. OK? I really want to be a hairdresser. I'm not about to mess that up.'

'Well, excuse me whilst I just run round the kitchen after my head.' I scowled. 'I was only asking.'

'When's your final exam, Jessica?' asked Mum, casting me a warning look.

'Next Thursday,' Jess replied, moderating her tone only slightly.

Mum glared at me. I got the message.

'I'm sorry, Jess,' I said reluctantly. I hated saying sorry to my sister. 'I didn't mean to upset you.'

Jessica shook her head slowly. 'It's all right for you, Tobey. You've never failed at anything in your life. God help you the first time you do fail, because you won't be able to handle it.'

'Then I won't fail.' I shrugged.

'And it's that simple, is it?'

'Yeah.'

I downed the rest of my orange juice and took my empty plate and glass to the sink. My appetite for more was gone.

seven. Tobey

The summer morning was already blindingly bright and blazing hot with a promise of a lot more sunshine to come. A heat haze rose up from the pavement, creating a muddled urban mirage of shimmering skyscapes and flickering, glistening buildings. To be honest, I was already sick of the heat. Roll on autumn. I pulled the strap of my rucksack further up my arm to rest upon my shoulder. The thing was heavy and uncomfortable and made me walk with my whole body tilted to one side. But that wasn't why I was in a bad mood.

Breakfast with Mum and Jessica had been bad enough. But then Callie had let me down. She must've decided to walk to school by herself today, in spite of telling me last night that she'd knock for me. I was so used to going to school with Callie that when it didn't happen, it felt strange, like I'd set foot out of my house and forgotten something vital.

But I shouldn't have been surprised. More often than

not these days, Callie was a silent companion. Since her nana had died, she'd changed. According to the newspaper reports, some anonymous Nought guy had died in the explosion as well. The authorities didn't seem to be straining themselves to establish his identity. Or maybe it'd been reported on page thirty-odd of the dead guy's local newspaper and hadn't managed to make it any further up the 'does-anyone-give-a-damn?' scale.

What had happened in that hotel the day Jasmine Hadley died? Was she really so unlucky as to be in the wrong place at the wrong time? Was life really that arbitrary? It would appear so.

An executive jet-black WMW – known as 'white man's wheels' – pulled up alongside me, its back window gliding down in expensive silence.

'Tobey Durbridge, isn't it?'

I stepped back, pulling my rucksack closer to my side. The WMW before me was almost limousine-like in its proportions. It had to be custom-made. The alloy hubcaps had been polished to a high shine and I could see my distorted reflection in them. I took another step back, as did my reflection. We both had the same idea.

A Nought man's face moved into view. I recognized him at once. Alex McAuley. Aka Creepy McAuley (only ever said behind his back) or Softly McAuley (occasionally said to his face by close friends only) because he could be kicking your head in and he'd never once raise his voice. No one – as far as I knew – had ever heard him shout. He didn't need to. His dark-grey suit covered a middleweight boxer's physique. He was still in shape, even though he was in his mid thirties. He wore his blond hair swept back off his face. His light-brown eyebrows framed hard, ice-blue eyes. The single yellow diamond stud he wore in his left ear twinkled like a giggle in the morning sunlight. He smiled at me, pulling back thin lips over perfect, high-price, sparkling white teeth. I fought my natural instinct to take another step back or, better still, do a runner. It wouldn't do any good anyway. I saw the silhouette of another Nought man in the back seat of the car next to McAuley. Between them was a state-of-the-art laptop, McAuley's no doubt, with a memory stick attached. The driver and the guy in the passenger seat were also looking at me. McAuley's car was full. The rumours were true. He never, ever travelled alone.

I answered the expectant look on his face. 'Hello, Mr McAuley.'

'Ah. So you know me?' he replied, his tone soft and lilting.

I didn't bother responding to that one. If he needed his ego stroked he'd have to find someone else to do it for him.

'I've been hearing a lot about you, Tobey Durbridge,' he said.

My heart flipped like a pancake. Didn't like the sound of that. Not one little bit.

McAuley raised his eyebrows when I failed to reply. 'Aren't you going to ask me what I've heard?'

I shook my head.

'You're not the least bit curious?'

'If it's bad, it'll crush my ego, in which case I'd rather not hear it. And if it's good, it'll make my head swell, in which case I'd better not hear it.'

McAuley considered me. I was pinned by his gaze like a lepidopterist's butterfly. 'Curiosity moves us forward,' he said.

Around McAuley, curiosity could also move you under – buried two metres under, to be precise – but I decided to keep that to myself.

'You know when to keep your mouth shut, don't you?' McAuley smiled, even though there was nothing to smile about. Mind you, if I'd forked out the kind of money he must've spent on all those porcelain veneers, I'd show them off too. 'Tobey, how would you like to work for me? I could always use a smart boy like you.'

I'd rather have my toenails extracted one by one without benefit of a general anaesthetic, but McAuley was just the man to make that happen.

'Well? I asked you a question, Tobias.' McAuley's eyebrows began to knit together and, if anything, his voice grew quieter.

'I'm still at school, sir.'

'I have little jobs that need doing over the odd weekend and a couple of evenings a month – nothing onerous. And I'm very generous, as you'll find out.'

I'm a fish and he's the fisherman and he's got his hook in my mouth. My silence will let him reel me in. Say something, Tobey. Godsake! Speak.

'I'd rather not, sir,' I replied quietly.

Inside McAuley's car, his crew began to laugh.

'You're very polite, aren't you? "I'm still at school, sir."
"I'd rather not, sir,"' McAuley mimicked. 'Three bags
full, sir.'

A single line of sweat trickled down from my left
temple in front of my ear, but I didn't dare wipe it away.
My heart was a punching bag being viciously pummelled
over and over.

'Tobey, you don't want to say no to me,' McAuley said
softly. 'I don't like that word. I mean, I *really* don't like
that word.'

A children's book. A first reader. My photo, legs pumping,
terror on my face. See Tobey run. Run, Tobey, run.

I stood still, my feet glued to my shoes, my shoes glued
to the pavement. My useless frickin' body. Adrenalin
coursed through me. Fight or flight? I couldn't do either.
Useless.

'I'm a good man to work for, Tobey.'

Why can't I just slide away on McAuley's oily
smile?

'I'm a loyal friend and I look after my own. Ask anyone
who works for me. Ask your friend Dan. But I think
you'll find I'm also a—'

'Tobey! How come you didn't wait for me?'

Callie's voice reached me before she did. That girl had
the ability to go from mute to surround sound in less than
a second. She trotted up to me, to stand between me and
McAuley.

'You were supposed to wait for me, toe-rag. Thanks for
making me run after you. Now I'm all sweaty.'

I pulled at her arm and stepped in front of her.

'What's wrong?' Callie frowned.

My eyes were still on McAuley. His gaze swept over Callie then back to me.

'This your girlfriend then, Tobey?' he asked. 'She's very pretty.'

'No. We're just . . . we walk to school together, that's all,' I replied.

'And we'd better get going, Tobey. We're going to be so late.' Callie grabbed my arm and pulled me after her. I had to trot to keep up. I trailed in her wake, forcing myself not to turn round and look into McAuley's glacier-cold eyes. Half a minute later, his black limo slid past us, the tinted windows now up. Callie and I carried on jogging until the car turned the corner. Callie let go of my arm and dropped her rucksack to the pavement, trying to drag air back into her lungs in rushed gasps.

'Tobey, are you OK?'

'Yeah.' I shrugged.

'You left without me.' There was no mistaking the accusation in her voice.

'I thought you'd already gone to school, that's why.'

'You can knock for me once in a while, you know. It doesn't always have to be me running after you. Would it have killed you to check?' Callie looked up and down the road. 'What did Creepy McAuley want?'

'He offered me a job.'

'Hellfire!' Callie turned to stare at me. 'You didn't say yes, did you?'

'I'm not entirely stupid,' I replied. 'Although saying no to that man might just be the stupidest thing I've ever done.'

'People who work for him usually end up in prison or dead,' said Callie.

Tell me something I didn't know.

'Which is why I said no, Callie.'

'D'you think he'll leave it at that?' Callie's teeth worried at her bottom lip.

I shrugged. 'Who knows? No point losing sleep over it. We'd better get going.'

I picked up Callie's rucksack and handed it to her. We walked to school without saying another word. Callie kept stealing glances at me, but I wasn't in the mood for conversation. She had known me long enough to figure that out for herself.

McAuley knew my name.

Worse than that, I was now a blip on McAuley's radar. It was hard to say which was spinning harder, my mind or my stomach.

'Tobey, you can't work for that man. You just can't.' Callie finally broke the silence between us. 'The Dowds run things around here. If they hear you're working for McAuley you won't be able to walk from your house to school without slipping.'

Slipping. The technical term for entering enemy territory. If I ever agreed to work for McAuley, it was only a matter of time before the Dowds got to hear about it, and then my house and my school and all the routes in between would mean I'd be slipping daily. That's what it was all about in Meadowview. The streets didn't belong to the government or the local authority; they'd been fought over between the Dowds and McAuley's mob. The Dowds ran practically every crooked operation on the east side of Meadowview. McAuley had carved out the west side for himself. He'd established his turf by speaking softly and ensuring that no one but himself and the few good men in his car knew where the bodies were buried. People who opposed him had the habit of 'disappearing' – including two of the Dowd family before an uneasy truce was brokered between them.

Now McAuley wanted me to work for him, even though he knew I lived on the Dowds' patch. And I didn't like what he said about asking my friend Dan for a reference. Surely Dan wasn't stupid enough to talk to McAuley about me? If McAuley didn't have any problem telling me that Dan worked for him, who else had he told? Dan only lived two streets away from me – in Dowd territory.

Damn!

How on earth was I going to extricate myself from this one? Dan might be one of my best mates, but he was stupid as a bag of rocks to get involved with McAuley. Now that I'd seen the man up close and personal, I'd have to try and persuade Dan to get out and stay out of McAuley's clutches. But most important of all, I had to make sure that McAuley kept his eyes off Callie.

Nothing bad was going to happen to Callie Rose.

Not on my watch.

eight. Callie

Tobey remained taciturn all day. It wasn't like him at all. He laughed everything off, never took anything seriously. But not today. After break, we sat together for our double science lesson, but try as I might I couldn't get him to open up to me. After the umpteenth mumbled monosyllabic response, I conceded defeat. Tobey stood over me as I put my stuff in my locker before lunch. We walked into the food hall together, but we peeled off in different directions once we'd got our lunch. I sat with Sammi and some of my other friends. Tobey sat by himself, but not for long. Some of his mates joined him, but from what I could see he still wasn't saying much. Tobey was a strange one. He didn't have many close friends, but that seemed to be by choice rather than design. He chose his friends carefully, but once he was your friend, he was your friend for life. And the mates he had were fiercely loyal in return. And I'm one of them. Every time I looked up, I caught Tobey watching me. I smiled a couple of times, but he immediately looked away.

For heaven's sake! I wanted to invite Tobey out for a meal or something the following night, but it was hard when he would barely speak to me. I mean, I didn't need three guesses to figure it out why. He was worried about

McAuley. And I couldn't say I blamed him. But why take it out on me?

McAuley was a lowlife, just like the Dowds. They climbed high up life's ladder by stockpiling the misery of others beneath them. Even the Liberation Militia were aware of their activities in Meadowview. At least, they were when I was a member. The Liberation Militia didn't bother with them over much. The L.M. considered themselves above that kind of petty wheeling and dealing. Drugs, prostitution, loan sharking, extortion – those kinds of criminal activities were left to the hag fishes, as McAuley, the Dowds and all other 'common' criminals were known within the L.M. – with the emphasis on common. The L.M. considered their cause more noble. They believed themselves to be freedom fighters. Their objective? Equal rights and equal justice for Noughts. And the means? By dispensing their own brand of justice to those they believed deserved it. And if you were innocent and got caught up, then tough luck. The world according to the L.M. The kidnap, torture and murder of the L.M.'s enemies was, in their eyes, honourable. If the government and the Cross-owned media didn't see it that way, if they chose to call the L.M. terrorists instead of freedom fighters, then so be it.

I wanted no part of any of them, not the L.M., nor the hag fishes. Never again. Uncle Jude was the worst. A hag fish masquerading as a warrior fighting for the greater good. The only greater good Uncle Jude had in his heart and his mind was getting revenge on my mother. So many things I knew now that I wished I'd known a few years ago. Even now my blood ran cold at the thought of what

I'd almost done so that Uncle Jude could have his revenge. Stupid. Stupid. Stupid.

But I'd been snatched back to sanity before I could fall irrevocably to Uncle Jude's scheme. In spite of knowing it was pointless, I still hated my uncle. And my loathing grew with each passing day. He was dead and I was still here, but it didn't make any difference. Each angry thought revolved around him. Uncle Jude was evil incarnate. He was so full of hatred that he could experience nothing else. The messages each of his senses sent to his brain were somehow transformed into one hundred per cent hate and nothing else. That was all his brain could register. When Nana Jasmine died, my uncle had died with her. I wondered about his last thoughts as the bomb he'd instructed me to make went off. That split second before his death, who had occupied his thoughts? Mum? Callum, my dad, and his brother? His family? His wasted life?

I knew it wasn't me, unless it was to curse me for fouling up his plans. I don't want to end up like him – but it's so hard. 'Cause Nana Jasmine isn't here any more. Where was the justice in that?

Mum and Aunt Minerva are going to talk to Nana Jasmine's solicitor, Mr Bharadia, again next week. They need to find out when they'll be able to hear her will and get probate, though it could be weeks still before that happens. When will it all be over?

It's taking so long because of the way Nana died and the length of time it took to prove conclusively that it really was Nana Jasmine who died in the explosion at the Isis Hotel. And then there were a number of other matters concerning her death to be sorted out first like the postmortem and the authorities releasing the body so that Mum and Aunt Minerva could arrange the funeral. And after the funeral, thank God for Tobey. Like Mum, he always seemed to be there when I needed company. I really don't know what I would've done without him.

I can't help wishing . . . but what's the point? Tobey is always going to treat me like the younger sister he never wanted. I'll just have to get used to it. I had hoped that maybe our kiss in his bedroom meant something to him. It meant something to me. But that's just me daydreaming. I all but held up a placard to tell him how I feel about him. I practically threw myself at him. For a moment there, when he pulled me closer, I could've sworn . . . Wishful thinking again. The best thing he could find to say about me was that I smelled of biscuits.

Biscuits! I ask you.

I was wearing the perfume he gave me last Crossmas and he thought I smelled of biscuits. I hope he didn't see how much that hurt. Biscuits . . . I'm not going to forget that one in a hurry.

It's funny, though. Even when I'm mad at him, I'm not really mad at him. Thinking of Tobey clears my head of other bitter thoughts. Thinking of him makes me smile. Maybe that's why I find myself thinking of him more and more often.

Maybe that's why . . .

nine. Tobey

✗ ✗ ──────────────────

'Happy birthday, Nana.' Callie kissed Meggie on the cheek and handed her a birthday card and a gift-wrapped box. At least, that's what it looked like from where I stood hovering in the doorway.

'What is it?' Meggie asked, putting the box to her ear and shaking it.

Callie teased, 'When you open it, you'll find out.'

Meggie smiled and began to carefully peel off the wrapping paper from one side of her present. Now if that'd been me, I would've just ripped the paper off. But according to Meggie, if it was removed with care, then 'the wrapping paper could have a repeat performance. Maybe several.' Godsake! It was only wrapping paper. Mind you, my current finances were such that I couldn't even afford to buy wrapping paper, never mind a present. I hadn't given Callie a present two months ago when it was her birthday and I still couldn't afford to buy her one. That really burned me. I wanted to buy Callie anything she wanted, but with what?

I looked around the sitting room, trying to find something to take my mind off the empty state of my pockets. I'd been in this room countless times before, but it never ceased to interest me how the room was a strange mix of old and new, past and present, Nought and Cross. Photos in frames lined the window sill and any available horizontal space. Photos of Meggie's family from a long time ago and another world away. Callie's Aunt Lynette occupied one photo by herself. I'd never heard anyone but Callie talk about her. Callie's aunt had died before Callie was born in some kind of road accident. Another photo on the side table showed all Meggie's children together – Lynette, Jude and Callum. They were all sitting right back on a sofa, none of their legs long enough to reach the floor. Callum couldn't've been more than two or three. It was kind of weird to think that that toddler in the photo was Callie's dad. There was a photo of Meggie and her husband Ryan together, their arms wrapped around each other as they both smiled at the camera. They looked so happy. I didn't know much about Meggie's life, but I knew she'd been through a lot and lost much – her husband Ryan and her children Lynette and Callum were now dead. It showed on every line on her face.

None of the oldies ever wanted to discuss the past, that was the trouble. Whenever I asked my mum about anything that happened more than ten years ago, she'd invariably say, 'Tobey, that was a long time ago. I can't remember.' But it seemed to me that most oldies remembered the past better than the present. They just didn't want to talk about it. Funny how Nought oldies never wanted to discuss the past and Cross oldies did nothing but. It seemed to me that the Crosses embraced their history in a way we Noughts very rarely did.

Callie's mum, Sephy, had her share of photos scattered around the room as well. Photos of her and Callie mostly.

There was one of Sephy and her older sister, Minerva, taken when they were both teenagers by the look of it. And one large photo of Callie's Nana Jasmine and Meggie sat self-consciously in the middle of the window sill. That photo was taken when they were young women. They stood side by side, arms linked as they both smiled at the camera. Every time I looked at that photo, I wondered what each of them had been thinking the precise moment the photo was taken. Callie once told me that her mum and dad, Sephy and Callum, were just kids when that photo was taken – certainly no older than nine or ten. How odd to think that two families with such different backgrounds could have their lives so intertwined.

At last Meggie got the wrapping paper off, revealing the dark-blue box underneath. I had never seen anyone take quite so long to get wrapping paper off. Meggie carefully removed the lid from the box. The surprise on her face was transformed to pure delight.

'I'm sorry it's not much,' Callie said apologetically.

'It's beautiful.' Meggie smiled at her before taking out her present. It was a gold necklace with a pendant shaped like a golden rose on a thornless stem. Callie had already shown it to me on the day she bought it, asking for my opinion.

'It's a rose from Callie Rose,' she told her nan, as if Meggie hadn't worked that bit out by now. 'It's so you'll always have something to remind you of me. You don't think that's too narcissistic, do you?'

Meggie smiled at her granddaughter. 'No, love, just unnecessary. I don't need a necklace or anything else to think of you. But thank you anyway. It's really beautiful.'

'And it won't turn your neck green,' I quipped from the door.

Meggie raised an amused eyebrow.

'Thanks for that, Tobey.' Callie scowled at me before turning back to Meggie. 'It's real gold, Nana. It's only nine carats, but it is real gold.'

'Callie, don't let Tobey wind you up, dear. It's lovely.'

'Tobey's got you something as well,' said Callie.

That was my cue to move further into the room. Reluctantly, I dug into my jacket pocket, pulling out a crumpled envelope. I handed it over, embarrassed. Meggie took hold of it and took out the birthday card. The envelope looked so manky, I wouldn't've blamed her if she'd held it gingerly by only one corner. But she didn't.

'It's a birthday card,' I mumbled, stating the obvious.

'That's very kind of you, Tobey.'

'It's not much,' I warned her as she took it out of its envelope.

Meggie looked at the expressionist vase of flowers on the front of the card and then read the words on the inside, which was more than I'd done when I bought it.

'Thank you, Tobey. It's lovely.'

The card was cheap and cheerful and had just about emptied my pockets. But Meggie was being great about it. She put it next to Callie's card on the side table.

Callie started chatting about the restaurant her mum and her nan were going to later and Meggie's face cleared as she listened. I admit I didn't contribute much to the conversation. Money was in my head again. It had to be in my head, I couldn't afford to keep it any other place.

Something had to change. I couldn't spend the next few years until I graduated from university like this.

Callie popped two lasagne meals into the microwave for us as we weren't going out to dinner with her mum and nan. We weren't invited because it was a school night. I mean, Godsake! Did I look like I went to bed before Meggie McGregor? But I wasn't going to argue. After all, it meant Callie and I could be alone together, which suited me just fine. After our meal, I asked Callie if she fancied going for a walk? The moment we stepped outside, the intense evening heat hit us like a slap round the face. We headed along our road, walking through a shock wave of rock music blaring out through the open living-room window of the house five doors along. The air smelled of chicken nuggets and bad temper. The irresistible urge to get something off my chest grew stronger with each step.

'Callie, I will get you something for your birthday. I promise.'

Callie was surprised. 'My birthday was ages ago.'

'I know. But I never got you anything.'

'It doesn't matter. I just want to forget my last birthday,' Callie said sombrely. 'Anyway, what brought that on?'

'I just . . .' I eyed the bracelet adorning her left wrist. The gold link chain set off the semi-precious lime-green stones that glinted against Callie's brown skin. It was beautiful. Just the sort of thing I'd've loved to have bought for her. Lucas and his deep pockets, no doubt.

'Tobey?' Callie prompted.

'I never got you a gift and I just wanted to let you know that I haven't forgotten. I will get you something.'

'Don't bother.' Callie shrugged.

'But I want to . . .'

'Tobey, it's no big deal. I don't want or need anything from you,' said Callie. 'At least . . . Never mind.'

'Go on. What were you going to say?'

'It doesn't matter.'

'What is it you want?'

Callie smiled. 'Let me come close to beating you at chess once in a while. That'll do.'

'Are you mad?' I replied, horror-stricken. 'Chess should be taken seriously, otherwise why bother?'

'It was just a thought.' Callie's grin broadened.

'Maybe it'll be a thought when it grows up?' I suggested.

Callie shook her head. We carried on walking.

'Are you still playing football this Sunday?' she asked.

'Yeah. You coming?'

'You mean, am I going to stand on a sweaty sideline at three on Sunday afternoon to watch you and your mates kick a ball around for ninety minutes?'

I nodded.

'I wouldn't miss it.' Callie smiled. 'See! I must really like you or something.'

We carried on walking in a companionable silence. There were all kinds of things I wanted to say, wanted to ask, but I'm useless at that kind of thing, so I did the same as usual and said nothing. I stole glances at Callie. Was she OK just walking beside me? Or did she wish she could be somewhere else? It was so hard to tell. She turned her head occasionally to catch me looking at her. Each time she'd smile like she knew something I didn't and we'd keep walking.

'Callie . . .' I began at last.

'Yes?'

'Have you . . . have you forgiven me for . . . telling you about your dad?'

I'd inadvertently revealed to Callie that her dad had been hanged as a Nought terrorist and for a long, long time afterwards she wouldn't even speak to me. It was the most miserable time of my life. After that I vowed that I'd never do anything to lose Callie's friendship again.

Callie stared at me. 'Tobey, that was a long time ago. Of course I've forgiven you. Like you said, we're friends.'

'It's just . . . I think about that day a lot. I didn't mean to hurt you.'

'I know you didn't. Let it go.'

'Easier said than done,' I sighed.

Callie nodded, her expression deadly serious. 'I know. You're not terribly good at letting things go.'

The sound of sirens split the air. And the sound was getting closer.

Callie's steps slowed. 'Sounds like we'd better head back,' she said.

Sirens were more common than birds chirping around here, especially lately. I was all for carrying on with our walk when three police cars screeched to a halt at the top of our road. Mrs Bridges was at it again. Everyone on our street knew she was dealing drugs. Punters would turn up and post money through her door, then she'd chuck the required merchandise out of a first-floor window. Her downstairs windows were barred and securely fastened, just in case some druggie fancied his or her chances. Most didn't, unless they were tired of having two working legs.

Everyone knew Mrs Bridges worked for the Dowds. Callie and I knew enough not to hang around. I took Callie's arm and practically frogmarched her back the way we'd come. For once she didn't argue.

'I hate this place,' Callie muttered from beside me. 'It never stops.'

She turned back to see what was going on. Even though the police cars were stationary, their lights were still flashing. The police were hammering away at Mrs Bridges's door. Good luck with that! Any drugs on the premises had been flushed away and were well on their way to the seaside by now. We quickened our pace away from all the banging and shouting.

'What d'you think is happening?' Callie asked.

'Who knows? What the cops would call N.H.I., no doubt.'

'N.H.I.?'

'No humans involved.'

Callie looked so profoundly shocked, I instantly regretted my cynical outburst. But I remembered the last time a Nought boy had been stabbed by another Nought around here. It was about three months ago, maybe four. I was on my way home from school when I turned a corner and saw a number of people and the flashing lights of police cars and an ambulance. Pushing my way forward, I stood rubber-necking like everyone else before we were all pushed back away from the scene. Some poor Nought boy of about my own age lay still on the ground, a slow pool of blood leaking out from beneath him. His hands were at his sides and his sightless eyes were staring straight into the sun. It was the first time I'd seen a dead body. I waited for some emotion other than sadness to kick in. What should I be feeling? Rage? Fear? Pity? Nothing stirred inside me. Taking one last look at the dead boy, I turned and walked away. I didn't run. I walked, my head down. I just wanted to get home. As I approached the street corner, I heard them before I saw them.

'So who got shot this time?' a woman's voice was asking. She might've been enquiring about the soup of the day in a restaurant for all the emotion in her voice.

'Not shot. Stabbed,' a younger male voice corrected. 'Just another kid. Some boy.'

'Noughts cleaning house again,' said the woman.

'The boy was still someone's son, someone's friend.'

'When you've been at this as long as me, you'll realize that all these Nought deaths are strictly N.H.I.,' said the woman.

'What does that mean?'

'No humans involved,' the woman replied. 'As long as it's blankers killing blankers, who cares?'

I turned the corner then. A middle-aged Cross copper was setting out cones to cordon off the road. Her younger Cross colleague looked at me, then away. It was one of those moments. They knew I'd heard them. I knew they knew. I carried on walking. N.H.I.? Was that what I was to them? Was that all I was? Something inside me began to uncoil – like something deep inside, asleep inside, was beginning to wake. I stopped walking, closed my eyes and took several long, deep breaths. Whatever had been stirring inside me settled and remained still.

It was better that way. Safer.

'Tobey, d'you think we'll ever get away from here?' asked Callie.

'I guarantee it,' I replied sombrely.

We reached my house first. I opened the door, bundled Callie inside and closed it firmly behind me.

'How can you be so sure?' asked Callie.

'Because there's no way I'm going to spend the rest of my life around here. And neither are you.'

Callie sighed. 'I wish I had your confidence.'

'I'm getting out of here, Callie. Just watch me,' I told her.

And I'm taking you with me.

ten. Callie

I loved walking to school with Tobey. He always made me laugh − when he wasn't in one of his quiet moods. And the morning was so light and bright, a promise of the day to come. The sunlight glinting on Tobey's dark-brown hair made it seem like he had occasional red highlights in it. Tobey's mum's hair was red so I suppose it was only natural that he would inherit some of her colouring. His hair used to fall in unruly waves almost to his shoulders, but at the beginning of our current school term he'd had it cut as short as I'd ever seen it. It was only two or three centimetres long now, if that, but it suited him. Made him seem older somehow. And now that his hair was shorter, it looked darker, to match his eyes. Tobey's eyes were the colour of strong coffee. But when he was angry, they grew so dark it was hard to tell where his irises ended and his pupils began. Not that there was much on this planet that could anger Tobey. He was Mr Sanguine. Tobey caught me looking at him. He smiled. I smiled back. Then I noticed something about him that hadn't registered before.

'Tobey, what's that on your chin?' I moved closer for a better look.

'It's my goatee. What d'you think?'

'That's your attempt at growing a beard?'

'A goatee.'

I shook my head. 'Tobey, I've seen more fuzz on a kiwi fruit. Lose it. It looks crap.'

'Thanks,' Tobey said sourly.

'If your best friend can't tell you the truth, then who can?' I asked. 'You look like you haven't washed your face this morning.'

'Thanks.'

I sniffed at his chin. He pulled back like he thought I was going to bite him or something. He should be so lucky!

'You smell reasonable, though,' I told him. 'Did you finally discover the meaning of life, the universe and soap?'

'You're real funny, Callie,' Tobey told me, his tone implying the exact opposite.

I smiled. 'You love me really.'

He reluctantly smiled back. 'Yeah, I adore you. Bitch!'

We both creased up laughing. Sometimes Tobey took himself a bit too seriously. And his attempt at a goatee really was wretched. We were having a good laugh, but were less than a minute away from school when all that changed. Tobey saw them before I did. I was too busy giggling at one of Tobey's silly observations about his sister's ex-boyfriend to see straight. But Tobey's accompanying laughter died on his lips and his eyes took on a hard yet wary look. I followed the direction of his gaze.

Lucas and three of his mates were standing on the steps of the school entrance, sharing a joke. I glanced between Lucas and Tobey and instantly smelled trouble. Lucas and his friends were weaving about like they didn't have a care in the world. Until Lucas spotted us. He said a few words to his crew, his eyes never leaving mine, and the laughter instantly stopped. I was too far away to hear what he said, but it had the desired effect. Lucas's friends all turned to face us, all trace of humour now gone. Tobey and I didn't alter our pace, didn't speed up, didn't slow down. Even though Tobey didn't say a word, I could sense the sudden tension in him.

I didn't understand Lucas. When he was on his own he was fine towards me. He acted like he still wanted us to be together. But when he was with his friends, it was a different story. The way they watched me and Tobey made me feel distinctly uneasy.

I broke up with Lucas soon after Nana Jasmine died. I couldn't cope with her death and Lucas as well. Being with Tobey was easy in a way that being with Lucas was not. It felt like Lucas was with me in spite of what I was, whereas Tobey couldn't care less that my dad was a Nought and my mum is a Cross. Between Lucas and me, silence was a high thorny hedge, something to be painfully overcome. But when I was with Tobey, silence embraced the two of us, pushing us together instead of driving us apart.

At first Lucas had tried to be understanding. But when I started hanging around with Tobey instead of him, our relationship changed. He was never overtly antagonistic, it wasn't that. But something about him made me . . . wary. I think if I'd been a dog, I would've held still and growled beneath my breath whenever he approached. Mum had told me that there were far more Noughts at Heathcroft School now than there ever were in her day, which was part of the reason she was happy for me to go there. And none of my friends were chosen according to their post-code or their skin colour, but I'd never seen Lucas hang out with anyone but Crosses. I guess his parents had had more of an influence over him and his thinking than either of us realized.

Steeling myself, I deliberately took hold of Tobey's hand. He instantly tried to pull away, but my grip on his hand tightened. I glared at him. He got the message and his hand faux relaxed into mine. Good thing too, or I'd never have spoken to him again. If Lucas and his friends wanted something to stare at then I was more than happy to provide it.

Tobey and I reached them. No one said a word.

'Morning, Callie,' Lucas said softly.

'Lucas,' I said, frost coating each syllable of his name. I didn't appreciate his intimidatory tactics. Not. One. Little. Bit.

'Is this "lead-a-blanker-to-school day" then?' asked Drew.

Tobey spun round to face him, pulling his hand from mine. 'Sod off, Drew,' he hissed, his hands clenched at his side.

So much for Tobey being Mr Sanguine! I was about to launch in with a few choice words of my own, but Lucas beat me to it.

'Drew, apologize,' Lucas ordered.

Drew looked at his friend like he'd lost his mind. And he wasn't the only one. I risked a swift glance at Lucas before turning my hostile glare back to the moron beside him.

'Say sorry to Durbrain?' Drew regarded Tobey with utter contempt. 'That'll be the day.'

Tobey took a step forward, as did Drew. Aaron, Yemi and Lucas moved to back up their mate. I pushed through to stand beside Tobey. He tried to step in front of me, but I sidestepped to stand beside him again. I stood with one leg slightly behind the other, taking up a strong, balanced stance, my arms at my sides, my hands poised. Thanks to Uncle Jude and his training programme for new recruits, I knew how to kick arse and take no prisoners – as Lucas and his cronies were about to find out. I assessed Aaron as the strongest of the group. He'd be the one to take out first.

'You should remember what side you belong to,' Drew told me through narrowed eyes.

'Oh, I do,' I said softly. 'And it'll always be the opposite side to you.'

'Like mother like daughter,' sneered Drew.

'What does that mean?' I asked.

'She had a thing for blankers too, didn't she?'

I was more than ready to slap Drew into a new post-code. All my previous training forgotten, I moved forward, but Tobey stepped in front of me again and Lucas moved in front of Drew. It didn't matter. Drew now had my full attention.

We were being given a wide berth by those arriving at school after us, but I was hardly aware of them. It was all about to kick off. And then Tobey, of all people, surprised the hell out of me.

'I'm not going to fight you, Lucas,' he said quietly. 'I'm not going to fight any of you. That's not what I come to school for.'

I watched in dismayed amazement as he slowly unclenched his fists.

'What's the matter, Durbrain?' Drew taunted. 'Chicken?'

'You must believe what you want to believe.' Tobey shrugged. 'Come on, Callie. Let's go inside.'

Tobey tried to take me by the arm, but I shrugged away from him. Out of the corner of my eye I could see Aaron and the others grinning disdainfully at Tobey, as if he was somewhere beneath contempt. And the studied calm I'd felt before burned away like dry paper on a bonfire. How could Tobey back down like that?

'Callie, it must be a comfort to know that Tobey Durbridge has your back,' Lucas scoffed.

I spun to face him. 'Lucas, why don't you—?'

'What is going on here?' Mrs Paxton's voice was like an icy deluge as the head emerged from the school building. She moved to stand to the side of all of us, and cast her trained eye over our still tension-filled bodies.

'Aaron, what's going on?'

'Nothing, Mrs Paxton,' Aaron mumbled, shuffling back, away from Tobey and me.

Mrs Paxton gave him a withering look before turning her attention to me and Tobey.

'Tobey?' she ordered.

Tobey looked her straight in the eye. 'Like Aaron said, there's nothing going on, Mrs Paxton.'

Mrs Paxton's lips tightened. 'All of you, go to your form rooms. At once.'

She stood aside as we trooped past her in silence. Tobey and I followed the others into school. I was still trying to work out who I was more angry at – Lucas and his friends or Tobey?

eleven. Tobey

'Why did you pull away from me?' Callie glared at me.

'What?'

'You heard.'

Well, that didn't take long. I glanced at my watch. Twenty-seven seconds into the building. I had hoped Callie would save it until we left school or, better still, till we got home. No such luck.

'It's very hard to defend the two of us with you holding one of my hands,' I told her.

'I don't need defending. I can look after myself,' Callie told me. 'And why did you back down? I wouldn't've given those gits the satisfaction.'

I shrugged. If I took on every prodigious arsehole who looked at me sideways, I'd spend my entire life with my fists clenched. I wasn't about to live like that, believing everyone was my enemy, getting my licks in first before others could touch me. That just wasn't me.

'Maybe you shouldn't be so combative,' I suggested.

The look Callie gave me would've speared right through to my vitals if I hadn't been wearing my kevlar underwear.

'Maybe you shouldn't let people walk all over you,' Callie countered.

'No one walks all over me, Callie,' I told her quietly.

The look on her face told me what she thought of that.

'There ain't one person who walks all over me,' I insisted.

Except maybe you, I added in my head.

Except probably you.

Except definitely you.

We continued to our lockers and unpacked our books for our first lesson in silence.

'I don't understand why you let them talk to you like that.' Callie shook her head.

I shrugged. 'Just because they're stupid as mud doesn't mean that I have to be.'

Callie glared at me. 'Tobey, when you throw me one of your infuriating "I'm-too-cool-for-this-earth" shrugs, I just want to kick your shins. Would you like me to teach you how to stand up for yourself? Because I'm volunteering.'

'I'm a pacifist.'

'Are you sure you don't mean another three-syllable word beginning with P?'

It took me a couple of seconds to work out what she meant.

'So I'm pathetic now, am I?'

'Tobey, what would it take for you to rise up from your laid-back, as in totally horizontal, position?' Callie was getting angrier by the second. The only way she was going to calm down was if I didn't take her seriously.

'As the Good Book says, "The meek shall inherit the Earth",' I told her, adding with a wry smile, 'With your permission, of course.'

'Tobey, it's not funny!'

My smile grew broader.

'Ugggh! Sometimes you drive me corkscrew crazy.' Callie raised her voice, causing some of those passing us to glance our way, curiosity written large across their faces. 'Don't you realize that by backing down you made that lot think that you're weak?'

'And why should I care what Lucas and his minions think of me?' I asked.

Plus I wasn't about to get kicked out of school for fighting. Mrs Paxton didn't put up with that from anyone, Nought or Cross. Getting booted out wasn't part of my five-year plan.

'You care too much about what other people think of you,' I said.

Callie's eyes carried enough mean heat to fry me where I stood. 'Don't you dare say that. I couldn't give a damn what Lucas and his cronies think of me. But I do care about being able to look at myself in the mirror.'

'Are you implying that I can't?'

Callie shook her head and returned to her locker.

'D'you think I'm weak, Callie?' I asked, no hint of a smile on my face.

Callie studied me. I wondered what she saw.

'Tell me the truth, Callie. D'you think I'm weak?'

Her answer mattered to me. Very much.

'D'you want me to be honest?' Callie asked at last.

Uh-oh! Whenever she asked that question it was because she knew I wouldn't like the answer. I nodded.

'Tobey, sometimes you look at me like you would stand beside me though any kind of rain, fire or shit storm. But sometimes, like today, I get the opposite feeling. Would the real Tobey Durbridge please stand up?'

'Is that a yes or a no?' I asked. Callie's words had scooped out a large part of my innards.

I shut my locker door and waited for her to answer. She always did that. When it was something she didn't want to say or she thought I wouldn't want to hear, she danced around her answer until I pushed. And I was pushing.

'Tobey, what would you do if someone said something derogatory about . . . us? The two of us? Together?'

Callie's face was turned up towards mine, the question mark in her head darkening her eyes and straightening her lips. What was it she wanted to hear?

'Callie, I'm not about to take on every brainless git who doesn't like the idea of the two of us together. People can say what they like.'

'I see,' she said. She turned away, but not before I saw the disappointment on her face. She muttered something. All I heard was the word 'together'. I took hold of her arm and turned her round to face me.

'Callie, what d'you want me to do? Punch out every idiot we come across?'

'No. But it'd be nice to know you've got my back.'

'I do. Don't listen to Lucas.'

Callie opened her mouth to argue just as the buzzer for assembly sounded. The harsh cacophony silenced whatever it was that she had been about to say.

'Callie Rose, I do have your back. You believe me, don't you?'

'Callie, there you are. You'll never guess what I just heard . . .' Samantha Eccles – or Sammi, as everyone called her – appeared from nowhere to link arms with Callie and drag her away.

A couple of metres further down the corridor Callie said something to Sammi, before turning back to me.

'Tobey, d'you want me to answer your question?' she asked.

I nodded. Did she really think I was weak? I was about to find out.

'The honest answer is – the jury is still out.'

She and Sammi carried on walking.

I didn't need to switch to genius mode to know that in spite of my best efforts, I'd messed up.

twelve. Callie

'Callie, are you even listening to me?' Sammi asked.

Not as such, no.

'Of course I am. Every word.'

'Yeah, right. What did I just say then?'

'Bliss is going round telling everyone how she and Lucas have a hot date this Saturday. He's taking her to the cinema and for a meal and to a party afterwards and it's going to be sooooooo divine.'

Sammi and I were the last ones to reach the athletics track. And I for one was glad to get there. Sammi had been going on about Lucas and Bliss for the last ten minutes, and to be honest, her assumption that I had to be upset was getting on my nerves. Mrs Halifax gave us a look, then tapped meaningfully at her watch, but for once she didn't have a go. The weather was over warm rather than over hot, so at least it wouldn't be like trying to exercise in an oven.

'Aren't you bothered?' Sammi whispered as we joined in with everyone else's warm-up exercises.

'Why should I be?' I frowned. Arms outstretched, I tipped over to one side then the other, stretching out my waist. What a waste of time. Compared to the physical training regimen the L.M. had put me through, this was a doddle.

'Well, you and Lucas used to be together.'

'With the emphasis on "used to be",' I pointed out. 'Lucas is free to go out with anyone he likes, though I pity his taste.'

'So it's definitely you and Tobey now, huh?'

'We'll be working on stamina today, so everyone five times around the track please,' Mrs Halifax called out.

Ignoring the groans coming from all directions, I immediately took off at a steady pace with Sammi beside me. I'd avoided her question rather nicely, I thought. Twenty steps later and Sammi was puffing like a faulty car exhaust.

'You . . .' – puff – '. . . didn't . . . answer . . . my question. Oh my God!' – wheeze – 'I'm dying!'

'Sammi, you need to exercise more and smoke less.' I frowned at her. 'Those cigarettes will kill you.'

'Answer . . . my . . . question . . .'

'What was it again?'

Sammi glared at me.

I smiled at her. 'Well, your nosiness, Tobey and I are just friends.'

'How boring,' said Sammi, disappointed.

Tell me about it!

'We shouldn't . . . have to run . . . in this heat . . .' Sammi rasped. 'This is . . . just cruel . . . and unusual . . . punishment.'

I took pity on her and eased my pace to a gentle jog, so gentle I was practically walking.

'You and Tobey . . .' – huff – 'd'you wish . . .' – puff – '. . . it was more?' Sammi asked.

I shrugged. Nana Meggie had a saying – if wishes were horses, beggars would ride. I glanced at Sammi, trying hard to keep my face neutral. I was running at about one-tenth of a kilometre an hour and Sammi was still having trouble.

'Why don't you just . . . tell him that?' Sammi coughed.

'It's not that simple,' I sighed. 'Tobey needs to figure it out for himself.'

'Oh, please. Callie, he's a guy. You'll have one foot in the grave before he catches on,' Sammi scoffed, finally getting her breath back.

'Then I'll wait.'

'You need to take him in hand, then take him to bed – not necessarily in that order,' said Sammi, winking at me.

'I don't think so.'

'I thought you liked him.'

I shrugged. 'I do. I more than like him. But that would be a bad idea.'

'Why?'

'If it doesn't work out, that's our friendship ruined. I don't want to risk that,' I admitted. 'Besides, there's no rush.'

'Except that Misty is determined to set more than just her eyes on Tobey,' said Sammi. 'So you'd better watch her – and him.'

'If Tobey really wants a girl who doesn't know a proton from a crouton, that's his business.'

'Wouldn't it bother you?'

Yes.

'No.'

'Misty says Tobey's one of the few boys in the school who knows what he's doing.'

'And the way she puts it about, she would know,' I replied with disdain.

This conversation was getting to me. I increased my pace, hoping Sammi would get too puffed out to talk so much.

'All I'm saying is' – wheeze – 'if you really like Tobey you'd better let him know and soon' – cough – 'or he's going to take what Misty keeps offering – if he hasn't already.'

'I'm not going to have sex with Tobey or any other guy just to keep him,' I argued. 'How pathetic is that. If that's what it takes then he's not worth having in the first place.'

'If you . . . say so,' wheezed Sammi doubtfully.

'I don't just say so, I *mean* so.'

I broke into a sprint which Sammi tried to match. There was no more talking as she tried to equal my pace. And she did try. But she didn't succeed. I finished my five laps with breath to spare. Sammi gave up after three, collapsed on the ground, and even Mrs Halifax's threat of a demerit slip couldn't shift her. By the time the lesson was over, I seriously wondered if Sammi was going to have a heart attack. We were back in the changing rooms getting dressed – well, most of us were. Sammi was sitting down with her head between her knees, dragging air into her burning lungs. I tied my jumper around my waist, before getting my bag out of my allocated PE locker. Glancing in the mirror, I saw my hair was all over the place. I used my fingers to unplait my ponytail, before digging out a comb. My hair reached well past my shoulder blades. During the forthcoming summer holidays I'd decided to get it cut short, more for convenience than any other reason. Plus Sammi reckoned short hair would suit the shape of my face.

'You should wear your hair loose more often,' Jennifer

Dyer, one of my Nought friends, told me. 'It really suits you like that.'

'Thanks, but—'

'Nah, it looks much better plaited up,' Maxine, another friend, interrupted. 'You look too much like a blank— I mean, you look like a Nought with your hair loose.'

The changing room went quiet. Jennifer's face was bright red. I turned to glare at Maxine. What a bitch!

'It's only hair, Maxine. And luckily for me I can wear it any way I want to,' I told her, pulling my hair back into a ponytail and re-plaiting it. I smiled at Jennifer. She returned my smile, gave Maxine a filthy look and carried on getting dressed. Maybe I'd put off cutting it for a while. Then again, maybe I wouldn't.

Sammi began to straighten up. She looked almost human again. 'Running is for horses, not people,' she complained. 'And anyone with boobs bigger than a thirty-two A should be excused from anything more strenuous than walking.'

I glanced down at my own boobs. According to Sammi's rule, I wouldn't have had one bit of serious exercise since I turned twelve.

'Callie, what's going to happen to the Isis Hotel bombing investigation now?' Talia asked, changing the subject.

My perplexed frown told her I didn't have a clue what she was talking about.

Talia dug into her bag and pulled out her mobile phone. A couple of screen taps later and one of the latest news items of the day was displayed.

The Nought man caught up in the bomb blast which killed Jasmine Hadley has finally been identified as Robert Powers, who was a guest at the Isis Hotel. With no known links to the Liberation Militia, the authorities have concluded that Robert Powers was unfortunate enough to be in the wrong place at the wrong time. Though flying glass and debris caused a number of roadside injuries, the Isis Hotel outrage claimed only two lives.

'So are the authorities no closer to finding out who planted the bomb then?' asked Talia.

'How should I know?' I raised my gaze from her phone to ask.

'There's no need to snap my head off. I was only asking.' Talia frowned.

'Sorry, it's just . . . I'm sorry,' I blustered. 'I have to go now.'

Snatching up my bag, I walked away from my friends without a backward glance. I had to get out of there. Right away from all of them. I needed to be alone. Behind me, Sammi rounded on Talia.

'What the hell is wrong with you, Talia? Callie's grandmother died in that blast. D'you really think she wants to be reminded of that every two seconds?'

I didn't wait for Talia's answer. I ran as fast as my school bag slamming against my back would allow.

Robert Powers?

Who on earth was Robert Powers?

I'd assumed that the Nought man killed with Nana

Jasmine was Uncle Jude. It had to be him. Did they find papers or a passport relating to Robert Powers on Uncle Jude's body? No, that couldn't be right. It would never have taken so long to identify him if they'd found identification papers. They must've had to reconstruct the Nought victim's jaw and teeth, and after that it was a question of finding the relevant dental records. And those records had revealed the dead man to be someone called Robert Powers. But Robert Powers and Jude McGregor had to be one and the same person. They just *had* to be. There was no other explanation.

Well, maybe just one . . .

What if it wasn't Uncle Jude who had died, but someone else? Oh, my God . . . What if some innocent man was in the wrong place at the wrong time and died because of the bomb *I* made?

And what if Uncle Jude was still alive?

thirteen. Tobey

As soon as I got home from school, I fixed myself a quick snack of scrambled eggs and beans on toast, then tried to settle down to my homework. But chemistry just wasn't lighting my fire the way it usually did. My head was too crammed with other thoughts.

Money!

Damn it! I had none and there was no prospect of any forthcoming.

Heathcroft School had provided me with a full scholarship, but just living day to day cost money. I only ever went on school day trips. My mum's pockets weren't deep enough for fortnights away skiing or singing abroad with the school choir. I'd even had to turn down the odd birthday party invitation or two because I couldn't afford to buy a decent birthday present. If only I could get the image of Dan's watch out of my head. I wasn't jealous. That wasn't it. I didn't want to own a watch like it or a designer jacket or any of that other nonsense.

I just wanted my share.

I wanted the choices, the options that money would give me.

My mobile phone roused me out of my mega-brood. Who was phoning me? I wasn't in a particularly talkative mood. But it was Dan. I took the call.

'Hi, Dan. You OK?'

'I'm fine,' Dan replied, 'but I need your help.'

'Help with what?' I frowned.

'I need to make some deliveries before eight tonight and I won't be able to do them all by myself.'

'Dan, I've already told you I'm not working for McAuley. And I don't appreciate you dropping my name to him either.'

'I didn't drop your name.'

'McAuley cornered me on the street a couple of days ago and he knew all about me.'

'Not from me, he didn't,' Dan denied.

Hmmm . . .

'Or at least . . .'

'Yes?'

'Well, I might've mentioned you in passing as a friend of mine who's cat-clever, but that's all.'

'Dan, you arse. To someone like McAuley, that's enough,' I said. 'So you can forget it. I'm not doing a damned thing for that man.'

'You wouldn't be doing it for him. You'd be doing it for me. You just need to drop off two packages for me whilst I do the other three and—'

'Which part of "no" don't you understand? The N or the O?'

'Tobey, it's just packages. You drop them off and that's it.'

'Why can't you deliver them?'

'I told you. I have to be somewhere at eight o'clock and I won't make it without your help.'

'What's in the packages?'

'I don't get told and I'm not stupid enough to ask,' Dan replied. 'It's healthier that way.'

'No frickin' way, Dan. This conversation is over.' I was about to hang up on him, but what he said next brought the phone back to my ear.

'I'll pay you. I'll give you half of what I make tonight.'

Half my brain told me to hang up anyway. But the other half turned my left hand into a magnet and wouldn't let me put down my phone.

'How much are we talking about here?' I asked at last.

The figure Dan mentioned made me catch my breath. No wonder Dan could afford designer threads and top-of-the-range watches. It would take me six months at my Saturday job to make the kind of money he was talking about.

'Come on, Tobey. It's just two packages,' Dan cajoled. He could sense that I was wavering.

Not wavering but drowning.

'Just two packages . . .'

I was on dangerous ground now. In my mind, two deliveries was already turning into a few. If all I had to do was deliver a few packages, then really, where was the harm? In fact, if I delivered a limited number of Dan's packages, think of the money I'd make. Enough to pay my university fees. Enough to live off when I was studying. Enough.

I liked the sound of that word. *Enough.*

I had to admit, the spectre of bank loans that I might never be able to pay back and debts up to my eyebrows didn't appeal massively. But there was no way I'd get to go to university otherwise. Mum just didn't have the money. And I needed to go to university like I needed to breathe. For too many Noughts and for far too long, the door to higher education had been locked, sealed and bolted. But others had given up blood, sweat and rivers of tears to kick that door open for me. How could I not walk though it? Failure just wasn't an option.

And more immediately, with the currency Dan was talking about I could buy a store-bought birthday card and a proper present for Callie. She deserved so much more than I could give her and she never once threw that fact back in my face. I still had one last year at school, plus university to get through before I could even hope to start making serious money. So where was the harm?

I mean, how long before Callie got fed up with me because I couldn't afford to take her anywhere or buy her anything? How long before money came between us? I hated money. The lack of bits of metal and paper was ruling, not to mention ruining, my life. But this . . . Dan's packages . . . Dan's world . . . this was something else again.

'It's just two packages?' I said, holding my phone like it was the enemy.

'Yeah, just two. I'll give you the easiest two,' said Dan. 'Thanks, mate. I knew you wouldn't let me down.'

'You knew more than me then,' I said sourly. 'Where are you and what time do we do this?'

'I'm outside your front door and how does now sound?'

Like the beginning of a long, slippery slope.

I sighed. 'I'll be right out.'

After a moment's thought, I took my lightweight hooded jacket out of my wardrobe and headed downstairs. 'Mum, I'm going out for a while.'

'Have you finished your homework?' Mum emerged from the sitting room to ask.

'Yeah. It's all done except chemistry and that doesn't have to be handed in until next week.'

'Where're you going?'

'Just out with Dan.'

'Where to? Another football match?'

'No. Not today. We're just going to hang out for a while. After all, it is Friday.'

'Tobey, I don't know about this . . .'

'We won't be long. A couple of hours at most,' I tried to reassure her. 'We'll probably go for a meal or something.'

'What's Dan up to these days?' Mum asked.

'Same old, same old.'

'Is he still working for the postal service?' asked Mum.

'That's right,' I replied, feeling distinctly uncomfortable.

'How come you hang around with Dan more than your other friends from school?'

That wasn't true. That was just Mum's perception 'cause she wasn't keen on Dan.

'Dan's been my friend since infant school.' I shrugged. 'Just because he didn't get into Heathcroft doesn't mean I'm going to drop him.' Besides, I didn't have to try to be something I wasn't when I was with him. At least, that's how I used to feel. I wasn't so sure any more. Now it felt like I needed to work out who I was, rather than who I wasn't. I wasn't the same Tobey I was six years ago. I'd changed. Dan hadn't.

Mum scrutinized me. 'All right, then. I'll see you later. Just . . . just keep your head down. OK? And if you see any trouble . . .'

'Walk away.' I finished Mum's mantra. 'I'll do my best.'

'Better than your best, Tobey,' she retorted. 'I don't want the police knocking on my door – for any reason. Understand?'

I nodded and headed out the door before Mum could say anything else.

Keep your head down . . .

I'd bet my next ten Saturday job pay packets that Lucas Cheshie was never told to keep his head down. I bet he was always told to do the exact opposite.

Dan wasn't lying. He stood outside my front door, bouncing impatiently from foot to foot. We immediately headed off along the street.

'Thanks, mate,' said Dan.

I nodded, ignoring the gnawing in my gut that kept telling me this was a *really* bad idea. Anything could happen.

If I got caught . . .

But all that money . . .

'Dan, I'm just helping you out because I need the money. OK? I don't intend for this to become a habit.'

Dan raised appeasing hands. 'Don't worry, blanker. I know you're just helping out a mate.' He grinned at me. 'But I really wouldn't mind your help on a few other deliveries I got lined up over the coming weeks. And at least I know I can trust you. You'd get fifty per cent of everything I make and that's more than I'd do for anyone else. Can't say fairer than that.'

'No, Dan.'

'You say no, but your empty pockets say yes. And after all, the desire for money is the most infectious disease on the planet.'

'It's not a disease I intend to catch. I need some money to tide me over and then that's it,' I told him.

'Whatever you say, Tobey.' The smug grin on his face was very eloquent.

'This is just to buy a belated birthday present for Callie,' I insisted. 'I'm not thinking beyond that at the moment.'

Dan smiled at me. We both knew that wasn't true.

fourteen. Callie

After school, I couldn't bear to face anyone so I hid away in the library for over half an hour, hoping that by then I'd be able to walk home in peace. I didn't want to be with anyone. I just wanted to be left alone, to think. I headed out of the school gates, every thought finding its way back to Uncle Jude. What if . . . ? What if he really was still alive?

'Callie Rose. Wait up.'

I turned round at the sound of my name. Lucas. I glared at him as he came running up to me, not bothering to disguise exactly what I thought of him.

'Hi, Callie,' he said diffidently.

'Hello, Lucas,' I replied. My tone could've frozen water. What did he want?

'I'm having a birthday party next week. Would you like to come?'

'Why?'

Lucas blinked in surprise at my question. 'What d'you mean?'

'Why're you inviting me?'

''Cause I'd like you to be there,' said Lucas, as if the answer was obvious.

But it wasn't, at least not to me.

'I'm not turning up at your party so you and your friends can make jokes at my expense,' I told him straight.

'We wouldn't do that.'

I raised my eyebrows.

'OK, *I* wouldn't do that. And I wouldn't let my friends do it either.'

'Yeah, I was very impressed with the way you reined them in this morning,' I said with contempt.

'I'm sorry about that,' Lucas said. 'I was just . . . I'm sorry.'

'You were just – what?' I prompted.

'I hate seeing you two together,' said Lucas. 'Tobey is trouble and you're going to get hurt.'

'What're you on about? Tobey is my friend. And my next-door neighbour. He wouldn't hurt a fly.'

'He's a Nought.'

Lucas had better not be saying what I thought he was saying. 'So?'

'Well, you're a Cross. It doesn't hurt Tobey's street cred to have everyone think of you as his girlfriend.'

I was a Cross now, was I? Funny how my status seemed to change depending on the eyes of the beholder. To Drew I was a Nought and would never be anything else. Lucas called me a Cross. Where did that leave me? On one side or the other or stuck somewhere in the middle?

'Lucas, what's your point?'

'I'm just trying to warn you to be on your guard. Tobey isn't the open book you seem to think he is.'

I shook my head, trying to figure out just what Lucas was playing at. Was it malice? Jealousy? What?

'And you know Tobey is with Misty, don't you?' Lucas

continued. 'Everyone in the school knows those two are an item.'

Well, Misty had told enough people, so that was hardly news.

'What's that got to do with me? I told you Tobey and I are just good friends,' I replied.

'The way you and I used to be "just good friends"?'

I frowned at Lucas. Where was he going with all this?

His eyes slowly narrowed. 'Or maybe Drew was right. Maybe us Crosses just aren't your thing.'

'Excuse me?'

Us Crosses? Lucas's exclusive club of which I was no longer a member? It hadn't taken much to get me kicked out.

'I guess you're more like your mother than I gave you credit for,' said Lucas.

I straightened up, trying to quash the tidal wave of hurt rising inside me. 'And that, Lucas, is why you and I together will never work,' I said quietly. 'Say what you like about Tobey, but he'd never, ever say something like that to me.'

Lucas looked genuinely remorseful, but it was far too little, much too late. He put out his hand to touch my cheek, but I flinched away from him. 'I'm sorry, Callie. That was . . . I didn't mean it.'

'Yes, you did,' I replied. 'You always make me feel like I have to constantly apologize for my mum and dad and for being who and what I am. Well, I'm not going to, not any more.'

I stepped round Lucas and this time he didn't try to stop me. A couple of steps on and I turned back. 'Lucas, you've never made me feel more than I am. But for your information, Tobey never makes me feel less. So thanks for your party invitation, but I think I'll pass.'

I headed home without another backward glance. Why did life have to be so complicated? Tears pricked at my eyes. First the news about Uncle Jude, then Lucas. What would Lucas say if he knew about my uncle? Probably think he'd had a lucky escape? Judge me as guilty by association? Or just guilty full stop?

Uncle Jude . . . Was he out there somewhere? Watching? Waiting? My uncle occupied every thought all the way home. Much as Lucas's words had hurt, Uncle Jude had the power to hurt me more. So where was he? Just waiting for the right moment to do the maximum amount of damage? He was really good at that.

Where was he?

'Hello, Ann. Is Tobey in?'

Tobey's mum shook her head. 'You've missed him by about twenty minutes. He went off somewhere with his friend Dan.'

'D'you know where?'

Ann shook her head again. 'Callie, are you OK? You look . . . out of sorts.'

My attempted smile slid right off my face. 'I'm fine. I just wanted . . . to talk to Tobey.'

'D'you want to come in and wait for him?'

I shook my head.

'He'll be back in a couple of hours if you want to come back then,' Ann told me. 'Jessica's off to a party later and I've got to go to work.'

Tobey's mum worked all kinds of unsocial hours. She was used to me coming and going in her house, just as Tobey treated my house like his second home. That's the way it had always been. Tobey's dad had gone off years before to 'find himself' and he'd stayed lost ever since. Jessica only mentioned him to curse him to hell and back. Tobey never mentioned him at all.

'If Tobey isn't in by the time you come round again, just use the spare key.' Ann lowered her voice even though there was no one around us. 'It's in its usual place.' Its usual place being under one of the plant pots in the tiny front garden.

'Thanks, Ann.'

'No problem. I'd much rather Tobey hung around with you than Dan. I don't trust Dan.'

'Why not?' I asked.

'Every time he comes into this house, he's always telling me how much everything cost – as if I didn't know already. Dan is a boy who knows the cost of everything and the value of nothing.'

I smiled faintly. I wasn't particularly keen on Dan either. Every time we met, he looked me up and down like he was working out how best to dissect me.

'If you see Tobey before I do, tell him I've left him some chilli in the fridge if he's still hungry. He just needs to heat it up. That goes for you too, Callie. Help yourself if you're hungry.'

'Thanks, I will,' I replied.

I turned round to head back home. Usually I would stand and chat with Ann, but not now, not today. Even though Tobey and I lived next door to each other, I still turned my head this way and that to see if I was being watched. Was Uncle Jude out there somewhere watching my every move? I shook my head, warning myself not to be so paranoid. It didn't help.

Usually I didn't mind coming home to an empty house – not that it happened that often. But today I did. The silence bounced off the walls and echoed around me.

I went straight up to my room. Sitting on my bed, I drew my legs up so that I could wrap my arms around them and rested my head on my knees.

Should I ask Nana Meggie when she got back home? Surely Uncle Jude would've got in touch with her by now? She was probably the only one on the planet who truly knew if Uncle Jude was alive or dead.

The bomb I'd made had killed an innocent man.

Uncle Jude could be out there, somewhere.

And if he was, nothing would be the same again.

fifteen. Tobey

Dan took me to a lockup I never realized he owned. It was secured with a combination-code padlock, opened by pressing a series of digits. Dan had to input his code three times before the thing finally clicked open. By his third frustrated try, accompanied by a lot of swearing and the muttering of several numbers, I had his code memorized –

not that I'd ever use it. So much for his security then! I walked into a small, windowless room which was a bit like a narrow garage. It smelled of damp walls and mould, like the air in the place was several months old. The only furniture was an old wooden table covered in packages and boxes of assorted sizes and shapes. The floor was strewn with rubbish, more boxes and carrier bags.

'So when did you get this place?' I asked. Thinking better of it, I raised a hand to ward off Dan's reply. 'You know what, don't tell me. I don't want to know.'

My two packages were covered in brown paper. Both were quite small. One was about the size of a bag of sugar, the other was the shape, size and weight of a pack of playing cards. Both had been wrapped to within a millimetre of their lives, with sticky tape covering the brown paper so that none of it could be peeled back to take a quick peek at what lay beneath. Dan placed both my packages in a supermarket carrier bag snatched up off the concrete floor. He gave me specific instructions.

'Guard those packages with your life. If some bastard thinks he'll take them off you, you make sure that doesn't happen. The only time that bag leaves your hand is if the cops put in an appearance. Then you drop the bag and run like the wind.'

Like I needed to be told that.

'I thought you said these packages were safe,' I said, liking this whole idea less and less with each passing second.

'I never said they were safe. That's your brain telling you what you want to hear.'

'So what's in them?' I asked again.

'I still don't know,' Dan said, a hint of exasperation in his voice. 'And asking too many questions in this line of work can get you into a whole heap of trouble.'

So whatever I was carrying, it wasn't something you'd pick up in the local supermarket. It was illegal and that meant dangerous, and dangerous meant I could end up in a youth detention centre or in prison. Or worse still, dead.

Just this once. Just this once and no more, I promise.

Please let me get away with it just this once.

Dan contemplated me.

'What?' I asked, irritated.

'D'you want some protection?' Dan asked slowly. 'Something to calm your nerves?'

'Like what?'

After giving me a scrutinizing look, Dan struggled to pick up one of the closed boxes off the floor, before dumping it on the only clear space on the table. I peered inside, then recoiled. The box was filled with mean-looking knives. I mean, double-edged, big-arsed, wicked-looking, eviscerating combat knives, switchblades, kitchen knives. In fact, every knife known to man was represented in that box.

'Godsake, Dan. What's with all the armour?'

'They're for protection.'

'Protection from which invading army?'

I couldn't believe what I was seeing. There had to be at least twenty blades in that box, maybe more. Probably more.

'Dan, are you off your nut?'

'I have to arm myself. The streets aren't safe,' he told me.

'Yeah, 'cause tossers like you can't set foot outside your house without tooling up,' I replied. 'Godsake! Why d'you need so many knives? You've only got two hands.'

'Carry one of these and no one will mess with you. D'you want one or not?' asked Dan, peeved at my lack of appreciation for his hardware.

'One what?'

'A knife? I have knives for every occasion.' Dan launched into a pseudo sales pitch. He picked up a knife at random. 'For example, this fine specimen is phosphate-treated and comes with a polymer sheath which is available in olive, camouflage and black.'

'Hell, no.'

'Tobey, I promise you, with one of these in your pocket, you'll—'

My response was heartfelt. 'No frickin' way.'

'Suit yourself.' Dan eyed me speculatively as he closed the box. 'I've got a couple of items even more effective than these knives . . .'

'Dan, don't even go there,' I warned. 'I'm not interested.'

'Suit yourself.'

'Thank you. I will,' I replied. I ran a shaky hand over my sweaty forehead. *Stop the world, I want to get off.* 'I need to get out of here. Just give me the relevant names and addresses before I see sense and change my mind,' I said.

Walk away. Walk away now, I told myself.

The answer? Not without my money. I was already thinking of it as *my* money.

★

The first stop was a forty-minute train ride out of Meadowview. The instructions Dan gave me seemed straightforward enough. Once I got off the train, I pulled up my hood, kept my head down and started walking. I thought it'd take me ten minutes max to get to my destination. Twenty-five minutes later I was only just turning into the right road. Each house in this area was detached and about a quarter of a kilometre from its neighbour – at least, that's what it felt like as I walked along. The front gardens were massive so I couldn't even begin to imagine how big the back gardens must've been. I stopped two or three houses away from my destination and looked up and down the wide, tree-lined street. Two women passed on the opposite side of the road, deep in conversation, but apart from that the road was deserted. My hood still in place, I cautiously looked up at the surrounding trees and at the tops of the lamp-posts in the vicinity. No CCTV cameras. Another glance up and down the road. I appeared to be alone.

Appeared to be . . .

Stop being paranoid, Tobey.

I headed for the designated house, trying to look a little less guilty and a little more like I had every reason to be there. My stomach was tumbling and copious beads of sweat were making my T-shirt stick uncomfortably to my back. The late evening hadn't begun to cool down yet. If anything the air had become more muggy, so that each breath was like inhaling after lifting a saucepan lid. I hated the summer.

This house was definitely upmarket. At least, it looked that way as I approached. But as I turned into the driveway, the weeds and moss sprouting up from between the paving stones were more evident. Somewhere overhead a crow cawed. I looked down at the parcel I was supposed to deliver. I guess drugs knew no boundaries and weren't confined to a single postcode or area or country come to that. One of the world's great levellers – along with love. And hate. And fear. I took another look around. It wasn't often that I made it out to the plush suburbs. Correction. I never made it out here. I tried to wrap my head around why anyone who lived here would need to haze their mind with drugs? I guess misery knew no boundaries either.

I rang the doorbell. I didn't hear any chiming inside. I pressed on it again. Silence. So I knocked as well, just in case the bell wasn't working. A baby started bawling its head off inside. Trying to ignore my racing heartbeat, I knocked on the door again, a lot harder this time. The door opened almost at once. The smell of nappies and toast hit me at once. A harassed Cross woman, in her mid-thirties, I think, answered the door. She wore white trousers and a yellow, sleeveless blouse. Her black hair was dishevelled, her onyx eyes wary.

'Yes?' she asked.

From the back of the house, the baby's crying was getting louder. She ignored it, her gaze darting nervously past me up and down the street.

'Are you Louise Resnick?'

'Who wants to know?'

'I have a package for Louise Resnick.'

'It's a little late to be delivering post, isn't it?'

I shrugged.

'Give it here then.' The woman held out her hand.

'I was instructed to only give it to the proper recipient.'

'Huh?'

'I can't give it to anyone but Louise Resnick.'

The unseen screaming baby turned up the bawling volume by quite a few decibels.

'Charlene' – the woman turned her head to scream back into the house – 'could you please do your job and stop Troy crying.' She turned back to me, her expression fraught, her eyes cold. 'I'm Louise Resnick, so pass it here,' she said impatiently.

The package stayed in my carrier bag.

'Oh, for heaven's sake,' said the woman. She picked up her designer handbag from beside the door. Annoyed, she retrieved her driver's licence and flashed it so close to my face that I had to pull my head back like a turtle. 'Happy now?' she asked.

I dug out the smaller package from my carrier bag as the woman replaced her licence and dropped the handbag onto the hardwood floor.

'Who's it from?' Louise asked suspiciously. She ran a shaky hand through her locks, making them even more untidy.

'I don't know,' I replied truthfully. 'I'm just delivering it.'

I held it out towards her. She took a half-step back, suddenly reluctant to touch it. She looked at me, trying to read my expression. I really didn't know what was in the package and it must've shown on my face because she finally stretched out her hand to take it.

'Thanks,' she murmured.

From one of the rooms behind her, the baby was now shrieking. Louise closed the door in my face without saying another word. I shrugged and turned away, heading back towards the train station. But once I reached it, I couldn't settle. I walked up and down the platform like my shoes were on fire. I made sure to keep my head down and my hood in place, just in case. The CCTV cameras placed at regular intervals along the platform would capture my jacket, jeans and trainers – and that was it. Hanging around anywhere near that woman's house was a really bad idea. I didn't know what was in the package and I didn't want to know, but every instinct I possessed screamed at me to get away, to drop my other package and run. But I couldn't. I'd agreed to help Dan and I had to see this through.

Focus on the money, Tobey, I told myself.

The train finally arrived to take me to my next port of call. Another forty-minute journey back to Meadowview and a twenty-minute bus ride later, I hopped off. This area was very different from where Louise Resnick lived. I looked around. If I ever had to draw Hell, then this was where I'd come for inspiration. Narrow streets, high-rise estates, no hint of green or any other colour except concrete grey. I'd been walking for less than five minutes when a car pulled up alongside me, matching my walking speed. The two Nought men inside, around my age or only slightly older, looked me up and down as they kerb-crawled beside me. After a swift glance at them, I looked straight ahead and carried on walking. One hand tightened around the carrier bag, the other was empty at my side. No hands in pockets. No sudden moves. No rude gestures. I forced myself not to speed up and run away or slow down either.

On the passenger's side of the car, a man with light-brown hair and dark-blue eyes looked me up and down, his expression suspicious and more. 'Which side of Meadowview d'you live on?' he asked.

'I don't,' I replied, still walking.

I skirted as close to the truth as I could get. I didn't live in Meadowview, on either side, on any side. I existed. On whose side were these two guys? Did they work for either the Dowds or McAuley? Or were they further down the pecking order than that? Did they claim ownership of a number of pages in the local map book, or just one page, or maybe just this street?

'I'm visiting a friend who lives around here,' I told them, forcing myself to look at both occupants in the car.

The man with the brown hair turned to the driver and said one word – 'Tourist.'

They drove off. The moment their car was out of sight, I stopped walking to give my heart time to stop punching my ribs. Existing was hard work. Existing wasn't much, but for the moment it was all I had.

A couple of minutes later, I reached my destination. This time it was a flat on the Chancellor Estate, a high-rise block that should've been demolished twenty years ago. Anti-social housing. I climbed up the concrete stairs, which stank of piss, vomit, disinfectant and paint, to the third floor.

Flat Eighteen was a third of the way along the walkway. I took a moment to look out over the balcony. A few people were milling about below, but no Crosses, so I was probably safe from the police. Unless they had some undercover Noughts watching me. I couldn't assume that the Noughts I saw weren't coppers. The police force was actively recruiting from 'all sections of society', as they put it in their ads. And it was working. So I had to be extra vigilant.

Careful, Tobey. You're definitely getting paranoid.

I mean, why should anyone be watching me? It's not like I'd done this before. It wasn't like I was going to be making a habit of this either.

Tobey, just deliver the package and go.

A deep breath later, I rang the doorbell. At least I didn't feel quite so close to spewing my guts out this time. The door opened after a few seconds. A man only a few years older than me opened the door. I'm tall, but he was taller. And broader. And heavier. The man wore denim jeans and a blue T-shirt beneath a black leather jacket. I wondered why he was wearing a jacket indoors, especially in this weather. Not that I was about to ask him. His designer trainers were clearly new because they were still out-of-the-box clean. His collar-length black hair was gelled back off his face and his dark-blue eyes were cold as deep, still water.

'Can I help you?'

'I'm looking for Adam Eisner.'

'That's me,' the man replied.

'Could I see some ID please?'

'Who are you?' A stillness came over the guy that instantly had me on my guard. He looked ready, willing and more than able to tip me over the balcony onto the concrete three storeys below.

'I've got a package for Adam Eisner and I've been instructed not to hand it over to anyone else.'

'And I've already told you, I'm Adam Eisner.'

'May I see some proof?'

The man's eyes narrowed. 'What's your name?'

I didn't answer.

'Who told you to deliver this so-called package?'

I didn't answer that either. Not that I could hear much over the sound of my heart trumpeting. This didn't feel right – at all. The man started to reach into his leather jacket pocket.

'Dan sent me,' I said quickly. 'I'm just helping out Dan. He's the one who told me not to give this to anyone else but Adam Eisner.'

The man's hand slowed, then stopped before emerging from his pocket, empty.

'So what's your name, kid?' asked the man.

No way was I going to answer that one.

The man unexpectedly smiled. 'You appear to have more brains than your friend Dan. So do yourself a favour, believe that I'm Adam Eisner and hand over the package.'

I did myself a favour.

Minutes later, I was out of the block of flats and heading back to the Wasteland. Dan and I had agreed to meet up there after all our deliveries had been made. When I felt sure that I was far enough away from the flats, I hopped on a bus to take me back to more familiar territory. I could've been mistaken for an owl, the way my head kept constantly turning round whilst I was on the bus. Two parcels and one evening of doing this and already I was acting like I was some kind of criminal. That said something in itself. I tried to tell myself that it was just nerves, that I was worrying over nothing, but somehow that didn't help. I obviously wasn't cut out for this line of work.

You know what? Sod this. No amount of money was worth this feeling of not being able to walk down the street without constantly checking over my shoulder. This was my first, last and only job for Dan. Ever.

When I finally got to the Wasteland, Dan was already waiting for me. He was standing on the sidelines of the football pitch. And he wasn't happy.

'Where the hell have you been?'

'Walking,' I replied.

'You should've been back thirty minutes ago.'

'Well, I'm here now.'

'Did everything go OK?' asked Dan.

That rather depends on your definition of OK, I thought.

'I delivered the packages like you asked me,' I said.

'Was Mr Eisner OK with that?' Dan swayed nervously before me like a mesmerized snake.

'Eventually,' I replied. 'He refused to show me any ID and because I'm fond of breathing, I didn't insist.'

'Tobey . . .' Dan was winding up for a rant, but I got in first.

'Don't start with me, Dan. The man was two metres tall, almost as wide, resembled a pit bull and I wasn't about to argue with him. You got a problem with that?'

'But he had black hair and was wearing a black jacket, right?'

I nodded. Dan sighed with relief.

'So where's my money?' I asked.

'When I get paid, you'll get paid,' said Dan.

I scowled at him. 'That's not what you said earlier.'

'I said you'll get half of what I make, but I won't get my money until tomorrow – or Sunday at the latest.'

I stood perfectly still and counted my heartbeats until the fire raging inside me began to dampen down. Dan kept looking away from my unblinking glare, still swaying uneasily.

'Dan, don't play me,' I warned him softly.

'I'm not,' Dan denied. 'I can't conjure money out of thin air. When I get mine, then you'll get yours.'

We both knew he'd implied otherwise. This wasn't part of our deal, not even close.

'When exactly will I get my money, Dan?' I asked.

'By the end of this weekend. Look, as we're mates, I'll pay you out of my own savings. How's that? I'll go to the bank tomorrow and get you what you're owed. Every penny. Be here at four tomorrow and I'll give it to you.'

'I work on Saturdays,' I reminded him.

'So work a half-day or call in sick,' said Dan. 'It'll be worth it.'

I regarded him without saying a word. At least if I went to work, I knew I'd get paid. If I turned up at four tomorrow afternoon and Dan was nowhere in sight, what then?

'Tobey, you'll get your money,' Dan said, exasperated. 'Trust me.'

'Why? 'Cause you've got my back?'

Now it was Dan's turn to remain silent.

'I'll see you tomorrow at four,' I sighed. 'Don't be late.'

I turned round. In my head I was already at home and stretched out on my bed.

'Tobey?' Dan began.

Wearily, I faced him. 'Yeah?'

A flush of red stole up Dan's neck and across his cheeks. If I didn't know better, I'd say he was embarrassed.

'You and I are friends, right?'

'Yeah.' At least, I used to think so.

'Well, I've gotcha. OK?'

I scrutinized Dan. His embarrassment couldn't be feigned.

'OK.' I nodded.

'I've got some more deliveries to make tomorrow if you want to double your money,' said Dan hopefully.

I frowned. So much for having my back. Only as long as I could be useful to him, by the sound of it.

'I haven't seen a single penny yet,' I replied. 'Two times nothing is still nothing.'

'Trust me.'

'No thanks, Dan. Today was enough for me. More than enough.'

'But you've seen how easy it is to make money. A couple of drop-offs here, a collection or two there. Nothing to it.'

'Nothing being the operative word. I'm not interested, Dan. Just give me the money you owe me tomorrow and we'll call it quits.'

Not wanting to prolong the argument, I headed home. I still couldn't shake the feeling that I'd just made one of the biggest mistakes of my life.

sixteen. Callie

I couldn't hide in my bedroom for the rest of my days. Was I really going to let my uncle take over my life again? I couldn't. I wouldn't. And yet I already had. Every thought, every breath I took was now wrapped around him. I sat and brooded as the hours crept by. More than once stray tears escaped to run down my face. I brushed them aside impatiently. That wasn't going to make my problem go away. But what should I do? At last I made up my mind. I took my phone out of my jacket pocket, but my index finger still hesitated before pressing the first digit.

Did I really want to do this?

What choice did I have?

I phoned Uncle Jude's private number, the mobile phone number that he gave out to very few people. But he'd given it to me when I was his soldier. When I was his puppet.

'The number you called has not been recognized,' some woman's toneless voice informed me. 'Please check and try again.'

I tried twice more, just in case I'd inadvertently or subconsciously called the wrong number, only to receive the same message. I was still alone. Mum was out with

Nathan and Nana Meggie was out with friends. I didn't want to be alone any more.

What if Uncle Jude was out there right now watching me? What was he planning? He didn't take a breath without plotting its speed and trajectory first. What did he have in store for me? Because one thing was certain: if he really was still alive, I'd be at the top of his revenge list. And Uncle Jude was a very patient man.

Maybe it was what I deserved.

Maybe it was all I deserved.

I went to my bedroom window to look out over the back of our house and our neighbours' houses. It was so still outside. A few birds swooped in the sky and the occasional plane flew in and out of view, but that was all. I went into Mum's bedroom and looked out her window. A number of people walked by over the next thirty-something minutes, Nought and Cross – but not Uncle Jude.

It didn't matter. I didn't have to see him to know he was out there. Somewhere. I wrapped my arms around myself. I was trembling. Actually trembling. Fear tore at me like some carrion bird.

Oh, Tobey, where are you?

I need you.

I need you to tell me that everything will be all right.

I need you to tell me I'm imagining things.

I need you to let me hide in your pocket. Bring me out for birthdays and holidays.

Tobey, where are you?

seventeen. Tobey

x x

'*Earlier today, Louise Resnick of Knockworth Park received a gruesome package. It contained the little finger taken from the left hand of a person, thought to be her husband. DNA tests are being carried out to confirm this. Louise Resnick's husband is Ross Resnick, a well-known businessman with alleged links to the Dowd family. Unconfirmed reports state that Ross Resnick has been missing for three days. It is thought that one of Mrs Resnick's three children immediately called the police once the package was opened. Louise Resnick was unavailable for comment . . .*'

Ross Resnick's smiling Cross face filled the TV screen. A photograph taken when he didn't have a care in the world. I switched off the TV. The ten o'clock news was making me sick. Physically sick. Icy sweat covered my forehead. The chilli I'd just eaten was bouncing up and down in my stomach. Taking the stairs two and three at a time, I raced for the bathroom and threw up. I mean, I erupted like a volcano. I vomited so hard and for so long, I was bringing up baby food.

That package . . .

There'd been a *finger* in the package I'd delivered.

Omigod! That woman, Louise Resnick, standing at her front door, taking the package from me. Had she opened it in front of her kids? Is that what happened? Did she scream? Drop it? Cry? Did she instantly know what it was? Who the finger belonged to? I knelt on the hard, tiled bathroom floor, my hands gripping the toilet seat. I was cold. When did it get so cold? And yet, sweat was still dripping off me.

A finger. I'd delivered a finger. Frickin' Dan. I was going to kill him. That poor woman. So much for ducking the CCTV cameras in the area. What . . . what if she gave my description to the police? What if the police thought I had something to do with chopping off her husband's little finger. Oh God . . . Suppose I couldn't prove I had nothing to do with it? One package, one delivery, and I might get banged up in prison because of it. What had been in the other package? Something just as bad? I'd assumed . . . what had I assumed? Drugs, I suppose. Or maybe money. But nothing like this.

I got up on auto-pilot to wash my hands and clean my teeth. I kept thinking about the package I'd held in my hands, the package that Louise Resnick had opened, the contents that her kids had seen.

Oh hell . . .

Don't shoot me, I'm only the messenger.

Don't blame me, I'm only the delivery boy.

Don't hurt me. I'm only seventeen. I only did it for the money. I just needed some money.

Shit.

I went back to my bedroom, made sure the door was

firmly shut and hit the speed-dial icon on my phone. Dan picked up after the second ring.

'Dan, have you seen the news?' I launched straight in.

'I didn't know what was in the package. I swear I didn't,' Dan protested.

Guess he'd seen the news then.

'You must've had some idea,' I said furiously. 'Louise Resnick knows what I look like. She'll describe me to the police and they'll do a photo-fit ID or something. Once a drawing of me hits the TV and the papers, how long before someone recognizes me and tells the police who I am?'

'Hang on. You're getting a bit ahead of yourself—' Dan began.

But I wasn't having it. 'You don't want to go there, Dan. You really don't.' I was that close to losing it completely. 'You're not in the frame for this. I am.'

Pause.

'Or was that the whole point?' I asked slowly.

'What d'you mean?' I could hear the frown in Dan's voice.

'It just strikes me as strange that suddenly you can't make all your deliveries and are desperately in need of my help. Quite a coincidence that the very first thing I deliver for you could land me in prison for assault or worse.'

'You can't think I set you up?' Dan said.

'All I know is I'm suddenly in a whole world of trouble,' I replied. 'Well I'll tell you something for free, Dan. If the police come knocking, I'm not going down alone. I'm not.'

The silence between us stretched out like razor wire.

'You shouldn't make threats like that,' Dan said slowly.

'It's not a threat. It's a promise,' I told him. 'I'm going to finish school, go to university and get a decent job. My plans for the future do not include a criminal record or getting banged up for something I didn't do.'

'It won't come to that,' Dan insisted.

'Damn right it won't,' I raged. ''Cause I'm not taking the fall for either you or McAuley. Not gonna happen.'

I disconnected the call without saying goodbye. The inferno raging through me during the entire phone conversation with Dan was rapidly burning itself out. And what it left was worse. I shouldn't have said what I had. It was a bluff, full of fury and frustration but a bluff nonetheless. Because if push came to shove, I couldn't turn against my friend — and he knew that. Which meant that if things did blow up in my face, I'd be on my own. I should've listened to my instincts — after all, that's why I had them. But I'd stomped on them instead. I wouldn't make that mistake again. But it was probably already too late.

I was in deep, deep trouble.

The doorbell rang and I shot up like a rocket. Was that the police already? Maybe I could lie low and pretend no one was in. But all the lights in the house were on. Damn it. Physically shaking, I slowly made my way downstairs. Taking a deep breath, I attempted, unsuccessfully, to calm my nerves. I opened the door.

It was Callie. She took one look at me and burst into tears.

eighteen. Callie

It was hard to say who was more shocked, me or Tobey. I never — and I mean *never* cried, at least not in front of other people. But the moment I saw Tobey, the tears just spilled out of me. After staring at me, Tobey took me by the hand and practically pulled me into his house before kicking the door shut.

'What is it? What's happened?' he asked urgently.

I shook my head, desperately trying to stem my tears. I lowered my gaze. I didn't want Tobey to see into my eyes. He'd seen far too much already. It wasn't fair to expect him to fill all the frightened, empty spaces inside me, and if he knew what was happening, he'd surely try. And probably fail. But try nonetheless. Uncle Jude said tears were a luxury of the weak. I couldn't afford to be weak, not now. But I felt like a dead girl walking and that was the truth.

Tobey pulled me close and wrapped his arms around me. He didn't say anything, for which I was grateful. He just let me get all the tears out of my system. When I finally pulled away, I was deeply embarrassed and Tobey's shirt was so wet it was practically transparent. Hesitantly, I looked around.

'Jessica's out. So is my mum,' Tobey told me.

I exhaled with relief, then tried to pull myself together, without much success.

'Callie, talk to me. What's wrong?' Tobey asked.

I shook my head, not yet trusting myself to speak. Tobey took my hand and led me into his kitchen. He made me a cup of coffee, ladling in three sugars even though I never have sugar in my coffee. He pushed the hot mug into my hands, ignoring me when I shook my head.

'Drink it,' he ordered. 'You look like you need it.'

Tentatively, I took a sip, but it burned my top lip. Fresh tears filled my eyes. Not because of the coffee – it wasn't that. But now that I'd started crying, I couldn't seem to stop.

'D'you want to talk?' Tobey asked.

I nodded.

'Come on then.' And Tobey led the way upstairs to his bedroom.

nineteen. Tobey

Callie sat on my bed, her fingers lightly tracing the lightning-fork pattern on my dark-blue duvet cover. Her lips were a straight line across her face, her forehead was furrowed. She picked up her coffee from my bedside table and forced herself to drink some more. Her now hazel-coloured eyes were staring straight through my floorboards, through the foundations of the house and down into the planet's core. I opened my mouth to offer her pocket change for her thoughts, then decided against it. I didn't need to be psychic or even terribly astute to know who was on her mind. Nana Jasmine.

How long before the memory of her nana stopped slashing at her? How long before the thought of Nana Jasmine brought a smile to her eyes instead of turning them a shimmering hazel? No one deserved to die the way Jasmine Hadley did. But Callie wore the memory of her death like a hair shirt. It was an accident. Why couldn't she see that? I sighed inwardly, wishing there was some way to lessen the hurt Callie was feeling. After all, we might be something less than lovers, but at least we were something more than friends. And I hated to see Callie this way.

But then there were my own troubles. With each second I expected the police to start hammering at my door. How stupid could one person get? A world of trouble was about to descend on my head and I had no one to blame but myself. And Dan. But mainly myself. I wondered about Ross Resnick, if indeed it had been his finger in that parcel. Where was he? Was he alive or dead? No doubt Louise Resnick's present had been courtesy of Creepy McAuley. The Dowds and McAuley's lot had been trying to wipe each other out for years and the police seemed to be no closer to putting a stop to it. McAuley or the odd Dowd or two occasionally made it to court, but that's as far as it ever went. Witnesses against any of them invariably developed the strangest forms of selective amnesia, or else they just disappeared like a magician's trick. In spite of my best efforts, I was now knee-deep in something I'd fought long and hard to avoid. And if Mum found out . . .

'Tobey, are you OK?'

I sat down beside Callie. "Course. But you're not, are you?'

Callie looked at me, her eyes momentarily unfocused. A smile, fake as silicon boobs, tugged her mouth upwards. 'I'm fine now.'

'Liar,' I suggested.

A hint of a genuine smile appeared. 'What makes you think something's wrong, apart from my tears showering you earlier?'

I bit back a smile. 'Hard as it is to read your poker face, I can see something's gnawing at you.'

Even without the tears, Callie seriously believed that she could suppress her every thought and feeling, that her face was like one of those classical masks. I didn't bother pointing out the obvious. We sat in silence. A couple of times, Callie opened her mouth to speak, but no words came.

'Callie, what happened to your nana Jasmine was a tragic accident,' I ventured at last.

'You think so?' Callie whispered. She looked up at me with the saddest eyes I've ever seen.

'I know so,' I replied. 'She just had the misfortune to be in the wrong place at the wrong time.'

Callie's gaze skittered away from mine. 'I guess.'

'Callie?' There was something else going on here. I frowned. 'What aren't you telling me?'

Callie looked me in the eye, her watchful gaze never wavering. 'Tobey, d'you remember that morning we spent together on Nana Jasmine's beach, the day of the explosion at the Isis Hotel?'

Callie's birthday and the day Callie's nan died. I nodded. Of course I remembered.

'I wanted to stay on that beach with you for ever. Especially when you kissed me. I was scared to leave you.'

'Why did you then?' I asked.

Callie could no longer look at me. Her gaze bounced off my rug, my painted walls, the navy-blue curtains, anywhere but me. 'D'you remember I had a carrier bag that day?' Her voice was so quiet, I had to move closer to hear her.

I frowned. 'Vaguely.'

Silence.

'Callie . . .'

'The carrier bag had a bomb in it. The same bomb that killed Nana Jasmine.'

I stared at her. Whatever else I'd been expecting, it sure as hell wasn't that.

'Are you sure?' I regretted the inane words the moment they left my mouth. 'I mean, where did you get it from?'

'I made it. Uncle Jude taught me how and he gave me everything I needed to make it.' Callie's fingers twisted relentlessly in her lap. Head bowed, I watched as a tear dropped onto the back of her hand, quickly followed by another, and another.

Jude McGregor . . . The Jude McGregors of this world swept through life, spreading poison like weedkiller over every person who crossed their path. I placed a hand under Callie's chin, turning her face towards my own. 'Who was the target?'

'Grandpa Kamal,' Callie said at last.

I inhaled sharply. 'How did your nana . . . ?' There was no good end to that sentence, so I left it trailing.

'Somehow Nana Jasmine guessed what I was going to do. She took the bomb and went to Jude's hotel to confront him with it. They both died and it was all my fault. But now . . .'

Silence.

'Yes?'

'The Nought killed in the explosion has been identified as some man called Robert Powers. Uncle Jude wasn't killed at all. Tobey, I killed . . . I murdered an innocent man.'

I shook my head, still trying to take it all in. 'Callie, it was an accident.'

'Robert Powers is dead because of me. I'm responsible. And Uncle Jude is still out there . . . He's going to come after me. I just know it.'

I stared at her. 'You haven't heard anything from him since the bomb went off, have you?'

Callie shook her head.

'Suppose, just suppose you're right and it wasn't your uncle who was killed,' I said carefully. 'If you haven't heard from him by now, there's no reason to think he'll come after you.'

Callie sighed. 'Tobey, you don't know him. He won't stop until he's had his revenge. Look at the way he waited years before using me to get back at my mum.'

'He won't get to you, Callie, because I won't let him,' I told her.

Callie smiled faintly, but said nothing. I knew what she was thinking. Much as she might appreciate the sentiment behind my words, she didn't think I'd stand much of a chance against the likes of Jude McGregor.

'Tobey, I think . . . I'm dying inside – all over again. And I can't bear it.'

'I'm here and I won't let that happen,' I told her, my arm slipping round her shoulders. 'Callie, you're not alone, I promise.'

'That's not how it feels, in here.' Callie's finger tapped repeatedly at the place over her heart.

'Callie, don't . . .'

'What, Tobey? Don't what? "Don't say that"? "Don't feel that way"? What useless advice d'you have for me?' Callie glared at me, but I wasn't about to spout platitudes – that was my sister's speciality, not mine. I knew better.

'I'm on your side, babe,' I said softly. 'You know that.'

Callie expression slowly softened. 'I'm sorry.'

She smoothed back her long curly hair with both hands. I watched her lick her lips before she turned back to me. Moments passed as I tried my best to put into words how I felt.

'You're not the only one . . . hurting, Callie,' I said at last.

Callie regarded me, taken aback. I met her gaze unflinchingly. I didn't try to hide anything.

'What's wrong, Tobey?' she asked.

'I . . . I got stopped earlier today on Chancellor Street. Two Noughts in a car . . .'

At once Callie's expression was all concern. I didn't need to say any more. She didn't need to hear any more. She understood.

'Are you all right?'

'I'm still standing,' I said, my pathetic attempt at a joke.

'What did they want?'

'The usual. Wanted to know what side of Meadowview was my spiritual home.'

'And you said?'

'"I don't live here. I'm just visiting a friend" – unquote.'

'What did they do?' asked Callie, her unease growing rather than lessening.

'Drove off. They lost interest.'

'What on earth were you doing round the Chancellor Estate?'

'I had to see someone,' I said reluctantly.

'Tobey, are you sure you're OK?'

'They didn't touch me,' I replied, adding to make a joke of it, 'I'll strip down to my hair follicles and you can check me over very slowly if you like – just to confirm it.'

Callie raised an eyebrow. 'Thanks, but I'll take your word for it.'

We sat still. Silent seconds were batted back and forth between us.

What does it mean when you can't even admit you live in a certain place any more in case you're caught slipping?

'Something is very wrong when your postcode could be the signature on your death warrant,' I said.

'You did the right thing—'

'The cowardly thing,' I interrupted.

'The *right* thing,' Callie insisted. 'Whatever it takes to survive, Tobey. You know that. And better a lie than a knife in the gut for being in the wrong place at the wrong time. You can't afford to be stupid – none of us can.'

'I just wish . . .' I began. I didn't finish the rest. It was pointless. Wishes didn't come true, not around Meadowview.

'So do I.' Callie knew what I was trying to say without me having to say it. She shook her head. 'Every time there's a fatal stabbing or shooting and it's Noughts involved, it's in the paper for a day, if that, and the politicians say it's tragic and then it's "as you were, everyone". And the rest of the country breathes a huge sigh of relief that it didn't happen in their back yard.'

Things had changed since my mum's day. Schools could no longer openly discriminate against us Noughts and everyone had to stay in school until they were at least sixteen – Nought or Cross. OK, so the Equal Rights bill currently wending its way through Parliament wouldn't change all attitudes overnight – especially in the blinkered wrinklies over thirty. But it was a start, a step. It's just . . . it was so hard to be patient when patience was taken as a sign of weakness or, worse still, a sign of acquiescence in the status quo. Dan, Alex McAuley, the Liberation Militia and even I had grown sick and tired of being patient. We all wanted our share and we wanted it now. And if we didn't get it, if it was denied us, well, why wait? Just take. The trouble was, everyone was taking. Nought, Cross, it made no difference. When you got right down to it, it was all about territory, for everyone on the planet. If countries could fight over it, then why not individuals? What's mine is mine, what's yours is mine. All together now. Everybody sing.

I thought of Dan and his box of knives and his protestations that the streets weren't safe. There was a lot of that kind of thinking going on. That kind of thinking had turned into a self-fulfilling prophecy.

'It's not right,' Callie said, sparks in her eyes. 'Those guys in the car and the others like them, they're all hag fishes. Uncle Jude was right about that if nothing else.'

We both sat in brooding silence.

'Callie, that's not the only thing that happened today,' I admitted.

'What else?' Callie frowned.

'I did something incredibly stupid and I have a feeling it's going to come back to haunt me.'

'What did you do?'

I opened my mouth to tell her, then thought better of it. I'd got into the middle of something and now I was up to my armpits in alligators. Did I really want to drag Callie into my mess?

'I'd better not say,' I replied, turning away from her.

Now it was Callie's turn to place her hand on my chin and turn my face back towards her own. 'Was it something really bad?'

I nodded. We regarded each other.

'So one way or another we're in the same boat?' asked Callie.

I nodded again.

'What do we do about it?'

I thought about all the things I could say, but none of them seemed even remotely adequate. She looked at me. I looked at her. Neither of us said a word. We spontaneously leaned towards each other. And I kissed her. Just my lips against hers to begin with. And though she was surprised, she didn't pull away. Her hands crept up my arms to hold my shoulders. That was all I needed, to wrap my arms around her. I opened my mouth, my tongue darting out to touch her bottom lip. Callie opened her mouth immediately. My tongue slipped inside. Maybe I should've licked or nibbled her lips first. But my tongue had other ideas. And to my surprise, Callie kissed me just as intently and as intensely as I kissed her. It was just meant to be friendly kissing, two friends comfort kissing because in that moment we both desperately needed to touch and be touched. We both needed to know that for just a few moments life wasn't a journey that had to be travelled alone. But with each second it became something more.

Callie snaked her arms around my neck, her lips still on mine. I wanted Callie so much, my body was aching. One of my hands moved up from her waist to cup her breast. And she didn't pull away to tell me to stop and she didn't slap my hand away. If anything she kissed me harder, her tongue darting back and forth into my mouth. I was trying with all my might to hang onto some semblance of reason, but it was fast flying out of my bedroom window. Callie was in my room, on my bed, kissing me, touching me, her hands slipping under my shirt. My mouth was suddenly dry. I wanted her so much, but I was scared. Scared she'd stop me. Scared she wouldn't. Scared all my dreams would come true and I'd be inside her for the very first time. Scared I'd be inside any girl for the first time and I wouldn't know what to do, how to move properly or make it good for my partner. For Callie.

Were we really going to do this? We sat next to each other on the bed. Callie looked at me, but didn't smile. I needed her. I moved to kiss her again, my hands moving restlessly over her body. She pulled away from me, placing a finger over my lips. I was immediately still, all except my pounding heart and the blood sprinting around my body.

'Tobey, d'you want me?'

Was she frickin' kidding? I took her hand in mine and placed it over my erection. Answers on a postcard please!

'Wow. Is that all for me?' Callie sounded worried.

'We'll take it slow,' I assured her.

'D'you have any condoms?' she asked.

I nodded. How about five packets, hidden under my mattress! I believed in thinking ahead. Callie moved her hand lightly over my groin, sending such shock waves of electricity through me that my body pulsed like a strummed guitar string. She leaned forward for another kiss. I met her more than halfway. Our lips together, our tongues swirled around and over each other. By the time Callie reluctantly pulled away from me, I was harder than I'd ever been before.

'I've never done this before,' Callie whispered.

My eyebrows shot up. Damn, every bit of my body was up.

'How come?' I asked, surprised.

'You never wanted me before.'

I looked into Callie's brown eyes and realized she really believed that. Damn, but I should bottle this poker face and sell it on a market stall. How many nights had I lain awake wondering about Lucas and Callie when they were an item? All those sleepless nights imagining them together, doing what we were doing now.

'I thought you and Lucas . . .' I began, still not quite able to believe it.

'Never.'

I couldn't help it. A grin broke out all over my face. Snubs to you then, Lucas!

'What's so funny?' Callie frowned. 'Now that you know I didn't do it with Lucas, you're not interested any more? Is that it?'

Why did girls always have to over-think everything? Godsake!

'Of course I'm still interested,' I said, exasperated. 'Has your brain stopped working?'

'Then why . . . ?'

I kissed Callie again. I admit the first few seconds were to stop her from talking bollocks, but after that it was 'cause it felt damned good. We carried on kissing whilst we tentatively undressed each other. It was awkward and fumbling and definitely not practised, but it didn't matter. We laughed together at our mutual eager clumsiness. And that made it even better somehow, like discovering a new place together. When we were both naked we lay on my bed, just kissing and hugging and tasting and touching each other. Her boobs were hot under my hands and soft and I didn't want to stop touching them. But there were other parts of her body I wanted to touch as well. From the way my body was throbbing, I knew I couldn't hold out much longer. I stroked up and down Callie's thighs before stroking between her legs to make sure she was ready for me. I had to get out of bed and fiddle under my mattress to find just one packet of condoms, which amused Callie no end. After finally putting on a condom, which was trickier than I thought and took three attempts, I moved over Callie to lie on her, my legs between hers. We kissed and just touched each other for long, loving minutes.

'D'you really want to . . . ?' I couldn't help asking. I needed to be sure that she wanted this just as much as I did. I was never going to risk losing her again.

Callie nodded. 'But only if you do,' she teased.

My upper body supported by my extended arms, I looked into her beautiful eyes as I pushed slowly inside her. God, it felt so good – until Callie winced. I was immediately still.

'D'you want to stop?' I whispered.

Say no. Please say no.

Callie shook her head. 'Just . . . wait a bit. Let me get used to you.'

I held as still as I could for as long as I could, reciting multiplication tables and bits of the periodic table in my head to calm down. Callie started to move slowly beneath me. I used that as my signal to go further, get deeper inside her. I moved slowly, pulling out a little and pushing on, doing my best not to rush. When she grimaced for the third time, I was ready to come out of her completely. I couldn't enjoy it if she didn't. As if she sensed what I was about to do, Callie's hands moved over my bum to pull me closer to her at the same time as she arched her hips. We both gasped as I slid all the way inside her. I lay still, only kissing her then, trying to silently tell her just what she meant to me, what being with her meant to me. I rose up to look at her. Callie's eyes were closed.

'Am I hurting you?' I whispered.

'Not so much now,' Callie replied softly. 'In fact . . .'

She wriggled her hips beneath me. Lightning jolts flashed through my body again. I couldn't help but groan.

'Tobey, are we having sex or making love?' Callie asked.

It was such a girly question that I had to smile.

'What d'you think?' I whispered, before nibbling on her ear lobe.

'Feels like making love to me.' Her hands stroked over my back as our hips slowly moved together. 'Does it feel like that to you?'

'Callie, you talk too much,' I groaned.

'Aren't we supposed to talk then?'

'Your mind should be on more than just conversation,' I rose up on my arms to tell her.

'It is.'

Callie's eyes closed as I withdrew and moved slowly inside her again. The little moan of pleasure she gave then lanced through me. I hadn't expected that, that giving her pleasure would actually increase my own.

'What else is on your mind?' I murmured.

Callie opened her eyes to look straight at me. 'How much you mean to me.'

My head spun with all the words I wanted to say, the way she made me feel inside and out. My mind was all corners and cracks and crevices, and thoughts and memories of her occupied every single one. How she looked when she was pissed off with me. The way she lowered her head before giving me one of her dirty looks. The way she raised her chin before she had a good laugh. A lifetime of memories, with spaces for an eternity more. I opened my mouth, but Callie placed a finger to my lips.

'Callie, I . . .'

'No words, especially not ones you feel forced into saying.' She smiled.

No force involved or required, but I didn't speak. Our fingers laced together at our sides. Our legs twined like vines. We were so connected that I couldn't feel where I ended and she began any more. Every sense was at work and heightened. I buried my face in the crook of her neck, mouthing the words that she'd forbidden me to say. Couldn't she feel how I felt about her? Couldn't she tell what she was doing to me?

Damn it, I had to say something. Just tell her the truth.

'Callie . . .'

Her eyelids fluttered open. She had a look on her face I'd never seen before. The light in her eyes made me catch my breath. And then we couldn't stop looking at each other as we moved together.

'You and me, babe, against the world,' I whispered.

Callie smiled and hugged me closer – and the rest of the world just fell away.

twenty. Callie

Wow! I'd done it. I'd actually done it. With Tobey. Ha! If anyone had told me six months ago that my first lover would be Tobey, I would've rolled on the floor, clutching my stomach. But we did it. And it was awkward and somewhere between uncomfortable and painful to begin with and hot and sweaty and messy and so damned wonderful to conclude.

'Are you OK?' Tobey asked, once he'd come back from disposing of his condom.

'I'm fine,' I whispered. I lay next to him, my head on his shoulder, with both his arms around me. 'It's getting late.' The last thing I needed was Jessica arriving home and bursting in on us. My face grew hot just thinking about it. 'Tobey, I should go home.'

Tobey held me that much tighter. 'What d'you have planned for tomorrow?'

I shrugged. 'Not a lot. Why?'

'Dan owes me some money. I'm meeting him at four o'clock tomorrow afternoon at the Wasteland to get it. Maybe you and I could do something afterwards to celebrate.'

'What are we celebrating?'

'Well, I can get rid of my V plates for a start.' Tobey grinned. 'That's definitely worth celebrating.'

I sat up, staring at him in wide-eyed disbelief. 'But what about you and Misty?'

Tobey lay back, his arms behind his head. 'How many times do I have to tell you that I'm not the slightest bit interested in Misty before you believe me?'

'But she's going round telling everyone how wonderful you are, especially in bed,' I informed him.

'How the hell would she know?' Tobey frowned.

That lying cow! I laughed and lay down on his shoulder again. His arms were instantly around me again. That was lovely in itself, like I belonged right there and nowhere else.

'Misty is pretty, though.' I could say that now I knew Tobey wasn't secretly lusting after her.

'If you like bubble heads who weigh about as much as one pound twenty pence,' Tobey said with disdain.

I stared at him. 'Ooh! Meow! Waiter, saucer of milk for Mr Durbridge please.'

Tobey grinned ruefully. 'Well, it's true. If she ever had an original thought it would die of loneliness.'

I burst out laughing. 'Tobey, that's harsh. Remind me never to get on your wrong side.'

'You can get on any side of me you like,' Tobey said hopefully.

'Where I am now is just fine, thank you.'

We lay in peaceful silence whilst time sloped past us.

'Tobey, d'you know what you are?' I ran a finger across his lips and down his nose and along the curve of his ear before cupping his cheek.

'What?'

Tobey looked at me. If I didn't know any better, I'd say he looked . . . nervous.

I whispered, 'You are . . . my mender of broken things.'

We looked at each other then. I mean, really looked. For just a few seconds, maybe a few plus, but it was enough. Enough for my heartbeat to quicken. Enough to make me catch my breath. Enough to quell any doubts trying to surface in my head. A slow smile swept across Tobey's face. He caught hold of my hand as it fell away from his face and kissed my palm.

'What was that for?' I smiled.

'Dunno. Maybe I mistook your hand for a biscuit,' he teased. 'Besides, you girls like that kind of thing, don't you?'

I snatched back my hand. 'This girl only likes it if you mean it.'

'I mean it,' Tobey replied, no hint of a teasing smile. He had a really strange look on his face. His gaze dropped from my eyes to my lips and stayed there. I ran my tongue over my lips and then my teeth.

'What?' I asked when I couldn't stand it any longer.

'What what?' asked Tobey.

'Why're you staring at my mouth? Have I got some food stuck between my tee—?'

Tobey kissed me. Really kissed me. Soft and gentle and long and loving and passionate. It was bloody lovely. Moments turned into minutes before I finally pulled away.

'I'll take that as a no!' I said, when I got my breath back.

Tobey just smiled. I glanced at the clock on his bedside table.

'I really should go,' I said reluctantly.

'Stay just a bit longer,' Tobey whispered, kissing my forehead and nose before moving to my lips. 'I've got five whole boxes of condoms under my mattress to get through.'

'Tobey, you must be drunk!' I immediately hopped out of bed and started to get dressed.

I ask you! Not even five condoms, but five boxes. What was he like? I turned to glare at him, but instead the frustrated look on Tobey's face made me burst out laughing.

I was laughing.

I was smiling.

You know what, Uncle Jude? Sod you. I'm happy and whatever happens now, you can't take that away from me. And I'll tell you something else. There'll be no more hiding away, no more feeling sorry for myself. Those days are over.

'Thanks, Tobey,' I said, pulling my T-shirt over my head.

'For what?'

'For listening to me. For being with me.'

'You're welcome,' said Tobey, adding hopefully, 'I was joking about using up all five boxes of condoms tonight. We've got all weekend to do that.'

'Omigod! I'm shagging a sexbot,' I exclaimed, sitting down again. 'Tobey, how about we give Mr Ever-Ready a rest for tonight? Besides, I'm sore.'

Tobey was immediately at my side. 'Are you sure you're OK?'

'I'm fine, I promise. I'm sore in a good way, not a bad way,' I tried to explain.

'How does that work?' asked Tobey sceptically.

'I'm not sorry we did it,' I told him. 'In fact, just the opposite.'

Tobey smiled and we kissed again.

'But don't go boasting to your friends about the two of us – and that includes Dan,' I added fiercely when I came up for air. 'Or Mr Ever-Ready will have only his memories to keep him warm. Understand?'

'Understood.' Tobey's smile grew broader.

'I mean it, Tobey. If you say one word about this to anyone, I'll kill you.'

'OK! OK! I said I understood, didn't I?' Tobey said, exasperated. 'Damn, but you're scary when you're annoyed!'

'And don't you forget it,' I replied. 'Are you going to get dressed or not?'

Tobey finally got his bum out of bed. He dressed in silence, but every time I looked at him, he had a ridiculous grin on his face. I had to bite my cheeks to stop myself from laughing with him. If he was a peacock, his tail feathers would be open like a fan and he'd be strutting!

'We still on for tomorrow?' said Tobey.

'If you're going to meet Dan tomorrow afternoon, does that mean you're taking the day off work?'

'Yeah.'

'Tobey, the stupid thing you did today, did that have anything to do with Dan?'

'It might've done.' Tobey was at once cagey.

'Are you going to tell me what you did?'

He shook his head, his expression sombre. 'Not now. Soon.'

Much as I wanted him to confide in me, if I pushed any more, he'd clam up completely. But that did it. No way was I going to let him meet Dan by himself. If I was there, I could at least try to stop him from doing another idiotic thing. I just wished I knew what he was talking about. He'd tell me, of course, but in his own sweet time and not if I forced the issue.

'I'll go with you to the Wasteland tomorrow afternoon. Then we can talk about how to spend the rest of our evening,' I said.

'It's a date,' said Tobey. 'In fact, what're you doing tomorrow morning?'

'Nothing much. Why?'

'Wanna do nothing much with me?'

'OK,' I agreed with a smile. 'Should I just come round here then? Or d'you want to come round to mine?'

Tobey considered. 'You come round here. Your nana Meggie makes me nervous.'

Oh my goodness! Tobey had actually made a decision. I opened my mouth to rib him, but decided against it. After all, I didn't want to put him off making another one at some point!

'Why're you putting on your trainers?' I asked as I watched him fasten them.

'I'm walking you home.'

I stared at him. 'I live next door, Tobey. I think I can make it from your front door to mine without too much trouble.'

'I didn't say you couldn't. But I'm still walking you home,' Tobey insisted.

I decided not to argue. To be honest, it was kind of lovely having Tobey looking out for me. He was definitely a lover, not a fighter. In a clash against Uncle Jude or anyone else come to that, he'd be about as much use as a chocolate frying pan, but it was still sweet.

twenty-one. Tobey

'Jessica, have you moved your bed in there?' I hissed through the locked bathroom door. 'You're not the only one with a bladder, you know?'

'W–why aren't you at work?' Jessica's voice sounded strange, husky, like she was still more than half asleep.

'I've got the day off,' I said, annoyed. 'Why aren't *you* at work?'

'I'm not feeling well,' said Jessica.

'Well, could you not feel well in your own bedroom and let someone else use the bathroom please?' I mean, I was sympathetic and all that, but Godsake! My bladder was about to explode.

If Mum wasn't back from her night shift and fast asleep in her bedroom, I'd've been battering at the bathroom door by now. What on earth was Jessica doing? She'd been in there for *ages*. Being the sole guy in a house with two women was a real test of my patience. After all the girly things I'd seen over the years in our family bathroom, it was a wonder I didn't need some serious therapy.

'Jessica, I need to use the bathroom. NOW!'

'OK! OK!' There came some strange noises from inside the bathroom.

When the door finally opened I launched myself into the room whilst trying to push Jessica out at the same time. She was wearing Mum's old dressing gown, which was at least three sizes too big for her, and she had the bath towel draped over her arm.

'Where're you taking that?' I asked, pointing at the towel.

'To the laundry basket.'

'Why?'

'It's wet.'

'What am I supposed to use?'

'Get another one.'

I frowned as I took a closer look at my sister. 'Godsake, Jessica. You look rough.'

'Thanks,' she intoned, her eyes half shut.

'You look like you've been left out in the rain all day and put away wet.'

'I'm tired. OK?' She glared at me.

'Then take some vitamins and try some eye drops. You look like a vampire.'

'Bog off.' Jessica strode off back to her bedroom. She bumped into the wall twice, though, so as a dramatic gesture it kind of failed.

Frowning, I sniffed at the bathroom.

'Why does it smell of vinegar in here?' I called after my sister.

'Nail polish remover,' Jess called back before entering her room.

Godsake! Couldn't she use that stuff in her own room and not the bathroom? My bladder dictating my pace, I ran to the airing cupboard, grabbed a towel from above the hot water cylinder, and ran back to the bathroom. It was not unknown for my mum or sister to slip into the bathroom ahead of me when my back was turned. And the fact that Jessica had only just come out wouldn't stop her from trying to pop back in. I was going to have a lovely long shower, wash my hair and shave before Callie arrived. I wanted to be clean and look neat without making it look like I'd been to a lot of trouble, or any trouble at all come to that. Time to get to work on making myself irresistible.

Callie didn't turn up until mid morning. I sat in the front room, listening to my favourite rock band with the volume turned down low so as not to wake Mum. I kept glancing out of the window, watching the passers-by. The moment I saw Callie go past my window, I sprinted into the hall. I opened the door before she had her finger halfway to the doorbell.

'Mum's asleep,' I gave as the reason why I'd come to the door so quickly. But to tell the truth, Mum had nothing to do with it.

Callie was wearing a light-blue, sleeveless, V-necked T-shirt and dark-blue jeans. She wore her hair loose for a change and it fell in curly waves around her face and down past her shoulders. Her earrings were gold, reflecting her skin tone. She smiled, her eyes warm brown today. She looked so good, my stomach kinda hiccupped. Every time that happened it took me by surprise. Wasn't sure I liked it much either. It made me feel . . . exposed, like wearing trousers with no bum to them. But I had no control over the way my body reacted to her, no matter how much I tried to rationalize my feelings or find a logical explanation for what she did to me.

'How are you?' I said, opening the front door wide for her to enter.

'I'm fine,' Callie sashayed past me. I was never really sure what that word meant until that moment when she did it. Then I knew all right!

I glanced up the stairs. No sounds, but I still lowered my voice. 'Are you OK after last night?'

Callie nodded. 'I'm fine.'

'I . . . you look . . .' I stopped babbling like an idiot and leaned in to kiss her. My arms wrapped around her, her arms wrapped around me and we kissed like we had less than one minute before the world ended!

When I finally let her go, Callie laughed. 'What was that for?'

'Just saying hello.' I grinned.

'I can't wait to see how you hold a conversation then?' Callie teased. 'Any chance of a coffee?' She walked ahead of me into the kitchen. By the time I got there, she was already taking out two cups. 'You gonna have one with me?'

'Yeah, go on then.'

I put on the kettle whilst Callie spooned coffee into both cups and two sugars into mine.

'Where's your sister?' she asked.

'In her room, probably on her phone where she'll be for hours.'

'What're we going to do after our coffees?'

'What would you like to do?' I asked.

I knew what I'd like to do, but there was no way Callie would go for that with Jessica in the house.

'Can we watch a DVD?' she asked. 'And can I choose it?'

Oh hell, no!

'We can't,' I said quickly. 'We have to go and see Dan soon.'

'Not for hours yet. Please, Tobey. I fancy relaxing on the sofa and watching a film or two,' said Callie.

'But, Callie . . .'

'Please. For me . . .' She started batting her long eyelashes in my direction. 'We could cuddle up . . .'

'Oh all right then,' I said, my heart sinking at the prospect of hours spent watching soppy films. 'Damn it, Callie, I must really like you or something.'

'Or something,' Callie agreed with a wink.

twenty-two. Tobey

'So where's Dan then?' Callie asked, looking around.

'I don't know,' I replied stonily. I checked my watch. Twenty minutes past four. I must've been truly dim to believe he would show up. I'd give him five more minutes. I looked around. There was a good-natured impromptu football match going on, mostly Noughts but also some Crosses. Callie and I stood on the sidelines, half watching as we waited for my so-called friend to put in an appearance. The Wasteland was pretty crowded, even for a Saturday afternoon. I glanced at Callie, taking in her slight frown as she watched the football. She hadn't said much as we'd walked to the Wasteland. Something was definitely gnawing at her.

Callie glanced up at the sky. 'Can we not stay here too long? I think it's going to rain.'

'Thank God,' I said.

The weather over the last two weeks had been diabolical, hot as hell and twice as fierce. We were all about due for a break. That was probably why the Wasteland was so crowded, because the air had cooled down a bit. Being outside today didn't feel so much like being an insect tortured under a magnifying glass.

'How much longer do we have to stay here?' Callie asked.

'No idea.'

'When is Dan going to get here?'

'How the hell should I know?'

'Well, excuse me all over the place,' Callie snapped back.

'Sorry, babe.' I leaned in to kiss her.

'You're forgiven.' She smiled when at last our kiss ended.

'Get a room!' some git called out from the football pitch.

Callie and I shared a smile and ignored the wolf whistles and ribald comments. Apart from Dan's vanishing act, the day hadn't been too bad. In fact, it'd been on the great side of good. Callie returned to her house and brought back a DVD which was a certain-sure cure for insomnia. The thing was so slow, I swear I could feel my hair growing. So whilst she was watching it, her back pressed against my chest, her feet up on the sofa, I wrapped my arms around her and made the most of holding her tight, touching and stroking her body, nibbling on her ear and kissing her whenever the film's plot slackened – and the plot wasn't exactly drum tight.

Plus whilst Callie had been watching the film, it had given me a chance to zone out and do some serious thinking about my predicament, as well as Callie's uncle. If Jude McGregor really was alive, if somehow he'd escaped the devastation at the Isis Hotel, then I would need money to get Callie away from him. With money, Callie and I could escape to some place where her Uncle Jude would never find us. It would mean missing school and my exams, but I'd do it in a heartbeat to keep Callie safe. I wouldn't tell her of my plans just yet. I had to get enough money together first. Deliveries?

Now if Dan would just show his face, Callie and I could be off and doing. I had plans for today. An expensive meal, a film or maybe even a theatre trip to impress her and then we'd take it from there. We had the whole evening ahead of us. And we could discuss our future together when the time was right. I'd have to pick my moment carefully. I looked at Callie and realized that we had our whole lives ahead of us. Callie and I, together.

A surprisingly chilly breeze brought me back to the Wasteland. The wind ruffled my hair and tugged at my T-shirt. I glanced up. The clouds were definitely getting darker. Callie was right. Rain was coming. Though I found it hard to care about the rain, the sun or anything in between at that precise moment. Callie's gold hoop-earrings glinted, catching my eye. Not that I needed her earrings sparkling in my direction to make me look at her. She was so damned beautiful it was hard to take my eyes off her. I put my arm around her, or at least I tried to. She shied away before turning to face me.

'What's the matter?' I asked.

'Tobey, when are we going to talk about what happened last night?' Callie began, albeit reluctantly.

'Why?'

What was there to talk about? Godsake! This wasn't going to be one of those girly 'let's-analyse-the-thing-to-death' talks, was it?

Callie looked here, there and anywhere but at me. 'I know . . . I know it probably didn't mean as much to you as it did to me, but—'

Whoa!

'Where'd you get that idea?'

'Well, you didn't mention it all morning,' said Callie.

'What was I supposed to say?' I frowned. 'Great shag?'

Callie glared at me. 'See! Everything is a big joke to you.'

What was she on about?

'What're you on about?'

Was Callie deliberately trying to pick a fight? Or maybe I'd been such crap in bed, she was trying to find a way to dump me.

'Tobey, I don't regret what happened last night, really I don't. But I've been thinking all morning that maybe we shouldn't do it again, at least for a while.'

'Why?' I asked, aghast. Looks like I'd been right. I know it hadn't been the world's most polished perform-ance, but it was my first time too.

'Last night was about comfort and getting lost in each other to shut out the outside world. I just don't think that's a good enough reason to carry on . . . doing it.'

'Is that all last night meant to you?' I asked, acutely disappointed. 'A bit of comfort and a way to take your mind off your uncle?'

'Don't you dare say that,' Callie rounded on me. 'You're the one who kept crowing about not being a virgin any more. You're the one who said you did some-thing really stupid yesterday, so being with me was obvi-ously just your way of forgetting your problems for a while.'

'That's not true,' I denied.

'Isn't it? OK, Tobey, no teasing, no jokes, no evasions, just the truth. How do you feel about me?'

I opened my mouth to tell her straight, only to snap it shut again. I wanted to tell her, I really did. But certain words were very hard to retract. Once they were out, they took on a life of their own and if I said them, they might turn round and take a chunk out of my arse. Callie was watching me intently.

'This is ridiculous. You're being really stupid,' I said at last.

'Thanks,' Callie said, not attempting to mask the hurt in her voice. 'That confirms what I thought.'

'Callie, I . . .'

'Forget it, Tobey. I was drowning, you threw me a life-line, now it's over.' Callie shrugged. 'I was stupid to hope it meant any more to you than that.'

'Hi, you guys,' Dan yelled out from several metres away.

'Look, we can't discuss this here,' I told Callie. 'Once Dan gives me my money, we can go for a meal and talk about it. OK?'

'Nothing to talk about,' Callie said coldly.

Why did I suddenly feel like I was clinging onto our relationship by my fingertips? Probably because that was exactly what I was doing. It was a choice between yanking open my chest and showing Callie my heart with all the risks that involved – or losing her anyway.

'Callie, we need to talk,' I said.

'Talk or listen to you insult me some more?'

'Talk.'

Callie didn't reply.

'I'm sorry I called you stupid,' I said, exasperated. 'Can we please just go somewhere and talk? Please?'

Callie didn't answer. Instead she turned to face Dan. I did the same, feeling like I was drowning. Dan approached us, a big, beaming smile on his face.

'What's the point of having a flash watch if you still can't get anywhere on time?' I snapped when he got close enough.

'I'm here now, aren't I?' Dan couldn't see the problem. 'Hi, Callie. You're looking fine, as always.'

'Thanks, Dan.'

'I mean it. You look real fit,' he said, moving closer to her.

Annoyance began to bubble inside me like a saucepan of water heating on a cooker.

'Callie, I can take you places and buy you things that Tobey hasn't even dreamed about.' Dan's smile was an oil slick on his face as he regarded her. 'Tobey's my mate and all, but when're you going to dump the loser and go out with me?'

Callie gave me a filthy look, then turned to Dan like she was seriously considering his offer.

'You even think about making a move on Callie and I'll break every bone in your body,' I told Dan straight. 'And when you're buried, I'll dig you up to break each bone all over again.'

Dan and Callie stared at me. Then they both burst out laughing. What was so damned funny?

'Someone's got it bad,' Dan said.

Callie looked at me, a strange light twinkling in her eyes. All the ice in her expression had melted. I turned away from her so she couldn't get the full effect of the blush cooking my face.

'Now you see, Tobey,' she said softly. 'That's all you had to say!'

'I don't know what you mean,' I mumbled, deciding to ignore them both till they stopped laughing at me.

Beyond the football pitch, across the grass, a black WMW pulled up. If I hadn't known any better I would've sworn it was McAuley's car. But what would McAuley be doing at the Wasteland on a Saturday afternoon? Two suited Nought men I'd never seen before got out and ambled across the grass towards the football pitch as if they didn't have a care in the world.

'So, Callie, when did you first manage to wrap my friend around your little finger?' Dan asked, holding an imaginary microphone to her face.

'Well, Dan, it all started when I was seven years old . . .' Callie squeaked out like her lungs were full of helium.

Dan had his back to the two men, who were slowly but surely heading in our direction. Something wasn't right. I looked around. A white saloon was parked on the opposite side of the pitch. Two men got out of that car, two Crosses. They also started heading towards the football pitch. I turned back to the two Nought men walking towards us. They were talking to each other, but the prickling on the back of my neck was getting worse. The two Noughts were only a few metres away now. They reached beneath their jackets – and then all hell was let loose.

'GET DOWN!' I yelled.

But my words came too late.

twenty-three. Callie

Several loud bangs sounded, like lots of cars backfiring in quick succession. Each noise made me jump. I looked around. The whole world reduced speed to ultra slow-motion. Every colour, every sensation was heightened except . . . except all I could hear now was my heart strumming. The world was slow, my heartbeat was fast. Strange combination.

All around us, people scattered like points on a compass. I could see their mouths move, watch their frantic expressions, but still the only sound was my own heartbeat, growing ever faster. It was like a drum inside me beating its own time. What on earth was going on? I looked around. Men with guns. Men with guns on either side of the pitch, shooting at each other. And all of us in the middle.

Get down, Callie.

Drop down.

Get down. NOW.

Two Cross men had their guns drawn and were shooting past us in the direction of the road behind us. I turned just in time to see McAuley, sitting in the back of his car, the back window all the way down. Flashes flared from inside the car. Bullets? *Bullets.* My head turned this way and that. Tobey was shouting at me, his mouth moving oh so slowly, too slowly to make out the words. But he was trying to tell me something important, something urgent. That much was evident in his eyes. And he was pulling at me.

Stop pulling me.

Dan was already on the ground.

GET DOWN, CALLIE . . .

From inside his car, McAuley fired his gun. And his gun was pointing straight at us. The gun jerked in McAuley's hand. He'd fired. And again. I didn't have time to warn Tobey or push him out the way. I stepped in front of him.

twenty-four. Tobey

'Godsake, Callie. Get down.' I hit the floor, trying to pull Callie with me, but she stood stock-still in front of me, staring across the park. I scrambled in front of her, pulling harder on her arm. Furious, I looked up at her, wondering why the hell she wasn't moving. Godsake! Bullets were now whizzing around us like mosquitoes round a blood bank. Godsake . . . Callie looked down at me. And that's when my world crashed to an abrupt halt.

A dark crimson stain was spreading out over the front of Callie's sky-blue shirt. More gunshots. Something glanced off the side of Callie's head and she toppled, her body falling like a house of playing cards.

'CALLIE . . .' I threw my body over hers, trying to protect her from stray bullets. McAuley's car screeched down the road, burning rubber as it went. The two Cross men who'd made a great show of strolling across the grass towards us were now racing back to their own car. Moments later, they too screeched out of sight. Everyone ran for their lives. Dan, who'd dived down beside me at the sound of the first bullet being fired, picked himself up and bolted. Within moments there was no one left on the Wasteland except me and Callie.

I sat up, pulling Callie with me. The crimson stain was

growing bigger, covering more of Callie's shirt. There was a circular hole on the left-hand side of her shirt, just below her shoulder. Blood ran down the side of her head, from her temple past her ears.

'HELP US! SOMEONE HELP US!' I yelled out.

Callie's eyes were closed and her breath left her nose and mouth with a strange rattling sound. I looked around at all the closed windows of the flats and houses that surrounded the Wasteland on three sides.

'PLEASE. SOMEONE HELP . . .' I pulled Callie to me, rocking her back and forth in my arms as we both sat on the ground.

Digging into my trouser pocket, I brought out my phone with one hand, laying it on the ground so I could dial the emergency services for an ambulance without letting go of Callie.

'Callie, hang on,' I whispered in her ear. 'Help will soon be here. Just hang on.'

The clouds separated and sunlight bathed us, so bright I was momentarily blinded. The rattling sound Callie was making suddenly stopped. No . . . She lay limp in my arms. And her sudden silence was far, far worse. In the distance I could hear the sound of a siren. Someone some-where must've phoned for help after all.

'Callie?' I whispered.

She lay so still, like a broken doll. My hands and clothes were covered with her blood. I hugged her to me, her cheek against mine, rocking her gently back and forth.

I've got you, Callie. I've got you. I'll never let you go. Never.

You and me, babe, against the world.

twenty-five. Tobey

The hospital corridor smelled strongly of disinfectant. Irregular beeps sounded all around me. Footsteps constantly hurried past me, but no one stopped. They wouldn't let me stay with Callie, no matter how much I pleaded. The paramedics who arrived in the ambulance didn't even want me to travel with them, but I held onto Callie's hand like we were super-glued together. Once we arrived at the hospital, Callie was whisked away to theatre. A nurse took me into a small room and asked me a number of questions about Callie's medical history, most of which I couldn't answer. I phoned Callie's mum, but she wasn't answering her mobile so I had to leave a message. I phoned Callie's home, but Meggie wasn't in either. No one was where they were supposed to be. All I could do was leave messages to say that Callie had been shot and was undergoing emergency surgery at Mercy Community Hospital. Not the sort of message I wanted to leave, but what choice did I have? I was ushered into the waiting room, which was heaving with people. There were no more available chairs so I leaned against the wall, texting my mum to let her know what had happened as I knew her phone would be switched off whilst she was working. She was somewhere in this hospital, but I didn't go looking for her. I needed to stay put so I could find out how Callie was doing the moment she was out of surgery.

Callie had been shot.

She might die.

Please don't let her die . . .

Even now I was still trying to work out what had happened. Images flashed like a series of snapshots in my head. The two Cross men in the fancy white car, they had to work for the Dowds. And McAuley and his men turning up at the Wasteland at exactly the same time, there was no way that was a mere coincidence. It hadn't kicked off in Meadowview like that in years. And now Callie was fighting for her life with a bullet in her. Maybe two. It was only just beginning to sink in.

Please don't let me lose her. Not now.

Not now . . .

Some instinct had me looking up, then around. My instincts hadn't let me down. Two officers were fast approaching, weaving their way through the others in the waiting room to get to me. They both wore suits, but I knew they were the police. One was a middle-aged Cross, the other a younger Nought, in his mid-twenties at a guess. The middle-aged Cross copper already wore a smile beneath his pencil-thin moustache. His dark eyes were watchful and shrewd. The Nought copper wore his blond hair buzz-cut. They got closer, their eyes never leaving mine. They were poised – that's the only word for it, poised – like they thought I was about to do a runner. I straightened up off the wall, then stayed perfectly still. When at last they reached me, they both stood directly in front of me. I wasn't going anywhere, even if I wanted to.

'You're the one who came in with the gunshot victim?' asked the Cross copper.

I nodded. 'Her name is Callie Hadley.'

The Cross copper extended his hand. 'I'm DI Omari Boothe. This is Sergeant Paul Kenwood.'

Warily, I shook the detective's hand. Sergeant Kenwood nodded in my direction, his blue eyes frosty, his hands staying firmly at his sides.

'What's your name, son?' asked the detective inspector, his tone even, as if he was asking for the time. Sergeant Kenwood dug out a notebook and pen from his pocket and flicked it open decisively.

'Tobey Durbridge.'

'Age?'

'Seventeen.'

'When are you eighteen?'

'In two months.' Why did he need to know that?

'Address?'

I told him.

'And the girl you came in with, you said her name is Callie Hadley?'

'Callie Rose Hadley, yes.'

'D'you know her address?'

'She lives next door to me in Johnstone Street, at number fifty-five.'

Sergeant Kenwood was scribbling furiously in his notebook, even though I hadn't said much.

'Can you tell us what happened?' asked Detective Boothe.

'I'm still not quite sure.' I shook my head. 'One moment Callie and I were watching a football match and the next moment bullets were whizzing round us like midges. It all happened so fast. A matter of seconds.'

'And where was this?'

'The pitch at the Wasteland.' I glanced at Sergeant Kenwood. He had yet to say a word. Perhaps they were playing chatty cop, silent cop.

'Who was doing the shooting?' asked the detective.

'No idea. When the bullets started flying, I was just trying to keep my head down.'

'What was Callie doing?'

'She was standing in front of me. I think . . . I think she froze.'

'How many gunshots were there in total?'

I shrugged. No idea.

'Under five? Under ten? Under fifteen?' prompted Detective Boothe.

'Maybe under ten,' I replied. 'I wasn't exactly trying to count them.'

'Did the shots all come from one direction or different directions?'

Careful, Tobey . . . I considered. 'Different directions, I think. That's why they seemed to be all around us. But I can't be sure.'

'Did you see any cars in the vicinity?'

I frowned at Detective Boothe and shook my head. 'I was watching the football match, so I wasn't paying attention to anything but that.'

'You didn't see anything?'

'No. Sorry.'

'Is Callie Hadley a friend of yours?'

'Yes,' I said warily. 'She's my girlfriend.'

Sergeant Kenwood snorted derisively at my words.

'D'you have a problem with that?' I asked belligerently.

'No. But she does, if you're the best she can do,' Sergeant Kenwood retorted. He looked at me like he wasn't looking at much. 'If that was my girlfriend lying on an operating table with a bullet or two in her, I'd want to get the bastard who did it. But all you Noughts in Meadowview have acute three-monkeys disease – see no evil, hear no evil, speak no evil.'

'All us Noughts in Meadowview have to live here when the police are nowhere around,' I replied.

'We can protect you,' said Detective Boothe quickly. 'You and your family, if that's what's worrying you.'

'I don't need protecting because I didn't see anything,' I insisted. 'I wish I had, but I didn't.'

The two coppers exchanged a look. They didn't believe a word.

'Is there anything else you can tell us about what happened?' asked the detective.

Pause.

'I—'

'Tobey? Tobey.' Callie's mum, Sephy, made a bee-line for me. 'What happened? Where's my daughter?'

'She's still in surgery,' I explained at once. 'I'm waiting to hear more.'

'You're Mrs Hadley?' asked DI Boothe, surprised.

'Miss Hadley,' Sephy corrected.

Both coppers looked Sephy up and down, before turning their speculative gaze to me.

'This boy claims that your daughter is his girlfriend,' said Sergeant Kenwood.

'She is,' Sephy dismissed. 'They've been friends for years. Could someone please tell me what's going on? Tobey, your message said Callie had been shot.'

'Your daughter was caught in the crossfire during an earlier incident,' said the detective before I could reply. 'I'm just trying to ascertain the facts from this boy, who was with your daughter at the time. But he claims he didn't see a thing.'

'Tobey?' Sephy turned to me, her eyes blazing, frown lines like train tracks marring her face.

'Don't you think I would say something if I could?' I protested.

'I don't know,' said Sephy. 'Would you?'

We regarded each other. I had to force myself not to look away. We both knew the way things worked in Meadowview.

'I need to see my daughter,' Sephy said at last, turning away from me. But not before I caught the intense disappointment clouding her eyes. It stung.

'Miss Hadley, if we could ask you one or two questions first,' insisted DI Boothe.

'Your questions will have to wait. I want to see my daughter,' Sephy insisted.

'It'll just take a minute, I assure you,' said the detective. 'Could we start by confirming your address, please?'

They led the way out of the waiting room. I could see their silhouettes through the frosted-glass window, but I was too far away to hear a word. I edged closer so that I wouldn't be across the room when Sephy came looking for me. I stood near the doorway, dreading the inevitable. After a minute or two, she came back into the waiting room, alone. My heart bounced at her approach. I knew full well what was coming.

'Tobey, I don't want any crap from you,' Sephy warned me, her voice hard with intent. 'Tell me what happened. And the truth this time.'

We regarded each other. Even though I towered over her, she still scared me to death. I admit it. Sephy was a lioness trying to protect her offspring and I was getting in her way.

'It's like I told the coppers, I hit the deck and stayed there when the bullets started flying.'

'And you didn't think to pull my daughter down with you?'

'I tried. It all happened so fast,' I said feebly.

'Did you see who did the shooting?'

I didn't reply. I couldn't lie to her, but there was no way I could answer the question either.

'Tobey, I asked you a question. Who was doing the shooting?'

Silence.

'I see,' Sephy said quietly. 'You told those police officers that Callie was your girlfriend. Did you mean a girl who just happens to be your friend or did you mean something more than that?'

'I meant both,' I replied quietly.

'But not enough of a friend for you to man up and do the right thing?'

'That's not fair—'

'Fair?' Sephy leaped on the word. 'My daughter has been shot. She could *die*. Don't you dare talk to me about "fair".'

What could I say to that? Nothing. Sephy looked me up and down, her expression bathing me with complete contempt.

'You know what? Callie can do without your so-called friendship. So why don't you go home? You're no use to anyone here. Now if you'll excuse me, I'm going to find out what's happening to my daughter.'

She was already turning round and heading out of the waiting room to find the nearest doctor or nurse. I caught up with her.

'I'll come with you.'

'No, you won't, Tobey,' Sephy turned to tell me. 'If you don't think enough of my daughter to tell the police who did this to her, then I have no use for you, and neither has Callie. Go home.'

Without waiting for my reply, Sephy strode away. After a few steps, she turned back with a look in her eyes I'd never seen before.

'Oh, and Tobey?'

'Yes?'

'You're no longer welcome in my house.' Sephy regarded me to ensure I'd got the message.

'Yes, Miss Hadley.'

The Fall . . .

twenty-six

'Tobey, can I come in?' Mum's voice was soft outside my door.

I didn't answer.

'Tobey, please.'

Silence.

I heard Mum sigh, but she respected the fact that my door was firmly closed and headed back downstairs. Mum had been knocking on my bedroom door at periodic intervals all morning – ever since she'd got in from work. How I wished she'd give up and leave me alone. I sat on the floor in the corner of my room directly opposite the door. I'd been sitting there ever since I'd arrived home the night before, with one knee drawn up, the other leg flat against the carpeted floor. In my left hand, my fingers worked at the super ball I usually kept on my desk. It was the size of a large marble and decorated with swirls of different shades of green and brown. Callie had given me the thing years ago, I can't even remember why. I hadn't moved from this corner all night, only shifting positions slightly when one leg or the other threatened to go numb. I'd never watched the dawn break before. In the middle of the night, the dark seemed so dense, it was easy to believe it would perpetually paint my room.

But the grey-blue light had pushed slowly but irrevocably against every shadow until they were all but gone.

And whilst watching the arrival of dawn, I'd been thinking. I'd been thinking a lot.

Callie's mum Sephy considered me gutless, as did the police. I wasn't about to argue with them. In spite of what Sephy had said to me the night before, I'd stayed at the hospital until Callie was out of surgery. I didn't sit with Callie's mum. She made it very clear that I wasn't wanted anywhere near her. I listened on the periphery when the surgeon finally arrived to tell us what was happening. Callie had been shot twice, once in the chest and one bullet had glanced off her temple. The bullet in her chest was out, but Callie was still in a critical condition.

'Callie has lost a lot of blood and there's considerable tissue damage, so she's not out of the woods yet. The bullet that entered her chest missed her heart by about a centimetre,' said Mr Bunch, the Cross surgeon. 'And the bullet that caught her temple caused a hairline fracture of her skull, but at least the bullet didn't penetrate. However, the next forty-eight hours will be crucial.'

'Can I see her?' I stepped forward to ask.

'She'll be unconscious for quite some time,' the surgeon warned me.

'I need to see her,' I insisted.

'No,' Sephy began. 'I don't think so . . .'

'Please, Sephy. Please.'

Sephy emphatically shook her head.

'I'll camp outside Callie's room or the ward or the hospital building if I have to until you change your mind,' I said desperately. 'Please let me see her. *Please.*'

Sephy scrutinized me for several seconds. Her gaze slid away from mine and a frown appeared across her forehead. When at last she looked at me again, she nodded, albeit reluctantly. I wondered what had made her change her mind, but I wasn't about to push my luck by asking. Mr Bunch led the way to the Intensive Care Unit. Callie was in a room by herself, the closest one to the nurses' station.

Nothing could've adequately prepared me for what I was about to see. Callie Rose was hooked up to all kinds of monitors and beeping machines. She had plastic tubing running into her mouth and an IV drip, plus a blood bag running into her arm. Her head was swathed in a bandage. Her whole body seemed so much smaller, like she'd shrunk in on herself. And all the paraphernalia around her was overwhelming. She was almost lost in the middle of it all.

I walked over to her and stroked the back of her hand which lay above the white sheets. For a long time I could do nothing but look down at her. Then I bent and whispered in her ear before kissing her forehead. I straightened up slowly, unable to take my eyes off her face. She looked fragile as crystal, like one more knock and she would irrevocably shatter.

Callie Rose, forgive me . . .

I took hold of her cold hand and held it in my own, never wanting to let it go. You see it in films and on the TV all the time. Someone's in trouble, dying, and their mum or dad or partner or best mate makes all kinds of promises and begs anyone who'll listen to swap places. Well, that's what I did. I would've swapped places with Callie quicker than a thought. But no one was listening.

She remained in the bed, hooked up to all those machines. I stood beside her, helpless.

My throat had swollen up, making it difficult for me to catch my breath.

Callie, if you can hear me, please . . .

But before I could finish my silent plea, the rhythm in the room changed. Where the monitors were beeping slow and steady before, now there was just a continuous droning hum coming from them. An alarm began to sound. Suddenly the room was full and I was shoved backwards out of the way. The pillow was whipped out from beneath Callie's head as a wave of doctors and nurses appeared from nowhere to swarm over her. And a continuous flat line continued its slide across the heart monitor. Sephy tried to get closer to her daughter, but they wouldn't let her stay either. The door was closed behind both of us. Sephy watched through the small window, her fists clenched against the pane as if she wanted to batter at it. She turned to me, her dark-brown eyes blazing.

'You . . .' she hissed. If words could kill, that one accusatory word would've butchered me where I stood. 'Who did this? *Tell me!'*

I looked through the window at the doctors and nurses still trying to resuscitate Callie, before turning back to Callie's mum. What would she do if I told her? Sephy was tough – with everything she'd been through in her life, she had to be. But she was no match for the Dowds or McAuley and his hired muscle-heads. If she went after them, which she undoubtedly would, Callie would end up an orphan . . . if Callie survived. *No. When* Callie survived. She just had to make it, and so did her mum. In that moment, I made my choice.

'I can't say 'cause I don't know.' The small words were outsized and razor-sharp in my mouth.

Sephy turned away from me. At that instant I ceased to be for her. We had nothing else to say to each other. I turned away and left the ICU and the hospital.

My grip on the super ball tightened. It wasn't like in films and games and on the TV. What had happened at the Wasteland hadn't been choreographed into chaotic elegance. No make-up person had drawn in cuts and bruises. No costume person had decided which knee of which pair of jeans needed to be torn. The bullets started flying, everyone started screaming and scattering and diving to the ground. The cuts and bruises had been all too real. Torn jeans and dirt-stained clothes had happened spontaneously. And the blood on Callie hadn't been sprayed on. It'd been pumped out. There was no one to shout: 'Cut. Great take,' or 'Let's do it again. Action.' Only now, for the first time, did I truly realize what Mum meant when she kept insisting that 'Life is not a dress rehearsal'. There were no rewrites, no retakes, no re-do icon to click on. Callie had been shot. Real life was agonizingly hard to handle. Real life was just agonizing.

I couldn't get the image of Callie lying on that hospital bed out of my head. I knew I never would. No one told me that helplessness made you feel so minuscule. At school, at work, even here in my own bedroom, I occupied very little space. Was it so wrong to want just a little bit more from life? I'd convinced myself that that was what Dan had been offering. Just a little bit more than I already had. And now everything had fallen to pieces. I stayed in my room throughout the night and most of the morning, only leaving when I needed to go to the loo. I didn't eat, I didn't sleep, I couldn't think straight. Jessica and Mum left me alone for the most part. Mum put a plate of ham sandwiches outside my door, even though I'd called out after at least ten minutes of her cajoling me to eat that I wasn't hungry. To get her off my back, I even tried one, but it was like chewing a crumpled-up page of printer paper. It didn't taste of anything and it wouldn't go down. So I spat it out into my bin and gave up. I greeted the following night lying on top of my bed, staring up at my ceiling. Closing my eyes, I waited for sleep to come and get me. But it was as if a switch had been flicked on inside my head and now my brain wouldn't stop whirling.

McAuley.

It had been McAuley's car at the Wasteland. McAuley's men had walked towards us on the football pitch. McAuley's men had shot first. And the two Cross guys who'd returned fire, they had to work for the Dowds. Was the shootout planned between them? Somehow I didn't think so. If they wanted to shoot it out, they could find somewhere better than a public park. So why had both groups turned up at the Wasteland? It didn't make sense. They weren't there to kill each other. One set of gangsters had to be there for another reason entirely. And the other lot – well they were there by either luck or design. I didn't know anything about the Dowds, except by reputation. They were ruthless and deadly when crossed, just like McAuley. All I knew about McAuley were the stories about him that were common knowledge and the things I'd learned from Dan. Had McAuley's men been after Dan? That didn't make sense. Dan had been working for McAuley for ages now. Dan and his deliveries. My luck had seriously run out from the time I agreed to . . . to . . .

Deliveries.

Ross Resnick.

I'd delivered the parcel to Ross Resnick's wife, just like Dan had asked. Was that the reason McAuley came after Dan? Because Dan should've delivered the package himself?

Or maybe . . . just maybe McAuley was after me?

Had Dan told McAuley what I'd said about not taking the fall alone if the police came knocking at my door? Was that what this was all about? Did McAuley decide I was far too dangerous to him? Godsake! I'd said a lot, but I hadn't meant it. It was just a lot of angry hot air released on the spur of the moment. I mean, as if I could take on McAuley. He had to know that I couldn't touch him. But McAuley and his men had evidently decided they needed to take care of business. McAuley'd be safe and I'd be too dead to be sorry. Was McAuley after both Dan and me? Was that the idea, to kill two birds with one stone? Or maybe I was the only one who was expendable. Either way, McAuley wanted me gone. Permanently.

That was the only explanation that made sense.

The only thing I didn't understand was how the Dowd family thugs had turned up at the same time. How did they know what McAuley had planned? There was no way they would've turned up just to save my sorry hide.

They didn't know me, and even if they did, I meant less than nothing to them.

I sought out some other more rational, reasonable explanation for what had happened – but there was none. The more I thought about McAuley coming after me, the more it seemed right.

The question was, what was I going to do about it?

As long as McAuley perceived me to be a threat, I was up shit creek with both hands and feet tied. I might as well just paint a bloody great target on my back. Is that how Dan was feeling? Where was he now? Hiding out somewhere? Or did he know he wasn't the intended target? Was he going to do a runner?

At long last, after three a.m., I finally passed out. It didn't last long. A couple of hours, according to my alarm clock. And no matter how hard I tried, I just couldn't get back to sleep.

Blood running down Callie's skin, spreading out across her blue T-shirt . . .

Blood running down the side of Callie's face . . .

Callie's eyes closing as she toppled over in front of me . . .

Gunshots like fireworks exploding all around us . . .

Those were the nightmares that forced me awake. Those were the images in my head that wouldn't leave, even with my eyes open. Especially with my eyes open. There was only one thing I could do. It was so dangerous – and not just for me but for those around me – but what choice did I have?

I had two options. I could either run and never stop, or I could get McAuley, before he got me.

Get McAuley?

Get real. Why didn't I stop all the wars on the planet and cure all diseases known to humankind whilst I was at it?

Get McAuley . . .

But I had to at least try. I owed Callie that much. He had to pay for what he'd done. And it was a simple matter of McAuley or me. What was that saying about keeping your friends close and your enemies closer? Experience was the greatest teacher. I had to get close to McAuley, convince him that I wasn't a threat.

And then it would be my turn.

There was one more week left before the school term ended. Not that it mattered. One week or one month, I just couldn't go back. My plans had to be changed completely. I had other matters to take care of now. I broke out my phone and speed–dialled. It took a good twenty seconds before my call was finally answered.

'Hi, Tobey,' said Dan before I could say a word. 'How are you? You OK? That was some shit on Saturday, yeah?'

Dan's tone was all friendly concern. It took a couple of moments before I could muster up a reply.

'Dan, I need to see you.'

'We're meeting this evening for football practice, so I'll see you then,' Dan pointed out. 'And we missed you at our football match yesterday.'

After everything that'd happened, that was all he had to say to me? My grip tightened around my mobile phone.

'You do know about Callie, don't you?'

'Yeah, I know.' Dan's voice took on a more sombre timbre. I for one was glad to hear the end of his jolly, bouncy tone. 'I'm sorry.'

Sorry . . .

So much I wanted to say. So much I couldn't.

'Where're we going to meet?' I asked quietly.

'When?'

'Now.'

'Now? But it's the arse-crack of dawn. What about football practice later? Aren't you going to come?'

'Not in the mood. I've got more important matters to deal with,' I said. 'I'll meet you in twenty outside the cinema. OK?'

'But it's not even open yet—'

'Dan, I'm not inviting you to watch a film,' I snapped. 'And by the way, did you tell McAuley what I said about grassing him up if the police came knocking?'

Silence.

'Thanks a lot.'

'You sounded like you meant it,' Dan protested. 'What was I supposed to do?'

You were supposed to have my back.

'You were supposed to know I'd never do that.'

'That's what I told Mr McAuley, I swear,' Dan rushed to explain. 'I told him it was just talk.'

I shook my head. Dan still hadn't connected all the dots. He was never very good on cause and effect.

'The cinema, Dan. Twenty minutes.' I hung up, then waited to see if he would phone me back. He didn't. It was only as I stared down at the phone on my lap that I realized with a start I was still wearing the same blood-stained shirt I'd worn at the Wasteland. Callie's blood had dried into the material, which had now stuck to my skin. And I could smell it. Why couldn't I smell it before? By the time I pulled off my shirt, I was shaking. Balling it up, I dropped it in the bin by my desk, then headed for the bathroom. I stripped off the rest of my clothes and got into the bath tub before turning on the shower. I didn't do my usual of allowing the water to run warm before I even let a toe get wet. The water was freezing, but I didn't care. It didn't matter. After a couple of minutes it was hot enough. I washed my hair and soaped my body. But it didn't matter how much or how hard I scrubbed, I could still feel Callie's blood sticking to my skin.

twenty-seven

I stepped out of the house, carefully closing the door behind me. Mum was still working nights so was fast asleep, as was my sister. Just recently, Jessica always seemed to be tired. Revising for her final exam this week, maybe? I didn't want to wake up either of them. Answering questions was not at the top of my list of priorities right now. I stepped onto the pavement when a question had me whirling around.

'Excuse me, but are you Tobey Durbridge?'

A tall, willowy Cross woman with braids falling like a waterfall round her face stood in front of me.

'Yes, I am.' I frowned.

Who was this woman? I'd never seen her before in my life.

'I understand you were with Callie Rose Hadley when she got shot?' said the woman.

'Yes, I was.' My frown deepened.

The woman's eyes lit up. 'Got one!' she called out. She brought her right hand out from behind her back. She was holding a microphone. A Nought man stepped out from behind the unmarked white van parked in front of our house. He was holding a TV camera. I stared in horror as the man came straight at me.

'Who are you?' I asked, taking a step back.

'Josie Braden. Channel Nineteen News,' said the woman as if she was delivering all I should want or need to know. 'You wouldn't believe how hard it's been to find a witness to Callie Hadley's shooting.' She turned to her colleague. 'Are we up and running, Jack?'

'In a moment,' Jack replied, checking his camera. A red light appeared at the front, like a small demon's eye unblinkingly focused on me. Jack hoisted the camera onto his shoulder and started pointing the thing at Josie.

'Three. Two. One,' Josie Braden counted down before speaking into the camera lens. 'This is Josie Braden outside Callie Rose Hadley's home in Meadowview. I'm here with Callie's neighbour Tobey Durbridge, who was with Callie Rose, Kamal Hadley's granddaughter, when she got shot.' Josie turned to face me, as did Jack's camera. 'Tobey, can you tell us what happened?'

The microphone was thrust under my chin. The red eye waited for me to speak.

I said nothing. Josie looked at me expectantly.

'Excuse me,' I said before turning round and heading off in the opposite direction.

A few steps on, I turned my head. Josie drew her hand across her neck. Jack lowered his camera. They both watched me, disappointment written in capitals on their faces. I was out of there. A medieval tongue-extractor couldn't've made me speak to the press. Hopefully she'd be the first and the last reporter to try and bother me and my family. Jess and Mum didn't know anything so what could they say? And if I said nothing then what could they report? All I could do was cross my fingers and hope against hope that my face and name didn't end up plastered across the TV or in the newspapers. It wouldn't take much more than that for McAuley to firebomb my house. The saying – there's no such thing as bad publicity? Well, that was crap. In Meadowview, there most definitely was such a thing as bad publicity. The kind of publicity that could get a person deader than a roast chicken.

'I must be mad,' Dan kept muttering. 'Mr McAuley's not going to like this . . .'

Dan had been whinging ever since we'd met up and I'd told him what I needed from him, which was an audience with McAuley. I didn't bother telling him about the reporter outside my front door. Dan was worried enough as it was. I buried my hands deeper in the pockets of my denim jacket, my hands clenched so tight, my knuckles cracked.

'You're going to get us both into big trouble,' Dan said, deeply unhappy.

'I'll explain it was my idea,' I said.

'Like Mr McAuley's going to give a damn about that.

We're both going to end up buried in concrete holding up a building somewhere at this rate.'

'How much further?' I asked, changing the subject.

'The other end of this road,' said Dan.

We'd travelled by bus for a good thirty minutes to get here, but this looked like an ordinary residential street – not the sort of place where you'd expect to find business premises. I frowned at Dan, but said nothing. We kept walking. Dan finally stopped outside an end-of-terrace house with a dark-blue door. It was nothing special. A three-up, two-down. The sort of house you'd pass a hundred times a day and never notice.

'McAuley's in there?'

Dan nodded, adding, 'This is a really bad idea. You're going to get us both killed.'

'Dan, change the tune, OK?'

'No, it's not OK. Mr McAuley doesn't like surprises.'

'He asked me to work for him, remember?'

'Yes, and you turned him down.'

'Well, I've thought better of it.'

Dan looked at me.

'What?' I asked, exasperated.

'Does this have something to do with what happened to Callie? Because Mr McAuley can sniff out bullshit at fifty paces.'

'It has nothing to do with Callie and everything to do with getting what's mine,' I replied. 'I want to make a lot of money and spend it whilst I'm still young enough to enjoy it. The shooting just woke me up to a few home truths, that's all.'

'Mr McAuley is not going to believe that.'

'Do you?'

Dan shrugged. 'It doesn't matter whether I believe it or not. It's not me you have to convince.'

'It's the truth, Dan. And if McAuley doesn't want me working for him, there's always the Dowds.'

Dan looked around fearfully. 'You don't want to joke about a thing like that. Around Mr McAuley, I wouldn't even *think* it. People have died for less.'

I gave Dan a look.

'Oh hell. I'm sorry.' Dan rushed through his apology. 'I wasn't talking about . . . I'm sorry.'

I shrugged and looked around. A black van sat outside the house. It had to belong to McAuley. The plush cream-coloured leather seats were a dead giveaway. Dan took a deep breath and headed for the front door. This was it. Once I set foot in this house, there'd be no turning back. Could I do this? Really go through with this? I could turn round and walk away and have this . . . this nothing inside me for the rest of my life. No self-respect. No pride. No Callie Rose . . . Or I could enter this house and never look back. Would McAuley believe me? Only one way to find out. Dan rang the bell three times, a pause, then twice more. The choice was made. The front door was opened by a Nought guy with light-brown, shoulder-length hair tied back in a ponytail. He wore a dark-brown suit with a crisp white shirt and was built like an army tank. If he exhaled too sharply, his clothes would fall apart around him. No way was anyone getting past him without his say-so.

'Hi, Trevor. Did you miss me?' asked Dan.

Trevor looked like he'd rip off Dan's head as soon as

look at him. I hung a few steps behind Dan and looked up and down the street. This house was the perfect disguise. No one would ever guess that McAuley's illegal activities operated out of such unassuming surroundings. He had an office for running his legitimate business in West Meadowview, on the industrial estate by the old railway bridge, but I'd put money on him visiting those premises maybe twice a year, if that. And I'd also put money on this not being the only house he used for his dodgy dealings. Very clever. Mrs Bridges at the bottom of my road dealt drugs out of her house, but she also lived there. This was a much better arrangement.

Dan waved me forward to stand next to him. 'Trevor, this is my mate, Tobey. Mr McAuley knows him.'

Mr I-Love-Steroids looked me up, down and sideways. He finally stepped aside to let us pass, but not without patting both of us down first. Godsake! What did he think I was packing? An Uzi? Dan headed into the first room on the right. A huge flat-screen TV sat on the wall like a piece of contemporary artwork. Two black leather sofas sat self-consciously facing each other on the hardwood floor. I chose to stand, as did Dan.

'So what happens now?' I asked Dan.

'We wait here until McAuley sends for us.'

A strange scraping noise sounded from overhead, like a chair being dragged across the floor. One bang and what sounded like a muffled groan later, and all was quiet.

'What was that?' I asked, pointing at the ceiling.

'Don't know – and don't want to know,' Dan replied.

I took the hint and refrained from saying anything else. After all, the room might've been wired for sound, for all

I knew. I wouldn't put anything past McAuley. My stomach twisted like an angry snake. In the history of bad ideas, this had to be the worst. There was no way this would work. But I had to do it. I had no choice. One minute turned into five before another muscle-head, bald this time, entered the room. He and Dan exchanged a cursory nod.

'All right, Byron?' Dan asked.

Byron didn't answer. He beckoned us forward. We passed through the small kitchen and out into a lean-to conservatory which held a small antique desk and two large potted plants. McAuley sat behind the desk in a huge burgundy leather high-backed chair like a king on his throne. There were two piles of papers on his left, a laptop in the middle of the desk and a cup of what smelled like fresh mint tea to the right of the laptop. Ignoring Dan, he looked directly at me.

'Tobey Durbridge . . . You're the last person I would've expected to come knocking at my door. What can I do for you?'

I took a deep breath. 'I wondered if your offer of work still stands?'

McAuley regarded me for at least half a minute. No one else in the room spoke or even moved a muscle. I forced myself to meet McAuley's gaze without flinching.

'Why're you here, Tobey?'

'For a job, sir.'

'Sir? Still so polite.' McAuley leaned forward. 'That's one of the things I like about you, Tobias Sebastian Durbridge. Always so polite.'

He'd been checking up on me. How else would he

know my middle name? I never told anyone – and I mean *anyone* – my middle name. Dan didn't know it. Even Callie didn't know it. McAuley had been checking up on me, and what's more, he wanted me to know it. But that was OK. McAuley was watching me for my reaction. I met his gaze and didn't even blink. I had to convince him that I had nothing to hide. Byron, McAuley's bodyguard, stood at his side, making no attempt to hide the gun in his hand. Byron might've been a big bloke, but I didn't doubt that his reflexes would be viper-fast.

'So you want a job? I seem to remember that you weren't interested,' McAuley continued.

'I've changed my mind, sir. I need the money.'

'What's changed between now and last week?'

'Reality has set in.' I shrugged.

'Now why don't I believe you?' McAuley was a study in stillness as he scrutinized me.

I opened my mouth to argue, then decided against it. McAuley was no fool. The worst – and last – mistake I could make would be to underestimate him. I shrugged again.

'In your shoes, I wouldn't believe me either,' I said.

McAuley sat back and smiled. 'At last, something we both agree on.'

I nodded slowly. 'Fair enough, Mr McAuley. I just thought I'd offer my services. I'm sorry to have wasted your time.'

I turned and headed for the door.

'How's your girlfriend? What's her name again? Callie Rose?'

'She's not my girlfriend,' I replied, still heading for the door.

'Wait,' McAuley ordered.

I turned round to face him. He beckoned me over and pointed to the spot where I'd been standing next to Dan. I walked back to my previous position. I felt like a naughty school kid made to stand in front of the head. No doubt that was just what McAuley was aiming for.

'Why d'you need money?' he asked.

'To get out of this place,' I replied. 'Out of Meadowview.'

McAuley's eyes widened. I'd succeeding in surprising him.

'To get away from people like me?' he asked softly with the merest hint of a smile.

'Yes, sir,' I replied without hesitation.

There was no mistaking the horrified gasp that came from Dan beside me.

'You don't harbour any dreams of being just like me when you're older?'

'No, sir.'

McAuley leaned forward over his desk, his index fingers touching at the tips to form a peak which he then tapped against his lips. Several seconds passed.

'You don't like me very much, do you, Tobey?'

'No, sir.'

Dan was staring at me like I'd lost every bit of my mind.

'But you're willing to take my money?'

'To earn it, sir.'

McAuley started to laugh. 'I like you, Tobey Sebastian Durbridge.'

I said nothing.

'So what are you prepared to do for me?' he asked.

'Whatever will make me the most money in the shortest amount of time.'

'And why should I trust you?'

'Because I'm loyal, hardworking, I do as I'm told. And I know when to keep my mouth shut.'

'It appears that you do,' McAuley agreed. 'But loyalty is the most important thing to me.'

'I understand, sir.'

'I hope you do,' said McAuley. 'Because if I find out that you – or anyone else who works for me – is abusing my trust, there will be no second chances.'

I got the message, loud and clear.

'If you give me a chance, I won't let you down,' I replied.

McCauley looked up at Byron, who was still at his side, and nodded. Byron carefully placed his gun on the desk, then sauntered towards us. *Trouble.* I watched Byron approach, knowing that danger was only a couple of steps away – and counting down. McAuley hadn't believed a word I'd said and if I left this place in one whole, living piece it would be a bona fide miracle. Cold sweat pricked my back and my armpits. What was Byron going to do? Kill me where I stood? What did McAuley expect me to do? Fight? Beg? What?

'Mr McAuley, I can vouch for Tobey. He's a good guy,' Dan said quickly before Byron reached us.

It was a valiant try, but everyone in the room knew that Dan was wasting his breath. I turned to look at McAuley. If I was going down, it would be facing him like a man. Byron stepped behind Dan and me. I held my breath. But to my surprise, I wasn't Byron's target. Byron grabbed hold of Dan's arms and pulled them back. Dan cried out in surprise and more than a little fear. He struggled to get free, but he was wasting his time. He wasn't going anywhere. A couple of quick yanks on his arms were enough to make him yell out in pain, but it had the desired effect. Dan kept still, whilst Byron stood directly behind him, still pulling back his arms. I turned back to McAuley, who was watching me intently.

McAuley pointed to the gun Byron had left on his desk. 'Pick it up.'

I moved forward to do as I was told. The stock was warm where Byron had been holding it and the gun was unexpectedly heavy. I adjusted my grip, keeping my finger well away from the trigger.

'D'you know what kind of weapon that is?' McAuley asked me.

It was a M1911 Series 70, single action, semiautomatic handgun, with a single stacked magazine that took seven .45 calibre ACP bullets, plus one in the chamber – that's if the thing hadn't been modified to take more.

'It's a gun, sir,' I replied.

'You know your stuff!' said McAuley dryly. 'That particular gun happens to be a classic. I keep telling Byron that he should use a more modern firearm, but that gun is one of his favourites.'

Why was he telling me all this? Like I gave a damn which toys Byron liked to play with.

'That particular gun is loaded with point four five calibre, non-expanding, Teflon-coated ball ammunition,' McAuley told me. 'I have the bullets made especially for me.'

I went to lay the thing back down on the table.

'Tobey, do something for me,' said McAuley silkily. 'Point that gun at Dan and shoot him.'

I must've misheard. 'Pardon?'

'You heard me,' said McAuley.

He picked up his cup of mint tea and started sipping it. The gun sat awkwardly in my hand as I looked from Dan back to McAuley. 'You want me to . . . ?'

'Kill your friend.' McAuley's voice was soft and slick as melted butter.

Dan stared at McAuley, horror-stricken. He struggled against Byron's python grip in earnest now, but there was no way Byron was letting him go.

'Well, Tobey?' said McAuley.

'Mr McAuley, please,' Dan pleaded. 'I work for you. I'm a good worker.'

'You brought a stranger to my house unannounced and uninvited,' McAuley turned to snap at him. 'Into *my* house. You never, *ever* bring anyone here without my permission, Dan. For that alone, you need sorting.'

'I'm sorry, Mr McAuley. I messed up,' Dan cried out. 'Tobey's my friend. And you offered him a job. I didn't think it'd do any harm.'

'You didn't think – full stop. You're a fool, Dan, and that makes you a liability,' McAuley replied. 'Tobey, either shoot him or give me the gun so I can take care of business.'

Would I be included in his 'business'?

Probably.

I looked at Dan, who was shaking his head frantically at me. The gun in my hand was so heavy. My dad had taught me about guns, before he left. He used to buy all kinds of gun magazines and he'd sit me on his lap as we looked at the photos and read the specifications together. Before he took off. But Dad would never have dreamed of having a gun in our house or anywhere near it – not a real one. He had a couple of replicas, but he said it was to study the engineering behind them. The last time he disappeared, Mum put the replicas in the bin. That's when I knew he wasn't coming back. And now I had a real gun in my hand, loaded with real bullets.

Slowly I raised my hand, pointing the gun straight at Dan's head.

'Tobey, no. I'm begging you. Don't . . . *Please* . . .' Dan fought like a wild thing to get out of Byron's grasp, but it was futile.

Though his lips were a thin immovable slash across his face, I could tell Byron was enjoying himself by the gleam in his green eyes.

'Tobey . . . no . . .' Tears streamed down Dan's face. A dark stain began to spread across the crotch of his light-blue jeans.

Sorry, Dan. I lowered my gaze, trying to get it together. My arm fell to my side. The gun was heavy, so very heavy.

Stretch out my arm.

Hold the gun steady.

If I'm wrong, if I've got it wrong . . .

Take aim, Tobey.

I raised my arm to aim the gun directly at Dan's heart.

'TOBEY, NO!' Dan screamed out.

Legs slightly apart, body braced, I concentrated on just one face.

And I pulled the trigger.

Nothing happened. Just a click. It dry-fired. No bang. No boom. No gun recoil. Just a click. The loudest click in the world. I hardly heard it over the sound of my heart racing like a jet engine. Byron released Dan, who fell at his feet in a crumpled heap, still sobbing.

I turned to McAuley, turning the gun round to hand it back to him by the stock. The slide hadn't even gone back when I'd fired. 'This gun doesn't work.'

'That gun doesn't have any bullets in it,' McAuley informed me. He took the gun from me, placing it on the table. He took another sip of his tea, as we regarded each other over his cup.

'You definitely remind me of me,' said McAuley. 'I'll have to keep my eyes on you.'

'Do I get to work for you now, sir?' I asked.

McAuley took out a phone from the top drawer of his desk and handed it to me along with a charger. He turned to Dan, looking down on him with utter contempt. 'Dan, you're lucky you're still useful to me, but if you mess up again . . .' McAuley turned back to me. 'Keep that phone with you at all times. I'll be in touch. Now get out and take your friend with you.'

twenty-eight

McAuley wouldn't even let Dan use the bathroom first to tidy himself up. Byron saw to it that we were out of McAuley's house less than thirty seconds later. It was weird leaving the house, like stepping out of reality into a fantasy world full of sunshine and promises, a world that felt fake and insincere. A world of people who didn't know the likes of McAuley existed, mainly because they didn't want to know. Ignorance provided countless nights of uninterrupted sleep in a way that knowledge never did. Once the front door was shut behind us, I took a deep breath, then another, and another. I'd entered the lion's den and got out in one piece. This time . . . So why wasn't my heart battering its way out of my chest? Why wasn't I puking my guts out? Maybe because my mind was racing ahead, whilst my body and my heart were stuck in the Wasteland with Callie. God help me when they caught up with each other. But until then, I had things to do. I pulled off my T-shirt and handed it to Dan.

'You can tie that round your waist,' I told him. The front of his trousers around the zip was still conspicuously dark blue.

Dan smacked my hand away. I couldn't blame him. He wiped his hands over his face, but didn't look at me. With each step away from McAuley, Dan's fear cooled and his rage towards me grew ever hotter. I could feel it radiating from him. There was an eruption coming. I put my T-shirt back on as Dan didn't want it. We turned the corner of the street and the explosion happened.

Dan shoved me against a wall and pinned me there, his forearm against my throat. 'You rotten bastard. You tried to *kill* me.'

'No, I didn't,' I replied as calmly as I could. 'The gun wasn't loaded.'

Dan pushed down harder on my throat. 'You didn't know that.'

'Yes, I d-did.' It was hard to get the words out with his arm pressed against my larynx. 'I knew it was a t-test.' If he didn't move and soon, I'd have to move him. My throat was beginning to hurt.

Dan's arm relaxed on my throat, but only slightly. 'How did you know?' Though his arm had relaxed, his expression hadn't.

'Byron was standing right behind you.'

'So?' Dan hissed at me, his spit spraying my face.

'McAuley said the gun was loaded with point four five calibre, non-expanding, ball ammunition.'

'So what?'

'If I fired the M1911 at that range, that kind of ammo would've gone straight through your body and probably straight through Byron's too. McAuley might not care about your sorry arse, but he wouldn't risk losing his minder that way. I knew it had to be a bluff.'

Dan stared at me. He slowly let go of me and stood back. But he wasn't happy. Far from it.

'You could've warned me.'

'How? McAuley and that Byron guy were standing right there. I had no choice but to do what I was told.'

'Suppose you'd been wrong?' Dan snapped.

'But I wasn't.'

'But suppose you had been?'

'But I wasn't.'

'You could've killed me,' Dan said, his eyes boring into mine.

'But I didn't.'

Casting one last fulminating look in my direction, Dan carried on walking. I fell into step next to him. I buried my hands in my trouser pockets and kept my eyes straight ahead. I was very aware of the filthy looks Dan kept giving me.

'What happened to Callie wasn't my fault,' he said belligerently.

'I never said otherwise.'

'But you blame me.'

'Dan, this is pointless,' I sighed. 'It was just one of those unforeseen things, that's all.'

'I didn't know what was in that package you delivered to Louise Resnick,' said Dan. 'I swear I didn't.'

I didn't reply.

'I know you don't believe me, but it's the truth,' he insisted.

'What makes you think I don't believe you?' I frowned.

'The look in your eyes when you pulled that trigger . . .' Dan was looking at me like he'd never seen me before. His words made me start.

'Dan, you're wrong. Besides, no one forced me to deliver those packages. It was my idea.'

And though we fell back to walking beside each other, each step took us further apart.

'Dan, you've got to believe me,' I tried. 'I knew the gun was either not loaded or else it had blanks in it. Besides, if our positions were reversed, are you telling me you wouldn't have pulled the trigger?'

'Don't you dare turn this round on me,' Dan raged. 'The point is, our positions weren't reversed.'

'You're the one who said—' I bit back the rest. No good could come from finishing that sentence.

'What?'

'Nothing.'

Damn, this was so hard. In the space of a few minutes, everything had changed between us. In the space of a few days, everything had changed between us. But I still had to rely on his friendship. I had no choice.

'Dan, will you do something for me?' I asked at last.

'I want to do bugger all for you,' Dan retorted. 'Except maybe kick your head in.'

'But you'll do this for me anyway.' I smiled faintly.

'What is it?'

'If anything happens to me, make sure my mum and sister are safe. OK?'

Dan didn't reply. I risked a glance at him. He met my gaze. Neither of us was smiling. Not even close.

'D'you promise?' I asked.

'Yeah,' he said at last. 'I promise.'

Two Nought girls of about our age or maybe a bit older walked towards us. Dan sidestepped, to walk slightly behind me, still conscious of the state of his jeans. The girls looked Dan and me up and down as they passed before turning to each other and giggling. Why do girls do that? Is it meant to make them seem more interesting? Attractive? 'Cause if so, then it misses by several kilometres. It just made them seem like airheads. Once they'd passed, Dan fell into step next to me again, not saying a word. The normal Dan would never have let two fit girls pass by without trying to get their mobile phone digits at the very least. His hands hung with false nonchalance over the dark patch at his groin. We approached a small parade of shops when I had an idea.

'Wait here,' I said to Dan, before popping into the newsagent. I bought two big bottles of water. Outside the shop, I grinned at Dan as I showed him the bottles. He frowned at me. I handed one bottle to him before unscrewing the top of the other one. I splashed the water over Dan's shirt and jeans.

'What the hell are you playing at?' Dan hopped about like the water was boiling. He tried to snatch the bottle away from me, but I wouldn't let him.

'The best way to hide one stain is amongst many,' I said.

He stopped dancing about after that, having finally clicked what I was doing. He wasn't happy, but he let me carry on. Once one bottle was empty, we swapped and I doused him with the second one. I clamped my lips together as I poured water over his head. The next thing I knew, we were both howling with laughter. People walking by gave us a wide berth – no doubt they thought we were both barking. By the time I'd finished, Dan was dripping wet with barely a dry patch anywhere on his clothes. His dark-blond hair was now darker and plastered to his head like a swimming cap. We looked at each other, and our laughter faded to nothing. Dan walked to the side of the pavement, put his hands on his knees to steady himself and vomited up his last ten meals. I watched him and there was nothing I could do. When he'd finally finished, he used the last remaining drops of water in my bottle to rinse out his mouth before spitting the lot onto the pavement.

'All right now?' I asked.

Dan's expression gave me the answer to that one. 'Tell me something, Tobey,' he began quietly. 'What would you have done if you had known the gun had real bullets in it?'

Dan and I looked at each other. How could I possibly answer that question?

'I don't know,' I replied. And that was the truth.

Dan nodded slowly but said nothing.

We headed for the bus stop.

twenty-nine

'Naturally I deeply regret that my granddaughter was shot. I will of course be praying for her,' said Kamal Hadley.

'But will you be visiting her?' asked one of the forest of journalists standing around him.

'I would sincerely hope that this current government keeps its promise and tackles the growing problem of gun and knife crime on our streets. If my granddaughter can get caught up in this, then anyone's child could find themselves in a similar situation. This government lacks the will, the expertise and, quite frankly, the guts to do anything about this situation. The people of this country need to rise up and reclaim the streets from the scum blighting all our live . . .'

'Yes, but will you be visiting Callie Rose in hospital?' The same reporter repeated his question.

'I have nothing further to say at this time.' Kamal smiled apologetically. 'I need to be with my family. Thank you.'

Kamal Hadley slipped back into his house, leaving the journalists outside barking more questions at him. I turned off the TV, my expression set like concrete. What a scumbag. There was no way he was going to set foot in Mercy Community Hospital, but he was so slick he'd implied otherwise. No doubt he saw this as his way of getting back into the political arena, in spite of the fact that it was mainly thanks to him that his party had crashed so humiliatingly in the general election a few months before. Callie had told me all about her grandfather. About the way he threw Sephy out of his house when she was pregnant with Callie. And how he'd slammed the door in Callie's face the one and only time she had tried to see him.

But I must admit, watching Kamal Hadley had been instructive. The way he held himself, the way he met the gaze of everyone who spoke to him like he had nothing to hide, the way he lowered his tone when asked a difficult question to indicate the depth of his sincerity. Callie's granddad was a true master of fake sincerity and subtle manipulation. I could learn a lot, just by watching him.

thirty

'OK, Tobey, why should this establishment hire you?' Mr Thomas, the deputy manager, glanced down at his watch as he waited for my reply.

This establishment . . . Godsake! What was wrong with calling it TFTM like everyone else?

Mr Thomas was a slight man, bald as an egg and shorter than me by at least a head, neck and shoulders. He wasn't exactly skinny, more like wiry. His dark-brown dome glistened like it'd been rubbed with oil or something. And in the space of fifteen minutes, the man must've glanced at me twice – if that.

After what had happened with McAuley and Dan a few days ago, I'd spent every spare moment during the rest of the week on the Internet and at the library. I'd barely been at home – hardly even noticed Mum going to work and back, or Jess heading off to take her exams. I needed information – as much of it as I could get. And from what I could tell from my research (which included frying my brain by reading celebrity and gossip magazines), the best way to get close to the Dowds was via TFTM, one of the top three restaurants in the city.

So on Saturday, I'd headed into town and filled in an application form for a job at TFTM. On the same day, they'd asked me to take what they called 'proficiency' tests, which consisted of English, maths and general knowledge. The tests were multiple choice and each was supposed to take thirty minutes. I finished them in half that time, but I wasn't stupid enough to broadcast the fact. TFTM, or Thanks For The Memories, as those with time on their tongues called it, struck me as the kind of place which wanted its employees to be only just smart enough. Too smart would not be welcomed. That was two days ago. This morning, overcast and early, I'd been invited in for a final interview.

Mr Thomas glanced up to glare at me with impatience. What was his question again? Oh, yeah!

'Well, sir, I'm a fast learner, I'm reliable and I'm a hard worker. And I worked in a restaurant during the summer holidays last year so I do have some experience.'

Which was the truth, just not the whole truth. But he didn't need to know that all I did for that job was clear tables and mop floors.

Mr Thomas flicked through the papers on his desk and didn't even bother to look at me. He must've heard the same reply a thousand times before. Of course he had. This was TFTM, one of the most exclusive restaurants in town. It consisted of a restaurant on the ground floor and a club called The Club (very ingenious – someone put a lot of thought into that one) on the first floor, accessible via a separate entrance and rumoured to have its own secret exit, to ensure that its famous clientele didn't have to deal with hangers-on or the paparazzi. The only way to get to the Club from the restaurant was via the kitchens at the back of the building. What it boiled down to was that no one was getting into the Club without an invitation. TFTM actively promoted the feeling of not needing anyone's patronage, no matter how famous – which of course made it *the* place to be. Not that anyone had shown me around yet. What I knew, I'd learned from reading local authority planning permission requests and building reports, reviews, celebrity gossip and basically anything and everything I could find about the place.

TFTM definitely needed no one.

I definitely needed TFTM.

I needed a job in this place like I needed to breathe.

Mr Thomas still wasn't looking at me. I needed to do something, say something to get this man to remember my name. I continued, 'Mr Thomas, I'd be perfect for TFTM because I do my homework and I know how to keep my mouth shut.'

Mr Thomas's head snapped up at that, his expression speculative. For the first time since this whole excruciating interview began, I had his full attention. First McAuley, now him. They were all interested in workers who knew how to keep their lips glued together.

'What d'you mean – you do your homework?' asked Mr Thomas.

'I looked up TFTM on the Internet before I came for this interview.'

Mr Thomas sat back in his chair, looking distinctly unimpressed. 'And what was the most remarkable thing you found out about us on the Internet?'

'I knew your restaurant was one of the best – that's why I really want to work here – but I didn't realize that the restaurant had achieved its third Michelin star earlier this year. Only five restaurants in the entire country can boast three Michelin stars.' I cranked up the enthusiasm and the wide-eyed admiration, wondering if I was overdoing it.

Mr Thomas's expression visibly relaxed. 'Oh, I see. You have ambitions in that area yourself?'

I nodded vigorously. 'I'd like to own my own place one day. Oh, nothing as fancy as this, but maybe a little bistro or a bed and breakfast on the coast somewhere. Who knows?'

'Indeed. Who knows?' Mr Thomas couldn't hide his condescending smirk.

'So I reckon a number of years at TFTM will teach me everything I need to know about starting my own . . . establishment. Just give me a chance, Mr Thomas. I won't let you down.'

'Hmm . . .' Mr Thomas glanced down again at my application form and my test results. 'OK, Tobey, you've got the job. When can you start?'

A smile of pure relief split my face – and most of it was genuine. 'Is tomorrow night too soon?'

'Tomorrow will be fine. You will work from Tuesday to Saturday and have Sundays and Mondays off. Your hours will be from six p.m. till one in the morning with two breaks to be negotiated with your supervisor, Michelle. You'll need to wear black trousers and a long-sleeved white shirt which you'll have to provide yourself. They are to be neat and clean at all times. We will provide you with a bow tie and two waistcoats. You will be responsible for keeping your waistcoats clean. If you lose them, the cost of any replacements will be taken from your salary. Your pay will be minimum wage, but what you make in tips you get to keep. And if you do well, the tips are excellent. Any questions?'

Tons of them. Like where was Ross Resnick, the manager of TFTM? Nothing had been seen of him in over two weeks, or rather only his little finger had put in an appearance. The rest of Ross Resnick had disappeared into what was generally suspected to be a McAuley-manufactured black hole. And how about the Dowds? How did they feel about the disappearance of their manager? After all, it was common knowledge that the Dowds owned TFTM. What were they doing about ensuring Ross Resnick's safe return? Any questions? What a joke.

I shook my head.

'Arrive at five-thirty tomorrow for orientation. Ask for Michelle – she'll tell you everything you need to know.' Mr Thomas stood up, indicating that the interview was over. He stretched out his hand which I shook with zeal. All this for a frickin' job as a waiter. Still, it was worth it. I'd got the job. I was in – and one step closer to my goal.

I started at TFTM on Tuesday night, after assuring Mum that it was only a holiday job and certainly not permanent. By the end of my Saturday shift, I ached in places I didn't know I had places. Ankles, calves, thighs, bum, the soles of my feet, even between my fingers – they were all screaming with fatigue and pain. I spent my evenings whizzing round like I had a rocket up my backside, as did all the serving staff, but some of the punters still complained that the service wasn't fast enough. My mouth more than ached from smiling when some jackass or other threw a casual insult my way, or complained that their food was cold when they were the ones who sat talking and ignoring their food for twenty minutes before picking up their bloody cutlery to eat. Zara, a Nought waitress in her mid-twenties who'd taken me under her wing, had been at TFTM for almost three years. And she swore each day would be her last. But it never was, for one simple reason.

'The money is too good. So I bite my lip and dodge and weave every time some git makes a grab for my arse or my tits,' Zara told me during one of our fifteen-minute breaks. I watched as she took off her shoes and massaged the balls of her feet. And I listened. When I was in the restaurant serving, as well as during the breaks, I did more of that than anything else. I listened.

'Some of the regular punters think that T&A comes free with their dessert,' Zara had continued with disgust. 'That's why we girls call this place Thanks For The Mammaries. On my last day here, an awful lot of customers are going to get the face slapping they deserve.'

Mr Thomas had been right. The tips were excellent. I made about three times more at TFTM each night than I ever did selling phones. Not that that was the reason I was so keen to work there, but it certainly didn't hurt.

There were two sets of changing rooms, male and female, and all levels of staff shared the same changing areas, but the staff who worked in the club upstairs rarely deigned to speak to us lowly serving staff from the restaurant. And I couldn't help noticing that most of the serving staff downstairs were Noughts, whereas most of the Club staff were Crosses.

I pulled off my bow tie and rainbow-coloured waistcoat and was just hanging up the latter in my locker when

Michelle the supervisor entered the men's changing rooms unannounced. A couple of guys had to grab for their towels to cover their jewels, but they never said a word. Not one person protested. It was obviously a regular occurrence.

'Angelo, we're short-staffed in the Club tomorrow so you'll be upstairs along with . . .' Michelle had a quick look around. 'Keith, and you as well, Tobey.'

'But I don't work on Sundays,' I said.

'You do now,' said Michelle.

TFTM was closed on Sundays. What was going on?

'We have a private party going on in the club from ten tomorrow till late,' Michelle explained.

'But Sunday is—' I began my protest.

'You'll get triple time, if that's what you're worried about,' Michelle interrupted with irritation. 'Now is there still a problem?'

'Whose party is it?' I asked.

'Rebecca Dowd.'

My stomach tightened, like a hand was squeezing my insides. Rebecca Dowd . . . Wiping all expression off my face, I asked, 'Who's she?'

Michelle's eyes widened. And she wasn't the only one. I was getting significant looks from everyone who'd heard the question.

'Vanessa Dowd's daughter? The sister of Gideon and Owen Dowd? Do those names ring any bells?'

The blank look on my face was obviously convincing. Michelle's expression morphed into one of pity. 'Damn it, Tobey, don't you know anything?'

'I'm here to learn.' I shrugged.

'Just be here at nine-thirty tomorrow night,' Michelle ordered.

'How will I get home?' I asked.

'Not my problem.' Michelle headed out as Angelo shook his head and Keith looked particularly hacked off.

Me? I was ecstatic. A late-night party on Sunday night running into the early hours of Monday morning meant I'd have one hell of a job getting back home. If I couldn't catch a night bus back to Meadowview I was in for a two-and-a-half-hour walk. But I didn't care.

I was going to meet the Dowds.

thirty-one

'Callum, I need your help. Yours too, Mum. If either of you are out there, somewhere, please watch over Callie. Please don't let my daughter slip away. I know it isn't written anywhere that life is supposed to be fair, but please keep Callie safe. And here. Meggie has been through so much. So have I. Taking Callie away from me wouldn't be fair. I know I'm being selfish, but I don't care.

'Callum, bring our daughter back. Her body is still here, but not the rest of her. The doctors are baffled as to why she hasn't woken up yet. One doctor asked me if Callie is a fighter. I put her right on that one. Of course our daughter is a fighter. Callum, you mustn't let her forget that. Remind her of all the things she has waiting for her in this life. Remind her just how much I love her.

'Mum, I miss your humour and your practical advice. I miss you. I talk to Callie every day. I tell her all the news and talk about things gone and things to come. I don't even know if she can hear the things I say, but I say them anyway. But if she can't hear me, I know she'll hear you. Send her back to me, Mum.

'Please.

'*Please* . . .'

I leaned against the wall, my head bent as Sephy's words trailed away into tears. I'd thought that at this time on a Sunday afternoon, I'd get to see Callie with no interruptions. But her mum had beaten me to it. When I arrived, the nurse at the nurses' station buzzed me onto the ward, then promptly disappeared before the door had shut behind me. Heading towards Callie's room, I'd heard Sephy before I saw her – and before she saw me. Her words were quietly spoken, but the ICU was quieter, just the hum of machines and the regular beep of the monitor coming at me from the middle distance like so much background noise. Maybe I shouldn't have stood outside Callie's room and listened to her mum, but I did. Part of me wanted to head into the room and share how we were both feeling, but that was impossible. Two of the nurses were heading back to their station. Decision time. I closed my eyes briefly.

Until tomorrow, Callie.

Time to leave.

thirty-two

On Sunday evening, all us waiters (no waitresses, just Michelle supervising) were taken into the Club fifteen minutes before the first guests arrived. We were told the schedule for the night and assigned to different parts of the Club.

'Tobey, you'll be circulating around the leisure area with various drinks,' Michelle informed me. 'Anyone who wants a specific order will have to go to the bar. Make sure your tray is never empty. You can take one ten-minute break at midnight and that's it.'

I nodded, only vaguely aware of what she was saying. I was still trying to take in everything. This was my first chance to see the Club – and it was something else. I'd never seen anything like it. Statues in various states of undress adorned the alcoves around the main room and the ceiling was draped with red, orange and yellow silk. There was a huge dance floor lit up with multi-coloured underfloor lighting to the left. Opposite, on the other side of the room, was the bar and beyond that the small kitchen which served snacks – or, as they called them up here, canapés. Dotted around the dance floor were tables and chairs, with sofas hugging the walls around the rest of the room. It smelled of flowers though I couldn't see a flower in sight. I went to the bar to get my first tray of drinks.

'Man, I hope you're wearing your titanium underwear,' Angelo whispered to me.

'What d'you mean?' I frowned.

'You'll find out,' said Angelo grimly.

The first guests began to arrive and the party officially started. I got Angelo to point out Rebecca for me. She was shorter than I expected, about five feet three or four and not exactly skinny but sure heading that way. She wore her hair in thin locks down to her shoulders and her make-up looked a bit overdone, but what did I know? She was wearing a sleeveless red dress with matching red high-heeled sandals and she looked stunning. The dress had a V at the front and the back and the skirt flowed around her thighs every time she moved. Even from across the room, her diamond earrings twinkled, as did the rocks around her neck. Happy eighteenth birthday! I took in every aspect of her appearance, drinking in her face – her cat-like dark eyes set slightly too wide apart, her burgundy lips, her high forehead. A tall but stocky Cross guy walked over to Rebecca and put his arm around her shoulders. She smiled up at him in amusement. He smiled down at her with genuine affection, the creases around his eyes deepening. He had to be thirty? Maybe thirty-two.

'Who's the guy with his arm around her shoulder?' I asked Angelo.

'That's her brother, Gideon, and don't let him catch you staring at his sister,' Angelo warned me. 'And I'll tell you something else. Gideon is a mean one, but he's a teddy bear compared to his younger brother, Owen.'

'Why? What's Owen like?'

'Ambitious. Focused. Ruthless.'

'Where is he? Is he here tonight?'

'He's the one in the blue suit who just walked in.' Angelo pointed discreetly.

I tried to get a good look at Owen, but only caught a glimpse before Rebecca hugged him. The place was beginning to fill up so it was tricky to get more than a partial view. I walked a couple of steps forward to get a better look, memorizing his face before I headed back to the bar.

'Why the interest in Gideon and Owen?' Angelo asked.

'I don't want to get into trouble by stepping on the wrong toes,' I replied.

Apparently Vanessa Dowd wasn't going to be present. Angelo told me that she very rarely ventured out of her house. From what he said, Vanessa Dowd sounded like a puppet-master, working from on high and pulling everyone's strings, including those of her own family. Especially those of her own family. It was time to get to work. I turned back to the bar to retrieve my tray and headed for the crowd that was growing by the second.

By midnight, Rebecca Dowd's eighteenth birthday party was in full swing. The music was blaring, the Club was heaving and most of the guests were already off their heads. Canapés and finger foods were doing the rounds, but the food wasn't as popular as the drink. My job was to weave in and out of the crowd with a tray full of assorted drinks, allowing empty glasses to be swapped for full ones. Every time my tray contained more empty glasses than full ones, I had to head back to the bar for more drinks. No one had to pay for a thing. Food and drink were on the house – or rather, on the Dowds. Looking around, I figured there had to be close to one hundred people in the Club – mostly Crosses, but at least a fifth of those present were Noughts. I wondered how many of them were Rebecca Dowd's real friends. My guess was ten or less.

Within the space of an hour my bum had been pinched purple and there wasn't a centimetre of my body that hadn't been thoroughly groped. Now I understood Angelo's titanium underwear warning. But my pockets were also being stuffed with money – amongst other things, like a few phone numbers. I didn't feel the least bit guilty about the money. Way I saw it, I was earning it and then some. When at last midnight rolled around, my head was pounding and I was about ready to drop. It was my break time so it was now or never. I weaved through the crowds, seeking my quarry. At last I found him, leaning against a closed door. Taking a deep breath, I walked straight up to him.

'Mr Dowd, may I speak to you?' I had to really raise my voice to be heard.

'About what?' Owen Dowd frowned.

'Alex McAuley.'

That got his attention. 'What about him?'

'May I speak to you in private?'

Owen Dowd looked at me, really looked at me.

'It'll be worth five minutes of your time,' I said. 'I promise.'

Owen took a key out of his jacket pocket and unlocked the door behind him. Once the door was open, he waved me in ahead of him. He wasn't taking any chances. I walked in and spun round immediately. I wasn't taking any chances either. Owen switched on the light and shut the door behind him with an ominous click. The sounds of the Club stopped immediately, like a radio being switched off. The room had to be soundproofed. I glanced around. It was a tiny office, with a poster-sized window behind an undersized desk. The window was covered with a dark-grey vertical blind which was shut. On the desk were scattered a few sand-coloured folders and a desktop computer sat self-consciously on one side. The floor was carpeted, a navy-blue carpet which made the room look even smaller.

'Now then, what's your name?' asked Owen.

'Tobey Durbridge,' I replied.

'So what's all this about?' said Owen. 'And it'd better be good or you're going to find yourself out of a job.'

So without wasting any more time, I told him.

I only had five minutes left of my break. The restaurant was closed and I didn't fancy chatting to anyone in the changing rooms, so I headed up the stairs to the flat roof, hoping fervently that the door would be open. It was.

The moment I stepped outside, I breathed a huge sigh of relief. After the heated chaos of the Club and the atmosphere in the air there, up here was cool and fresh. The air-conditioning unit sat hulking in the middle of the roof, growling away like some great wounded animal. I walked to the nearest edge to peer over the side. Beneath my feet, I could feel the music thumping, vibrating through my body. I looked up. The stars were the furthest away they'd ever been. I looked down. Two storeys down to the ground. The longer I stared, the closer the pavement seemed to get. But I didn't want to look away. This was better than looking up and only seeing Callie looking down at me, blood spilling over her chest. Better this than closing my eyes and seeing Callie in the hospital as the nurses and doctors fought to bring her back to life.

'Are you going to jump?'

The woman's voice had me spinning round. It was Rebecca Dowd, standing beside the air-conditioning unit. How long had she been up here? I stared at her like I'd lost my mind. Rebecca smiled, amused at my goldfish impersonation. I snapped my lips together and tried to look like my IQ was greater than my shoe size.

'Sorry,' I said ruefully. 'You took me by surprise.'

'You're not going to jump, are you?' Rebecca sounded worried.

'The thought hadn't crossed my mind, no.'

'Good.' Rebecca breathed a huge sigh of relief. 'Because I'd have to try and talk you out of it and I'm useless at that kind of thing.'

'Fair enough.' I smiled, and looked up at the night sky again, drinking in the peace above before I had to head back down to the throng below.

'Are you OK?' asked Rebecca. 'You look . . . out of it.'

'I'm fine. Just a million kilometres away.'

'Nowhere pleasant by the look on your face.'

'I'm just missing my girlfriend,' I admitted.

'Oh? Where is she?'

How to answer that one? 'We're not together any more.'

'Oh. I'm sorry.'

I shrugged. Time to change the subject. 'So what brings you up here?'

Rebecca sighed, walking over to me. 'I came up a while ago for some peace and quiet.'

'Me too,' I said. 'But if I'm disturbing you I can leave.'

'No, that's OK. You can stay.'

I smiled. 'I'm Tobey.'

'Becks,' said Rebecca, holding out her hand.

I stepped forward to shake it.

'Hi, Becks. So what d'you think of the party then?'

'It's OK.' Rebecca's response was distinctly lukewarm. 'I'm not really a party person. What about you? What d'you think of it?'

'Well, I'm not exactly a guest,' I pointed out, indicating my waiter's uniform.

'All the better to get an objective opinion,' Rebecca replied.

I considered. 'I'm not really a party person either. I'd much rather see a good film and go for a meal afterwards.'

'Me too.'

Rebecca and I shared a smile.

'But as parties go, most of the people downstairs seem to be enjoying themselves. Mind you, in the morning they won't remember whether the party was good, bad or indifferent.'

'Yeah, so what's the point?' said Rebecca, antipathy in her voice.

'Excuse my asking, but aren't you Rebecca Dowd? Isn't it your birthday party?'

'It's supposed to be, but it's more for my mum's benefit than mine. My party will appear in all the right celebrity magazines and a tabloid or two, with photos of all the usual suspects, and Mum will deem my party a success.'

'The usual suspects?' I queried.

'All those people who would go to the opening of a fridge door as long as it got their faces in the papers and the gossip mags.'

I contemplated Rebecca. I'd thought she'd be some spoiled little princess who thought the sun revolved around her and who'd have nothing worse to bleat about than the merest wrinkle in her dress or a scuff mark on her shoes.

'What?' Rebecca ran her hand over her hair.

'Nothing. I just . . . you're not what I expected,' I said.

'Is that good or bad?'

'Definitely good.' I smiled.

We stood for a few moments looking out across the centre of town. The traffic, the lights from the buildings, the occasional siren, they were all just background, but vibrant background. I wanted to reach out my hand, snatch it all up and put it in my trouser pocket. But I deliberately turned my back on it to face Rebecca.

'So what did you get for your birthday?' I asked.

Rebecca's hand moved self-consciously to her neck. 'This necklace – amongst other things.'

'It's beautiful.'

'D'you really like it?' she asked doubtfully.

'Well, I wouldn't wear it,' I replied. 'But it looks good on you.'

'I thought it was a bit . . . ostentatious, but Mum insisted that I should wear it.'

'There are worse things to wear,' I said.

I deliberately took a step closer. Rebecca didn't back away. I lifted the necklace away from her neck for a better look. The metal beneath my fingers still held the warmth of her skin. The necklace was either white gold or platinum. I'd've put my money on the latter. It certainly wasn't mere silver. Adorning the chain was a cross set with at least nine diamonds and I reckoned each diamond had to be at least half a carat. Not that I'm into diamonds or anything like that, but I did occasionally glance in the odd jeweller's shop window with dreams about the watches I could buy myself and the everything else I would buy Callie if I ever had any money. Rebecca's necklace would've been dazzling around Callie's neck, complementing her beige skin.

'Tobey . . . ?'

I snapped out of my reverie and immediately released Rebecca's necklace. 'Sorry. I went offline.'

'Were you with your girlfriend again?'

I shrugged, not denying it.

'Did you love her?'

That was something . . . the one thing I couldn't lie about, couldn't even talk about.

'Like I said, it's over now.'

'Maybe you—'

'Tobey, what d'you think you're doing? Your break was over ten minutes ago.' Michelle looked about ready to fire my arse.

'Michelle, please don't blame Tobey. He was just being kind and keeping me company.'

'Oh, Miss Dowd. I'm so sorry. I didn't realize it was you.' Michelle did everything but curtsey.

'I do hope Tobey won't get into trouble because of me,' said Rebecca.

'Of course not,' Michelle hastened to reassure her. 'Tobey, take all the time you need.' She turned and headed for the door to go back downstairs.

'No, that's OK, Michelle. I'll get back to work,' I called out quickly. I wasn't ready to lose my job quite yet. I turned to Rebecca. 'It was nice to meet you, Becks.'

Michelle had already left the roof and was on her way back down to the Club. I guess it didn't pay to upset the Dowds, any of them.

'It's a shame we were interrupted. I was enjoying our chat,' said Rebecca.

Something in her voice made me stop. 'You make it sound like not a lot of people talk to you,' I said, surprised.

'They don't,' Rebecca replied. 'They talk at me or through me or around me. Very few people talk *to* me, and even less listen to what I have to say.'

'I like to listen,' I told her.

'I noticed that,' said Rebecca. 'Your girlfriend must be mad to dump you.'

I didn't bother to correct her.

'I'd better get back. I just hope I have the stamina to last until the party finishes.' I smiled to lighten my words, but more than meant them.

'Don't worry,' said Rebecca. 'I reckon this party only has another hour's life left in it – at most. Then you can go home.'

I sighed. 'Well, it'll take me nearly three hours to walk home from here, so that'll be something to look forward to.'

'Three hours? Why? Where d'you live?'

'Meadowview. But I didn't realize until I checked this afternoon that there are no night buses that run to where I live at this time on a Monday morning.'

'Oh, I see.'

'Anyway, enjoy the rest of your party, Becks.'

'I'll try,' Rebecca replied. 'It was nice talking to you.'

'You too,' I said. And I went back downstairs.

When I finally left the club it was nearly three in the morning. I'd be home long after dawn and all I wanted to do was crash into my bed now. My feet were killing me. What would they be like after a three-hour walk? Damn!

I'd even asked Michelle about kipping in the changing rooms until the buses started running again, but she shot that idea down in flames.

'You can't,' she told me. 'It's against health and safety regulations, plus you'd set off the alarms, plus Mr Dowd would never allow it.'

The fuss she made, I regretted ever asking her.

'Shouldn't've asked,' Angelo whispered to me. 'Should've just done it.'

Well, it was too late now.

After saying my goodbyes to the other waiters, I set off. The idea of sleeping in some doorway until my body, and especially my feet, recovered grew more and more appealing. I'd only been walking for a couple of minutes, though, when an executive saloon car pulled up beside me. The back window slid down.

'Hi, Tobey.' Rebecca leaned out to talk to me. 'Would you like a lift?'

I glanced past her to the Cross driver, who kept his eyes

facing forward. I looked up and down the sleek lines of the luxury vehicle. A lift in this car? Hell, yes!

'Thanks, Rebecca.' I grinned. 'I'd love one.'

Rebecca Dowd was taking me home. What a strange night.

thirty-three

Mum nagged and nagged until I gave in and let her make me some mid-morning breakfast.

'I know your job pays well,' she said, 'but I'm not happy about the hours you have to work. You're a growing boy. You need regular sleep and proper meals.'

'Mum, you're fussing,' I sighed. 'And the job is only until school starts again. Until then I'll survive. And anyway, I'm not back at work until tomorrow night.'

Though to tell the truth, I was still so tired, all I wanted to do was get myself something to eat, then fall back into bed. Jessica was at work and Mum had one of her rare days off. When Mum wasn't working at the local hospital, she did agency nursing to make extra money. Jessica's college fees and all the extras I needed for school meant that she spent every spare hour working. One day that'd all change. I'd be the one looking after her and buying her all the things she deserved.

'I want you to give up your job a week before school

starts. OK?' said Mum. 'You'll need to get back into the habit of sleeping at night and waking up at a reasonable hour each morning.'

'Yes, Mum,' I said.

It wasn't worth arguing. Besides, Mum needed to take her own advice more than I did. She was losing weight and was looking and acting distinctly brittle. Whilst Mum went off to make me something to eat, I had a quick shower.

After my wash, I put my pyjamas back on. Heading downstairs, I went into the living room. I switched on the TV and flicked from channel to channel, searching for something to watch. Mum walked in and handed me a plate with a fried egg toasted sandwich on it. She frowned at me.

'You do intend to have a shower sometime today, don't you?'

'I've already had one,' I replied smugly.

'And you put your pyjamas back on?' Mum's eyebrows were doing a disapproving dance.

'Yep!'

'How can you have a shower and put your jammies straight back on?' asked Mum.

'Like this, Mum,' I said, indicating my clothes. 'And what's more, I'm going back to bed after this.'

'All right for some,' Mum sniffed.

I took a bite out of my sandwich whilst using my other hand to change the TV channel again. I flicked onto a news bulletin and was about to keep flicking when Mum snatched the remote away from me.

'Leave it there,' she said quickly.

She sat down next to me to watch the news, sipping at the coffee she held in her other hand. I tucked into my food.

'. . . *Earlier this morning the Liberation Militia set off a car bomb outside the Department of Industry and Commerce in Silver Square, only two kilometres from the Houses of Parliament. A warning was phoned through one hour before the bomb was due to explode. The emergency services had to evacuate all the surrounding buildings in the area. The car bomb was detonated in a controlled explosion by the army. No one was injured. We can now talk to the Minister for Commerce, Pearl Emmanuel, who is in our Westminster studio. Tell me, Minister, what do you think——?*'

Mum pressed the button to switch off the TV.

'What on earth is wrong with those people?' She frowned.

'What d'you mean?' I asked, my half-eaten sandwich slowing on its way to my mouth. I looked at the blank screen. Why'd she turn it off? Even the news was better than nothing.

'The Liberation Militia,' said Mum, almost angry. 'The Equal Rights bill is about to be passed. Why don't they give the government a chance?'

'Maybe they want to make sure this government doesn't go back on its word?' I ventured. After all, it had happened before with the last lot.

'Of course they won't break their promises,' said Mum. 'This government would have to be stupid or suicidal to withdraw the Equal Rights bill now. The Liberation Militia are about to get what they're supposedly fighting for. So why're they still blowing up stuff?'

'Maybe they're trying to remind the government that they're still around and watching them?' I said, before taking another bite of my sandwich.

'If the L.M. aren't careful, they'll turn people against the bill. They're not helping our cause, not any more,' said Mum.

I took another bite of my sandwich.

'You know what this is?' she went on, eyes narrowed. 'It's the last gasp of a terrorist group who're about to become obsolete.'

'Maybe they have a job lot of explosives and need to use them up before the bill is passed,' I said flippantly.

Mum glared at me. 'It's not funny, Tobey.'

'I know,' I sighed. 'But it's not like the old days when they used to blow shit up with no warning whatsoever.'

'They shouldn't be blowing up anything at all. And stop swearing.'

'How is "whatsoever" swearing?'

'Ha bloody ha!' said Mum. She handed me the mug of coffee before getting to her feet. 'That's for you.'

I peered down inside the empty cup. 'You've drunk it all.'

'I know.' Mum grinned at me before ambling out the room.

'Ha bloody ha, Mum,' I called after her.

'Stop swearing!'

I washed my empty plate and Mum's empty mug before heading back to bed. I'd barely pulled up the duvet when my mobile started to ring. I checked to make sure it wasn't the phone McAuley had given me. It wasn't. It was my own personal phone. I decided to change the ring tone on

McAuley's phone so that when it rang I'd instantly know who was calling me.

'Hello?'

'It's me. I've been thinking about your proposal.'

Not even a hello. It didn't matter, I recognized Owen Dowd's voice at once. I sat up, waiting to hear his decision.

'The way I see it, I've got nothing to lose.'

'That's absolutely right, Mr Dowd,' I agreed. 'You don't.'

'And you seriously believe that you can deliver?'

'I know I can.'

'OK, I'll play. For now.'

'You won't regret it,' I said, my relief intense.

'No, but you might if you're playing some kind of game,' Owen warned. 'When you get me the information you promised, I'll take that as proof that you meant what you said last night.'

'Fair enough, Mr Dowd.'

'And if anything goes wrong . . .'

'I'm on my own. I know.'

Pause.

'Don't, under any circumstances, try to contact me. D'you understand?'

'Yes, sir.'

'I'll be in touch.'

He hung up. No hello. No goodbye. I didn't expect anything else.

I pressed the button to disconnect the call and let my mobile drop onto my bed. The previous evening hadn't gone quite as I'd planned, but that was OK. On the way back to my house, Rebecca and I hadn't stopped chatting. She was very easy to talk to, very easy to like. Too easy. I had to keep reminding myself that she was a Dowd. All the way home, I wondered if maybe I was reading too much into her offer of a lift. When we pulled up outside my house, we chatted for ages. I was the one who had to make my apologies, otherwise we would've been talking until the dawn broke over the car bonnet. And I'm sure that when I told her I had better head indoors, I hadn't imagined the disappointment on her face.

Rebecca's birthday party couldn't have come at a better time. What an unexpected bonus. I got to meet her brother faster than I would've done otherwise. I took it as a sign that out there, somewhere, someone was on my side.

thirty-four

Just before noon on Tuesday, the phone McAuley had given me started to ring. The unfamiliar ring tone threw me for a moment until I remembered. It took a few seconds to track down the phone, which was in the pocket of my denim jacket, hanging on the nail I'd hammered into the back of my bedroom door.

'Hello?'

'Good morning, Tobey. How are you?' asked McAuley.

I was instantly on my guard.

'I'm fine, thank you, Mr McAuley.'

'Sleeping OK?'

Pause. Now what did that mean? Some damage limitation was required.

'Sleeping just fine, sir. I've got some news actually. I wanted to phone you sooner, but I didn't know how to contact you as you didn't leave a number on this phone and I didn't want to turn up at your address unannounced.'

'It's a wise man who learns from the mistakes of others,' said McAuley, spouting the cliché like he'd only just made it up. How pathetic was that? 'What news d'you have for me?'

'I managed to get a job at TFTM.'

Silence.

'Mr McAuley?' I was the first to break the strained quiet between us.

'Why did you do that when you work for me?' McAuley asked softly.

'I thought it might be useful to you to have someone working in a place owned by the Dowds. I didn't mention it beforehand because I wasn't sure I'd get the job.'

Silence. Again.

'Just say the word, Mr McAuley, and I'll give up my job there straight away,' I said earnestly. 'I just thought it might be useful to you.'

'And it might be, Tobey. It just might be,' said McAuley. 'What exactly will you be doing at TFTM?'

'I've been employed as a waiter in the restaurant. I'm not up in the Club unfortunately, but that's what I'm aiming at.'

No need to tell him I'd already started working there. Let's put it this way – what he didn't know wouldn't hurt me.

'I see. I want you to report back to me regularly,' said McAuley.

'I don't have your phone number, sir.'

'I'll phone you,' said McAuley.

'Yes, sir.' I made sure to keep my sigh of relief inaudible. He'd bought it.

'And Tobey?'

'Yes, sir?'

'I do the thinking around here, not you. Understand?'

'Understood, sir.'

'Are you working there tonight?'

'Yes, sir. My hours are from six p.m. till one, Tuesdays to Saturdays.'

'Good,' said McAuley. 'Because I have a job for you before then. A delivery . . . no, actually, make that two deliveries, that need to be made before this evening. Can you do that?'

What kind of deliveries?

Ask no questions, hear no lies.

But no more body parts. Please.

'Yes, sir. Where and when?'

'Byron will meet you at the Wasteland in thirty minutes. He'll give you all the details.'

'Yes, sir.' But McAuley had already hung up. He didn't need to wait to hear that I would do as I was told. Besides, I would never have hung up on McAuley first. Little things like that meant a lot to him. The smaller the person, the smaller the things that mattered.

With a sigh I got dressed. So much for my lazy morning in bed. My lazy morning the day before had gone down a treat and I was so looking forward to another one. Ah, well.

Not surprisingly, the Wasteland didn't contain too many people and less than a handful of children. If I'd had kids, I wouldn't be taking any chances either, not after what had happened. I looked around, but there was no sign of McAuley's lieutenant. I wasn't exactly sure where I was supposed to meet Byron so I headed for the deserted football pitch, the first time I'd been there since . . . since. Just looking at it made my heart jump erratically. My eyes were drawn to the ground, the exact spot where Callie lay after she'd been shot. There was nothing to indicate she'd ever been there, not even the flowers that'd been brought to this place by friends and strangers alike after that day. Either a cleaning crew or the one day of rain we'd had since the shooting had washed away every trace of her blood. That was all it took – a shower of rain, the slam of a door, the thrust of a knife or a gunshot – and just like that, a person could be gone with nothing but the memories of others to show that they'd ever existed. Life was too fragile.

'Come with me, Tobey.'

Byron's voice in my ear made me jump. I hadn't even heard him approach. Already he was heading away from the football pitch and towards the road. He walked towards a black saloon car with tinted windows. Was this another set-up? Was the black car Byron's? Byron turned his head, impatience written all over his face. I followed him.

'Sit in the front,' he told me once we reached his vehicle. I hesitated only momentarily, and I certainly didn't argue. Byron headed around his car to get behind the wheel. The moment he was inside, he pressed a button to lock all the doors. The loud clunk made me flinch.

Tobey, take a deep breath and get it together.

I was altogether too jumpy. It made me look guilty of something. Byron turned in his seat to face me.

'Mr McAuley wants you to deliver a parcel and a letter. Can you do that?'

I nodded.

Byron produced a white envelope from his inside jacket pocket. He held it out for me to take. There was no address or name on the front, no markings of any kind.

'Who's this for?' I frowned.

'Vanessa Dowd.'

Vanessa . . . Was he joking? From the expression on his face, unfortunately not. Vanessa Dowd never came to TFTM. How on earth was I supposed to get the letter to her? I didn't know her home address and there was no way anyone at TFTM would just give that to me.

Was this some kind of trick to catch me out?

Godsake! I was being too paranoid. But being around people like McAuley and the Dowds could easily do that to you. I swallowed hard before taking the envelope and putting it in my inside jacket pocket.

'How am I supposed to get this to Vanessa Dowd?'

'You'll have to figure that out for yourself,' said Byron, totally unconcerned.

'Well, what's her address?' I asked.

Bryon shrugged. 'McAuley doesn't know. You'll have to figure that one out too. But my boss has every confidence in you. He knows you're a smart guy.'

There was no answer to that – and no mistaking the sneer in Byron's voice either.

'Oh, before I forget,' he said, handing me another envelope, much fatter than the last one.

'Who is this one for?'

'You,' said Byron. 'Payment for doing as you're told.'

I hesitated for a moment or two before taking the envelope and stuffing it into another pocket.

'Aren't you going to open it?'

'Later,' I replied. 'Could you thank Mr McAuley for me?'

Byron nodded, his eyes appraising me.

'What about this parcel I'm supposed to deliver?' I said.

'It's for Adam Eisner, Flat Eighteen, same address as before,' said Byron.

'What address would that be?' I asked without missing a beat.

Amusement lit Byron's green eyes. 'D'you really think my boss doesn't know that you delivered two of Dan's packages a while ago? One to Adam and one to . . . someone else.'

'Who told him that?'

Was it Dan or Adam Eisner himself? It seemed impossible to keep secrets from McAuley.

'You need to stop asking so many questions,' said Byron. 'It isn't healthy.'

A chill chased up my spine. Message received and understood. I looked around the car. The back seats were empty and Byron wasn't making any strenuous moves to hand me anything.

'Where's this parcel for Mr Eisner? Am I allowed to ask that at least?'

'It's in the boot. Get out and I'll pop the boot for you,' said Byron.

I did as directed, walking round to the back of the car. I had a good look around before I stepped up to it. The boot opened with a loud clunk, then rose to the sound of constant beeping. A package wrapped in brown paper and about the size of a car manual lay on the left. A supermarket carrier bag filled with food sat next to it. I lifted up the parcel. The moment I was clear, the boot descended. I looked through the back window. Byron was watching me via the interior mirror, no hint of a smile on his face. He drove off just as the boot clicked shut.

There I stood at the edge of the park, two unaddressed envelopes in my jacket pockets, an unaddressed parcel in my hands and the distinct feeling that I was being followed. The prickling of my nape left me in no doubt about that. I looked around nervously.

The question was, who was watching me?

thirty-five

I spent the next couple of hours hopping on buses and trains that took me all over Meadowview and beyond. A lot of the time, I didn't even know where I was. But when that happened, I just leaped on the nearest bus, getting off at the first place I vaguely recognized. I kept telling myself

I was being ridiculous, I wasn't in some spy novel. But I decided it would be better to waste a couple of hours by being over-cautious than to be nabbed by the police whilst carrying a parcel containing I-don't-know-what inside.

I could just see it now – 'Honestly, officer, I didn't know I was carrying two semiautomatic weapons . . .'

Yeah, right!

I took two trains into town and three back out again. I scanned the faces of my fellow passengers for those that were too familiar, those that I'd seen one too many times today. Only when I was convinced that I was no longer being watched or followed did I head for Adam Eisner's flat. Even as I climbed the stairs of his estate building, I couldn't help wondering what was inside the parcel I was delivering. If anyone had asked me, I would've sworn that my fingers were tingling just from touching it. It didn't matter whether the tingling was real or merely my mind playing tricks, I could still feel it. And it didn't feel right. I rang the bell. The front door opened almost immediately. Adam Eisner stood there, his black hair combed back off his face, his dark-blue eyes shooting poison darts.

'Where the hell have you been?' he roared at me.

There was no other word for it. It was a definite roar. He pulled me into his flat, slamming the front door behind me.

'I was expecting you over an hour ago,' he said, his face mere centimetres from mine.

'I'm sorry I'm late, Mr Eisner, but when I collected your parcel, I got the feeling someone was watching me, so I travelled around until I was certain I was no longer being followed,' I explained quickly.

Eisner backed off a bit, his expression wary. 'Who would be following you?'

I shrugged. 'I have no idea. Probably no one. Like I said, it was only a feeling, but I figured it was better to be safe than banged up.'

Eisner headed for his front door and opened it. He looked up and down the corridor outside his flat, before crossing it to peer down at the ground below. He scanned all around the block for a solid minute before returning to his flat, closing the door quietly behind him.

'You should've phoned someone to tell them what you were doing,' Eisner retorted.

Phoned who exactly? None of them were exactly on my speed-dial list. I held out his parcel to him.

'Bring it into the kitchen,' Eisner ordered.

I inhaled sharply. I just wanted to get out of there. I had an envelope which was burning through my jacket pocket and scorching my flesh. And I still hadn't figured out how I was going to pass it on to Vanessa Dowd.

I followed Eisner into the kitchen. Four Nought men sat around a farmhouse-style table, all stark naked. A number of small plastic bags covered the table, most empty, some half-filled with white powder.

'Put the package on the table,' said Eisner.

I couldn't wait to get rid of it. I dropped it like the thing was white-hot – which I now realized was exactly what it was. A set of electronic scales sat in the middle of the table along with a bigger bag of a dull-white powder. What was in the bigger bag? Flour? Sugar? Powdered baby milk? One of the men was weighing out exact amounts of the merchandise before carefully pouring it into the small bags, while the others were adding the same amount again from the bigger bag. They were cutting drugs. That's why they were all sitting around naked – it cut down the number of places they could hide the stuff for themselves.

Eisner picked up a small knife and cut a slit down the brown parcel like he was a surgeon making the first incision. White powder gently spilled out on either side of the cut. My heart was beating hard and heavy. Eisner turned to smile at me.

'I see McAuley was right about you. You have a smart head on your shoulders.' Eisner picked up one of the tiny bags filled with white powder which hadn't yet been added to and held it out to me. 'Take that for your trouble.'

I shook my head. Cocaine? No way.

'Take it,' said Eisner. 'You won't find better blow anywhere in Meadowview.'

I took the bag and stuffed it into my trouser pocket.

'I have more deliveries to make.' Was that really my voice playing back at me, so low and so calm? It had to be.

Eisner nodded and led the way out of his flat. I walked along the corridor towards the stairs, knowing that Eisner was watching every step. I headed away from his block and just kept going. Everything inside me was still, like my heart and my head and my very soul were all holding their breath.

As I turned some anonymous corner, a couple of bins came into view outside some local shops. I strode up to the nearest one and pulled the plastic bag out of my pocket, careful to keep the contents hidden in my hand. I stretched out my arm, my hand poised over the bin.

Let it go, Tobey. Before it's too late. Let it go.

But I couldn't. I just couldn't.

thirty-six

Hello, Callie. How are you feeling today? You look a little better. Your face isn't quite so ashen. They tried to suck the life out of you, didn't they? But you're strong, Callie Rose. Stronger than even you think. So hang in there. You don't have to wake up today or tomorrow or even this week. You'll come round in your own good time.

But you will come round.

And when you wake up, I want to be the first face you see. That's why I visit you every day, even if it's only for a few minutes. When you awake you'll see me smiling at you and nothing else will matter. My guess is that you've been through so much over the last few months that it all finally caught up with you and you're just dealing with it in your own way. Your mind is . . . resting, recharging. I'm not worried about you being in this place. I'm not worried about the fact that you haven't regained consciousness yet.

I think . . . I feel you're waiting for me. So don't wake up yet. I haven't finished what I need to do. Just sleep – and wait for me.

I had to see you today, Callie. I had to take that chance. You're the only one I can talk to. My pockets are full, Callie – and they're weighing me down so much I can hardly stand upright. I've got one jacket pocket filled with money. Blood money. Another pocket contains a letter that I'm afraid to deliver. And in my trouser pocket there's . . . there's . . . something that clings to my hand like superglue and no matter how hard I try, I can't shake it off my fingers, I can't get rid of it.

I'm scared, Callie.

There! I've admitted it. Just between you and me, I'm bloody terrified. But one thing keeps me going – you.

Just you.

Only you.

I'll hang onto that and do what I have to do. Whatever it takes, eh, babe?

So how am I doing? Well, the weekend was kinda strange. I met a girl. Her name is Rebecca, Rebecca Dowd. She's Vanessa Dowd's daughter. Yes, *the* Vanessa Dowd. I had to work on Sunday at TFTM. It was Rebecca's eighteenth birthday party. Private function. I got triple time plus tips so I made a whole heap of money. A few more weeks of this and I'll be able to buy you the birthday present I've been promising you for ages. Anyway, Rebecca gave me a lift home and we chatted and had a good laugh all the way back to my house. I think she likes me. I surprised her and that's a good thing. I don't know what she was expecting, but I kept up with her conversation and I even managed to tell her one or two things that she didn't know. And when she found out I was going to Heathcroft High . . . ? You should've seen the looks she kept giving me after that. My mum was right – that school is like a passport.

When we arrived outside my house, we sat in her car

for almost an hour, just talking. Reading between the lines, it sounds like she thinks most guys are more interested in getting to know her family's money than her. Of course I didn't ask for her phone number or for a date or anything. I think that surprised her too. I have to admit, though, Rebecca was all right. I think you'd like her. But enough of her. Besides, I'll probably never see her again.

Callie, I'll come and see you as often as I can. It's tricky because I can't let anyone know that I'm here. And I sure as hell can't let your Aunt Minerva, or worse still, your mum, find me here. Your mum is waiting for me to man up and tell the police what I know. And with every day that passes with my silence, I know she despises me more. But this is something I have to sort out for myself.

I'm going to make McAuley pay for what he did to you.

I'll get him.

Or die trying.

The trouble is, I can't do it without help – Owen Dowd's help. He's the only one with the money and the resources and the will to help me. I just wish I could get over this feeling that I'm crawling into bed with the devil to catch a demon. Crawling into bed metaphorically speaking, of course. I tell myself that it's the end result that counts, nothing else. Oh, I know what the end result needs to be, *has* to be. But it's the getting there that's tricky. Isn't it always? I have a vague plan and the will to succeed, but that's it. It will have to be enough. Trouble is, I feel like I'm stumbling through some improvised dance that I'm kinda making up as I go along. But that's OK, I'll survive. I hope.

Y-you have to live, you know that, don't you, Callie? I don't know what I'd do without you. I've . . . cared about you for so long, I don't know how to do anything else. I wouldn't tell this to anyone but you. Hell! I wouldn't even tell you if you were conscious enough to hear it and play it back to me.

But I do . . . care about you. Very much.

You force my heart to beat.

So don't ever scare me like that again.

When you got shot, it was as if . . . as if the bullet that got you had escaped your body to hit me right between the eyes. I survived, though, because you did. But when your heart stopped . . . When that happened, all hope inside me started to wind down like a broken toy. I guess everyone has their Achilles heel. Why should I be any different?

Hang in there, Callie. Remember, it's you and me against the world. I'll deal with McAuley, and when you wake up we'll go away together. Somewhere far away where Jude McGregor will never find us. You just sleep, Callie Rose. Sleep until it's all over. And don't fret about what happened to you. Trust me, Callie. I'm taking care of that. Whatever it takes.

And if it doesn't work, if I get jammed up, just know that it was worth it.

You were worth it.

thirty-seven

Vanessa,

I'm sure the last thing either of us wants or needs is a resumption of hostilities. The last turf war between us created casualties on both sides. But I will take out you and yours if your family try to muscle in on my patch. You need to rein in your sons. Once I have ALL my territory back, your manager will, I'm sure, find his way home.

And not before.

M.

thirty-eight

I arrived for my job at TFTM at least fifteen minutes too early, waiting for the opportune time to put my plan into action. Inside the restaurant, I saw a few very late-lunch diners with only a couple of staff visible through the tinted windows, but they were at the back of the restaurant and hadn't even noticed me – which was just the way I wanted it. I stood outside, glancing at my watch, tapping it periodically and holding it to my ear, strictly for the benefit of the person who was watching me. 'Cause I was now in no doubt that I was being followed. And I had a good idea who was acting as my shadow.

I looked up and down the street, waiting for the right moment. And I didn't have long to wait. A middle-aged Cross woman who reminded me a bit of Callie's aunt Minerva was walking towards me. The woman wore a dark-grey suit and a mustard-yellow blouse and she carried a laptop briefcase. Her braids were pulled back and styled elegantly on top of her head.

'Excuse me,' I asked, stepping in front of her.

'Yes,' asked the woman, slight suspicion in her voice. But at least she had stopped.

I took another small step towards her. 'I'm sorry, but my contact lenses are playing up,' I smiled. 'Could you tell me what address is on this letter please?'

With my back half towards the restaurant window, I pulled the envelope for Vanessa Dowd out of my inside jacket pocket and handed it to her. Sidestepping slowly, I watched as the woman looked down at the envelope. I had to make sure that she was seen with the letter first rather than me. She looked at the front of the envelope, then turned it over in her hand.

'There's no address on this letter.' The woman frowned.

'That explains why I can't read it then.' I grinned apologetically. 'I'm sorry to have troubled you.'

'That's OK.' She handed back the envelope, looking at me like my deck was short of more than a couple of playing cards.

'Thanks anyway,' I said.

The woman hurried on without another word. I looked down at the envelope and turned it over as the woman had done. Painting a frown on my face, I looked up, just as Michelle and Angelo arrived for work. The letter charade with the suited Cross woman had been for their benefit alone. I could only hope it'd worked.

'Oh, hi,' I said.

'You're early,' said Michelle.

'My watch is running fast.' I showed it to them so they could see for themselves, the letter still in my hand.

'Then for goodness' sake buy yourself a new watch,' Michelle snapped.

'What's that?' asked Angelo, nodding at the letter I was waving about.

'Oh, this. A woman just asked me to give it to Vanessa Dowd.' I pointed up the street in the direction of the woman who'd just left. 'I told her she doesn't work here, but she insisted that Mrs Dowd's son Gideon did. She wouldn't take no for an answer.'

'What is it?' asked Michelle.

I shrugged. 'Haven't a clue. Does Gideon Dowd work here then? Is there any way I can get this to Mr Dowd to give to his mum?'

Angelo held out his hand. I eagerly handed over the envelope. Fingerprints. I wanted the envelope to be covered in a whole database full of fingerprints. That way I could hide mine amongst many – just in case the Dowds had the means to check them out.

'I wonder what it is,' Angelo mused aloud before handing it back.

'So is Gideon Dowd coming here today?' I asked.

'As a matter of fact Gideon will be in later,' said Michelle cagily. 'He sometimes comes in to do business with Mr Thomas.'

'Oh, I see.'

'But how did that woman know?' Michelle looked worried.

I shrugged. 'Michelle, can I give this to you to pass on to Mr Dowd so he can give it to his mum?'

Michelle wasn't happy, but what could she say? She reluctantly took the letter from me. From what I'd heard, Gideon and Owen Dowd both kept small offices somewhere upstairs in the Club where I wasn't supposed to go without an explicit invitation or reason. I'd already seen Owen's office and I was in no hurry to see his brother's. Evidently Michelle wasn't happy about me delivering the letter to Gideon in person either. Rather her than me.

I left TFTM, shift over, in the early hours of Wednesday morning. At least, because it was a week day, the night buses were running so I could get fairly close to home. The bus would drop me about a fifteen-minute walk from my house, but that was better than having to walk the whole way. I was grateful for small mercies. The night was warm like a blanket around me. I looked up. The moon was a crescent and I could make out the odd star plus the lights of a plane flying high overhead. But there was too much city light pollution to see much more than that.

With a sigh, I started on my way. I'd taken five or six

steps when I heard, 'Get your filthy blanker hands off me.'

I spun round. Charles, a barman who worked up in the Club, was the one doing the shouting. The object of his wrath was a middle-aged Nought guy who sat cross-legged on the ground, a cup in his hand to collect the spare change of passers-by. On a piece of card in front of him, were the words: HOMELESS AND HUNGRY. PLEASE HELP. The homeless guy obviously wasn't doing very well if he was still asking for change at this time of night. But catching late-night revellers and staff heading for home must've seemed like a good ploy. The seated guy wore a woolly hat, despite the warm weather, with a plaid shirt and jeans, all assorted shades of grubby and dark.

'Sorry. I'm sorry.' The guy with the cup raised a placating hand.

What was he apologizing for? What had he done?

'Don't ever touch me again.' Charles carried on mouthing off, whilst brushing down the lower leg of his trousers. I couldn't see anything on them. Maybe he was trying to wipe off fingerprints. A number of TFTM employees had gathered around by now, wondering what all the commotion was about.

'Look at you,' Charles said scathingly. 'You're an embarrassment. Get off your arse and get a job, you worthless blanker.'

There were some gasps, but no one spoke.

'And what are you?' asked the homeless man, his gaze never leaving Charles.

I'd been wondering the same thing myself. Charles was as white as the homeless guy. As white as me.

'I'm not a blanker, I'm a Nought,' Charles announced.

Behind him, some of Charles's Cross colleagues started to snigger, a couple of them pressing their lips together real tight to stop themselves from laughing out loud. The seated guy stood up slowly, his cup still in his hand. He and Charles never took their eyes off each other. The homeless man slowly shook his head. Charles's eyes narrowed. He stepped forward. So did I.

'Here you are,' I said, handing the homeless guy a couple of notes from my trouser pocket. 'Go and get yourself a warm meal.'

The man took my money without a smile. I didn't expect anything else. Charles couldn't get to him without shoving me out of the way first, which he was probably prepared to do. And he had ten years and quite a number of kilos on me, but I wasn't going to budge – well, not without him body-charging me first. The homeless man ambled off like nothing was bothering him, which it most likely wasn't. I went to follow in his direction, but Charles grabbed my arm and spun me round to face him. He glared at me. I said nothing.

'Takes a blanker to know a blanker,' he said softly.

He let go of my arm and marched off. All the TFTM people who'd been watching the show faded away like a sigh. In mere moments, I was alone.

Noughts and daggers. Crosses and blankers. Noughts and blankers. Crosses and daggers. Circles within circles. Divisions and yet more divisions. No black. No white. Just myriad shades of grey, one shade for every person on the planet. I didn't like where my thoughts were leading me, but my mind was full of sharp things. Sharp words like blanker, sharp sounds like the Crosses laughing at Charles, sharp sights of Charles and the homeless guy regarding each other, and homeless smells and textures like needle points. Only with Callie could I be comfortable. I shook my head. Something about the encounter between Charles and the homeless guy had left me feeling... hollow. I needed Callie to fill all the empty spaces inside of me. But she wasn't here. At that moment, I felt incredibly lonely. I hadn't realized until this moment how loneliness could eat away at you so much that it actually hurt. I needed to get home. I'd barely taken ten steps away from the place when an unfamiliar silver sports car pulled up beside me.

'Fancy a lift?' Rebecca's voice reached me before the passenger window was even halfway down.

Poking my head through the open window, I grinned at her. 'Love one. Whose car is this?'

'Mine.' Rebecca smiled. 'An eighteenth birthday present. Check out the licence plate.'

I took a couple of steps back to do just that. The registration read BECKS 1.

'Very nice,' I said, wryly wondering what Mum would get me for my eighteenth birthday in a couple of weeks' time.

'Hop in then,' said Rebecca.

I did just that, grateful for the car and the company.

Once we were on our way, I asked, 'Not that I'm not grateful, but how come you're driving when you've only just had your eighteenth birthday?'

The government had recently changed the law so that you couldn't even take driving lessons until you were eighteen minimum. Yet Rebecca had been given a car for her eighteenth birthday and was happily driving around.

'Private lessons on private roads for the last year,' she said. 'I took my test on my birthday and passed. Mum said if I passed first time I could have a car, I just didn't expect to get one quite so quickly.'

Oh, the joys of having money. All together now. Everybody sing!

'So were you at the Club again tonight?' I wondered.

'Nope. I just happened to be driving past . . . Well, actually, that's a lie. I was waiting for you.'

I stared, stunned. 'Why?'

'I wanted to give you a lift home.'

'Are you thinking of starting up your own taxi service?'

Rebecca laughed. 'Not as such.'

'Why did you want to give me a lift then?'

'I wanted to talk to you again,' said Rebecca, looking straight ahead.

'About what?'

She shrugged. 'Whatever you like. I don't mind.'

Huh?

'Oh. I see,' I said embarrassed. Slow or what?

We exchanged a brief smile before Rebecca turned her attention back to the road. I sat back into my seat and relaxed. Wow! She really did like me.

'It's a shame you didn't come into the restaurant this evening,' I began. 'It must be International Have-A-Moan day 'cause we had them all in tonight. We had one guy who chose the woodland fruit strudel for dessert, then complained it was too dry. It came with a jug of apple and cognac custard and I came that close to pointing out that if he bothered to pour the custard on his strudel, it would be wet, so what was his problem?'

'I can imagine how that would've gone down,' said Rebecca wryly.

'Yeah, like a lead balloon,' I agreed. 'But it was so tempting!'

I spent the next thirty minutes telling her about some of the other restaurant customers I'd come across so far. It was very indiscreet, but what the hell. I was very good at impersonations and voices, and let's face it, TFTM provided some great material. At one point Rebecca was laughing so hard, we started to drift across the road. An angry beep from an oncoming car persuaded me to tone it down a bit. Finally we pulled up outside my house.

'Thanks for the lift, Rebecca. And the company. I appreciate it.'

'You're welcome.' She smiled.

I got out and headed for my front door. Giving her a wave, I went inside.

The next night, Rebecca was once again waiting for me outside TFTM. This time I held her hand as a thank you before I got out the car. When she dropped me home the night after that, I thanked her by kissing her cheek. The night after that she turned her head so that I ended up kissing her lips. It was brief, mainly because she surprised the hell out of me.

'What was that about?' I couldn't help asking.

'Tobey, for a bright guy you're surprisingly slow about some things,' Rebecca said, exasperated.

'OK, what am I missing?' I frowned.

She took a deep breath. 'Are you going to ask me out or not?'

I stared at her. 'D'you want me to?'

'Why don't you ask me and see?' Rebecca said patiently.

'Becks, I don't suppose you'd like to see a film or something with me some time?' I asked doubtfully.

'God! I thought you'd never ask.' She laughed. 'If the kiss hadn't worked, I was contemplating dancing naked on your doorstep tomorrow.'

'Damn! Now she tells me.' I grinned – then my smile faded. 'What about your brothers?'

'What about them? They're not invited,' Rebecca replied.

'What're they going to say about the two of us going out together?'

We both knew what I was asking.

'It doesn't matter what my brothers think, because it's my life and I'm the one going out with you, not them,' Rebecca said.

Question answered, but I decided to keep pushing.

'What would your brothers say if they could see us now?' I asked.

Rebecca took a deep breath. 'Quite frankly, it's none of Gideon's business and Owen couldn't care less if I dated the head of the Liberation Militia.'

'I'm sure Owen does care about you, in his own way.' Even I winced at that platitude.

Rebecca's brown eyes twinkled, though she did her best to hide the smile on her lips.

'OK, work with me here. I wasn't sure what else to say,' I said dryly.

Rebecca smiled. 'I appreciate the gesture. But Owen cares about Owen, no one else. He does love me and I love him; it's just that we don't like each other very much. Or at all. And as for Gideon, he's like Mum. He likes to run things, including my life.'

I nodded, without saying anything else.

'Tobey, you don't strike me as the kind of person who'd let anyone stop you from getting or doing what you really want. But if being with me is going to make you uncomfortable, just say and we'll forget all about it.'

'No, it's not that,' I rushed to reassure her. 'I'd like to go out with you. In fact, I'm glad I had the idea.'

Rebecca laughed and this time I joined in.

'So what would you like to see?' I said.

'Tell you what. Why don't we go to one of those multiplexes where they're showing lots of films and then we can decide.'

'OK. Sunday or Monday?' I asked.

'How about both?' Rebecca winked at me.

'Both it is,' I agreed with a grin.

I asked for her mobile number and she gave it to me without hesitation. I actually had Rebecca Dowd's digits! After one final kiss which lasted a bit longer this time, I got out of the car. I waved at her as she drove off, but the moment I turned to my front door, my smile vanished.

thirty-nine

Hi, Callie.

I bought these for you. Sorry they're a bit squashed and some of the petals have fallen off . . . well, a lot of the petals have fallen off, but I had them under my jacket. It's not that I'm ashamed of bringing you flowers or anything. It's just . . . I was keeping them safe inside my jacket in case the wind caught them before I could get to the hospital. Anyway, enough of the flowers. I'll leave them at your bedside and I'll ask one of the nurses to put them in a vase just before I leave. I know how much you like flowers.

So how are you today?

You're looking better. I know I always say that, but you really are. Was that a flicker of a smile I saw just then? Callie, I must admit, I sort of envy you. Nothing that's happening in the outside world can touch you now. You're above and beyond all that. I know when you wake up, it'll all be here waiting for you, but at least for now you don't have to worry about the world and everything going on in it.

Sometimes I look around and I wonder, 'Is this it? Is this all there is?'

But then I think of you. I remember the way you smile at me.

And my question is answered.

forty

'Rebecca, why don't you just come out and tell your mum that you want to be a teacher?'

'Because it wouldn't do any good,' Rebecca sighed.

She took a sip of her fizzy mineral water and looked around the Mexican restaurant. It was a bit on the loud side and probably not as upmarket as she was used to, but if I was paying half the bill for our meal – which I'd insisted on – then it'd have to do. We'd decided to dine today and go to the cinema the following day instead. And in all fairness, Rebecca had been enthusiastic about eating at Los Amigos. I was the one with doubts, which had proved to be unfounded. The restaurant was about one-third full. Not bad for a Sunday night.

'If you did go to university, what would you study?' I asked.

'History. Or maybe History and Politics. But what's the point of talking about it? It's never going to happen.'

'Why not?'

'Mum won't hear of it. As far as she's concerned, she and my brothers are working hard so that I'll never have to. She reckons I should – quote – find a good man, get married, produce grandchildren and enjoy myself – unquote. What d'you think of that?'

'Sounds like hell!' I replied truthfully.

Rebecca laughed. 'My sentiments exactly. Mum thinks that having money and having ambition are somehow mutually exclusive.'

'Have you tried to tell her otherwise?'

'Until I'm blue in the face,' she said. She took another sip of her mineral water, then sighed. 'I would've made a good teacher.'

'So you're going to give up? Just like that?'

'You don't know my mum.'

Was she kidding? Vanessa Dowd was a formidable woman and an implacable enemy. Everyone knew that. And her sons Gideon and especially Owen were cut from the same cloth. If you got in their way, they'd run you over and never spare you a first thought, never mind a second one.

'My mum always says that this life isn't a dress rehearsal,' I began carefully. 'Mum says that regret is an underestimated emotion that can eat away at you just as much as jealousy or anger.'

'Your mum says a lot,' Rebecca said ruefully.

'Ain't that the truth!'

'You want something so you just . . .' She made a gesture with her hand like a rocket zooming upwards. 'You just go for it. It's that simple?'

'Yes, it is – if you want it to be,' I replied. 'I mean, look at you and me. To some people this is complicated. But not to me. What could be more simple than the two of us sitting here, enjoying a meal together? Mind you . . . Never mind.'

'Go on,' Rebecca prompted.

'I can't help wondering why you agreed to have dinner,' I admitted. 'After all, I am younger than you. Isn't that the kiss of death?'

'You're only younger by a few weeks. That's not much,' said Rebecca. 'Besides, you look much older than me.'

'Thanks,' I said dryly.

'No, I meant that as a compliment,' she rushed to explain. 'Some guys look younger than their age or they act all juvenile and silly, but you're much more mature. And I look younger than I really am, so you looking so much older than me works, don't you think?'

'Thanks. I think.'

'Oh hell, that didn't come out the way I wanted at all. What I mean is—'

'Tell you what,' I broke in. 'How about we change the subject?'

'I'd like that,' Rebecca agreed gratefully.

We grinned at each other. My smile faded first.

'Tobey, tell me more about your friends at—'

But she was interrupted by our first course arriving – a large bowl of guacamole sitting on a plate surrounded by mountains of nachos which we'd decided to share. I was so busy concentrating on the food being carefully placed between us that I almost missed Rebecca's gasp. I looked up immediately. She looked down, but not before I caught the expression on her face.

'What's wrong?' I frowned.

'Nothing.' The reply was terse, verging on a snap.

I looked around. There were people at the bar, Noughts and Crosses, mostly couples or small groups, but one or two people were drinking alone. More people were sitting down at tables, eating. No one was even looking at us. Nothing seemed out of the ordinary. I turned back to Rebecca. Something was still troubling her.

'Becks, I'm not a complete idiot, only half of one! So what's going on?'

'I'm so sorry, Tobey. This wasn't my idea, I promise you.'

'What?'

'We're being watched,' Rebecca admitted.

I only just managed to stop myself from spinning round. I took a deep breath, then another.

'Who's watching us?' I asked when I trusted myself to sound relatively calm.

'It doesn't matter,' she said, her head bowed.

'It does to me.'

'The man at the bar, the one wearing glasses. He works for my brother.'

'Which one?' I said sharply.

'I told you, the man wearing glasses . . .' Rebecca frowned.

'No, which brother does he work for?'

'Gideon. But what difference does it make?'

All the difference in the world.

'Why is your brother having us followed?'

'I don't know. I . . . I may have mentioned you, once or twice.' Rebecca was staring at her nachos like they were sprouting wings. 'Maybe more than twice. But I never thought he'd stoop so low as to have us followed.'

'What does he think I'm going to do to you? Kidnap you?'

'Look, I'm really sorry.' Rebecca still couldn't look me in the eye. 'If you want to bail on me, I'll understand. I would, in your shoes.'

Her expression was a cocktail of various emotions. Her lips kept twisting in a parody of a smile and she was blinking an awful lot. I realized with a start that she was on the verge of tears.

I forced a smile. 'I'm not going to bail, Rebecca. I like you. But this has to be the most original date I've ever been on.'

Rebecca's smile was more genuine than my own. 'Wait here. I'll be right back.'

She practically bounded from her chair and marched across to the bar. I swivelled in my chair and watched as she tapped the Cross guy wearing glasses on the shoulder. He turned, polite query on his face. Nice try! Rebecca's voice was too low for me to make out what she was saying, but her expressive face conveyed the conversation just as well as any words. Her words were flowing thick and fast, her expression thunderous. The guy tried to act innocent, but soon gave up on that when it became clear that Rebecca wasn't buying it. They had a heated discussion for a couple of minutes. Had this guy been following me when I met Byron? If it was him, then what had he seen? I'd lost him before reaching Adam Eisner's house, I was sure of it. And he couldn't've seen much through Byron's tinted car windows, but even so.

I stood up, wondering if I should join them. I dithered about for a few moments before making up my mind, but the moment I set foot in their direction, the guy headed for the exit. Rebecca walked back to me, her lips pursed together.

'Everything OK?' I asked as we both sat down again.

'It is now,' she replied.

'Does your brother do this every time you're on a date?' I asked.

'Not after today he won't. I'll make certain of that.'

'Can I ask you a question about your family?' I began tentatively.

'Go on then.'

'Now that your family are . . . successful, wouldn't it make more sense for them to give up all the . . . less legal stuff and go legit?'

'I regularly ask Mum that same question,' sighed Rebecca.

'And what does she say?'

'There's no guarantee that a legitimate business will succeed — too many external, uncontrollable variables. But there will always be a market for the illegal. That's as predictable as the sun rising each morning, plus it's a faster way to make money.'

'Is that you or your mum talking?' I frowned.

'My mum, of course,' said Rebecca sharply. 'With a bit of Gideon thrown in.'

A faster way to make money? For the likes of the Dowds and McAuley maybe. For the ones who worked for them, it was a faster way to end up rotting in prison — or rotting in a cemetery, more like.

'Besides, Mum's got some high-up Meadowview cop in her pocket, so we don't get troubled too much,' Rebecca added.

'You do stay away from that world, though, don't you?' I asked, anxiously.

'Of course. Nothing to do with me,' Rebecca said, suddenly looking concerned as though she realized she was saying too much. 'Besides, Mum wouldn't let me get involved, even if I wanted to.'

I could only admire the way Rebecca brushed off her family's business. Nothing to do with her – except that she dressed in it and drove it and ate it and slept on it and under it and every jewel she wore was paid for by it. I had to find out a few things before this went any further.

'How is Gideon going to react to you going out with one of his employees?' I asked, deliberately changing the subject.

'If it doesn't interfere with your work at TFTM, what difference does it make?' Rebecca frowned.

'The quality of my work will be irrelevant,' I pointed out. 'Your brother isn't going to like this.'

'Does that bother you?' Rebecca asked.

I shook my head. 'Not if it doesn't bother you.'

'It doesn't. I really like you, Tobey – in case you hadn't already noticed. And you're the first guy to treat me like Rebecca instead of Rebecca Dowd.'

'That means a lot to you, doesn't it?'

Rebecca nodded. 'Yes, it does.'

I lowered my gaze and bit into another nacho. She was with me because she thought her surname didn't matter to me. I was beginning to realize just how lonely Rebecca truly was.

'We should make this a regular thing,' I ventured. 'Our Sunday night dinner together.'

'I'd like that.' Rebecca grinned.

I grinned back. 'D'you wanna swap email and IM addresses?'

'Fine with me,' she said. 'If you give me your phone, I'll key in all my details.'

Once we'd swapped info, I checked my phone to make sure that all the information was saved. Rebecca had given me all her details, including her home address. I put my phone back in my inside jacket pocket.

I dipped a nacho into the guacamole and held it out to Rebecca. She grinned at me before opening her mouth. We fed each other until the guacamole bowl was empty. This dinner date had been more successful than I could've dared to imagine. The Dowds owned a copper – and not just a constable or a sergeant by the sound of it. I'd rapidly changed the subject when Rebecca mentioned it, especially as she looked so worried about what she'd revealed. The last thing I wanted was for her to think I'd latched onto what she'd said. But I'd taken it in and filed it away. My inner euphoria was fading somewhat, though. OK, so I knew at least one Meadowview copper was corrupt. One slight problem: I didn't know who. And until I did, I couldn't use the information to my advantage. And I sure as hell couldn't trust any of them. Should I risk trying to get a bit more information from Rebecca? Then I realized what I was contemplating and the direction of my thoughts startled me.

Don't do it, Tobey.

I needed the information, but part of me – a big part of me – was loath to use Rebecca like that. I didn't want her to think I was just like every other guy she knew.

I looked around the room, forcing myself to think of something else.

So Gideon was having us followed, was he?

Let him do his worst. I had plenty to hide, but neither Gideon nor any of his employees would ever find it.

forty-one

I'd only been home for ten minutes when my phone, or rather McAuley's phone, rang.

'Hello, Mr McAuley,' I said the moment I accepted the call.

'Hello, Tobey.' McAuley's oily voice sent a chill tap-dancing across my skin. 'You've been working at TFTM for long enough now. What've you got for me?'

Nothing.

Except . . .

'I've found out something interesting, sir,' I began.

'Oh yes?'

I took a deep breath. 'There's a crooked cop working at Meadowview police station, high up by all accounts, who's on the Dowd's payroll.'

'Who?' McAuley said eagerly.

'I haven't found that out yet,' I admitted.

'Why not?'

'My source didn't know the name of the bent copper.

Reb— I mean, er . . . regarding the bent cop, my source didn't have any other information.'

'I need a name, Tobey, and sooner rather than later, or your information is worse than useless,' McAuley snapped.

'Yes, sir. I'll see what I can do.'

'I want a name, Tobey,' he reiterated.

'Yes, sir.'

McAuley hung up. Damn it. Talk about providing the guy with steel-capped boots so he could give me a good kicking. What had I been thinking? Plus I'd almost given Rebecca away by saying her name. How stupid was that? McAuley wouldn't leave me alone now until I told him the name of the crooked cop who worked for the Dowds. I needed to find out who it was. And fast.

But how?

forty-two

Another Tuesday evening rolled around all too soon again. Tuesday evenings were beginning to feel just like Monday mornings used to. But at least my weekend had been OK. Dinner with Rebecca on Sunday and the cinema yesterday – some chick-flick she chose. The poster called it a 'romantic thriller', but it was thriller-lite as far as I was concerned. After the cinema we had a bite to eat and walked for a while, talking about anything and everything before Rebecca finally drove me home. The fifteen minutes we were parked outside my house were spent synchronizing lips rather than chatting. It was OK, I guess. Nothing like kissing Callie . . . but OK.

Until I got out of the car and saw Sephy watching me. We regarded each other silently. With a scornful toss of her head, she turned away first, dumping the bulging black bin liner in her hand into the wheelie bin for collection the following morning. She walked back into her house without saying a word to me. I stood on the pavement long after she'd gone indoors. I could see myself exactly as she saw me. It wasn't a pleasant picture.

So here I was back at TFTM, my mind full of questions and doubts and worries – and very few answers. I put on my multi-striped, multi-coloured waistcoat, trying not to take too many lingering looks at the thing before it brought on a migraine. Every time I saw my waistcoat I had to remind myself about all the money I was making. I was just fastening up my matching bow tie when Michelle came marching into the men's changing rooms. Luckily it was the beginning of the shift rather than the end, so most of us were dressed or heading that way. Michelle, however, had eyes for no one but me.

'Tobey, Gideon Dowd wants to see you in his office,' she told me.

'Now or after my shift?'

'Now.'

This was either about Rebecca or McAuley's letter to Vanessa Dowd. I knew which one I'd rather it was.

'Where's Gideon's office then?' I asked.

'That's Mr Dowd to you. Go upstairs to the Club. The office door is next to the upstairs kitchenette.'

I headed up to the Club via the back stairs and made my way to Gideon's office door. At the top of the stairs, I came to an abrupt halt. Someone was coming out of Gideon's office, someone I recognized. I only caught sight of his face for a second before he turned his back to me and strode towards the customer exit. He hadn't seen me – too busy scrutinizing the piece of paper in his hand. But it was him, I was sure of it. Frowning, I decided to keep what I'd seen to myself. At least until I could use it for my own purposes.

Now that I was back in the Club, I took another look around. The silk awnings had been removed, revealing the smooth white ceiling that hadn't been apparent before. All the statues in the alcoves had been replaced with huge potted plants. I shook my head. They shouldn't have bothered with the statues for Rebecca's party: she would've much preferred the plants. I guess the statues photographed better for all the glossy magazines. The Club was still relatively empty apart from a couple of guys taking an inventory behind the bar. I knocked twice on Dowd's door and waited to be invited in.

'Come!' came the gruff voice.

Entering the room, I closed the door quietly behind me. The smell of cigarettes and coffee instantly pummelled my nose. Godsake! Didn't the man believe in cracking a window to let in some fresh air? I turned round, taking in the tiny room at a glance. There were no windows. That explained a lot. How could Gideon stand to work in an office with no windows? The man himself was poring over some papers on his desk. He leaned back in his chair the moment he heard me move further into the room. Now I was close to him, I saw he had short black hair, carefully shaped around his face and ears like it had been measured using a ruler before being precision cut. His face and jaw were square, his lips thin like he was too mean to show any more than he had to. This was the closest I'd been to him. Too many other people had been in the way at Rebecca's party.

I stood. He stared. He stared. I stood.

'Have a seat, Tobey,' said Gideon, his eyes narrowing.

I sat.

'I'll get right to it,' he began.

No chance of a cup of coffee then?

'This thing between you and my sister has to stop.'

Or a chocolate biscuit or two? No? Oh well!

'Rebecca and I are just friends,' I began.

'I'm not interested in your view of your relationship,' Gideon interrupted. 'Rebecca is getting too attached to you and I won't have it.'

I sat back in my chair. 'Don't you think Rebecca is old enough to make her own decisions?' I asked.

'Of course not. Rebecca is totally naïve. She thinks everyone is who or what they say they are.'

Now just what did he mean by that?

'With me, what you see is what you get,' I replied.

'Tobey, this isn't a debate. You're to leave my sister alone. Quite frankly, she can do a lot better.'

'We're just having the odd meal together or trip to the cinema,' I tried. 'We're not doing any harm.'

'I don't want to hear it. I'm telling you to stay away from my sister.'

'And what does Rebecca say about all this?' I said.

Gideon looked me up and down, like he was seeing me for the very first time. 'Tobey, you don't want me as your enemy. You really don't. If you don't back off, you're out. And I can make it impossible for you to get any kind of job, anywhere – and that's just for starters.'

'I know that, Mr Dowd.'

'So what's it to be?'

I shrugged. 'No contest.'

Gideon smiled for the first time since I'd entered the room. 'I knew you'd make the right decision. You may go back to work now.'

Gideon bent his head, returning to his papers. I stood up and started to unbutton my waistcoat. It was only as I was pulling it off that Gideon noticed I was still in his office.

'What d'you think you're doing?' He frowned at me.

Saying goodbye to my university fund.

'You told me to choose between my job and Rebecca,' I said, laying my waistcoat on Gideon's desk. I took off my bow tie and placed it on top of the waistcoat. 'So I've chosen.'

Gideon's eyes narrowed. 'Tobey, you've just made the biggest mistake of your life,' he said softly.

No chance of a job reference then?

I left the room.

forty-three

Hi, Callie,

How're you feeling today? You look much better, babe, like you're only sleeping. A sleeping beauty. Godsake! I'm getting frickin' mushy. But at least most of the tubes going into your mouth and into your veins have now gone. That's a good sign – right? So you must be getting better. You're just not . . . waking up. Not yet. But you will. You have to.

I miss you so much, Callie. So much. I wish you were awake so I could tell you everything that's happened since you were . . . you were brought into hospital. I need to talk to you. You're the only one who'd understand what I've been going through, what I'm trying to do. Trouble is, I'm not sure who I am any more. I need you to remind me.

Now when I look in the mirror, a stranger stares back at me. I only feel like I'm me, the real me, when I'm in this room with you. I can't help wondering what you would say or do if you knew what I was up to. Would you try to stop me? Or would you urge me on? Six months ago, I would've said I knew the answer. Now I'm not so sure.

Your hand is warm in mine. We kind of fit together,

don't we, Callie? Like a two-piece jigsaw puzzle.

Oh my God! You squeezed my hand. I felt it. You definitely squeezed my hand. Open your eyes, babe. Please, just open your eyes and look at me.

Please.

OK then. Small steps. Maybe you're not ready to open your eyes yet, but you definitely squeezed my hand.

Small steps.

Promise me something, Callie. Promise me that when you do open your eyes, you'll recognize me. I couldn't bear it if you of all people didn't recognize me.

forty-four

The body of Ross Resnick, the manager of the well-known restaurant – Thanks For The Memories – was found in woodland this morning by two campers. Although Ross Resnick had been missing for over a month, initial forensic examinations revealed that he had only been dead for three or four days. The cause of death has not yet been established. Ross Resnick's wife, Louise, recently . . .

I switched off my phone. I didn't want to read any more news. I stared out of the bus window, watching the rest of the world pass by without a care in the world – at least that's how it felt. I was on my way home and I couldn't wait to get there. I just wanted to crawl into bed and hide away.

I no longer had a job at TFTM, but it didn't matter because the object of that exercise was to make contact with Owen Dowd. Working there and earning some extra money had just been a bonus. Meeting Rebecca had been a windfall. An innocuous date or two had turned into my sure-fire way of getting information about her family. I'd made a couple of deliveries for McAuley, but nothing I couldn't walk away from. At least that's what I'd told myself.

But now McAuley wanted more from me. He wanted to know the identity of the copper owned by the Dowds. I'd dangled that carrot in front of him because it was all I had. But all I'd gained was McAuley snapping at my heels for more. And I didn't have any more, nor the first clue how to rectify that.

And Ross Resnick was dead.

I didn't even know the man and yet somehow his death weighed heavily on me. Was he the one making all that noise in the upstairs room when Dan and I had visited McAuley's house? I'd suspected then, as I suspected now, that it had been him. And if Ross had been the one upstairs, he was probably bound and gagged and worse.

What else had they done to him before he died?

It didn't bear thinking about, but I couldn't get the question out of my head. I told myself all this was just guesswork on my part. I told myself a lot of things. But inside I *knew* Louise Resnick's husband had been alive and in the upstairs room when I heard the scraping noise.

Could I have prevented his death if I'd just phoned the police? Ross was no saint – he worked for the Dowds and they were just as bad as McAuley. But did anyone deserve to die the way he had – in pain and alone? Before Callie got shot, I'd've said an emphatic no.

Not any more.

And that scared me.

Once I got home, I headed straight for my room. I stripped off and crawled into bed, knowing that I'd have trouble sleeping. And I was right. Sleep and I remained strangers. I lay awake for the best part of the night, trying to see beyond my desire for retribution. Maybe Gideon was right about my making a mistake . . . And what about Rebecca? She was OK, much nicer than I expected her to be. What right did I have to drag her into the middle of all this? Especially as Callie was getting stronger every day. She'd squeezed my hand earlier, I was sure of it. If only I could clear my head of the image of Callie looking down at me, blood spilling out over her chest, then maybe I could let all this go. Maybe.

I had to find a way to walk away. I wanted to be around when Callie woke up. She needed me, almost as much as I needed her. I groaned inwardly as I thought of the day's events. Ross Resnick had lost his life. I'd lost my job. My problems were trivial by comparison. I'd quit my job at TFTM . . . Even now, part of me couldn't believe what I'd done. When I walked out of Gideon Dowd's office, I'd practically broken my arm trying to pat myself on the back. But now reality had set in. I mean, dramatic gestures were all very well, but what if Rebecca bowed to her brother's demands and decided not to see me again? Why did that thought bother me so much? It wasn't as if I was attracted to her or anything, but I liked her friendship. Or was it something more basic than that? Did I really like her friendship, or was it just useful? And if the answer was the latter, what did that make me? A man on a mission? Or a user like everyone else?

Rebecca always picked me up after work to drive me home so she had to be aware that I'd lost my job, but she hadn't tried to phone me. Maybe that was the end of that, but I didn't want to think so. She liked me, really liked me. That was flattering in itself. And I liked her company. So I'd give her a day and if I didn't hear anything, then I'd phone her for a chat. Perhaps I'd invite her out to dinner or maybe a film. No big deal.

And if she said no?

I'd dance across that bridge if and when I got to it.

I finally fell asleep, my head full of Rebecca, my heart full of Callie Rose.

I awoke the next morning far earlier than usual, and I still had no answers.

Let it go, Tobey.

Walk away from the Dowds and McAuley and that world – before it was too late. I headed straight for the shower to try and make sure I got my share of the hot water, but I needn't have bothered. Mum's bedroom door was open so she'd already left for the day. And there was no music or TV blasting so Jessica must've gone to college. Sweet! I had the house to myself, just the way I liked it.

I got myself a fresh towel from the airing cupboard and headed towards the bathroom. I glanced down at my pyjama bottoms doubtfully. Should I put them in the laundry basket or did they have another few days of wear left in them? I decided to keep wearing them. These ones were just moulding nicely to my body shape. I opened the bathroom door. Jessica was sitting on the floor, her back against the bath tub.

'Godsake, Jess. Suppose I'd walked in here naked? I thought you'd . . . gone . . .'

On the lowered toilet lid sat Mum's best teapot, plus a cook's blowtorch from one of the kitchen cupboards. A faint coil of smoke, like a dying mist, emerged from the teapot spout.

What the hell . . . ?

'Jessica . . . ?' My whisper of disbelief somehow got through to her. Her eyelids fluttered open and she looked at me, her pupils the size of pinpricks, her gaze unfocused.

Jessica opened her mouth to say something, but the words got lost somewhere in her head. She blinked twice like her eyelids weighed as much as her entire body, then she closed her eyes. She slumped over and would have hit the floor if I hadn't been there to catch her. Propping her up with one hand, I took the lid off the teapot with the other. A dark-brown stain coated the bottom of the pot. An unfamiliar smell wafted up to greet me. Vinegar . . . I looked at the cook's blowtorch and the teapot and my sister, and only then did I realize what I was seeing. And even then I still couldn't believe it.

What had she taken? From the look of it, Jess was smoking junk. But she couldn't, she wouldn't be that stupid. I looked round the base of the toilet then checked the bin. A crumpled piece of paper, like a waxed sweet wrapper, lay on top of all the other rubbish. She hadn't even tried to hide it. I picked up the wrapper and gingerly raised it to my nose. There was no smell to it. I guessed you had to burn the stuff to get the vinegary smell. I'm sure we were told at school that heroin gave off a sweet smell. Maybe it depended on the type. The inside of the wrapper was sticky, gummy beneath my tentative finger. What had Jessica mixed this stuff with? Crumpling up the wrapper, I dropped it back in the bin, vigorously wiping my fingers on the legs of my pyjamas.

Jessica was using. How long had she been doing this? And how had both Mum and I missed it? Should I phone for an ambulance? Was this a normal state for a drug-taker or had she overdosed? I tried to think back to the drugs education lessons we'd had when I was thirteen. Wasn't it harder to overdose by inhaling junk rather than injecting? Harder, yes, but by no means impossible. I hadn't paid much attention to the lessons at the time. I was sure I'd never be stupid enough to chase the dragon or inject or snort or any of that other stuff, so why bother listening? Now I wished I'd listened to each and every word the teacher had said. Was Jessica going to be OK? I had no way of knowing. The teapot sat there, mocking me. Me and my deliveries.

'Jess, open your eyes. Come on, Jess. Just open your eyes,' I begged.

I shook her and gently patted her face. Her eyelids fluttered open, a spark of recognition in her eyes. Without warning, she launched herself at the toilet bowl. The torch clattered to the floor and I only just caught the teapot as the toilet seat was pushed up out of the way before Jessica puked her guts out. Squatting down, stroking Jessica's back, I pulled her hair back off her face. She closed her eyes and slumped back against me. She was out of it again.

My sister was still breathing and her pulse seemed steady, but that was it. That did it. Time to phone for an ambulance. I couldn't take the chance of Jessica having a bad reaction to the stuff she'd inhaled – or vomiting again whilst she was unconscious. My thoughts must've communicated themselves to my sister, 'cause she opened her eyes. Coffee. Should I make some coffee? No, that was for hangovers. Godsake! Exactly what use would coffee be to my sister now? I wasn't thinking straight.

'Jess, listen. When did you use this stuff? Five minutes ago? An hour ago? When?'

I might as well be talking Martian for all the good it did me. It couldn't've been that long ago, not if the smoke was still coming out of the spout when I entered the room. I checked Jessica's arms. No needle marks. At least she wasn't shooting up. Yet.

Mum. Should I phone Mum? That's right, Tobey – this is all Mum needs to brighten her day. I wouldn't phone her unless it was absolutely necessary. But suppose Jess collapsed whilst I was dithering about desperately trying to make up my mind what I should do? Godsake, what did I know about drugs and all that stuff?

Don't shoot me, I'm only the delivery boy.

Just let my sister shoot up instead.

It was useless to say sorry and even more useless to think it, no matter how heartfelt. I looked at my sister and it was like every blood cell had turned into tiny shards of razor-sharp glass which were now dragging their way through my veins. Useless or not, I had to say it.

'Jess, I'm sorry.'

I checked her pulse and breathing again. Slow but steady.

'Jess, open your eyes,' I ordered when she tried to slump again. 'Jess, look at me.'

Godsake. How much of the stuff did she inhale?

I thought of all those half days in and full days off Jessica was always claiming to have. Is this what she'd been doing with all that time at home? Did she still have her job? Or did she just spend her days inhaling Meadowview Oblivion – or MO, as it was known around here? Two friends I'd known since primary school were addicted to MO, but I never for one second thought my sister had joined them. I still couldn't quite understand how I hadn't noticed what was going on. But then, what did I expect? I'd been so wrapped up in other things, I wouldn't've noticed if she'd sprouted another head in the last few weeks. Guiltily, I remembered that I hadn't even bothered to wish her luck in her exam – even though I'd known how important it was to her that she passed.

What should I do?

If I phoned for an ambulance, Mum would find out. But maybe that's what my sister needed – for Mum to find out and help her. My head was spinning. What to do for the best? Jess's eyes were open, she was looking at me.

'Jess, I'm going to phone Mum.'

Jess slowly shook her head. 'No,' she whispered. 'Please.'

'Jess, she needs to know.'

'No. Promise.'

I started to shake my head.

'Promise,' Jessica urged.

'OK,' I replied reluctantly.

'Promise.'

'I . . . I promise.'

'Y-you should . . . sh-should be asleep.' Jess's eyelids kept fluttering shut.

And I would've been if I'd still been working at TFTM. Getting home late from that job meant that I slept until past noon each day. Was that what Jessica had been relying on? She wasn't to know that I'd lost my job. Early to bed meant early to rise. Too early as far as my sister was concerned. I sat on the floor with her, cradling her in my arms as I waited for her to come out of it. There was nothing else I could do.

Deliveries.

forty-five

When my legs threatened to die under me from sitting on the cold bathroom floor for so long, I managed to stand up and half carry, half drag my sister to her bedroom. She was totally lethargic. Laying her on the bed, I covered her with the duvet. I sat down next to her and kept watch all morning. The house was so quiet, it didn't feel right. Jessica went from fitful sleep to long moments when she didn't appear to be breathing at all. I had to keep getting up to take her pulse or put my ear to her nose to feel her breath against my skin. It was only around midday that she finally started sleeping normally. I had to risk leaving her alone so I could have a shower and tidy up before Mum came home, but I popped into her room every few minutes to check on her.

I vacuumed the whole house, tidied the kitchen and the bathroom and scrubbed out the teapot. Mum only broke out this particular teapot once or twice a year, but I didn't fancy the idea of any of our elderly relatives getting high or, more likely, poisoned. A teapot . . . Godsake! Just what did my sister think she was doing? All I could do was hope that Jessica hadn't peed the bed or puked or done anything else that would be a dead giveaway. Whilst she was asleep, I searched through my sister's wardrobe, then her chest of drawers. In the right-hand corner of her bottom drawer, at the back, were two more wrappers. I opened one up. It contained a grey-brown lump, about the size of a chewy mint. Even though I'd heard all about the stuff – and who hadn't, living in Meadowview? – I'd never seen it up close and personal like this before. I tried to remember all I knew about this stuff, the different kinds manufactured around the world. It was sticky, highly addictive, extremely potent – that's about all that came to mind. The wrapper shook in my hands. I searched around for more paper wrappers in Jessica's bottom drawer, but there were no more. Heading for the bathroom, I emptied the contents of the two wrappers down the loo, dropping the wrappers in after them. I flushed the toilet, but whilst the contents disappeared, the wrappers didn't. It wasn't going to be that easy. A second flush, and then a third, and the waxy wrappers still wouldn't go down. They just floated on top of the water. I ended up having to stick my hand down into the toilet bowl to retrieve them before Mum came home and saw them. I washed my hands over and over for a good five minutes afterwards, but they still felt dirty. I sat on the toilet lid for ages, just trying to think straight.

I headed back to Jessica's room and sat at the foot of her bed.

'Jessica,' I said softly, not wanting to scare her into waking abruptly. 'Jess, wake up.'

My sister finally opened her eyes. For the first time in hours her gaze was focused and she knew who I was. I had my sister back. She sat up, then groaned, her hand flying to her head.

'What time is it?' she whispered.

'It's just after one.'

Her gaze grew watchful. Silence.

'Are you going to tell Mum?' she asked at last.

'No,' I replied.

Jess breathed a sigh of relief. The smile she turned on me was full of gratitude.

'But you are,' I told her.

Her smile vanished. She started to shake her head, but quickly stopped. She closed her eyes like she was in pain. 'I can't.'

'Yes, you can, Jess. 'Cause if you don't tell her, I will.'

'No, you mustn't. Please, Tobey.'

'I'm sorry, Jess. I'd keep quiet about most things, but not this. You need to get help before it's too late.'

Jessica's eyes narrowed. 'Stop looking at me like that. This is only the third time I've smoked the stuff,' she snapped. 'I can handle it.'

'That's what they all say,' I replied. 'Godsake, Jess. A teapot? Are you so desperate you had to use Mum's teapot?'

'He said it would be easier than trying to inhale the smoke off foil. He said the teapot would cool down the smoke and I could inhale it when it came out the spout.'

'Who's "he"?' I asked sharply.

Jessica turned away from me. 'I was just trying it,' she said, trying to defend herself. 'I'm not an addict. Addicts inject. I don't inject.'

'Smoking that crap leads to injecting, you know that. This is non-negotiable, Jess. You've got to tell Mum before it gets worse.'

'If you make me do this, I'll never forgive you.'

'That's up to you,' I replied. 'But I'm not going through another morning like this one. Never again, Jess.'

'You didn't need to spy on me. I didn't ask you to. Just sod off and mind your own business.' Jessica was getting more and more angry.

'You're my sister, so you are my business,' I told her. Ironic words, considering how much I resented them each time Jessica said them to me. I headed for the door before turning back, a frown biting into the corners of my mouth.

'Why did you do it? Godsake, Jessica. You know what that stuff does. Why put yourself through that?'

'You wouldn't understand.'

'Try me.'

Jessica shook her head. 'Just leave me alone.'

'Jess, how could you be so stupid?'

'That's right!' she screamed at me. 'I am stupid. Stupid Jessica who can't do anything right. Stupid Jessica who can't learn anything, can't be anything.'

I stared at her. 'Is this . . . is this about your hairdressing course?'

'Don't be stupid,' Jess dismissed. 'No . . . hang on . . . that's me, isn't it? I'm the brainless one in this family. I've spent my entire life running to catch up with you, Tobey.'

'So all this is my fault?'

'This isn't about you. Not everything is about you.' Her voice grew quieter. 'Tobey, just go away.'

I recognized that look on Jessica's face. She wasn't going to say anything else – nothing I wanted to hear at any rate. I headed for the door, but something else occurred to me.

'Jess, where did you get the gear from?'

'None of your business.' She lay down again, turning away from me.

I walked over to her, placing my hand on her shoulder and turning her round to face me. 'Who sold you that stuff?'

Jess sat up and glared at me. 'D'you really want me to tell you?'

In that moment, I knew – but I had to hear her say it.

Jess said one word, the one word I dreaded. 'Dan.'

Dan.

Icy fingers clutched at my stomach as I stared down at my sister. If my so-called friend had been standing in front of me right then and there, I'd've ripped his head off with my bare hands. Jessica staggered to her feet and headed for the bathroom. Moments later I heard the sound of the shower running. At least she was up and about now, making an effort before Mum arrived. But for how long? And she was going to seriously lose it when she discovered what I'd done to the rest of her junk. I still had the bag of cocaine Adam Eisner had given me, but that was hidden away where no one would find it. I sure as hell wasn't going to use it, but I hadn't thrown it away either. I had no such qualms about my sister's stuff.

And as for Dan . . . he was going to pay.

Him and McAuley.

They profited by biting huge chunks out of all of us in Meadowview. It was time for someone to bite back.

forty-six

The following morning brought cooler weather, which was welcome, and some unexpected visitors who were not so welcome. Two guests, to be precise. DI Boothe and Sergeant Kenwood. Like I didn't have more than enough on my plate already. Mum wasn't too thrilled, to say the very least. Not only did she get woken up early, but it was the police. Mum was always warning me that she didn't want the police knocking on our door for any reason. At least the police car outside our front door was unmarked. I was grateful for that, otherwise I would never have heard the end of it. I don't know why they sent the same two coppers who'd interviewed me at the hospital. Maybe their bosses thought we'd established some kind of a rapport!

'Would anyone like a cup of tea?' Mum asked, more out of politeness than anything else.

'I'd love one, Miss Durbridge,' said Sergeant Kenwood.

'It's Mrs,' Mum bristled.

'Mrs Durbridge,' he corrected with a false smile.

'I'd love a cup too,' said the detective. 'Two sugars. If you're sure you don't mind?'

'No trouble at all,' said Mum, her tone indicating otherwise. 'Tobey?'

I shook my head. Mum headed off.

Sergeant Kenwood sauntered over to shut the door. All my senses ratcheted up another gear, though I didn't turn round to watch him directly. The cups of tea were obviously a ploy to get my mum out of the room.

'We wondered if you'd had a chance to remember anything else?' asked the detective.

I shook my head. 'I've told you everything I know.'

'But I don't believe you,' he said.

Well, that was hardly my problem, but from the look on his face, the detective was about to change that.

'I think it would be best if—' He didn't get any further.

My sister Jess flung open the door and stalked into the room.

'Is Tobey in trouble?' she asked straight out.

'And you are . . . ?' asked Sergeant Kenwood, breaking out his notebook.

Jess walked over to him to stand at his side as he wrote. 'Tobey's sister, Jessica,' she said. 'That's J-e-s-s-i-c-a.' She peered over the sergeant's arm to make sure he spelled her name right. 'God, that's rubbish handwriting. Don't you have to rely on what you've written when you go to court? How can you even read that?'

And in spite of everything that had happened the previous day, I don't think I've ever felt closer to my sister than I did at that moment. I loved the way she refused to let Sergeant Kenwood intimidate her. Jessica smiled at me. It was uncertain, as was mine, but at least it was shared. We had our moment of connection which had been missing the day before.

'Paul, put your notebook away.' Detective Inspector Boothe sighed.

The sergeant reluctantly did as he was told, by which time Mum had come back in with two cups of tea. She handed them to the officers before turning to my sister.

'Jessica, this doesn't concern you. Could you go to your room, please?'

'Mum, don't send me to my room like I'm a child,' Jessica argued.

'Then go to the kitchen, go into the garden, go and sit on the roof if you want, but I don't want you in here,' said Mum.

Jess and I knew that tone of voice. Mum only brought it out a mere handful of times a year, so it was seldom used, but very effective. Pouting like a trout, Jess flounced out. Mum turned back to the coppers.

'Now then, is there a problem, officers?' she said, getting straight to it.

'Mrs Durbridge, we'd like your son to come down to the station to make a second formal statement,' said DI Boothe.

'Why does he need to do that?' asked Mum, clutching her dressing gown even more tightly around her. 'He's already told you everything he knows.'

'We need a new formal statement,' Sergeant Kenwood reiterated. He turned to me, his blue eyes cold as a winter sea. 'Tobey, you're the only witness we've got. Apparently, you and Callie Hadley were the only ones in the park at the time of the incident – apart from the shooters of course. Amazing, that. Saturday afternoon and only you and your girlfriend in the park. Who would've thought it?'

Sarcastic git. He made it sound like his lack of witnesses was my fault. But then wasn't I doing the same as everyone else when it came to not telling the police what had really happened?

'My son isn't going anywhere without me,' said Mum.

'Of course, Mrs Durbridge,' soothed the detective.

'If you could wait here please,' said Mum firmly. 'I have to get dressed.'

Without waiting for their reply, she headed back upstairs. No way was I going to stay in the living room with the two coppers. I bolted, mumbling something about getting my jacket. I went to my room and sat on my bed, waiting until I heard Mum head downstairs again. Formal statement, my eye. I wasn't going to say anything that I hadn't already said, so why drag me and my mum all the way down the police station? This was harassment. Or intimidation. Or both. But if they thought they were going to scare me into saying anything detrimental to my health, they were very much mistaken.

When we reached the police station, Sergeant Kenwood ushered me and Mum into an interview room and left us there. I waited for the explosion from Mum, but she didn't speak, not one word. In a way, that made it worse. I sat there with the weight of her disappointment pressing down hard upon me. We sat on one side of a table. Recording equipment had been set into the adjacent wall. A CCTV camera sat self-consciously in one corner of the room, attached to the ceiling like some great black beetle.

After about ten minutes, DI Boothe entered the room with some Cross woman I'd never seen before. She wore a black trouser suit with a light-blue shirt and lace-up black shoes with low heels. Her hair was cut ultra short and neat. And though her face was expertly made up, she was pretty average looking. If I'd passed her in the street, I wouldn't've looked at her twice. She and DI Boothe sat down and the woman pressed the record button before even looking at me. Mum and I exchanged a look.

'Interview room three, twelfth of August, the time is nine-fifteen a.m. Detective Chief Inspector Reid and Detective Inspector Boothe in attendance, interviewing Tobey Durbridge, aged seventeen. His mother Mrs Ann Durbridge is also in attendance.'

DCI Reid faced me and I immediately revised my opinion of her. The rest of her might've been nothing to write home about, but her eyes were ruthlessly sharp and shrewd and didn't miss anything.

'Tobey, could you tell me exactly what happened on the afternoon of the tenth of July when Callie Rose Hadley was shot.'

So once again, I told my story. And throughout the whole retelling DCI Reid kept checking her watch. If I didn't know any better, I'd've said she didn't have the slightest interest in what I was saying. The moment my statement was over and signed, DCI Reid thanked me and announced to the recording that DI Boothe was leaving the room. The detective stood up and did exactly that. DCI Reid stopped the recording and we all sat in silence. DCI Reid didn't take her eyes off me. Not once. What was going on? Less than a minute later, Detective Inspector Boothe was back. A quick nod of his head and a thank you from the DCI and we were escorted from the interview room.

The scratching claws in my stomach told me that something wasn't right here. What was all this about? Why drag Mum and me all the way down here to make a statement they already had and obviously didn't want again? They hadn't challenged me on anything I'd said. They hadn't tried to make me change my story. There was none of the usual stuff I'd seen on the TV.

So what was going on?

The claws in my stomach grew more vicious with each passing second. This just didn't feel right. And then I saw him coming towards me, flanked by two Cross coppers.

McAuley.

In handcuffs.

'I'm going to sue everyone here for wrongful arrest and malicious prosecution.' McAuley's voice held quiet menace as he spoke to one of the officers at his side. 'This is harassment, pure and simple. I haven't done anything so you have no right to arrest me.' He was so steaming mad, I'm surprised the paint didn't blister on the walls. He saw me and did a double take. Then he smiled slowly. One of his all-knowing little smiles. Recognizing him, Mum gave McAuley one of the filthiest looks she could muster, but he only had eyes for me. As we passed each other in the corridor, he didn't take his eyes off me, not for a second.

'Don't worry about the police, Tobey,' he said, low enough so that only I could hear. 'Once I'm out, I'll take care of you.'

My heart went into free fall.

I'd been set up.

'What did that animal say to you?' Mum asked angrily once McAuley was out of earshot.

'Nothing, Mum.'

'Don't give me that,' she argued. 'He clearly said something. You're as white as a white thing. Did he threaten you?'

I shook my head. 'He just recognized me as Dan's friend. That's all. Dan knows him.'

Mum didn't look entirely convinced, but she let it slide. And as for me? A potent cocktail of fear and fury had me shaking inside. All that crap about making a statement. The police just wanted to have McAuley and me in the same place at the same time to make McAuley think that I'd been telling tales. And if the expression on McAuley's face was anything to go by, it had worked.

forty-seven

When we got to the front desk, DI Boothe asked me, 'Are you ready to revise your statement now?'

'No,' I snapped.

DI Boothe took me to one side and lowered his voice as Mum signed the necessary paperwork at the desk. 'Tobey, we're the only ones who can protect you from McAuley. Tell us what really happened at the Wasteland. Be smart.'

DI Boothe and his colleagues had thrown me into the lion's den and were now telling me they could shield me? Yeah, right.

'I'll be fine,' I told him, knowing the words were a lie before they even left my mouth. I was a dead man walking.

DI Boothe shook his head pityingly.

'You want me to trust you? For all I know you could be the one working for the Dowds,' I said bitterly. 'Is that why you set me up? So McAuley can deal with me? Are you acting on Gideon Dowd's orders?'

The detective stared at me, genuinely shocked. It quickly morphed into anger. 'Are you suggesting I'm on the take?'

'It's well known that the Dowds own some high-up

copper at this station – no doubt someone who warns them about forthcoming raids and sting operations and undercover cops and the like. That's why the Dowds are untouchable. And then you wonder why no one in Meadowview will talk to you?'

DI Boothe was taking in everything I said like he'd never heard of such a thing before. He was either a great actor or he really had no idea there was at least one crooked copper, and probably more, on his patch.

He looked around quickly. Mum was still at the reception desk and no one else was close enough to hear our hushed conversation.

'Tobey, you can trust me,' said the detective. At my look of scepticism, he added, 'I know I would say that anyway, but it's the truth. All I want is to bring down Alex McAuley and the Dowds. We in Meadowview deserve better.'

'*We* in Meadowview?' My eyebrows were raised as high as they could go.

'Yes, *we*,' the detective emphasized. 'Because contrary to what you may think, I live here too. Tobey, talk to me. Tell me what you know.'

'All I know is, McAuley thinks I've been in here, singing my head off, thanks to you. Strange that, don't you think? Gideon Dowd warns me to stay away from his sister and when I refuse, the next thing I know I'm dragged in here for McAuley to see. What a great way for Gideon Dowd to make sure McAuley does his dirty work for him. And now I'm supposed to trust you to protect me? You're a bent copper in Gideon Dowd's pocket and we both know it.'

'I don't work for the Dowds or Alex McAuley,' DI Boothe denied vehemently. 'It wasn't even my idea to bring you in.'

'Then whose idea was it? 'Cause that person is probably working for Gideon Dowd,' I said.

Boothe didn't answer.

I glared at him, saying scornfully, 'And I'm supposed to trust you?'

'It's safer if you don't know who arranged to have you brought in. I'll look into it,' he said, his lips a determined slash across his face.

'You do that,' I said with scepticism. 'Oh, and are you having me followed?'

DI Boothe didn't reply.

'Is that a yes?' I asked, knowing full well it was. 'May I ask why?'

Boothe considered whether or not to answer my question.

'We needed to know who you were covering for – the Dowds or McAuley. We were hoping to catch you in conversation with one or the other.' He smiled without any real humour. 'But you like to fly with the birds and swim with the fishes at the same time, don't you? As far as those following you could tell, you were working with both.'

'Tell your officers to stop following me,' I said angrily. 'For one thing, they're not very good at it. And if you want to know who I'm working for, all you have to do is ask.'

'I'm asking,' said the detective.

I smiled. 'I'm working for myself. No one else.'

'And if I don't believe you?'

'That's your problem. In the meantime, I'm outta here.'

'Let us protect you,' Boothe tried again.

'Thanks, but no thanks.'

'I personally give you my word that no harm will come to you or your family.'

'I can take care of myself,' I replied.

DI Boothe shook his head. 'Tobey, you're a fool. Don't you realize I'm on your side? When you finally figure that out, give me a call — but don't leave it too long.'

He walked away just as Mum approached us and before I could say another word.

By the time we got back home, Mum was livid at the police for, as she put it, 'dragging us down to the station for no good reason'. I left her still ranting as I headed for my room. I couldn't forget the look on McAuley's face when he saw me. Surely he knew that I wouldn't blab? I wasn't stupid. Everyone was using me, and if the police didn't get me, McAuley or the Dowds would. I needed some insurance — not for me, but for my mum and sister. I wasn't going to let anything happen to them.

If it was just me, then I could tell them all to go to hell. But it wasn't just me. Anything I did to McAuley or the Dowds would be returned tenfold by those who worked for them. They'd make sure that it wouldn't just be me who suffered. My family, my close friends, they'd all be fair game too. That's why I had to tread so carefully. I wasn't ready or prepared to take on McAuley yet. So I had to get things straightened out with him. This thing with Rebecca had resulted in me taking my eye off the ball. It was time to remedy that.

I lay down on my bed, staring up at the ceiling. What had started off as a tentative saunter down this particular path had now turned into a roller-coaster ride over which I had absolutely no control. I'd known that if I started this, it would be very hard to stop, but no one had warned me it would be impossible.

Would that have stopped me from embarking on this course of action?

Probably not.

I lay still for almost an hour, just trying to gather my thoughts together into some semblance of order. What exactly was I letting myself in for? I was blundering into the unknown, but I wouldn't've turned back, even if I could.

The mobile McAuley had given me started to ring. I hadn't expected anything else. I knew the moment he got out of the police station, he'd be giving me a call. The moment I pressed the talk button, he launched in.

'I want to see you,' he said.

'Yes, sir.'

'I'll be outside your house in ten minutes.'

'Oh, but—' I began, thinking of the wobbly Mum would throw if she saw McAuley parked outside our house. He would be even less welcome than the police.

'Yes?' McAuley said brusquely.

'Nothing, sir. I'll be waiting.'

McAuley disconnected the call.

Ten minutes . . .

The countdown had begun.

forty-eight

I stopped outside Mum's closed bedroom door. She was probably fast asleep by now and wouldn't thank me for waking her up. Jessica had gone out somewhere. I so desperately needed to say goodbye to someone. Anyone. But there was no one. With a sigh, I headed downstairs, leaving Mum undisturbed. I headed out of the house, my hands deep in jacket pockets. I looked up at the blue sky, hoping . . .

But I didn't get my wish.

McAuley arrived right on time. I cast an anxious glance up at Mum's bedroom, but her curtains were closed against the daylight. Byron was the only other person in the car and he was driving. McAuley pointed to the seat next to him in the back. I got in. The door was only just shut when Byron drove off. And with each second, the hollow space inside me grew bigger and bigger.

'Mr McAuley, you have to believe me, I never said a word to the police,' I launched in immediately. 'They dragged Mum and me down to the station to make a statement, but I didn't tell them anything because I don't know anything. They're trying to set me up so that you'll think I've been telling tales.'

McAuley leaned back against the luxurious leather seat, his laptop on the seat between us, a newspaper on his lap as his gaze dissected me. Was it just me or was it uncomfortably hot in his car?

'Why would the police set you up?'

'To make you think I'm a danger to you. That way, with you after me, they reckoned I'd have no choice but to co-operate with them.'

'Co-operate?'

'The police think I know more about the shooting at the Wasteland than I'm saying. But I don't.' I looked McAuley in the eyes as I spoke, desperate for him to believe me. 'When the shooting started, I hit the ground and stayed there. I didn't see a thing.'

McAuley studied me for a long time. I didn't look away or flinch from his gaze. Not once. Because that would've been fatal. My heart was skipping like a boxer in training.

Don't throw up, Tobey. For God's sake don't throw up.

Especially not in McAuley's car.

Or worse still, over him.

At last McAuley's expression relaxed, although his eyes stayed hard as ever.

'How's your job at TFTM?'

What was he up to now? Were his unpredictable conversational leaps designed to catch me out? Careful, Tobey . . . Impatiently, I wiped my forehead with the palm of my hand. Would it kill him to turn on the air conditioning or to open the windows? But why should he? McAuley didn't have a single bead of sweat on him.

'I don't work there any more, sir.'

'Oh? Why not?'

I decided to keep my story as close to the truth as possible. 'Gideon Dowd fired me.'

'Why?'

'For going out with his sister.'

'Rebecca.'

'Yes, sir.'

'And you two are still together?'

'I don't know, sir. I haven't heard from her in a while.'

'D'you like her?'

I shrugged.

McAuley contemplated me. 'So you're sleeping with the enemy.'

I opened my mouth to deny it, only for my mouth to snap shut. Even if McAuley didn't mean literally, he meant figuratively. It was the same difference to him.

'Mr McAuley, if you tell me not to see her again, then I won't,' I said after a moment's pause. 'I'm only with her to try and find out the name of the bent copper in the Dowds' pocket. Rebecca was the one who gave me that information in the first place.'

'You still haven't found out who it is yet?'

'No, sir. But I will. I just need more time.'

'And you don't think you've had enough already?'

'I will get you the information, sir. I guarantee it.'

McAuley turned to his driver. 'What d'you think, Byron? Is Tobey a man of his word?

Byron shrugged. 'I think he's too clever by half – or at least he thinks he is.'

McAuley smiled. And his smile sent a chill ricocheting around my body. Where were they taking me? What were they going to do? McAuley picked up his PC and placed it on his lap over the newspaper, before analysing the screen. His memory key was attached to one of the two USB ports at the side. Why did he need to carry his laptop around with him all the time? Was it just for effect? To make him look more businesslike? Or was there actually stuff on it that he needed at a moment's notice? I carried on watching him, but he completely ignored me. He appeared to be reading emails, but I couldn't exactly lean in for a closer look. Our conversation, such as it was, was over. At least for now.

I swallowed hard. Should I say something? Press my case? Did he believe what I'd said or not? I looked out of the window. I didn't recognize where we were and I didn't have a clue where we were going. After about twenty minutes of total silence in the car, I risked another glance at McAuley. His laptop was back on the seat between us and he was watching me. Sweat was dripping off my forehead.

'Too hot for you, Tobey?' asked McAuley.

'A little,' I admitted, taking off my jacket before I melted into a puddle on the floor. I put it on the seat between us.

'I like it hot,' said McAuley. 'I find I think better when the heat is on.'

I didn't doubt it. With a smile, McAuley picked up his newspaper and started reading.

Where the hell were we now? Somewhere countrified by the look of it. There were no houses now, just fields in various shades of green as far as the eye could see, and trees to my left, lining up on the horizon. Thoughts drummed in my head like rain on a corrugated roof. My intestines were tying themselves in knots. *Where were they taking me?*

Byron turned left onto a single-track road and we drove for another few minutes. More and more trees appeared all around us. Byron turned the car to the left and took us off-road. The suspension on the car must've been state of the art, because I did little more than bounce a couple of times.

'Bryon, stop here,' McAuley ordered, closing his newspaper and folding it neatly.

The car came to a smooth halt. Byron had stopped the car, but the engine was still running. We were in the middle of leafy nowhere. Trees surrounded us like sentinels, silent witnesses to whatever was about to go down. I couldn't even hear the odd bird chirping. I didn't recognize where we were at all. We'd only been travelling for slightly under an hour, but this might as well have been another planet.

This was it.

'Tobey, d'you know where we are?'

I shook my head.

'Neither does anyone else,' said McAuley, adding silkily, 'You do understand, don't you?'

Oh, yes.

'Mr McAuley, I work for you now,' I said quietly. 'There's no way I would ever betray you.'

'Loyalty means everything to me, Tobey. Everything. I've told you that before.'

'Yes, sir.'

'Maybe you should give him a test, Mr McAuley? See which side he's really on,' said Byron.

'Maybe I should at that,' McAuley agreed slowly.

I glanced between Byron and his boss. What kind of

test? Had I been granted a reprieve or set on the path to hell? Or was I already on my way?

'But maybe he just isn't worth it,' mused McAuley.

He smiled, enjoying the power he had over me. My life lay in his hands and he was making sure I knew it. And I did. He didn't have to bring me all the way out here to the arse end of nowhere to make his point.

'You're going to have to prove yourself to me, Tobey. I think that's only fair, don't you?'

'Yes, sir.'

The hollowness inside was gnawing away at me now. Godsake. What was McAuley going to make me do?

'First I want you to tell me everything, and I mean *everything* that happened at the police station earlier,' McAuley ordered. 'And take your damned jacket off my computer.'

'Sorry, sir.' I retrieved my jacket.

'That's a serious piece of kit and you just chuck your jacket over it?'

'I'm sorry, Mr McAuley.'

I slipped the object in my hand into my jacket pocket, trying to make my movements as unnoticeable as possible. If I never made it beyond this forest, at least . . . I was getting ahead of myself. One step at a time. I needed to survive. So whatever McAuley asked me to do, whatever test he gave me, I would do it.

No. Matter. What.

'Cause it had to be better than the alternative.

I told McAuley everything he wanted to know. I didn't leave out anything. He interjected with the occasional question, but that was it. When I finished, he scrutinized me some more.

'Well, Byron?' asked McAuley, never taking his eyes off me. 'Is he telling the truth?'

'I'd say so, sir,' Byron replied.

'You're still useful to me, Tobey – lucky for you.'

'Yes, Mr McAuley.' Very lucky.

'Take us back, Byron,' said McAuley.

And those words were like hard-rock music to my ears. Byron carefully turned the car round and headed back the way we'd come.

'Byron, I do enjoy my visits to the countryside, don't I?' said McAuley.

'That you do, sir.' I caught Byron's tiny smile in the driver's mirror.

The rest of the journey home was achieved in complete and utter silence. I looked out of the window, but had to wait over half an hour before I saw a landmark I recognized.

Once we arrived at my house, as I turned to open the car door, McAuley said, 'I've thought of a way you can prove yourself to me, Tobey.'

My hand froze on the door handle. 'Yes, sir?'

'When you've found out the identity of the crooked officer who works for the Dowds, I want you to make another delivery.' McAuley's smile held smug satisfaction. He was incredibly pleased with himself.

'Another package for Mr Eisner?'

'Not this time.' McAuley shook his head. 'I'll want you to make this delivery to me personally.'

'To you, sir?' My words were sharper than intended. What could I possibly bring him that he didn't already have?

'You have access to something that I can't get near. Rebecca Dowd, Tobey. I want you to bring me Rebecca Dowd.'

And just like that, the hollow, gnawing sensation deep inside me ceased. There was nothing left inside. I was now hollow all the way through.

Rebecca . . .

'Yes, Mr McAuley.'

'So you'll do it.' It wasn't a question.

'Yes, Mr McAuley. Anything you say.'

'I'll let you know where and when. Keep the phone I gave you with you at all times.'

'Yes, sir. I always do.'

McAuley turned away from me. I was dismissed. I got out of the car. Byron drove off the moment the door was shut. I watched the car until it turned the corner and was out of sight. And still I stared after it. Rebecca Dowd was now a package scheduled for delivery. And I was the one who had to deliver her. I couldn't jeopardize all my plans for Rebecca. I just couldn't. What about Callie? McAuley had to pay for what he did to Callie.

But could I really sacrifice Rebecca?

Yes.

No . . .

I didn't know. That was the scary thing. I really didn't know.

I entered my house, heading straight for my bedroom. Even with the door shut behind me, I couldn't relax. I flopped down on my bed, my head in my hands, willing the tension headache between my eyes to dissipate. Minutes passed before I stopped shaking. I emptied my pockets onto my bed. McAuley's memory key shone up at me, the one I'd swapped for my own. In his car, I'd really believed I wouldn't make it home again, at least not in one living piece. But if I was going to die, I wanted to make sure McAuley wouldn't get away with it. So using my jacket for cover, I'd switched his memory key for my own corrupt one. The fraught actions of a desperate man. And all the time I was swapping the memory keys, I expected to feel his hand around my wrist, followed by Byron's gun at my head. But I'd got away with it.

I wasn't even sure what I'd been thinking. Something about my body being found with McAuley's memory stick in my pocket. If that didn't directly incriminate him, then I'd hoped there would be something on it that the police could use to bring him down. Not exactly the way I originally had it planned, but I'd had to improvise.

So now what?

I had McAuley's memory stick.

And he had mine . . .

I sat bolt upright, staring a hole through my wall. Was there anything on that stick to link it back to me? I thought long and hard. My memory key was completely corrupt, totally unreadable. But what if McAuley found a way to retrieve data off it? Then he'd find my chemistry homework and the history presentation Callie and I had been working on. If he managed to retrieve just one file, I was screwed.

I forced myself to calm down. I'd tried every trick in the book to retrieve data off that stick and I was no slouch when it came to computing. If I couldn't do it, then surely he couldn't? I'd just have to hope I wasn't indulging in wishful thinking. I was safe. Was I safe? Until I heard otherwise, no news had to be good news. In the mean-time, I maybe had something I could use against him. And I had to work fast before I was forced to do something monstrous.

My admittedly naïve initial plan had been to get close to McAuley. To follow orders – any orders – until I learned something I could use against him. I'd planned to become another Dan, with my eyes wide open and my mouth tight shut. But now I had the memory stick, I'd be stupid to pass up this opportunity.

My phone rang, just as I was about to switch on my computer.

'Hello, Dan,' I said coolly, after reading the caller ID.

'Tobey, can you be at my house in five minutes?'

'Why?'

'I need your help,' said Dan.

It only took me a moment to decide.

'I'll be there,' I told him.

He disconnected the call, like he expected nothing less.

forty-nine

Five minutes later, I was standing outside Dan's door. I hadn't forgotten Callie. Or my sister. I'd never forget the way Jess looked when I opened the bathroom door. It kept playing on repeat in my head, along with Callie being shot. Even now I was afraid I'd give myself away with every word I said to Dan and every look I gave him. Why would I even think about helping him? Friends close. Enemies closer.

'Hi, Dan,' I said, the moment he opened the door.

'Hi, Tobey.'

Dan shifted from foot to foot. I stood perfectly still. I'd never really noticed the way Dan fidgeted before. For the first time I wondered if he was sampling his own merchandise.

'So what's the problem?'

'Mr McAuley just phoned and gave me a job to do, but I can't do it alone,' said Dan.

'What's the job?'

'Some dagger, name of Boris Haddon. He owes Mr McAuley money and I'm being sent to collect it. Mr McAuley warned me this is my last chance. He told me if I screw this up, then I'd better crawl under a rock and stay there.'

'And you want me to help you strong-arm some guy into giving you money? I don't think so, Dan. That's called five to ten years in prison.'

'I just need some backup. I'll do all the talking and none of us will come to any harm. He'll hand over the money and we'll be on our way in less than a minute. But if I'm alone, Haddon might be tempted to try something stupid.'

'Who is this Boris Haddon?'

'He owns a bakery in North Meadowview. It's doing very well by all accounts.'

Hence a vulture like McAuley circling.

'Does Haddon know you're coming?'

"Course not,' Dan scoffed. 'At least . . . at least, I don't think so.'

'So are you supposed to go to his house or his shop or what?'

'Mr McAuley said Haddon would be in his shop till six this evening, but I thought we could go now before the lunch-time crowd hits the place.'

'Wouldn't McAuley have warned him to have the money ready to hand over?' I argued. 'In which case, Haddon does know you're coming.'

Dan considered. 'I suppose that makes sense,' he said grudgingly.

'Did McAuley tell you to ask for my help?' I frowned.

'No.' Dan looked puzzled. 'Why would he? I'm asking you as a friend.'

A friend . . .

'Are you going to help me then?' Dan asked. 'Please, Tobey.'

Pause.

'OK, I'll do it.' But my reasons weren't exactly altruistic. Not even close.

'Tobey, are you ready to get your hands dirty? 'Cause you're no use to me if you're not prepared to back me up.'

'I'll give you all the backup you'd give me,' I replied.

Dan's eyes narrowed. I forced a smile.

'We're cool,' I told him. 'So how do we get to Haddon's shop?'

Dan frowned. 'By bus. How d'you think?'

I only just managed to stop myself from creasing up. Two hard-guy wannabes getting heavy with one of McAuley's victims, then making good their escape on the local bus. Oh yeah, we were really threatening! If this Haddon guy managed to pick himself up from the floor when he'd finished howling with laughter, then he just might find the energy to boot Dan and me out of his shop.

'You'll need this,' said Dan, holding out a sheathed knife, its handle towards me.

And all at once, it wasn't so funny any more. I hesitated. Dan thrust it towards me. I took it.

'Am I likely to need it?' I asked.

'Probably,' said Dan. 'We have to show Haddon that we mean business.'

'And if he has a gun?'

'He wouldn't be that stupid, not when he knows that we work for Mr McAuley.'

Then why did we need knives? Dan sounded like he was one hundred per cent sure this Haddon guy wouldn't put up a fuss or a fight. But fear or desperation often drove people to do things that stupidity alone would never make them consider.

'Once you tell Haddon who you work for, surely you won't need any kind of hardware?' I pointed out.

'It's for protection, just in case.'

I stuck the knife in my jacket pocket.

'I'll get my jacket,' Dan said, heading into his house.

The moment his back was turned, the mask-like expression on my face slipped. My friend, Dan. The friend to all – if the price was right and it didn't cost him anything. And I had to hide my true feelings because I still needed him. Hiding my true feelings was so hard, but I was becoming a master at it. Dan grabbed his jacket off the banister and left his house, slamming the door shut behind him just as hard as he could. I was amazed the glass didn't fall out of it.

'Is your mum at home then?'

'Yeah, and fast asleep, but not alone.'

'Anyone you know?'

'Nope. She rolled in around three o'clock this morning, pissed as a newt with some guy in tow. I locked my door and left them to it.'

We walked in silence. In a world of changes, Dan's mum was a constant. She'd been that way for as long as I could remember. There'd been a time, before Dan started working for McAuley, when the only decent meals he got were round at my house. He used to bring his clothes to ours to be washed as well, before he made enough money to pay for a washer-dryer of his own.

My friend, Dan.

'Dan,' I began, 'what's your ambition?'

'What d'you mean?'

'I mean, what'll you be doing in five years' time, ten years, fifteen?'

'I don't know, do I?'

'Will you still be working for McAuley?'

'Hell, no,' Dan said vehemently. 'I'll have my own business by then. I'll be running things.'

'So you're not in McAuley's pocket?'

'I'm not in anyone's pocket. There's only three things in this world I care about – me, myself and I.'

That I could believe.

Less than fifteen minutes later, Dan and I hopped off the bus at the High Street. It was less than a minute's walk to Haddon's bakery. I was about to walk in, but Dan's hand on my arm stopped me.

'Tobey, are you OK with this?'

I nodded. 'Let's just get it over with before I come to my senses.'

We walked in. The smell of fresh bread and sticky cakes wafted enticingly around me. The shop was bright and airy and spotlessly clean. Behind the counter was a door, half wood, half frosted glass. Adjacent to the counter against one wall was a huge fridge filled with sandwiches and various drinks in bottles and cartons. Opposite, against the other wall, were bakery racks filled with different kinds of loaves, rolls and pastries, with tongs next to almost every item that wasn't already wrapped. The cream cakes were behind glass next to the counter and they looked good. I could see why the shop was so popular. A Cross man and a Nought woman were serving. Dan ambled about looking at the sandwiches and pies. I stood by the door as we'd agreed on the bus. When the last of the three customers in the shop finally paid for her cottage loaf and left, Dan nodded to me. I turned over the sign hanging on the door to indicate that the shop was now closed, just as a Cross man tried to enter the shop.

'Sorry, mate,' Dan called out. 'We're closing until we catch all the mice that are running around over the shop floor.'

The customer – ex-customer – looked horrified and hurried off. I stood in front of the door so that no one else could walk in uninvited.

'What d'you two think you're doing?' the Cross guy who I assumed was Boris Haddon exclaimed angrily.

'It's OK, Mr Haddon,' Dan said amicably. 'Mr McAuley sent us.'

Boris glanced uneasily at the Nought girl standing next to him.

'Sophie, take the rest of the day off,' he told her.

'But, Mr Haddon . . .'

'Just do as I say,' said Boris. 'OK?'

Sophie looked from her boss to Dan and me and back again. 'OK, Mr Haddon,' she replied nervously.

Boris gave her a studied look. Sophie pulled off her hat and her apron, throwing them beneath the counter, before bending to retrieve her jacket from the same place. Alarm bells started pealing, only the cacophony was inside my head, not in the shop. No employee kept their jacket beneath the serving counter if there was somewhere else to hang it up. Leaving personal possessions on the shop floor was a guaranteed way to get them nicked. And from the look of it, this shop had a private room behind the counter. I shifted my position to try and see through the frosted glass that led to the private room, but Boris moved almost imperceptibly in my way. Almost, but not quite.

'Who did you say you two worked for?' Boris asked.

'Mr McAuley sent us,' Dan began. 'You need to pay my boss what you owe—'

'Dan, I think we've got the wrong shop.'

Dan turned to me, frowning. 'What're you on about? Of course we haven't . . .'

I tried a different tack. 'Dan, your boss only asked you to request that the debt be paid within the next thirty days.' I turned to the shop owner. 'Mr Haddon, we're sorry to trouble you. We just wanted to politely request that you send a cheque to . . . that you send on a cheque at your earliest convenience.'

'Tobey, what the hell d'you think you're doing?' Dan rounded on me.

'It's time for us to go,' I told him.

'The hell it is. I'm not leaving here without the money this dagger owes Mr McAuley.' Dan's hand was already in his jacket pocket as he started behind the counter.

I raced across the shop to step in front of him. Furious, he tried to shove me out of the way. Eyes wide, mouth open, Haddon took a couple of steps back. Dan's hand was emerging from his jacket pocket, but his hand was no longer empty. So I hit him. Less than a second later, he fell to the ground, more from surprise than any other reason. I certainly hadn't hit him that hard. I squatted down beside him, holding out my hand to help him up, my other hand also busy as it moved over his jacket pocket. Dan scowled at me.

'Dan, I'm sorry about that . . .'

He pushed me aside as he struggled to get up under his own steam.

'I apologize for the disturbance, Mr Haddon,' I said. 'Dan, we should leave—'

'Is this what you call having my back?' Dan asked with contempt, shoving me backwards – hard.

He was starting towards me when the door behind Boris Haddon opened and a swarm of coppers flooded out.

'DOWN ON THE GROUND. NOW.'

'GET DOWN.'

The orders were coming from all directions. I dropped to the floor immediately. One copper knelt hard on my back as he wrenched my arms back to slap handcuffs on me. My head to one side, I glared at Dan. Slow or what?

Couldn't he pick up on what I'd been trying to tell him? Boris Haddon knew we were coming all right. And he'd set up a welcoming committee. There was only one reason for Sophie, Haddon's employee, to keep her jacket under the counter and that was because she didn't want to reveal who was in the back room by opening the door. If Dan had ever bothered to find himself an everyday, honest job he'd have been able to work that out for himself.

I groaned as I was pulled to my feet, but it wasn't so much the handcuffs or the pain in my back which made me cringe. It was something else entirely. I was heading back to the police station. Mum was going to do her nut! Both Dan and I were patted down. Apart from two mobile phones and some money, my pockets were empty. The copper patting down Dan quickly found two knives on him, one in each of his jacket pockets. Stunned, Dan stared at them. He turned to me, shocked. But we had no time to do more than exchange a look before we were both bundled out of the shop and into separate police cars.

fifty

I ended up with an official reprimand as apparently I wasn't old enough (by less than one month) to receive a formal caution. I had trouble working out exactly what the reprimand was for. As far as I could tell, the charge was affray – which was totally specious, not to mention bogus as far as I was concerned. What it did mean though was that I was fingerprinted and a swab was taken from my mouth to provide a DNA sample. I was told the records would be destroyed after five years if I stayed out of trouble, but I wasn't holding my breath on that one. Everyone knew the police were trying to build up a DNA database of all the Meadowview residents, especially us Noughts. It was only a matter of time before the DNA of everyone in the whole bloody country was held on some computer or other.

But I knew I should count myself lucky. Dan was charged with carrying offensive weapons and remanded on conditional bail. It could've been worse. He could've been charged with extortion or whatever the proper legal term for that is, but apparently he didn't say enough to make an extortion charge indisputable. He'd had a damn good try, though. I still couldn't believe how slow on the uptake he'd been. So the charge of carrying offensive weapons was the best the police could do. Dan was taken back to a cell to await the arrival of his mum. Knowing her, he'd be waiting an awfully long time.

And if Mum was angry before, she was spitting nails and breathing fire by the time she came to get me. One look at her face, and staying in a cell seemed almost preferable. She didn't waste a breath before she started.

'What did I say to you about not bringing the police to my door?' she stormed. 'And not just once but twice in one day. Are you aiming for some kind of record?'

'I'm sorry, Mum,' I mumbled.

'Sorry? *Sorry?*' That just made her even more angry. 'I

don't want to hear sorry. And what were you doing in a bakery in North Meadowview?'

'It was just a misunderstanding, Mum,' I said. 'Dan and I were just mucking around. Mr Haddon overreacted.'

'What were you doing with Dan in the first place?'

'Just hanging out. Mum, I didn't think it would do any harm—'

'And this is exactly how it starts.' Mum shook her head. 'Tobey, tell me something, does Dan work for McAuley?'

'I . . . I think so, but Mum, *I* don't. You've got to believe me, McAuley has got nothing that I want. Absolutely nothing,' I said quietly.

'I don't want you hanging round Dan. He's going nowhere fast and I don't want you tagging along for the ride.'

I looked around to make sure no one was within earshot. 'Mum, you're gonna have to trust me. Please, just trust me.' I don't know what it was – the expression on my face, some note in my voice – but something halted her tirade. She studied me long and hard.

'Tobey, what're you up to?'

I looked around again, nervous as a cat in a room full of rocking chairs.

'Nothing, Mum.'

'Don't give me that, Tobey. I know you. And I know when you're up to something,' said Mum.

'Mum, I—'

'Has all this got something to do with Callie getting shot?' she said slowly. 'Tobey, please tell me you're not—?'

'Mum, I'm not about to do anything stupid,'

I interrupted. 'Besides, I've got you to keep me on the straight and narrow.'

'Tobey, this isn't funny,' said Mum.

I sighed. 'I know. I'm sorry.'

'If I had any sense, I would ground you for the rest of the holiday.'

'Mum, I won't get into any more trouble, I promise.' At least, I promise I'll try not to. 'Besides, I want to visit Callie later. Please?'

'Hmmm . . .' Mum wasn't the least bit convinced, but she didn't follow through with her threat to ground me. I hadn't yet told her that I no longer worked at TFTM, which helped. I suspected that was the only reason she wasn't confining me to the house.

'So when you wake up later, if I'm not at home, that's where I am – OK?' I said, pushing my luck.

We took a couple of steps towards the door, but I couldn't go any further, much as I wanted to. And I really, *really* wanted to.

'Mum,' I began, 'I need a favour.'

Mum stared at me like one of us had lost our mind and she was trying to figure out which one. 'Tobey, I'm fighting a really powerful urge to explain all about the biological structure of nerves and their abundance in the human body.'

'Why would you want to tell me about nerves?' I frowned.

'So that when I tell you you're getting on every last one of mine, you'll appreciate just how serious that is,' she replied.

Godsake! Sometimes Mum was too much of a nurse. 'I really need this favour, Mum.'

'Tobey, you've got more cheek showing than a maternity ward. You drag me down here – twice – and you think you've got a favour coming?'

'It isn't for me, Mum. It's for Dan. He's still locked up in this place and you know what his mum is like. She'll let him rot in here.'

'And what has that got to do with me?' asked Mum testily.

'Mum, we've got to help him. He's in trouble.'

'He is trouble, never mind anything else,' she snapped.

'Mum, this is important. Please. He doesn't have anyone else.'

'Dan is not my concern. You are,' Mum argued.

McAuley had given Dan one last chance and Dan had messed up. For the life of me, I didn't understand why I should feel any anxiety for him. Rotting in a cell was no more than he deserved. But if I left him here, the only other person who'd bail him out was McAuley. And no matter what Dan had done, I couldn't leave him to McAuley's tender mercies. I had enough on my conscience already.

'Mum, we have to get Dan out of here.'

Mum frowned at me, her frown deepening as she scrutinized my face. 'Has this got something to do with Dan and McAuley?'

I nodded, albeit reluctantly.

'They're not going to release Dan into my custody. I'm not his mother.'

'Yes, they will,' I argued. 'The prisons and the police cells are already overcrowded so they're not going to keep anyone for longer than strictly necessary. As long as you say you'll take responsibility for him and sign the necessary paperwork, they'll let him go. Just tell them that if they don't release him into your custody, they'll be looking after him until his next birthday.'

'Take a seat,' said Mum after a few moments. 'I'll be back in a minute.'

'I'll come with you,' I said.

'No you won't. If you want me to help Dan, you'll do as I say. Sit down and stay put. I mean it, Tobey.'

'OK,' I agreed reluctantly.

I stayed put, but remained standing as I watched her head over to the reception desk. She and the woman behind the desk had a long and heated discussion which looked like it was veering dangerously close to an argument at times. Finally the officer called over one of her colleagues to help behind the desk whilst she headed off somewhere. Ten minutes later she emerged with Dan walking beside her, followed by DI Boothe, who barely glanced at me. The scowl on Dan's face when he saw me could've soured honey. He watched Mum sign the forms for his release, then we all left the police station together with Mum walking slightly ahead of us.

'Am I supposed to be grateful?' Dan asked belligerently.

'No,' I replied.

'Mr McAuley warned me not to screw this up,' he said, an edge to his voice. 'He already thinks I'm a liability. When he hears about this . . .'

'It's not your fault Haddon called in the police,' I said.

'Mr McAuley won't see it that way,' said Dan bitterly. 'So now I've got McAuley on my left and the cops on my right, thanks to that stunt you pulled. You had my back all right, just so you could stab me in it.'

The words I wanted – needed – to say were burning holes right through me. But I kept most of them inside. Forcing myself to stay calm, I said, 'Dan, since we're discussing backstabbers, explain to me why you felt the need to sell smack to my sister.'

Shocked, Dan took a half-step back. He put out his hands to ward me off even though I hadn't moved a muscle. 'Tobey, your sister came to me, not the other way round, I swear.'

'And that makes it OK, does it?'

'She said if I didn't sell her some gear she'd find someone else who would,' Dan rushed on. 'I thought if she got it from me, at least I could make sure she wasn't smoking something harmful . . .'

''Cause smack isn't harmful?'

'I told her she didn't want to start up with that stuff, but she wouldn't listen.'

'So you figured if someone was going to make some money from Jessica, it might as well be you?'

'No, you've got it all wrong. I was just trying to help.'

Help? Was he serious? My eyes narrowed.

'Tobey, listen. Please. Jess came to me.'

'When?'

'What?'

'When did she first come to you?' I said patiently. 'How long have you been selling that stuff to her?'

'I've only sold to her twice. The first time was four or five weeks ago. That's it.'

I studied Dan, my eyes never leaving his face. Did I ever really know him? He sure as hell didn't know me. Once again, all the words burning inside my head had to stay there. I couldn't even clench my fists. The definition of growing up – hiding what you truly feel, suppressing what you really want to do. Unless you were McAuley or the Dowds. I was beginning to see the attraction of their particular way of life. There was a definite appeal to living by your own set of rules. A very definite appeal.

'Dan, listen carefully 'cause I'm only going to say this once,' I said, once I trusted my voice to stay calm. 'Stay away from my sister.'

'OK, Tobey. OK,' Dan agreed.

He kept shifting from foot to foot. I stood like a statue, watching him. Ice was crystallizing in my veins and moving irrevocably through my body. Dan was nervous. I wasn't. We stood in thorny silence, regarding each other. And in that moment I knew that I'd lost him. No matter what happened now, we'd never go back to the way we once were; we'd never fully trust each other again. One day I might forgive him for what he'd done, but I'd never forget. He was probably feeling exactly the same way. In spite of the warmth of the day, that realization made me cold and sad.

We started walking again, though now we were way behind my mum.

'When did you slip the knife into my pocket?' asked Dan.

'When I was trying to help you up. I couldn't be caught with it,' I said, my voice edged with reluctant apology.

'And I could? Thanks a lot.'

There was nothing I could say to that. The silence between us continued to eat away at our friendship.

'Dan, I'm sorry.'

'No, you're not,' Dan shot back. 'Sorry implies that if

you could go back, you'd do things differently. We both know that you wouldn't change a thing.'

I didn't say anything because he was right. Dan looked at me, such a look that I stopped walking and reluctantly faced him to hear what he had to say.

'This isn't about your sister, though, is it?' Dan said quietly. 'Jessica added fuel to the fire, but what happened to Callie started it. I never realized till now just how much you hate me for what happened to Callie Rose.'

He had my full attention.

'I thought you blamed McAuley and the Dowds,' he continued. 'But you blame me as well. I was the one who asked you to deliver that package to Louise Resnick and there was no way the Dowds were going to let McAuley get away with the torture of one of their own.'

'We've already been through this—'

'Yes, but I'm seeing the real you now,' said Dan. 'McAuley's driven by greed and pride and the lust for power. With you it's different.'

'What d'you mean?'

Dan studied me like he'd just had a revelation. 'All this started because Callie was shot, and maybe you even managed to convince yourself for a while that she was the one you were doing all this for. But that's not true any more, is it?'

'I don't know what you're talking about.' I frowned. I wasn't sure I wanted to find out either.

'This has stopped being about Callie. It's not about Jessica. It's not even about me. You've moved on from that. This is now about you.'

'How sad are you?' I laughed derisively. 'Is this how

you manage to get through each day? By blaming everyone but yourself?'

'If this was about your sister, you would've taken me apart the moment you saw me earlier. If this was about Callie Rose, you would've come after me the moment you left the hospital after she was injured. That's what *I* would've done. But that wasn't enough for you. It still isn't.'

'Maybe I didn't come after you when Callie Rose was shot because I didn't blame you,' I ventured.

'But that's just my point,' said Dan. 'You *did* blame me. Not just me, but me included. And you were prepared to use me to get what you wanted. It was all about you and your revenge.'

Not true. This had nothing to do with me and everything to do with what had happened to Callie Rose. She was the one I cared about. She was the one I was doing this for . . .

'So because I didn't act the way you would've, I don't care about Callie and my sister? Is that it?' I said angrily. 'You're talking bollocks.'

Dan shook his head. 'You just don't get it, do you? You're getting too much . . . satisfaction out of all this. You've developed a taste for being the puppet-master and we're all − what's the word? − expendable. That's why you're so dangerous.' He gave a bitter laugh. 'McAuley doesn't know what he's in for.'

'Dan, you're wrong—' I began, but for the life of me, I couldn't think of anything else to say.

'Are we even now, Tobey?' asked Dan quietly. ''Cause if anyone but you had done this to me, I'd be back at my lockup getting ready to do some damage.'

'So what should I expect, Dan?'

Dan gave me a look. He opened his mouth to speak.

'Could you guys hurry up?' Mum called to us. 'I would like to try and get at least five minutes sleep before work today. Dan, I'll drop you home first.'

'There really is no need,' Dan replied. 'I can get the bus home.'

'Nonsense,' said Mum. 'Besides, I told the police I'd make sure you got home safely.'

Dan and I sat in the back of the car. Mum didn't even start the engine until she'd made sure we'd put on our seatbelts. Then we were on our way. And the entire journey back was achieved without Dan and I saying a single word to each other. I stared out of the window whilst Dan's words played round and round in my head like a song on repeat.

This wasn't about me. This was about Callie.

It was . . .

'Mum, can we stop off at our house first?' I asked as we got close to our road. 'I have something of Dan's that I need to give to him.'

'What?'

'Something,' I replied, reluctant to elaborate.

'As long as you hurry up,' said Mum.

When Mum stopped in front of our house, I was in and out in less than a minute. But now what? I didn't want to hand over what I'd retrieved in front of her. I got back in the car, doing up my seatbelt.

'Mum, could you drop both of us off at Dan's house?' I asked. 'And I promise I'll be home within fifteen minutes.'

I caught Mum's look in the driver's mirror. She didn't

need to speak, her expression said it all. If I wasn't home in fifteen minutes, she'd come looking for me and if she had to do that . . . I got the message. Less than five minutes later we were outside Dan's.

'Dan, you are going to stay out of trouble, aren't you?' asked Mum.

'I'll do my best.' Dan smiled faintly.

After one last warning look cast in my direction, Mum turned the car around and headed home.

The moment she was out of sight, I took out the envelope that Byron had given me, the one full of money, and placed it in Dan's hand. 'This is yours,' I said.

Dan's eyes narrowed. 'What's this?'

'McAuley gave it to me, but . . . but it's yours.'

Dan's fingers folded slowly around the envelope.

'OK?' I said.

'OK.' He turned abruptly and walked away, straight past his own front door.

Where was he going? To his lockup? What was he going to do?

'Dan,' I called after him.

He stopped, but he didn't turn round.

After a moment's thought, I said, 'We're even now.'

Dan carried on walking.

fifty-one

Back at home, I had to wait till Mum went back to bed before I could get down to what I really wanted to do. I connected up McAuley's memory stick and started scanning it. And what did it contain? Letters of complaint to the Inland Revenue and other government bodies about a shipment of rugs imported nearly a year ago and still being held by Customs. A spreadsheet comparing the price of rugs from around the world. More letters of complaint. An inventory of the contents of McAuley's warehouse. Godsake! The files contained stale, boring stuff that was of absolutely no use to me at all. And each file I checked after that was more of the same. They all contained import/export details of artefacts and luxury knick-knacks and other rubbish. It was beginning to look like swapping the memory sticks had been a complete waste of time. When I thought of the risk I'd taken, I felt sick. There were only three more files to check and from the file names, I didn't hold out much hope that they'd be useful.

The next file I opened was called *Schedule*. Only one problem – it was completely empty. Why on earth would McAuley keep an empty file? What a waste of disk space. I opened up the last two files. The first was more twaddle about misshapen figurines and sculptures. The second file contained the bank account details of McAuley's lieutenant, Byron Sweet. I couldn't believe that Byron, Mr Pit-bull himself, had the surname of Sweet. That was about the only interesting thing in the last file. I learned Byron's bank, his branch code and his bank account number – which were all worse than useless.

And that was it.

I slumped back in my chair. Now what? There was nothing in any of the files that was the least bit illegal, unless I was missing something. I listed all the files, in case there was one I'd missed and hadn't read yet. But there wasn't. I read them all again, every word, but there was nothing remotely worthwhile. I held my head in my hands and tried to think. There was no way I'd get another crack at McAuley's computer. I looked at the list of files on my screen, desperately willing them to turn into something I could use.

Something I could . . .

Something . . .

I leaned closer to the screen. *Schedule*, the file with nothing in it, was almost one hundred kilobytes big. Why would a file with nothing in it be so large? I opened the file again. It consisted of eight blank pages. I scrolled all the way down then back up again. The file was definitely empty. Or was it? A light bulb started flashing in my head. Mouth dry, heart thumping, I clicked the option to select everything in the file, then changed its colour to black. The file was immediately filled to overflowing with text and a grid that must've been from a spreadsheet.

Oh, yes!

'Very clever, McAuley,' I muttered.

I mean, credit where credit was due. The colour of the

words in the file had been changed to white. White words on a white background. No wonder the file looked blank. I tried not to get too excited, but this looked far more promising. I settled down in my chair and started reading. I read the file from top to bottom, then read it again to make sure I hadn't misread any of it.

According to the spreadsheet in the file, McAuley had invested every penny he had in three shipments coming into the country within the next few days. He'd euphemistically referred to his shipments as 'X'. The first shipment was due the day after tomorrow. Two more shipments were scheduled to arrive after that, each at intervals of three days. Each shipment was going to a different address, where they would be stored until McAuley arranged collection. He wasn't taking any chances. From the look of it, it seemed the Dowds had taken away more of McAuley's business than anyone suspected and he wasn't quite as loaded as we'd all assumed.

Why on earth hadn't he quit when he was ahead?

And then I realized. He couldn't quit. It wasn't just the money that McAuley craved, it was the sense of control and power it gave him. He was like a pathetic despot, looking out over the portion of his kingdom called 'half of Meadow-view' and longing for it all. And the Dowds were exactly the same, two wings of the same bird. They targeted those who had little and made sure they ended up with less. And Dan's attitude to McAuley was 'at least he's one of our own'. I shook my head, wondering if he still felt the same way.

The file contained details of delivery addresses, times, the initials of a number of people who were going to pay for 'X' and the amounts of money involved. And I mean, large, eye-boggling amounts of money. I finally had something I could use. The question was, how? I could just tell the police, but there was no way to link the shipments to McAuley unless he was found with the stuff and McAuley was much too smart for that. After it was delivered, he'd have his minions do his dirty work for him. And even if there was some way to link the shipments to him, a smart lawyer could claim that McAuley didn't know what was being imported in his name or that it wasn't even his property. I could tell the police and they'd confiscate his shipments, but that wasn't enough. I admit it. It wasn't anywhere near enough. I wanted McAuley's world to unravel slowly but irrevocably. So I'd have to find some other way to use this information to his disadvantage.

It was time to make a phone call.

Phone call concluded, the next thing I had to do was protect the information I had. I printed off all the sheets, then placed them in an A5 envelope, which I addressed to Callie Rose. I took a second-class stamp from Mum's handbag and stuck that on the letter. This letter would be my insurance policy – just in case. I knew Sephy would never open her daughter's letters, and once Callie was out of hospital the letter would be easy enough to retrieve – if I got through this.

Once that was done, I tried to figure out my next move. I finally decided on a course of action. It wasn't smart and it sure as hell wasn't foolproof, but it was all I had.

I headed for my local library, memory stick hidden in the cuff of my jacket – just in case McAuley or the police decided they couldn't do without my company. At the library, I booked a computer for an hour and started working on my first letter. It would probably be the most significant one of my life. I decided to use a handwriting font that I didn't have on my computer at home. I couldn't take any chances. If the letter was ever traced back to me . . .

To the Dowds,

This letter contains information about Alex McAuley and his business interests that you will hopefully find useful. McAuley is expecting a shipment to be delivered to 3 Londridge Street, Meadowview on 14th August at 4.30 p.m. The shipment will arrive in a home food shopping delivery van. I don't know the route the van will take before it arrives at the above address. This delivery, one of the smaller ones scheduled to arrive in the next couple of weeks, is worth over three-quarters of a million pounds. How you decide to use this information is of course entirely up to you. If you do decide to act upon the information in this letter, I will supply you with the times, dates and venues of all McAuley's other consignments for the rest of the month – but only if you decide to act on the information contained herein.

I thought my use of the words 'consignment' and 'herein' was a good touch. No one ever used those kinds of words in real life. Hopefully those words and the way I'd phrased certain other sentences would make it seem like someone much older than me had written the letter. And possibly a woman? After a lot of deleting and rewriting, I decided the letter was ready – except for one thing. The Dowds would never believe the information I was giving them was genuine if I didn't ask for some kind of reward. As far as they were concerned, altruism – especially criminal altruism – didn't exist. So I added:

Once the above shipment is yours, I would expect payment of 10% of the gross worth of the product before I part with any further information about other future deliveries. I feel 10% is fair. I would expect this money in cash. I shall provide further instructions regarding the payment of my money once McAuley's goods are in your hands.

I had no intention of taking a penny from the Dowds, but they needed to believe I was just as avaricious as they were. I printed off the letter, making sure to hold it with a tissue so that my fingerprints wouldn't get on it. Folding it, I placed it in the envelope I'd brought with me. The question was, should I post it to Gideon Dowd at TFTM or should I post it to Vanessa Dowd? Thanks to Rebecca, I now had her home address. But I suspected I was one of a mere handful of people who knew it. If I posted the letter to Rebecca's mum, it might be easier to trace. Giving it to Owen wasn't part of the plan. Besides, I wanted as little as possible to do with him. TFTM it was then. I would just have to hope that Gideon Dowd would be at the Club the following day to receive the letter. I could've sent it as an email, but Gideon could trace the email back to this library and it was in my neighbourhood, plus it had twenty-four-hour CCTV. With Gideon's connections, he could easily get hold of the footage and discover that I'd been in the library around the time he received the email. No, far better to send it via snail mail. Slower but safer.

My second letter was far easier to write. I used the same font and took the same precautions to make sure that my fingerprints didn't appear anywhere on it. This letter was much simpler, though. This one gave details of McAuley's second shipment. What should I do about the third scheduled delivery? Tell the police? Tell the Dowds?

Tell no one?

I took the latter path. It would take expert timing, but maybe I could move the shipment, or at least part of it, to some place where no one but me would ever find it.

I mean, why not me?

Why not?

It's not that I fancied myself as another McAuley. Far from it. But I had to think ahead. I had to think. I had to look out for myself. No one else would.

I'd make no snap decisions about the third shipment. The answer would come to me. But one way or another, all this should start to hit McAuley where he would feel it the most. I wasn't finished with him yet.

Not even close.

fifty-two

Hello, Callie Rose.

I . . .

Today I . . .

I have nothing to say.

fifty-three

As I walked down the hospital steps, my whole body felt as if it was made of lead. I'd sat with Callie for over thirty minutes – and I couldn't think of anything to say. What was happening to me that I couldn't find anything to say to her? I pulled my T-shirt rapidly back and forth away from my sweaty chest. The sky was white-grey and the air was really humid and sticky. This damned weather was really getting to me. Time to head back home. My letters were posted and I'd managed to visit Callie again without getting caught. Mum must've set off for work by now, and as for Jessica . . . ? Well, I'd barely seen her recently. We'd been avoiding each other. But Jess wasn't uppermost in my mind. I had other matters to attend to. First a shower, then phone Rebecca to ask her for a date. I hadn't heard from her in a while and I needed to know where I stood now that her brother had banned us from being together.

Why couldn't I speak to Callie?

Head bent, I was lost in my own thoughts as I left the hospital grounds, so they saw me before I saw them. I only knew I had company when they appeared in front of me. Three sets of feet belonging to three morons – Lucas, Drew and Aaron. After a cursory glance at them, I tried to walk round them. I just wanted to be left alone. Drew deliberately stepped in front of me.

Godsake . . . I wasn't in the mood for this, I really wasn't.

'Hello, Durbrain.' Drew smiled.

That nickname was so old and tired it needed a walking stick. Was that really the best he could come up with? I tried to step past him, but he moved to block me again. OK, now he was officially pissing me off.

'Callie's not here to protect you,' Drew taunted.

I smiled faintly. He just didn't get it.

'Are you satisfied now?' Lucas asked, moving to stand directly in front of me.

My eyes narrowed. What was he on about? I took a half-step back so I could keep Drew and Aaron in sight as well.

'Thanks to you and your fellow blankers, Callie is in hospital,' said Lucas. 'I warned her that she'd end up getting hurt or worse hanging around you.'

'She could do better than you at the local pig farm. You're just about the same colour as a pig, aren't you.' Aaron turned to his mates, a stupid grin plastered over his face. He really thought he'd said something profound.

Lucas, however, never took his eyes off me. 'I told her not to trust you, that you were no good. And when she regains consciousness, she'll realize I was right all along and dump you like the steaming pile of dog—'

My fists shot out. Both of them hit their target – Lucas's stomach, followed by his face when he doubled over. He dropped like a stone. Aaron charged at me. I sidestepped him, then stuck out my foot to trip him. He hit the pavement like a felled tree. Not that he stayed there long. For a guy with such a big build he was surprisingly agile.

'Blanker, you'll pay for that,' Aaron hissed at me.

He came at me, arms up, fists clenched. So I kicked him where it'd do me the most good. This time he went down and stayed down. By which time Lucas was back on his feet, though holding his nose, which was bleeding. Aaron was still rolling on the ground.

'Who's next?' I asked quietly.

No one spoke. I stepped over Aaron and continued on my way. Maybe now Drew would realize it was never me Callie was protecting, even if he – and Callie – had thought otherwise.

Once I got home, I sat on my bed, rubbing my forehead with the palm of my left hand, trying to ease away the headache that was lurking behind my eyes. It was not the time for my phone to ring. I glanced down at the screen, checking the caller's ID, but it said 'Private'. At least it wasn't McAuley bothering me. I could guess who this was. Did I really want to speak to him? I had no choice. Even so, I let it ring seven or eight times before I answered.

'Hello?'

'I thought you weren't going to answer,' Owen Dowd said at once. 'It's far too late to have second thoughts.'

'No second thoughts. No third ones. I was in the bathroom washing my hands, that's all.'

'Did you do as we agreed?'

I sighed inwardly. This man certainly didn't believe in pleasantries.

'Yes, I did. And I made sure the letter was addressed to your brother as we discussed earlier.'

'Good. Excellent. Leave the rest to me.'

I had every intention of doing just that.

'Is there anything else you want to tell me?' Owen asked.

Like what?

'I don't think so,' I replied. 'It's all working out the way you wanted.'

'That doesn't mean that either of us can get complacent.'

'No, Mr Dowd.'

'You're sure there's nothing else you want to tell me?' he said.

'Nothing, sir.'

The existence and destination of my second letter, I intended to keep to myself. Or was this his subtle way of telling me that he already knew what I was up to? But he couldn't know anything about the second letter. I'd been very careful. Owen Dowd only knew about the first shipment. Unless I'd overlooked something . . .

Tobey, calm down, I told myself. *He's just fishing.*

I decided not to rise to his bait.

'What other information did you find?'

'Nothing of use. Lots of complaining letters to the tax office, I think. Oh, and Byron Sweet's bank account details. He's one of McAuley's minions. But there was no password information in the file or even how much money he has in the bank. It was just . . . just . . .'

And that's when it occurred to me. Ideas flowed one after the other like the tide coming in.

'I know a way we can use Byron's bank account to our advantage,' I said, trying to dampen down my excitement in case Owen didn't go for my plan.

'I'm listening,' he said.

'It will require quite a lot of money,' I warned.

'Doesn't it always?' he replied sourly.

So I told him what I had in mind. There was a significant pause when I'd finished.

'I'll think about it,' he said at last.

I released the breath I didn't even realize I'd been holding.

'Anything else?' he asked.

'When will I be paid?'

'Once I have what I want, you'll get your money.'

'I'll look forward to it,' I replied.

'You're going to be a very rich man, Tobey.'

'Yes, sir.'

'I'll send you a banker's cheque as we agreed. Don't spend it all at once!' Owen rang off, his laughter ringing in my ears.

It was lucky for both of us that he couldn't see my expression as I disconnected the call. Just listening to him made me want to go down to the kitchen and scrub out my ear with the saucepan scourer.

Rich people were so predictable. They reckoned everyone wanted money, that everyone had their price. And for rich people there was no such thing as 'rich enough' – at least not for people like the Dowds and McAuley. Too much was never enough. That was why I was going to succeed and they were going to fail. And there wasn't enough money on the planet to stop me now.

fifty-four

The whole of Meadowview was buzzing. McAuley's latest shipment had been hijacked by 'persons unknown'. The news was that, en route to its destination, a home shopping delivery van supposedly filled with food had been intercepted and relieved of all its contents. There was an awful lot of speculation as to what those contents might be. Some said drugs. Some said smuggled immigrants brought in as cheap labour. Some said dodgy electronic gear. All said illegal. None said food. The job was sweet (apparently), 'cause it wasn't as if McAuley could go bleating to the police about his lost merchandise. And the best thing of all was that everyone was having a really good laugh at his expense.

That, if nothing else, was enough to put McAuley on the warpath. He had to be asking himself some hard questions by now. Like how had the Dowds known about his shipment – for who else would have the brass nerve to take what belonged to McAuley? How did they know the route? Even I didn't know the answer to that question. I didn't have that information, so how did the Dowds get it? There was no way McAuley could let the hijacking of his goods stand. If he did, every minor-league, two-a-penny thug would try their luck against him. So once the laughter ceased, the whole of Meadowview would be holding their breath to see how McAuley would retaliate. He was going to declare war on the Dowds over this. Still, that wasn't my problem, at least not yet. I had a more pressing dilemma.

Like, did McAuley suspect me of any involvement in this? Well, I was still breathing and walking around on two working legs, so I guessed not. But surely it was only a matter of time . . . ? I'd tried to be careful and cover my tracks, but now was not the time to get complacent. If McAuley suspected me of being involved in the loss of his merchandise, then it would only be a matter of time before I got the Ross Resnick treatment.

fifty-five

Mum had the evening off, Jessica wasn't off to a party or to one of her friends' houses and I no longer had a job, so for once we all ate together. Mum made us spaghetti bolognese and we had a small bowl filled with grated cheddar cheese to sprinkle on top of it if we wanted. Mum reckoned she wasn't going to buy stinky cheese (as she called any cheese that originated in another country), just so she could sprinkle some on spag bol the once a fort-night we had it. We sat around the tiny table in one corner of our living room. Mum's eyes were trained on the TV in the opposite corner as she watched the early evening news. My eyes never left my sister. And it was getting on her nerves.

'What?' she silently mouthed at me, venom darting from her eyes and mouth.

'Are you OK?' I mouthed back.

Jessica glared at me and concentrated on her food. 'Mum, is there any orange juice?' she asked.

Mum turned back to the table. 'Didn't I put any out?' There were three non-matching glasses but no juice carton present. 'I'll just go and get some,' she said. She stood up and headed for the kitchen.

'Where's the rest of my stuff?' Jessica barely waited for Mum to leave the room before she started.

'What stuff?'

'Tobey, don't muck about. Where's my stuff?'

'I don't know what you're talking about?' I popped a forkful of spaghetti into my mouth.

'Tobey, I'm warning you.'

'Have you told Mum yet?' I asked.

Jessica drew back slightly. 'Not yet, but I will.'

'When?'

'When I'm ready.'

'You'll never be ready,' I said. 'If you don't tell her by this weekend, I will. I mean it, Jessica. You've had long enough.'

'Tobey, give me back my stuff. I need it.' Jessica's voice was half plea, half demand.

'Is this the same stuff that you only use occasionally and that you can handle?' I asked.

'I don't need a lecture from you,' said Jessica. 'Just give it back.'

'Can't do that,' I replied. 'I flushed it down the loo.'

She stared at me, then glared at me. Without warning, she launched herself across the table, knocking the glasses and her plate flying. My chair tipped backwards and I almost ended up on the floor. Jessica was on her feet and trying to pummel all bloody hell out of my body. All I could do was try to protect myself from her feet, hands and knees. I didn't want to hurt her by seriously trying to defend myself. Mum came running into the room and tried to separate us, but Jessica was like a wild animal. She was ready to knock Mum over just to get to me.

Mum grabbed my sister's arms and shook her violently. 'Jessica, what the hell is the matter with you? What's going on?'

'He . . . He . . .' The wild stare left Jessica's eyes and she slowly returned to normal, her breathing slowing down.

'Jessica?' Mum frowned. 'D'you want to tell me what's going on?'

'Yeah, Jessica. Why don't you do that?' I said, getting to my feet. I touched a tentative finger to my mouth. I was right. My lip was bleeding. Godsake! Jessica scowled at me like she hated me, which at that moment she probably did.

'I'm waiting, and this had better be good,' said Mum. 'Which one of you is going to tell me what this was all about?'

Silence.

'Tobey has started working for McAuley, delivering drugs,' Jessica said viciously. 'He's a drug dealer.'

Huh? I stared at Jessica like I'd never seen her before. I had to hand it to my sister. I hadn't seen that one coming. At all.

'Mum, that's not true,' I protested.

'It is true, Mum. Ask anyone around here,' Jess insisted. 'Ask Dan.'

Mum looked so shocked, my heart sank. She was already three-quarters of the way towards believing my sister.

'Is that why McAuley spoke to you at the police station?' asked Mum. 'Why the police arrested you?'

'The police didn't find a thing on me, Mum. You know they didn't,' I said. 'I'm not a drug dealer. Jessica's lying.'

'Why would your sister say something so outrageous?' asked Mum.

I looked at Jessica. She scowled at me, totally defiant. We both knew that if I now told Mum what Jess had been up to, Mum would never believe me. She'd think I was just trying to get my own back.

'Tobey, are you mixed up in drug dealing in any manner, shape or form?' asked Mum. 'And I want the truth.'

One package. One frickin' package with drugs inside. That's all I'd delivered. That didn't exactly make me a drugs baron. But it didn't make my hands squeaky clean either. Suppose something had happened to Jess? What if the first package I'd delivered to Adam Eisner had contained smack and she had overdosed on the stuff I'd ferried across Meadowview? How did I know that someone else out there hadn't, no matter what drug was in the package? I looked from Jessica to Mum, unable to say a word.

Mum burst into tears.

I don't know who was more shocked, me or my sister.

'Tobey, I've shown you how that stuff destroys lives.' Mum was so disappointed in me, her words came out choked and full of sorrow. 'After all my warnings, all the things I've told you about drugs? How could you?'

I tried to put my arm around Mum, but she shrugged me off and headed out of the room. She went upstairs, her steps slow, almost like she had to drag herself upward. I listened as she closed her bedroom door. Silence surrounded me like fingers pointing. I turned to my sister. All this because she didn't want Mum to know that she needed help. Jessica actually looked ashamed of herself, but so what?

'OK, Jess. You know what? You win,' I said. 'But do me a favour? When you move on to injecting junk instead of inhaling it, do it somewhere where Mum and I won't find you if . . . when it goes wrong.'

I went into the hall, grabbed my jacket and headed out of the door. At that moment, I needed to be as far away from my sister as I could get.

✕✕

fifty-six

BLAZE DESTROYS TFTM

At around 3 a.m. this morning, a fire broke out in the well-known exclusive celebrity eatery – Thanks For The Memories. The restaurant's sprinkler system failed, leading to extensive damage of the restaurant and the famous Club above, but no one was injured as the building was empty at the time. Although local firefighters were at the scene within ten minutes, they still had to battle for over two hours to control the inferno. Police had to be called in to control the watching crowds.

'There is some water, smoke and fire damage to the furnishings and the décor, but the structure of the building remains mostly unaffected,' said Mr Thomas, TFTM's deputy manager. 'I'm looking forward to welcoming our regular customers and all newcomers to the new and improved TFTM. We shall return bigger and better than ever before.' Mr Thomas stated that he expects his restaurant to be open for business within the next couple of months. The fire is being investigated by the police and the fire service. A spokeswoman for the Fire Department stated that because the fire took hold of the building and blazed so quickly, arson has not been ruled out.

It had begun.

× ×

fifty-seven

There was something I needed to sort out for Callie whilst I still had the chance. And if I could just find this out for her, then I'd have something to say the next time I visited her. Was that what Callie was waiting for? News as to whether or not she was safe from her uncle? Is that what she needed to wake up?

I didn't want to put it off any longer. I headed next door, even though the thought of being dissected by Sephy Hadley's penetrating gaze didn't appeal. At all. I could still remember her expression when she saw me kissing Rebecca. But it wasn't Callie's mum I needed to see. I took a deep breath and rang the doorbell, hoping against hope that Sephy wouldn't be the one to open the door. Surprise! Surprise! For once, good luck was running with me.

'Hi, Meggie.'

'Hello, Tobey.'

'I wondered if I could have a word with you in private.' I looked past Meggie up the stairs, then into the kitchen at the end of the hall.

'Sephy's at the hospital visiting Callie, if that's who you're looking for,' Meggie said, amused.

'No,' I denied quickly. 'It was you I wanted to speak to.'

Meggie looked surprised, but she ushered me into the

living room. After waiting for me to sit down, she sat opposite. It took her a bit longer than it took me. Once she was comfortable, she looked at me expectantly.

'Meggie, I need to ask you something.'

'Oh, yes?'

'It's about your son.'

Meggie's gaze was instantly watchful. 'Which one?' she asked.

'Jude.'

'What about him?'

There was no easy way to say this, so I'd just have to spit it out.

'Is Jude alive? Has he been in touch with you?'

Meggie sat back in her chair and regarded me long and hard. The silence scraped against my skin like a cheese grater.

'It's just . . . it's just that before Callie was injured, she thought that her uncle died alongside her Nana Jasmine,' I rushed to explain. 'Only then the news began talking about some guy called Robert Powers. Callie was terrified her uncle would come after her again.'

'Callie told you this, did she?'

'Yes, she did,' I replied. And in as many words. I looked at Meggie, waiting for her answer.

'When my granddaughter comes out the hospital then I will give her a direct answer to that question,' said Meggie.

'So is Jude alive then?' I asked.

'I'll discuss that with my granddaughter, not you.' Meggie's voice wasn't anywhere near a snap, but I still felt like I'd been firmly put in my place.

I wasn't poking and prying into Meggie's business for my own sake. I just wanted to have something to tell

Callie the next time I saw her. Hopefully something good. But Meggie was going to keep the subject of Jude as something only she and Callie would discuss.

I was excluded.

fifty-eight

Over the next couple of days, the tension at home was unbearable. I wasn't talking to Jessica, Mum wasn't talking to me. We might have been ghosts passing through each other for all the contact we made. I seriously thought about telling Mum to search through Jessica's room – as she probably had more 'supplies' by now – or to check her best teapot if she wanted to know the truth about who was using and who wasn't. I mean, I might've scrubbed the thing out, but surely there was some chemical or other that Mum could get from the hospital which could test for smack, no matter how little was left or how microscopic the residue? But then Jessica would accuse me of using as well as dealing, and what proof would I have that she was lying? That would just make a bad situation even worse. I couldn't do right for doing wrong, that was the trouble.

The only silver lining in a sky full of dark clouds was that Rebecca still wanted to see me, though it took some doing to persuade her that I didn't hold her responsible for losing my job at TFTM.

'That's why I haven't been in touch,' Rebecca admitted when I phoned her. 'I felt sure you'd blame me for what Gideon did.'

'Don't be daft. Of course I don't blame you,' I insisted. 'And to prove it, I'll buy you dinner.'

So it was all arranged.

We met in town and went for a pizza. In about half a minute, Rebecca scanned the menu, then closed it and put it down. Five minutes later, I still hadn't made up my mind.

'Are you OK, Tobey?' Rebecca asked. 'You seem preoccupied.'

'What? Oh, sorry. I've just got a lot on my mind at the moment,' I said.

'I'm really sorry about you losing your job,' she said quickly. 'I wish you'd let me help, at least until you find a new one.'

I shook my head. 'Rebecca, I'll be fine. I've some money saved and something will turn up. Besides, I wasn't thinking about my job, I was thinking about my sister, Jessica.'

'Is something wrong with her?'

'Yeah. And I'm still trying to figure out how to put it right.'

'Can I help?' Rebecca asked doubtfully.

I smiled. 'No. But thanks for the offer. I appreciate it.'

'If you need any money—'

'I don't,' I interrupted. 'It's not that kind of problem. And stop worrying. I'll find another job.'

'Gideon had no right to sack you,' Rebecca fumed.

'He didn't sack me. I quit,' I amended.

'OK, but he had no right to force you to quit,' she said.

'Rebecca, I promise it's OK,' I said. 'Besides, you're worth it.'

Rebecca switched on a smile bright as a lighthouse when I said that. I returned to my menu, focusing on the task at hand.

'Tobey, promise me something,' Rebecca began hesitantly.

'What?'

'Promise me you won't ever lie to me.'

Pause. 'I promise. What brought that on?'

Rebecca shrugged. 'I just need to know that you're being honest with me.'

'Fair enough,' I replied, studying my menu again so she couldn't see my eyes.

Rebecca waited until I'd ordered and was tucking into my garlic bread starter before she told me her news. For one hopeful moment I thought she was kidding, but her earnest expression indicated otherwise.

'You're serious! Your mum . . .' I coughed to clear the squeak in my voice. 'Your mum wants to meet *me*? But why?'

''Cause I told her all about you.'

'What on earth for?' I asked, aghast.

''Cause I like you.' Rebecca shrugged. 'You're the first guy since I was a kid to talk to me like a normal human being.'

'What about your brothers?'

'They don't count,' Rebecca dismissed. 'Besides, they don't talk to me. They dictate and command and argue.'

'What about your dad?'

'My dad and my uncle were killed when I was nine.' Rebecca's dark-brown eyes clouded over. At that moment, she so reminded me of Callie Rose. I turned away. I didn't want her to remind me of Callie or anyone else for that matter. This was already hard enough without thoughts like that making it harder.

I offered my sympathies. My reply was inadequate, but what else could I say? Rebecca's dad and uncle were the two Dowds that McAuley was rumoured to have taken care of. No wonder Vanessa Dowd and her family hated Alex McAuley so much.

'What about previous boyfriends?' I asked, to change the subject.

'I went to an all-girls school and whilst my friends were happy to come round to my house, very few of them ever invited me back. And as for the brothers of the few friends I had, well, I think my surname was either more than enough to put them off or the only reason they wanted to be with me in the first place.'

'More fool them then,' I said.

And I meant it. Rebecca was nothing like the rest of her family. Any idiot could see that. I knew she'd had at least one proper boyfriend and it hadn't ended happily, but I didn't want to push her any further into unhappy memories.

'Rebecca, do you—?' I began.

'Tobey! I thought it was you. How . . . er . . . how are you?'

My heart sank like a big stone in a small pond. 'Hi, Misty.'

'Are you . . . er . . . eating here too? Me and my friend Erik over there have just arrived.'

I glanced across at Erik, who was scowling at me. Erik was a Nought in our year, but in a different class.

'Misty, this is Rebecca. Rebecca, this is Misty. Misty

and I are in the same class at school.' I thought I'd better make some introductions. I didn't want Rebecca to get the wrong idea.

Which was what exactly?

Why was I so worried about what she might think? Misty didn't even bother to look at Rebecca. Her eyes were still trying to pin me to my chair.

'If you like pizza, maybe we could . . . you know . . . come here next weekend or something . . .' Misty began, adding a blatant wink. 'I'm still hoping to get you alone . . . on a date.'

'I . . . er . . . Well, I . . .' I began.

'Oh no, you didn't!' Rebecca couldn't believe her ears, her eyes or any of her other senses from the sound of it. 'You didn't just ask Tobey out when he's so obviously on a date with me?' She glared at Misty, and if looks could kill she'd've been banged up for life – Dowd family connections or not.

'Tobey's dating *you*?' Misty's eyebrows launched into the air at that news. 'I don't think so. Tobey wouldn't go out with a dagger.'

Rebecca jumped to her feet. 'Listen, bitch . . .'

I jumped up. We were attracting all kinds of attention, the last thing I wanted. I stepped between the two before the hair-pulling began.

'How about I kick your skinny arse?' Misty said, trying to duck round me.

Godsake!

Rebecca was about to hurl herself across the table. 'I'm going to bury my stiletto where the sun don't shine,' she said, pulling off her earrings.

Things were getting serious. When a girl pulls off her

earrings, then lightning and thunder are about to hit and hit hard. Anyone with a sister knew that.

'Tobey, you can do much better than this dagger skank,' Misty told me scathingly.

Whoa!

'Misty, enough. I *am* on a date actually,' I said firmly. 'And Erik's over there waiting for you, so maybe you should head back to him.'

'But, Tobey . . .'

'Bye, Misty.'

Misty frowned at me, then cast Rebecca a filthy look before taking the hint and heading back to her date.

I sat down. After a few seconds, so did Rebecca.

Silence reigned between us.

'I'm sorry about calling your friend a bitch,' said Rebecca quietly. 'It was inexcusable. I lost my temper. I guess I'm more sensitive than I realized.'

I shrugged. 'Forget it.'

'It was rude of me,' she went on unhappily. 'I really am sorry.'

'Rebecca, it's OK. Really it is.' I leaned across the table and brushed my lips against hers. 'Don't let Misty spoil our dinner. Besides, you were right. She is a bitch!'

Rebecca laughed as I'd wanted her to. I returned to my garlic bread. All that excitement had worked up quite an appetite. I couldn't believe Misty. She was on a date, I was with someone, and she still wanted to start some drama. Godsake!

'Tobey, you were about to ask me something, before we were interrupted,' Rebecca prompted.

I put down my bread half-eaten. 'Becks, d'you trust me?'

'Of course.'

'Why?'

The question took Rebecca by surprise. 'I just do.'

'But why?' I persisted.

'Because you didn't chase after me. If anything it was the other way round,' said Rebecca. 'You're quite happy to be seen with me in public and you don't try to hide me away like some shameful secret. You're the only guy who hasn't insisted that I pay for everything. Are those enough reasons to be going on with?'

'They'll do.' I smiled.

Poor Rebecca. She'd been so unlucky with the guys she'd met in the past. And her luck hadn't changed.

'So are you up for meeting my mum?'

'When?'

'How does tomorrow night sound?'

Like Hell on earth. I swallowed hard. 'Tomorrow night sounds fine.'

fifty-nine

Hi, Callie.

I'm sorry I haven't been to see you for a couple of days. Things have been a mess at home with Jessica and I couldn't get away. You're looking so much better, though. You really do look like you've just dozed off.

I've got some news for you. The police intercepted one of McAuley's shipments today. Apparently a little bird told them when, where and what to look for. There are little birds singing all over Meadowview! So that's the second shipment McAuley has lost. Once is bad luck, but twice is bad habits. Unfortunately there was nothing to tie the shipment to McAuley, but everyone – including the police – knows exactly who was running that delivery. By now McAuley is going to be a desperate man, and his desperation will make him even more dangerous than before. I'm definitely going to keep my head down.

I'm going on another date with Rebecca tonight. I'm off to meet her mum. And no doubt, Gideon and Owen will be present too. Gideon has already warned me off so I'd better wear full body armour and a box. Something tells me I'm going to need them. Rebecca is trying to make out that her mum can't wait to meet me, but I think—

'Tobey . . .'

The sound of Callie's voice made me jump out of my skin. I'd been looking down at her hand in mine as I spoke so I missed any signs that she was waking up. I could do nothing but stare as her eyelids fluttered open. She turned her head to focus her gaze on me.

'Callie!' I leaped to my feet and pulled her up to hug her just as hard as I could.

'Ow!' Callie croaked out her protest. 'Too tight.'

I loosened my grip, but no way was I going to let her go. My mouth was already beginning to ache from grinning so hard. I'd wanted my face to be the first one Callie saw when she woke up and I'd got my wish. I lay her back down on her pillows, then kissed her. I only shifted when she started pushing weakly against my shoulders. When I lifted my head, she gasped to drag some air back down into her lungs.

'What're you . . . doing? Are you' – Callie tried to swallow past the dryness in her throat – 'trying to kiss . . . me . . . until I pass out?'

I shook my head not yet trusting myself to speak.

'Besides' – Callie couldn't raise her voice above a whisper – 'my breath . . . is smelly.'

Godsake! Like I gave a damn!

'Water please,' she said. Her voice sounded deep and hoarse, but I've never heard anything so wonderful in my life.

I poured out half a tumbler full of water and held it to her lips to help her to drink. Callie took a few sips before collapsing back onto her pillows as if just sitting up and drinking had exhausted her. She reached for my hand and held it in her own.

'Tobey.' She breathed my name, like just saying it eased her pain.

Callie was looking at me like the last few weeks had never happened. I had what I'd been waiting for. To her I was the same. I was sane. I was safe.

'How're you feeling?' I asked. I really couldn't stop smiling.

'Got a headache.' Callie raised a hand to her temple.

The bandages had long since come off, but she still had a scar to show where the bullet had struck her skin. I bent to kiss it.

'You're very kissy all of a sudden.' Callie frowned.

I laughed. 'You'll be OK now, Callie Rose,' I said. 'Let me go get a doctor.'

Callie's grip on my hand tightened as she looked around her room. 'Tobey,' she said. 'Am I in hospital?'

My frown mirrored Callie's as I nodded.

'W-why am I here? And who's . . . who's Rebecca?'

sixty

I didn't want to be here. I wanted to be back at the hospital with Callie. When I explained about TFTM and meeting Rebecca Dowd, Callie had got more and more agitated. I backtracked and spoke about her getting injured. Just one problem. She didn't remember getting shot. She didn't remember even going to the Wasteland that day. She didn't remember anything that had happened in the days before the shooting either. It had all gone. When Callie found out how long she'd been unconscious, she started to freak. It'd taken two nurses and a doctor to calm her down and sedate her. After she succumbed to sleep, the doctor tried to reassure me that it was natural for those emerging from a coma to feel completely disorientated for a while. But I couldn't help looking at Callie and feeling that I'd just messed up. Again.

I really didn't want to be here with Rebecca. But I'd

started this thing so I had to see it through to the end. She'd picked me up from outside my house at six o'clock and at ten minutes past seven we were pulling up to an electronic gate with two CCTV cameras trained on it. Rebecca took out a small device like a mini remote control from the cup holder between our seats and pointed it at the gate, which then swung back like wings preparing for flight. We drove along a paved driveway before stopping outside her home. I looked up at it, impressed in spite of myself. It was only slightly smaller than Jasmine Hadley's old home, but then so were most public museums. Double-fronted and with copious windows on all three storeys, it looked like it could house half of my street.

I got out of the car, still looking up at the building.

'Ready?' asked Rebecca.

'As I'll ever be,' I replied.

She took my hand. 'Don't worry, you'll be fine.'

We'd see about that. The front door opened just as we reached it. A pocket-sized Cross woman wearing a lilac-coloured flowery dress stood in the doorway. I had to force myself not to pull my hand out of Rebecca's.

'Hi, Mum,' said Rebecca. 'This is Tobey.'

So this was *the* Vanessa Dowd, was it? She wasn't at all what I'd expected. Except maybe her eyes. Her dark-brown eyes were cold and calculating. She looked me up and down like she was appraising a piece of jewellery.

You'll know me next time, I thought. But I was careful to keep my expression neutral.

'Mum, stop that,' sighed Rebecca.

Her mum suddenly smiled. 'Well, so far he's lasted longer than most.'

'See! And Gideon couldn't intimidate him either.'

I was getting a bit tired of both of them talking about me as if I wasn't there. I stepped forward. 'Hello, Mrs Dowd. Pleased to meet you.'

Mrs Dowd shook my hand before stepping to one side. 'Come in, come in.'

Said the spider to the fly . . .

Rebecca and I waited till her mum had shut the door so that she could lead the way.

'Let's go into the drawing room,' said Mrs Dowd.

At home, it would've been called the front room! We entered a space as big as the whole of the downstairs of my house. It was amazing, with a fireplace big enough to walk into and two of the largest sofas I'd ever seen placed on either side of it. 'It's a lovely room,' I said sincerely.

'It does,' said Mrs Dowd.

It does indeed!

She indicated that I should take a seat. Once I sat down, Rebecca sat next to me and her mum sat on the sofa opposite.

'Tobey, how much—?' Mrs Dowd got no further.

Gideon and Owen came in. Gideon had a glass of something amber-coloured in his hand. Owen was on the phone.

'What's he doing here?' Gideon asked the moment he clapped eyes on me. 'I don't want him in my house.'

'Whose house?' Mrs Dowd asked quietly.

Gideon's lips tightened. 'He doesn't belong here.'

'For once I agree with my brother,' said Owen, his free hand clasped over his phone.

'I don't give a damn what you think, Owen,' Mrs Dowd rounded on him.

'Tell me something I don't know, Ma,' Owen said with sarcasm.

Owen was younger than Gideon but taller and more lean. I had to hand it to him. No one would ever guess that we'd met before.

'Owen and Gideon, you both promised me you'd behave. I live here too and Tobey is my guest,' said Rebecca. 'You two should have some manners.'

To my surprise, both Owen and Gideon looked suitably chastened. They really did dote on their little sister.

'I quite agree,' said Mrs Dowd evenly. 'Tobey, I apologize for my sons' distinct lack of class.'

I shrugged.

'Can I get you a drink?' Vanessa Dowd continued. 'Coffee? A soft drink? A glass of wine or lager perhaps?'

'No, thanks. I'm fine,' I replied.

Owen moved to stand over by the window so he could finish his conversation in relative privacy. Gideon sat at the other end of the same sofa as his mum.

'Now where was I? Ah yes . . .' Mrs Dowd smiled. 'Tobey, how much did McAuley pay you to deliver Ross Resnick's finger to Louise Resnick?'

Game, set and match to Vanessa Dowd. I hadn't even touched the ball.

Beside me, Rebecca gasped. 'Mum, what on earth . . . ?'

My blood began to run fast and hot through my body. Vanessa Dowd was a real piece of work. I turned to Rebecca and shook my head before turning back to her mum.

'Mrs Dowd, I delivered the package for a friend, not

McAuley. I didn't know what was in the parcel and it was the one and only delivery I made. Afterwards McAuley paid me three hundred pounds. I gave every penny away.'

I could feel Rebecca's eyes burning into me. I turned to face her, one of the hardest things I'd ever had to do.

'Y-you work for McAuley?' she asked. 'Ross . . . Ross was a friend of mine and you work for McAuley? How could you?'

Don't, Rebecca. Don't lump me in with all the other guys who lied to you and used you. I'm not like that . . .

Except that I am.

'No, I don't work for him. I did that one delivery and that was it,' I tried to explain. 'After the business with Ross Resnick and especially what he did to my sister, I made it clear I wanted nothing more to do with McAuley and I went looking for another way of making some money. That's when I started working at TFTM.'

And those were all true events – they just didn't happen with the motivation I'd implied. Rebecca drew away from me. It was only a slight movement, but it was enough. I looked from her to Mrs Dowd and back again. Nodding briefly, I stood up. Thank you and goodnight.

'I'm sorry you don't believe me, Rebecca. I've told you the truth, but I guess you have no way of knowing that.'

I turned back to Mrs Dowd. She watched me, a tiny smile of satisfaction on her face. She was slicker than Gideon, that was for sure. Where he used a sledgehammer, she used a razor-sharp stiletto. In a way I admired her. Here was an object lesson in how to get a job done.

'What . . . what did McAuley do to your sister?' asked Rebecca.

'Thanks to McAuley and one of my so-called friends, my sister Jessica is now doing heroin,' I said, adding bitterly, 'I have a lot to thank McAuley for.'

I looked around. Owen was off the phone and I had everyone's full attention.

'Tobey, I haven't figured out yet what your game is,' said Gideon. 'But don't worry, I will.'

'There's no game, no nefarious plans, no cards up my sleeve,' I told him. Gideon Dowd could sod off and die as far as I was concerned. I took a deep breath. 'It was nice meeting all of you,' I said, my tone implying the exact opposite. 'If you don't mind, I'll phone for a taxi and wait outside until it arrives.'

I started for the door.

'Tobey, have a seat,' ordered Mrs Dowd.

Like McAuley, she didn't need to shout. I stood for a moment or two, seriously thinking about defying her. But then I sat down again next to Rebecca, who didn't move away. What was going to happen now?

'Rebecca?' her mum prompted. 'Is your guest staying for dinner or not?'

I looked at Rebecca steadily. To look away would've been to appear worse than guilty.

'Would you like to stay?' she asked at last.

'Only if that's what you want,' I said.

'Then stay.'

'Very touching, I'm sure, but the blanker obviously can't be trusted,' said Gideon. 'And he worked for McAuley for goodness' sake. For all any of us know, he still does. Am I the only one in the room with any sense?'

'I worked for McAuley – past tense,' I said. 'And it was once and only once.'

'So you say,' Gideon dismissed.

'It's the truth.'

'Are you arguing with me?' he asked through narrowed eyes.

'Yes, I am,' I replied.

To my surprise, Mrs Dowd burst out laughing. 'Good for you, Tobey,' she approved.

Which was the last thing I'd expected from her. What on earth . . . ? I glanced at Gideon. His expression was very eloquent. If he could've punched through my chest and ripped out my heart to hand it, still beating, back to me, he would've done so – in a hot big city second.

'Mrs Dowd, dinner is served,' said a Cross man in a dark suit who seemed to appear from nowhere.

Who was this guy? He couldn't be a butler. I mean, Godsake! Who had a butler in this day and age? Ah! Apparently the Dowds did.

'Mum, I need to freshen up,' said Rebecca.

She looked fresh enough to me.

'Good idea. I'll join you,' said Vanessa Dowd. 'Morton, we'll be right there.'

'Yes, Mrs Dowd.' The butler headed out of the room, followed by Rebecca and her mum.

After giving me a filthy look, Gideon followed them. I stood up, unsure what I should do. I went to follow them, hoping to stumble across the dining room some time before morning but Owen blocked my way.

'Tobey, we need to talk,' he said.

Owen looked around to make sure we were truly alone, then he handed me a folded slip of paper. Frowning, I opened it and quickly read. I stared at him, completely shocked.

'Is this for real?'

Owen nodded. 'I had that amount deposited in Byron's account, just as you suggested. This had better work, Tobey. That's a lot of my money sitting in that blanker's account.'

Owen was such a tosser. He was talking to a Nought, but thought nothing of insulting us Noughts to my face. I looked down at the confirmation slip in my hand. Owen had transferred a mind-boggling amount of money to Byron's account, far more than I'd suggested.

'It'll work.' I nodded. 'Besides, you got McAuley's first shipment, didn't you? So that's your money back, plus interest.'

'I didn't get the shipment,' Owen dismissed. 'My brother did.'

'But you're poised to take over McAuley's entire operation,' I reminded him. 'And think how much money you'll make then.'

'I shall enjoy being out from under Gideon's shadow,' mused Owen. 'I have quite a few ideas of my own . . .'

I just bet he did.

Owen emerged from his reverie to tell me, 'I must admit, when you first came to me with this scheme, I thought you were either barking or a genius.'

'The jury's still out on that one,' I said, handing back the confirmation slip.

Owen smiled. 'Oh, before I forget, I need the name of

a straight career copper. Not a PC Plod, but not anyone too high up who'll be more interested in covering things up either.'

Surely he'd know more of the coppers in Meadowview than I did? Why was he asking me?

'It can't be anyone even vaguely connected with me. It can't be anyone I know,' explained Owen, taking another swift look around to ensure we were still alone. 'I've got to play this smart. Gideon is gonna go down and if Ma suspects I had a hand in bringing down her favourite son, I'm as good as dead.'

Happy families.

'I think Detective Inspector Boothe at Meadowview police station is straight,' I ventured.

'You're sure?'

'As sure as I can be. But it's not guaranteed.'

'DI Boothe, eh? Never heard of him, so he'll do.'

What was Owen planning? At that moment, I thanked God that I wasn't his brother.

'I like you, Tobey.' Owen grinned at me. 'I knew you and I could do business.'

'How did you know?' I couldn't help asking.

'Because I recognized you for who and what you are at once,' he replied.

'And what's that?'

'My mirror image.'

Inside my body, every drop of blood lost its heat. That was a damned lie. There was no way I was Owen's mirror image.

'I hear another shipment of McAuley's got . . . shall we say, diverted?' said Owen.

'Yeah, I heard that too,' I said. 'Something about the police getting it?'

'What a shame I didn't get to hear about it first,' said Owen, his eyes never leaving mine.

'Yeah, it is,' I agreed.

'You only got details of the one shipment in the file you retrieved from McAuley's memory key?'

'That's right,' I said. 'And I gave you all the information I had. Maybe the police bugged McAuley's house.'

'Maybe they did,' said Owen.

Silence.

'May I ask you something?' I began.

'Go ahead.'

'How did your family find out I delivered that package to Louise Resnick?' I asked.

Owen allowed himself a tiny smile. 'Whatever McAuley knows, sooner rather than later it finds its way to us as well.'

'Oh, I see.' That confirmed it. Someone in McAuley's employ was working for the Dowds. That question was answered. Wasn't there anyone in this whole crummy little world who could be trusted?

'So is that how you knew where and when to send your men on the day of the Wasteland shooting?' I asked. 'One of McAuley's men told you beforehand what he was planning?'

'It might've been,' said Owen. 'Tobey, I don't like a lot of questions.'

I had to bite back my response to that one.

'Fair enough. What are we talking about?'

Owen looked puzzled.

'We're not with the others. You obviously kept me

here to talk about something,' I said. 'Rebecca or your mum might want to know what.'

Owen studied me carefully before he said, 'Tell them I warned you that if you're lying and you really are working for McAuley, I will kill you myself.'

Silence.

Owen suddenly smiled and my blood ran like icy slush. He said, 'Now let's go eat.'

sixty-one

Dinner with the Dowds was excruciating. Owen completely ignored me. Rebecca was very quiet, only speaking when spoken to. Gideon spent the entire time either on his mobile or directing snide remarks my way. Only Vanessa Dowd seemed to be completely at ease and enjoying herself. The food reflected the ambience around the table. Shark's-fin soup was the starter, followed by the rarest steak I'd ever had. The thing was so rare I'm surprised it didn't moo on my plate. No one bothered to ask me how I wanted it cooked – I was definitely a well-done kind of guy. But I wasn't about to complain.

Rebecca's mother watched with amused interest as I chewed my first bloody mouthful. 'Tobey, I'm afraid it's one of the things I insist upon,' she said. 'Steak should be eaten very rare, otherwise it's ruined.'

'Rebecca, you like your meat rare too, don't you?' Gideon said pointedly, looking from Rebecca to me and back again.

Tosser.

'I'm a vegetarian, Gideon – as you very well know,' Rebecca replied.

I chewed on another mouthful. The steak was served with matchstick-thin chips and assorted vegetables. I cleared my plate. The dessert was lemon tart served with lime sorbet. It was foul, bitter and nasty. But I ate all of that too.

After dinner, Rebecca barely said five sentences to me. I gave it half an hour, but when she still wouldn't talk to me I decided I'd truly outstayed my welcome. I was quite prepared to phone for a taxi, but Rebecca insisted on driving me home. All the way home, she'd only speak to me when spoken to, so we quickly lapsed into an uncomfortable silence. Doubt had raised its ugly head and Rebecca was backing away from me.

As we pulled up outside my house, I tried one last time to get her to talk to me properly.

'Rebecca, would you like to come in and meet my mum and sister?' I asked.

She looked surprised, then pleased, but the light in her eyes soon faded. 'No, I . . . No, thanks. Better not.'

I sighed. 'Look, Rebecca, I never lied to you.'

'You never told me the truth either,' she replied. 'And you promised me, Tobey. Look, I have to go home. Mum's orders.'

'Can we meet up tomorrow? We need to talk.'

Rebecca started to shake her head.

'Please. I need to talk to you.'

'All right then,' she said reluctantly. 'When and where?'

'How about tomorrow outside Los Amigos at seven?'

'I'm not sure I want a meal.'

With me.

'Well, we can meet there and find a coffee shop nearby.'

'OK. I'll see you at seven.' At least it wasn't a straight-out no. Rebecca drove off the moment I was clear of her car.

I was getting the chilly treatment and, to be honest, I didn't blame her. I should've told her up front about McAuley. I'd thought about it, I really had, but had decided it would look too much like I was just trying to manipulate her. Big mistake.

I entered my house and went straight up to my room. Sitting on my bed, I thought through everything that had happened since Callie was injured. Before then, my life had seemed so neatly stitched together. It scared me just how easily everything fell to pieces.

There was a knock at my door. Before I could answer, Jessica walked into my room. Her typically unruly, spiked hair lay un-gelled and tamed in a pixie cut framing her face. And for once she wasn't wearing make-up. She smiled at me, albeit hesitantly. I was instantly on my guard.

'Have you come to get me into more trouble with Mum?' I asked with belligerence.

'Don't be like that . . .'

Was she serious?

'Jessica, what d'you want?'

'I want us back to the way we used to be,' she said.

'Then tell Mum the truth,' I replied.

Jessica looked me in the eye. 'I did. At least, part of it.'

'Jess, I'm not the one in this family who's into drugs,' I pointed out.

'No, you're just into money,' she said. 'And it's all right for you, 'cause you're smart. You have a real chance to make some and get out of this place. What're the rest of us supposed to do, Tobey?'

'I don't know. But you'll never find the answer in waxed paper wrappers.'

'I'm not looking for the answer.'

'Then what are you looking for?'

'A way to not mind so much about the question.'

'Jessica, that stuff will stop you minding about anything, except more junk,' I said.

'I know.'

'Then please stop taking it.'

'It's that easy, is it?'

'No. But Mum and I are here to help you.'

'I'll think about it.'

So much for that then. 'D'you want me to tell Mum for you?'

Jessica's eyes narrowed. 'Is that a threat?'

'No,' I said, exasperated. 'I'm trying to help. Can't you see that?'

'No, I can't,' said Jessica. 'You only want to help me your way, not my way.'

What was she on about? I really wasn't in the mood for a big argument so I let it slide.

I sighed. 'Are you still using?'

At first I thought she wasn't going to answer. 'Tobey,' she said at last, 'I'm not one of your maths problems. OK?'

'Meaning?'

'Meaning not every problem has a solution.'

'I know that.'

'No, you don't. That's the trouble. In your world A plus B equals C. It works for maths so you expect it to work for people too.'

'That's not true.'

'Isn't it?' asked Jessica. 'You assume you've got me all figured out. I bet you even think you know why I started on smack in the first place.'

'I thought maybe it had something to do with your course at college,' I admitted.

'You think I'm going to fail?'

I shrugged. It seemed logical.

'Tobey, I did my exam and submitted enough course-work to scrape a pass. My marks won't be setting any college records, but I did pass,' Jessica told me. 'So what does that do to your theory now?'

'All right then. Tell me why you started taking that stuff,' I challenged.

Sadly, she shook her head. 'Tobey, I did just tell you.'

'I don't understand.'

'I know,' said Jessica. 'And you never will until you experience the one thing that drunks and druggies and all the miserable, lonely, unhappy people in this world share.'

'And what's that?' I asked.

'Work it out.'

And she was gone.

sixty-two. Callie

How can I have slept for so long? It feels like I just nodded off, like I've been out of it for a day, maybe two max. I stopped. The world didn't. Time moved on without me. So did Tobey.

Who is Rebecca?

Just a girl? His girl friend? Or his girlfriend? I thought . . . Tobey and me . . . I thought . . . But I was wrong. He has someone else now. Rebecca. And what do I have? Uncle Jude and this hospital bed. I'm trying so hard to be glad for Tobey. I'm trying so desperately hard not to mind – or care. But though I've never met Rebecca, I hate her. I hate her for taking Tobey away from me, for being there when he needed someone.

I've woken up to find all the bad things in my life have been waiting patiently for me and all the good things have gone. Uncle Jude is out there, biding his time. I'm surprised he didn't visit me when I was unconscious and finish the job. Or maybe he wants me wide awake to fully appreciate when he takes his revenge. I still have to live with the fact that an innocent man is dead because of me. That hasn't gone away either. That fact has eaten an even bigger hole inside of me, because I'm still here, I've survived. And Robert Powers didn't. Is this karma? In the world of 'what goes around, comes around', maybe I'm getting what I deserve. I just wish someone would tell me when it'll stop hurting so much.

All I want is for Tobey to hold me tight and tell me that everything will be all right between us. Who am I trying to fool? All I want is Tobey.

But he's moved on.

And I'm stuck here.

And I've never felt so alone.

sixty-three

The following morning, me, Mum and Jess all sat down to have breakfast together again. Mum sipped at her orange juice. Jessica picked at her cereal. I stirred my coffee round and round. For once I didn't have much of an appetite. Every time I looked up, Jessica was looking at me. Should I say something to Mum? Should I try? I still hadn't worked out what my sister had been trying to tell me the night before. And I was desperate not to make things any worse.

'Mum, I lied to you about Tobey,' Jessica said unexpectedly.

Mum frowned at her. 'Pardon?'

'Tobey hasn't been dealing drugs. I only told you that because he threatened to tell you . . . to tell you that I'd been s-smoking . . . smack.'

'Jessica, please tell me you're joking,' Mum said, appalled.

Jessica bowed her head, unable to say a word.

'You've been taking drugs?' Mum whispered. 'Oh, Jessica.'

A tear followed in quick succession by a host of others fell from Jessica's eyes onto the table.

I looked from Mum to my sister, holding my breath.

'Oh, Jessica . . .' Mum got up and hugged Jess to her. Jess fell into her embrace and started to sob her heart out.

'Tobey, could you leave us alone for a while?' Mum asked.

I headed for the door, wondering what had happened to make Jess change her mind about telling Mum. Maybe she'd meant it about getting things back to the way they used to be. God knows that was all I wanted as well. But somehow it felt like those days were over, never to return.

Jessica and Mum were in the living room with the door shut for over an hour, almost two. I went up to my room and wrote an email to Callie. An email I knew I'd never send, but I had more than a few things to get off my chest. And it helped – a little. A very little.

I couldn't put it off any longer. It was time for another letter. I didn't have time to go to the library again so my own computer would just have to do. And this was just the sort of carelessness that could get me caught, but I had to do it now before I changed my mind.

Wearing a pair of my mum's rubber gloves this time to ensure I ended up with a sheet of fingerprint-free paper, I drafted my third and final letter. My brain must've been temporarily scrambled by a cosmic ray to believe I could use McAuley's last shipment for my own ends. Either that or scrambled by greed. But not any more.

I wanted no part of it.

My letter to the police was short and to the point, telling them everything I knew about McAuley's last drop-off. The man would be out of business, but it still didn't feel like enough. I was beginning to realize that nothing ever would. I placed the letter in a printed envelope addressed to DI Boothe. Time to get out of the house. Besides, I couldn't stand the silence any longer. Grabbing my jacket off the banister, I thought about just heading out the door without saying a word. But I couldn't do that to my mum. That was my dad's trick.

'Mum, I'm going to see Callie at the hospital,' I called through the still closed living-room door.

After a few seconds the door opened. Mum stood there, her eyes slightly red. She'd obviously been crying. And from where I stood in the hall, I couldn't see my sister.

'Are you OK, Mum?' I asked.

Mum nodded.

'If you want me to stay, I will.'

'No, that's OK. Say hello to Callie for me.'

'Is Jess OK?' I lowered my voice to ask.

'No. But she will be,' Mum said with determination. She looked up at me and stroked my cheek. 'I love you, Tobey. You know that, don't you?'

Whenever Mum told me she loved me, my response was invariably, 'I know.' As it was today. But today my usual response didn't feel like nearly enough.

'Mum, I . . . I . . . I have to go.'

She smiled at my discomfort, stroking my cheek again. 'Give Callie my love.'

'I will.' I practically sprinted out of the door.

I'd wanted to say it, I really had. But I'd never said those words to anyone in my life and I couldn't just start now. But Mum knew. She had to know. And now that she knew the truth about Jessica, everything would be OK. It had to be.

Now it was time to put things right between Callie and me.

sixty-four

Dropping my letter in the postbox outside the hospital, I headed into the building. Five minutes later, I took a deep breath and walked into Callie's room. Every cell in my body told me this was a bad idea, but I needed to see her. Her head was turned away from the door. She was looking out of the window towards the park beyond. I stood in the doorway, watching her, drinking in her stillness. Apart from the occasional blink, no other part of her body beneath the bedcovers moved.

'Hello, Callie,' I said softly.

'Hello, Tobey,' Callie replied without looking at me.

That hurt. I swallowed hard before I could trust myself to speak again.

'May I come in?'

Callie nodded.

I entered the room and sat in one of the chairs by her bed. She still wasn't looking at me.

'How're you feeling?' I asked. 'Have you remembered a bit more?'

Like the night we spent together?

Please remember being with me, Callie. Please remember making love with me. Otherwise I'll start to doubt my own memories. I'm already beginning to wonder. Maybe the whole thing was a dream, wishful thinking, nothing more than a fantasy.

Callie shrugged. How I wished she'd look at me.

'How's Rebecca?' she asked.

All kinds of explanations raced through my head. But that's where they stayed.

'She's fine,' I replied. 'We're having dinner once I leave here.'

Godsake! Why did I say that? To get a reaction? Because I have a big mouth? Or, God help me, to get back at Callie for not remembering our night together?

Callie turned to look at me. I had to force myself not to look away.

'Will I get to meet her?'

I shrugged. We regarded each other.

'My doctor says I can go home later today,' said Callie. 'Once I'm strong enough, maybe you, me and Rebecca can get together.'

'OK,' I agreed, knowing full well it'd never happen.

Rebecca wasn't stupid. One look at Callie and she'd know which way the wind was blowing. Head bent,

Callie laced her bedsheet in and out of her fingers. She wasn't the only one who was nervous.

'I've got most of my memory back now,' she said, looking at me again. 'I still don't remember the time around the shooting. But I remember everything else.'

'Oh.'

The time around the shooting? How did Callie quantify that? Two minutes before the shooting, or two hours or two days or two weeks before?

'Is that it?' she asked. 'Is that all you have to say?'

'What would you like me to say?' I asked.

Silence. The tension between us expanded like a balloon too full of air. An explosion was about to happen. I didn't have long to wait.

'Tobey,' My name burst from Callie's lips. 'Why did you—?'

Sephy and Meggie chose just that moment to walk in. Thank goodness for bad timing. Callie's look of frustration didn't go unnoticed. Sephy kissed her daughter's forehead before sitting down. Meggie did the same.

Sephy glared at me, her brown eyes giving me frostbite.

'Hello, Tobey,' said Meggie.

'Hello.' I wasn't sure what else to say.

I knew I should leave, but I didn't want to. Not now. Not yet. Meggie looked from Callie to me and back again. She sighed.

'Callie, I . . . I have something to tell you,' she began. 'And I don't want to put it off any longer.' She and Sephy exchanged a look before she continued. 'It's about . . . Jude.'

Callie flinched as if the word was a physical thing that had struck her.

'Tobey told me that you're . . . worried my son is alive and that he'll come after you.'

Though Callie didn't reply, Meggie had her full attention. I watched Callie avidly.

'Tobey, could you wait for us outside, please,' said Sephy. And it wasn't a request.

'No, Mum. I want Tobey to stay,' said Callie.

'But this is private family business,' Sephy began.

'I have no secrets from Tobey.' Callie looked at me as she spoke, her expression sombre. The words were said almost in a monotone, yet she still managed to make it sound like an accusation. Then she sighed. 'Will you stay, Tobey?'

I nodded. I wasn't going anywhere. Not whilst Callie needed me.

Meggie took a deep breath, closed her eyes momentarily, then spoke. 'Callie, love, Jude is dead. He died in the Isis Hotel bomb blast along with Jasmine.'

Callie shook her head. 'Uncle Jude isn't dead. The news said some man called Robert Powers . . .'

'Robert Powers was the alias Jude used. My son was infamous, notorious – and proud of it.' Bitterness hardened Meggie's voice. 'He knew that he wasn't going to die in bed of old age. He set up an alternate identity, complete with dental and doctor's records, a driver's licence, the works – and all under the name Robert Powers.'

'But how could he get an ID card and driver's licence?' asked Sephy. 'You have to produce a birth certificate to obtain those.'

'The real Robert Powers was born in the same year as

Jude and killed over fifteen years ago in a road accident. Apparently it's a well-known Liberation Militia tactic. Send off for the birth certificate of someone who has died and then use it to get all kinds of official documentation like passports,' said Meggie. 'So that's who Jude became and I was sworn to secrecy. He told me that if anything happened to him, his false ID would make sure that I wasn't hounded by the police and the press.'

'But the police must've had Uncle Jude's fingerprints.' It was as if Callie was afraid to let herself believe it. 'They had to be on a police database somewhere.'

'Callie, the explosion took out the top floor of the hotel. Jude's body was too badly damaged to identify using fingerprints. All the police had to work with were some teeth to match to dental records,' said Meggie. 'Please believe me, Callie, my son and Robert Powers are ... were ... one and the same person. I paid anonymously for Robert Powers's headstone. I even visit his grave occasionally to lay some flowers. Jude is dead.'

Meggie bowed her head. Sephy slipped an arm around her shoulder and whispered some words of comfort into her ear. I glanced across at Callie. Tears were flowing down her cheeks like a waterfall. I sprang up to go to her, but she shook her head, impatiently wiping the tears from her face.

'I'm OK,' she told me. 'I need to do this, before I bottle out.'

I knew what was coming. I moved to stand beside Callie's bed. Sephy looked from me to Callie, suspicion creeping into her eyes.

'Callie?' she prompted.

'Nana Meggie, you need to know something,' Callie began, fresh tears spilling onto her cheeks. 'The bomb that killed Uncle Jude and Nana Jasmine, I . . . I m–made it.'

Meggie stood up slowly and bent to kiss Callie's forehead. 'I know,' she said.

Callie stared at her. 'You . . . you know?'

'I've always known.'

'I don't understand.' Callie shook her head. 'Did Mum tell you? Why did you never say anything?'

'Your mum never said a word.' Meggie hastened to reassure her.

'Besides, what was there to say?' asked Sephy, as she moved to stand next to Meggie. 'I didn't realize what Mother was going to do until it was too late. I thought . . . Well, it doesn't matter what I thought.'

'Nana Meggie, how did you know if Mum didn't tell you?' asked Callie.

'Jasmine told me what my son was making you do,' said Meggie. 'She got in touch with me . . . and told me.'

'Do you know what happened that day?' Callie asked. 'Did Nana Jasmine decide to confront Uncle Jude? Did the bomb go off by accident?'

Callie turned to me, uncertainty written on her face, so she missed the swift look Sephy and Meggie exchanged. But I didn't. Callie's mum and grandma were both hiding something.

'Mum?' Callie prompted.

Sephy said gently, 'Love, I wasn't there. I was with you,

remember? But I'm sure it happened something like that. Callie, you mustn't blame yourself.'

Meggie added, 'It was an accident, love.'

'You think so?' Callie whispered. 'You really think it was an accident?'

Sephy and Meggie glanced at each other again. There was so much shared history between them that all they needed was a passing look to exchange volumes.

'Callie, we love you very much,' said Meggie. 'And Jasmine felt the same. She went to confront my son and . . . and the bomb went off. And the last person you should blame is yourself. I knew what my son was. So did Jasmine. He's responsible for what happened, not you.'

'But two people died . . .' Callie began.

'An accident. A tragic accident and not your fault,' Sephy insisted.

'Mum, did you know what Nana Jasmine was going to do when she left us in her house on my birthday?' asked Callie.

'Of course not. I would've stopped her,' Sephy said.

Callie was too busy looking at her mum to notice the look in Meggie's eyes at that question. With a start, I realized that even if Sephy hadn't known what Jasmine was up to, Meggie did. Meggie glanced at me. In that instant I knew the truth. And Meggie knew I knew. But I would never, ever tell Callie – and that was a fact.

'Mum, do you hate me?' Callie whispered.

'Oh, sweetheart, of course I don't hate you.' Sephy swept Callie into her arms. 'I told you before, there's nothing on this earth or beyond that could make me hate you.'

Callie and her mum hugged each other for a long time. When at last Callie let go, she turned to Meggie.

'Nana Meggie, I'm so sorry,' she said. 'I never meant for Uncle Jude or Nana Jasmine to get hurt. I was so lost and confused, I didn't know what I was doing.'

'I understand, dear,' said Meggie. 'All I want in this world is for you to stop blaming yourself.'

'Easier said than done,' Callie told her.

'But you've got to try,' said Meggie. 'Jude is dead, Callie. Don't let him ruin the rest of your life. You have to do what I did and let him go.'

Meggie looked down at the bed, but her gaze was somewhere in the past. An unhappy past. A couple of blinks later and she was back in the present, but her eyes still held a profound sorrow I was only just beginning to understand. Sephy stroked her daughter's hair. Meggie forced a smile. And though Callie tried to smile, it wobbled precariously on her face.

She turned to me, and the look in her eyes made my throat tighten so much I could hardly breathe. 'Tobey, you're going to be late for your dinner date,' she said quietly.

'I don't mind staying.'

'It's OK. I'm OK – or I will be. You should go.'

I knew a dismissal when I heard one. But even so, I couldn't help asking, 'Are you sure?'

Callie nodded. 'I'll see you . . . when I see you.'

And she turned away from me. Deliberately. Sephy watched me, a satisfied expression on her face.

I left Callie's room. Sephy followed me. Closing the door behind her, she walked a few paces along the corridor so that there was no chance of us being seen through Callie's window.

'As you can see, my daughter is now awake,' she said. 'So you needn't feel you have to visit her any more. I found out from one of the nurses that you've been here almost every day, in spite of what I told you.'

'How could I stay away? Callie is my best friend—'

'Oh, please,' Sephy scoffed.

'She is. I'd do anything for her.'

The look Sephy gave me was withering.

'It's true,' I insisted.

'Tobey, how stupid d'you think I am? D'you really think I'm going to stand idly by and watch you hurt my daughter?'

'I'd never do that—'

'But you did, Tobey. And you're still doing it. Don't forget, I saw you and your new girlfriend.'

'And you told Callie?'

Sephy's eyes narrowed. 'I didn't tell my daughter a damn thing. You did enough boasting about your new girlfriend on your own.'

'Rebecca isn't my girlfriend.'

'Tell that to her tongue and her tonsils,' Sephy replied with sarcasm. 'What is it with you? Off with the old and on with the new? Then keep the old as backup? Well, not where my daughter is concerned.'

'If you'd just let me explain . . .'

'Go on then.' Sephy folded her arms as she waited.

But I had nothing – at least nothing that was safe to share. No explanations. No excuses. No reasons. Nothing.

'That's what I thought.' Sephy's voice dripped with

contempt. 'Tobey, you obviously don't feel the same way about my daughter as she does about you. So do us all a favour and leave her alone.'

'That's not true,' I said. 'I . . . I do care about Callie.'

'Oh, spare me your lukewarm protestations.' Sephy raised both hands, her palms towards me as if she was warding me off. 'You know what, Tobey? I'm not getting into a debate with you. Callie doesn't need your guilt-inspired visits. I believe my daughter just made her feelings clear on that subject. I know I have.'

I closed my eyes briefly. The faster I ran towards Callie, the further away I got. Maybe I should just stop running.

'Miss Hadley, why are you doing this?'

'Because actions speak louder than words. When my daughter needed your help, when she needed you to tell the police what really happened, you turned your back on her. You let those responsible for harming her get away with it.'

Tell her, Tobey. Tell Sephy the truth . . .

'You walked away, Tobey. So keep walking. That's about all you're good for. Meggie and I have come to take Callie home. From this moment on, you leave her alone.'

And with one last look of pure disdain, Sephy headed back to her daughter.

sixty-five

Even though the sky was cloudy and rain threatened, I made my way back to the Wasteland. I had nowhere else to go. I glanced up at the darkening grey clouds. They filled the sky to overflowing. I sat on a park bench and watched the world pass me by. I was so close to getting everything I'd tried to achieve, and I'd never felt so far away from everything I believed in. It wasn't supposed to work that way.

I sat still for I don't know how long. Only the first fat splash of rain on my forehead roused me. I glanced at my watch. It was time to meet Rebecca. It was also time to draw a line under our relationship, such as it was. Maybe we could still at least be friends, though no doubt her brothers and her mum would do their best to make sure that didn't happen. But even if we couldn't stay friends, was it too much to hope we could part that way?

On my way to Los Amigos, the phone McAuley had given me started to vibrate in my pocket. Godsake! Much as I wanted to throw the mobile into the nearest bin, I couldn't. Instead, against my better judgment, I answered it.

'Hello, Mr McAuley.'

'Tobey, I'm deeply disappointed in you.'

Hello to you too. Had he finally figured out that I'd had a hand in the disappearance of his shipments?

'I don't know what you mean, sir,' I said cautiously.

'Tobey, don't make things worse by treating me like a fool. You were supposed to get me some information,' said McAuley. 'Where is it?'

It took me a second to catch up. He was talking about the bent cop on the Dowds' payroll. I was still safe. For now.

'I haven't been able to find out. I don't work at TFTM any more. Gideon got rid of me.'

'I'm not interested in your excuses. I'm very disappointed, Tobey. Now if you want to get back into my good books, you'll bring Rebecca Dowd to my warehouse on the industrial estate at ten o'clock tonight without fail. I can use her to get my shipments back from her family. Is that clear?'

Silence.

'Did you hear me, Tobey?'

'I'm sorry, Mr McAuley, but I can't do that,' I replied.

'Tobey, when you're in a hole you don't keep digging,' McAuley said silkily. 'You'll do as I say or you'll force me to show you what I do to those who let me down.'

'I'm sorry, Mr McAuley, but Rebecca has nothing to do with this and I think you should leave it that way. So I'm not doing it.' I disconnected the call before McAuley could make his threats more specific. I must be mad. This had to be the very definition of painting yourself into a corner. I dropped McAuley's phone on the pavement and ground it under my heel, enjoying the satisfying crunch it made as the plastic shattered. No more phone calls. No more orders. He was finished and I wanted nothing more to do with him or any of them. I knew what I had to do now. And I had to act fast. Time had just about run out.

sixty-six

At the coffee shop, Rebecca and I sat at a table by a window. Outside the rain was beginning to pelt down. Usually I loved the rain. It calmed me down. But not today. My brain felt hot-wired. My filter coffee sat untouched. Rebecca sipped at her skinny latte. She wore denim jeans, a red blouse and a denim jacket – and she looked the business. Her braids were tied back in a ponytail, but she seemed unaware or unconcerned about how pretty she looked. Conversation between us flowed like boulders travelling uphill. Neither of us had quite plucked up the courage to say why we were here. Rebecca took another sip of her coffee, then placed the tall glass down on the stained wooden table.

'Tobey, d'you like me? And please be honest,' she asked.

'I like you very much,' I replied at once.

'D'you love me?'

I thought of Callie. 'No,' I said.

'D'you think you could ever love me?'

All kinds of lines about not being able to tell the future and the like skipped into my head. But I couldn't lie to her. It wouldn't be fair.

'I don't think so,' I said. I took a deep breath and must-ered up a straight answer rather than a prevarication. 'No.'

'I didn't think so,' Rebecca said. 'I'm your rebound girl.'

'My what?'

'You split up from your last girlfriend and I came along at the right time to stop you being lonely,' she explained.

'That's not true,' I protested. 'I mean, there was more to it than that.'

'Let's be honest, Tobey. You like me, but it'll never be more than that – and we both know it. I think it takes a lot for you to love someone, but once you do, that's it for you,' said Rebecca. 'Your ex-girlfriend doesn't know how lucky she was.'

'Rebecca, I didn't set out to use you,' I said at last. 'I want you to believe that.'

'Oh, I do,' she said. 'In fact, I want to thank you for helping me to realize that I'm more than just my mother's daughter.'

'You don't give yourself enough credit,' I told her. 'You can do anything, be anyone. The only person stopping you is you.'

'You really believe that? It's that simple?'

'Yeah,' I replied at once. 'When you get right down to it, it is that simple. And you're in a better position than most people. You don't have class or status or money holding you back. You just need to get out of your own way. Godsake! That sounds like something my sister would say!'

Rebecca laughed. I'd told her about Jessica's meditation and inner-peace phase. I just hadn't mentioned how much I missed it compared to Jess's latest kick.

'I love the way you have such faith in me,' said Rebecca.

'What's not to believe in?' I smiled.

'To be honest, I've already made enquiries about teacher training courses at university,' she said, almost shyly. 'I haven't told my family yet, though.'

'That's fantastic,' I said. 'You'll be a great teacher. You have a lot of patience.'

'Except with certain girls called Misty,' Rebecca laughed.

'You're not alone in that one,' I told her.

We both finished our coffees.

'I don't work for McAuley, Rebecca. I want you to know that. I detest the man.'

'I know. And I'm sorry about your sister.'

I licked my lips as I tried to frame what needed to be said next.

'I've heard that McAuley blames your family for the loss of some shipments he recently arranged. You need to be on your guard, Rebecca. McAuley's a filthy piece of work who'd roll a tank over his own mother if she got in his way. And his back is against the wall, which makes him even more dangerous.'

'Don't worry,' Rebecca said with a confident smile. 'Mum and I are off on holiday tomorrow so McAuley won't be able to get anywhere near me.'

I sighed, relieved. That was OK then. To my surprise, Rebecca leaned across the table and kissed me. It was short but sweet.

'So you and me, we're still friends?' I asked.

I guess I wanted to have it all, but I really did like her.

Rebecca placed her hand over mine on the table. 'Of course we are. Nothing's going to change that.'

'I'm glad.' I smiled. 'Fancy another coffee?'

She considered. 'Oh, go on then. But I can't stay long.'

'Fair enough,' I said, standing up. 'Want a cake to go with it?'

'Tobey, you're a bad influence,' she admonished with a smile.

I grinned at her. 'I know!'

Over the next thirty minutes, I told her about Jess and finding her on the floor in the bathroom at home. Rebecca told me about the long-running feud between her two brothers. Apparently they'd been at each other's throats since they were kids. Reading between the lines, it sounded like their antagonism towards each other had been fuelled and fanned by their mother, but I wasn't about to spoil the affability growing between us by saying so.

Rebecca glanced down at her watch. 'Tobey, I have to go now,' she said reluctantly. 'Mum's expecting me back home. I have to finish my packing.'

Which was a real shame because both of us were enjoying our time together.

I said, 'Make sure you send me a postcard, OK?'

'Every other day,' said Rebecca.

'One will do,' I replied. It was only when I caught the smile on her face that I realized she was teasing me.

I paid for our coffees. We walked to the exit and hugged.

'Want me to walk you to your car?' I asked.

'No, don't bother. I'm only a couple of minutes up the road. I managed to find a parking bay. It must be my lucky day,' Rebecca smiled. 'Tobey, can we meet up for another coffee when I get back?'

'I'd like that. Very much,' I replied truthfully.

Outside the coffee shop, Rebecca dug into her bag and pulled out an orange and yellow umbrella. The thing was up and over her head in two seconds flat. My sister didn't like her hair to get wet in the rain either. Another hug made a tad awkward by the brolly, then a wave and we set off in opposite directions. The rain was still pitching down, but after the heat wave we'd had I was now kind of enjoying it. I'd always liked the rain. I was actually smiling! My meeting with Rebecca had gone better than I deserved. When she got back from her holiday, I'd definitely take her out for a meal or something, rather than a measly coffee.

A black van drove past. It was only after about five more steps that I realized where I'd seen it before – outside McAuley's house. Was McAuley following me? I turned. The van was heading away from me. I was sure it was McAuley's, but in that case, why hadn't he stopped? Even with my hair plastered down and the rain falling like a barrage of arrows, he must've seen me.

Rebecca.

No . . .

I raced back to the coffee bar and saw Rebecca and her brolly about twenty metres ahead of me, heading back to her car.

'REBECCA,' I called out, trying to make my voice heard over the teeming rain and the roaring traffic.

'REBECCA, WAIT . . .' I sprinted towards her.

Rebecca spun round to face me, just as McAuley jumped out of the passenger side of his van.

'BECKS, LOOK OUT!' But I was still at least six metres away. And McAuley was right behind her. A slight movement of his arm was all it took. Rebecca didn't even have a chance to look surprised before she fell to the pavement. Her umbrella rolled away from her. She lay motionless on the ground as McAuley stood there, his arms at his side, a dripping knife held in his right hand. I skidded to an abrupt halt less than two metres away from him and stood stock still, unable to move. And even though the rain kept slanting into my eyes, I'll swear until my dying day that McAuley smiled at me. A brief, satisfied smile.

'You let me down, Tobey,' he said. 'My warehouse at ten tonight, or I'll come to your house – and through your family, if necessary – to get you.'

He climbed back into the van. It drove away at an unhurried pace. Those closest to Rebecca's prone body rushed to her aid, her discarded umbrella an indicator that something was very wrong. And still I couldn't move. Rebecca lay face down on the ground, her head to one side. Raindrops fell into her open, sightless eyes, but she didn't even flinch. She stared across the pavement and into the gutter. The world went very still, very quiet. Just for an instant, but it was enough. Cold sweat and warm rain drenched my body. My stomach began to fold in on itself. I tried to take a breath, but my body had forgotten how. It was only when my burning lungs were howling out for air that I managed a horrified gasp. Then all the sounds around me were amplified to such a degree that the noise was painful, deafening.

Through the drumming rain came cries for help, calls for an ambulance and pleas for witnesses. The crowd was getting bigger all the time. Most were still trying to figure out what had happened. One Cross man turned Rebecca over onto her back and tried to administer mouth to mouth and CPR. His actions were frantic, one breath away from pure panic. His face . . . the glasses he wore . . . familiar . . . he'd been in the coffee bar with us. Following us? I instinctively knew who he was. Rebecca's bodyguard — assigned by Gideon to keep his distance but protect. Too much distance.

He'd failed.

I'd failed.

My mistakes. Expensive mistakes. Costly. Priceless. I couldn't afford the price, so Rebecca paid. She was motionless. No blood . . . why was there no blood? The rain snatched it up and escaped away in every direction with it. I stared down at Rebecca and the world grew colder and quieter. It was only when a distant siren split the air that the blood started racing around my veins again.

My body shaking, I turned and walked away.

I was good at that.

I only made it halfway along the road before, without warning, my stomach erupted. I was sick all over my shoes and the pavement. I wanted to lie down and curl up in a ball until the image of Rebecca's unseeing eyes left my head. I wanted to lie down spread-eagled in the rain until I was washed clean again. But there wasn't enough water on the planet.

First Callie Rose. Now Rebecca.

Oh, God . . .

Rebecca.

No more. Please no more.

sixty-seven

My mobile started to ring. I answered it on auto-pilot, my hand trembling. My whole body was shaking. Breathe in, breathe out. Calm down, Tobey.

Rebecca . . .

Breathe out, breathe in.

Tobey, get it together.

Rebecca.

Rain washed over my hand and my phone, but I didn't care. Why couldn't I stop shaking? Keep walking, Tobey. Whatever else happens, keep walking.

'Tobey? This is Detective Inspector Boothe.'

'Yes, Inspector?' I said faintly.

'I have some good news for you.'

Good news for whom? Had he got to McAuley . . . before I could?

'Good news?' I prompted.

'We found our corrupt cop. She's been arrested, along with Gideon Dowd.'

'I don't understand.'

'Acting on an anonymous tip-off, we were able to place surveillance equipment and use undercover personnel from other regions to catch Gideon Dowd discussing future payoffs with DCI Reid. In return she gave him details of a raid on his house and one of his business premises planned for two days' time. DCI Reid was the one in the Dowds' pocket.'

DCI Reid . . . Where had I heard that name before?

'The woman who interviewed me at the police station?' I remembered.

'That's right,' said DI Boothe. 'I believed what you said, Tobey. And as it was DCI Reid's idea to bring you in, I went over her head to get permission to lay a trap for her. And she walked right into it.'

I shook my head, which felt like it was stuffed with cotton wool.

'I . . . I don't understand. You got an anonymous tip-off?'

'Yeah. Some public-spirited citizen provided us with chapter and verse. We know all about DCI Reid and her involvement with Gideon Dowd. We were sent files documenting meeting times and payoffs, offshore bank account details and all the operations she scuppered on Dowd's behalf. We also got information tying a whole shipment of hijacked drugs to Gideon. He was stupid enough to store them in the basement of his town house. With the data we were sent and the surveillance evidence, that piece of trash Reid and her scumbag lover Gideon will both be dining on prison food for twenty years minimum.'

'I see.'

'I did wonder if I have you to thank for the files I was sent?' Boothe enquired ingenuously.

'Nothing to do with me,' I replied slowly.

No, DI Boothe needed to thank Owen Dowd.

Gideon was out of the way. McAuley was on the ropes and busted. Owen Dowd now owned it all.

Meadowview was out of the frying pan – and into the fire.

Well done, Tobey.

What was my mantra? Whatever it takes?

All I had to do now was head up to the top of the tallest building in Meadowview and wait for one and all to thank me. With a psycho nut job like Owen Dowd now running things, the thanks would pour in.

'So are you prepared to talk to me now?' asked Boothe. 'Will you testify against McAuley?'

'Why would I do that?'

'Because we both know he's the one responsible for your girlfriend ending up in hospital. Testify against him and I can guarantee you and your family will be protected. We can even relocate you if necessary,' said DI Boothe.

'It's too late,' I replied.

'What d'you mean?' I could hear the frown in Boothe's voice.

'I mean, it's too late tonight. Ask me tomorrow.'

I disconnected the call.

sixty-eight

I tried phoning Dan, but his phone just rang continuously. There was only one thing left to do. I headed for his lockup. It was only on my second attempt that I accurately remembered the combination to his padlock. I went in, coughing against the smell of stale air and stale hopes and stale dreams. The single bulb didn't cast enough light to sweep the corners of the place. No matter. I knew what I needed. I found it in a box in the far corner of the room, a P99 military semiautomatic – the 9mm version. It had a green polymer frame – an eco-friendly colour, I told myself. I checked the magazine. It was fully loaded. Making sure the safety was on, I put the gun in my jacket pocket. I spun around and halted in mid-step. Dan stood at the entrance to the lockup, watching me.

'Dan, I need your help,' I launched in at once. 'McAuley killed Rebecca Dowd and now he is after me.'

'What d'you plan on doing about it?'

'It's me or him,' I said quietly.

'Finally gonna get your hands dirty?'

'Dan, please. Will you help me?'

The smile Dan gave then was a long way from friendly. 'Why don't you just call the police?'

''Cause then McAuley will find a way to make my whole family pay, not just me.'

'Why should I care about you or your family?' asked Dan.

'It's not about me, Dan. My mum and sister don't deserve what will happen if McAuley gets hold of them.'

'Says the man who started all this in the first place,' he said bitterly. 'You wound us all up like your little dancing dolls and now you're complaining because we're not dancing the way you want us to.'

What could I say to that? Nothing.

'Dan, please. McAuley's at his warehouse, but he's not alone. I can't do this by myself.'

'You're gonna have to.' Dan shrugged. 'This isn't my fight.'

'But McAuley's men will all be armed to the teeth.'

'Not my problem,' said Dan. 'And *now* we're even.'

So much for that then. The faint glimmer of hope I'd felt when I turned round and saw Dan standing there flickered and died. Only desperation had made me believe that he might help me. Far too much had passed between us.

'Can I take your P99?' I took the gun out of my pocket to show him.

'Are you going to bring it back?' he asked wryly.

Probably not.

'If I can.'

'Then go ahead. Take a couple of extra magazine clips, just in case.'

We could've been talking about comic books or sausages rather than guns. I took an extra magazine clip out of the box and headed for the exit.

'You won't change your mind and help me?' I tried one last time.

Dan shook his head, adding, 'You do know you won't get past Byron and the others packing a gun, don't you? It'll never happen.'

I looked down at the gun in my hand and shook my head. What did I think I was doing? I'd never fired a real gun in my life. Targets at a fairground and pellet guns with my dad were about my speed. What did I think was going to happen? I'd go in, guns blazing like some Cross cowboy in a film, and save the world from McAuley? Yeah, right.

I walked back to Dan's table and put down the P99 and the extra clip.

'Ah! Going to use a new technique against McAuley and his crew, are you? Gonna poke them in the eyes or swear at them? Or were you thinking of throwing the odd shoe?'

Dan was right – and I resented him for it.

I didn't stand a chance with a gun.

I didn't stand a chance without one.

'Welcome to the dance floor, Tobey,' Dan said with satisfaction. 'The song is called "Survival".'

And I was about to get crushed underfoot. I left the lockup and headed for McAuley's warehouse.

sixty-nine

As I walked, I tried not to think and I certainly didn't want to feel. It wasn't far, only thirty minutes from Dan's lockup, and at least the rain had eased off. I looked up at the sky, knowing I'd never enjoy rain again. I just wished I could've spoken to Callie one more time before seeing McAuley. Just one last time. I wasn't happy about the way things had been left between us, but then whose fault was that but my own? If I didn't know who or what I was any more, then what chance did she have of figuring it out.

At last I arrived at the warehouse. The industrial estate contained seven or eight units, most of which were empty and boarded up. At this time of night the place was deserted. The railway bridge beyond the estate was the only sign of irregular life in the whole place. Four or five street lamps had to illuminate the entire estate and were failing miserably. Two Nought security guards dressed in dark blue or black stood outside McAuley's warehouse, chatting. One wore a wool hat pulled tight down over his head, the other was smoking a cigarette. The guard wearing the hat was showing the smoker something on a mobile phone. I inhaled deeply, allowing the smell of tar and rubbish and traffic fumes to fill my lungs, then walked straight up to them.

'I need to see Mr McAuley. Could you tell him that Tobey Durbridge is here?'

The two guards exchanged a look. The smoker stubbed out his cigarette, grinding it under the toe of his thick-soled shoes. He looked me up, down and sideways as he broke out his walkie-talkie. Turning away from me, he spoke into it, his voice a low monotone. Thirty seconds later, he signed off and turned back to me.

'Turn left inside and head for the far end of the ware-house. The office is on your right. Mr McAuley is expecting you,' he told me ominously.

'Thanks,' I replied, though I had no idea why I was thanking him.

He opened one of the warehouse doors and left me to it. I followed his instructions, passing vast crates and boxes stacked on top of each other. The warehouse was dimly lit and eerily silent, a silence so deep it echoed back at me. The rest of McAuley's men had to be in his office already. I took out my phone, pressing the speed-dial icon to get through to DI Boothe. I was wasting my time. From within this warehouse, it was impossible to get a signal. Every nerve in my body screamed at me to turn back. There was no way I could take on the likes of McAuley. It was foolish to even try.

Don't think about that, Tobey. Just keep going.

Whatever it takes.

I knocked on the office door before I could change my mind. 'Mr McAuley, it's me – Tobey,' I called out. 'I have some news you need to hear.'

The door opened slowly. Byron stood in the doorway, gun in hand. He took a quick look around to make sure I was alone, then stepped aside to let me into the room. McAuley sat in the chair at his desk. My gaze zipped around his office like a pinball. Byron stood next to me at the door. Trevor, the guy from McAuley's house, and two other muscle-heads I'd never seen before were dotted around the room.

'So you came?' said McAuley. He turned to Byron. 'I told you he'd come. Search him.'

He stood up and sauntered towards me whilst Byron patted me down from head to toe, not missing a centimetre in between.

'Mr McAuley, I've got something to—'

McAuley threw his whole weight behind a punch to my stomach. It felt like a wrecking ball had hit my innards. I dropped to my knees, clutching my belly and coughing my guts out. Another punch to my head and I was down on the floor, seeing stars and the whole solar system whizzing round my head. My cheek was on fire. I could taste blood in my mouth. McAuley ambled back to his original position behind his desk.

'Byron, get rid of him.' McAuley's voice reached me through the ringing in my ears.

'No. W-wait. P-please. Wait.' My breathing came shallow and fast and sharp. Sweat coated every centimetre of my skin.

This is it, I thought. I tried to swallow, but nothing could move past the jagged rocks in my throat.

It's all over. I'm done.

Byron grabbed my arm and hauled me to my feet. I struggled to stay upright, holding my stomach, which still roared with pain. It felt like my stomach muscles or maybe my spleen had been split wide open. And my cheek was on fire.

'Mr McAuley, I f-found out s-something from Gideon Dowd.' I could hardly catch my breath to speak. But silence would kill me for sure, or maybe just sooner. 'Something you n-need to know.' I had to get the words out whilst I still had the chance.

'If it's the identity of the bent cop, I already know. It's been all over the late-night news,' said McAuley. 'You should've been the one to provide that information, Tobey, not a newsreader. You let me down on that score as well. And ignoring my instructions about Rebecca Dowd? Not smart, Tobey. Not smart.'

'I'm s-sorry about Rebecca, sir. I shouldn't have disobeyed you. It won't happen again.'

'That's right,' said McAuley softly. 'It won't.'

'But the information I have is something far more interesting than a bent cop, sir,' I rushed to assure him. I managed to stand upright to face him. Something was trickling down my cheek. I touched my fingers to my face. Blood. His punch had cut my cheek, inside and out. My hands dropped back to my side.

Silence.

'I'm listening,' McAuley said brusquely.

'It's private,' I said, deliberately looking at each of his squad in turn.

'I have no secrets from my men. I'd trust them with my life.'

'Would you really?' I asked carefully.

McAuley might've been a lot of things, but slow wasn't one of them. He glanced at Byron, who shook his head. I wasn't carrying any hardware, so I was no threat. It wasn't luck that had made me leave Dan's gun behind – it was a sense of self-preservation.

'Maybe you should get three of your men to guard the warehouse entrance, just in case?' I suggested. 'One of Dowds' men saw you – what you did to Rebecca. They'll come calling.'

McAuley stood up, his ice-blue, ice-cold eyes burning into me. 'Trevor, take Dave and Scott and go do as he says. And when you're outside, you'd better phone for some reinforcements.'

The three men left the room, albeit reluctantly. That was perfect. I hadn't had to engineer it so Byron was left behind.

'So what is it?' said McAuley.

This was it. The moment of truth, half-truths and downright lies.

'One of your men is working for the Dowds.'

'Bollocks!' McAuley didn't believe it for a second.

I remembered what he'd said about demanding the loyalty of the people who worked for him. He was like Rebecca that way. Loyalty was everything.

'I have proof,' I said.

'It'd better be watertight,' McAuley said silkily, the threat evident in his voice.

'Can you go online with that computer?' I asked, pointing to the one on his desk.

McAuley's eyes narrowed. 'Of course.'

'Ask Byron to log on and show you how much money he's got in his bank account.'

'What the . . . ?' Byron piped up. 'What is this?'

'Byron is working for the Dowds,' I explained. 'The proof is in his bank account. After today he was going to turn tail and run out on you.'

'I don't believe a word of it,' said McAuley.

'Then check his account. If I'm wrong, then you can hand me over to Byron.'

Byron marched over to me. 'I'm going to enjoy breaking your scrawny neck,' he hissed, spraying spit in my face.

I stepped back, wiping my face with the back of my hand.

'Just check, Mr McAuley. Unless of course you want Byron to get away with it.'

'Alex, you don't believe this bullshit, do you?' Byron turned to his boss.

'Of course not,' said McAuley.

My heart nose-dived. I was screwed.

'But it wouldn't hurt to check, would it?' McAuley continued. 'Log onto your bank account, Byron.'

Byron stared at his boss, unable to believe his ears.

'And once you've proved that Durbridge is lying, he's all yours,' McAuley added.

Byron gave me a look I'd never seen before, and if I lived to be two hundred I never want to see again. If Owen had been lying about putting the money into Byron's account, I was deader than a Sunday roast. Byron marched round the desk and started slamming his fingers down on the keys. I moved round the desk to see the computer screen along with him and McAuley.

Byron input the requested three digits from his four-digit pin code and the requested first, fifth and ninth characters from his password. They all came up as asterisks on the screen so I couldn't hope to learn or guess what his pin code and password might be. Not that it made much difference now. A new screen appeared, showing details of Byron Sweet's current account. It contained six figures, a very healthy six figures. Owen hadn't lied – thank goodness.

Behind Byron, McAuley straightened up.

'T–that can't be right,' Byron spluttered. He clicked on the refresh icon to redisplay the page. The amount of money in his bank account didn't change. He sprang to his feet. 'Alex, I don't know what's going on, but I have no idea how all that money got in my account. I really don't.'

I moved out from behind the desk. If things were about to kick off, I didn't want to get caught up in it.

'That's a lot of money, Byron,' said McAuley quietly.

'It's not mine. You've got to believe me, Alex,' Byron protested. He looked around as if searching for someone to back him up, but there was just him and McAuley – and me. He pointed at me. 'Tobey did it. He must've put it in my account.'

'Where would I get that kind of money from?' I scoffed.

'Boss, I—'

The gun blast made me jump. Byron's hands flew to his throat, but blood squirted out from between his fingers like a fountain. It splashed over McAuley's suit and sprayed his hair. Byron fell backwards like a felled tree. He was dead before he hit the floor. McAuley stared down at him, eyes wild. My mind was screaming. I didn't expect . . . I clamped my lips together so that no sound could spill out of my mouth.

Omigod . . .

McAuley was going to kill me next. I saw it in his eyes as he slowly turned to look at me, his gun still in his hand.

'I'm sorry, Mr McAuley, but I thought you should know,' I said quickly. 'I heard Gideon Dowd talking to one of your men on the phone when I worked at TFTM. Gideon called him by his surname, Sweet. But I only found out earlier today that Byron's surname is Sweet. I'm really sorry, Mr McAuley.'

Trevor, Scott and Dave burst into the room. McAuley was covered in blood, but Byron's body was behind his desk so they couldn't see it from the door. The three men looked me up and down, wondering how I was still standing, wondering where all the blood on their boss had come from. McAuley put his gun down on the desk so he could button up his bloodstained jacket, like he thought that would tidy him up.

'Get rid of the body,' he told them, still buttoning up his jacket.

The three men went round the desk. They stared down at Byron's body, shocked. Two of them bent down to pick him up. I saw it on the desk, my one and only chance. I snatched up McAuley's Glock 23 before any of them could make a move. I hadn't planned on this, but the gun was lying there just asking to be claimed. And I'd rather be at the stock end of it than the barrel end.

'All of you, just stay right there. And keep your hands where I can see them.' The gun was trained on McAuley and his men, who were standing together for the first time since I'd entered the warehouse. From what I could figure out, apart from McAuley and these three, there were just the two security guards at the warehouse entrance. But for how long? McAuley had sent for reinforcements. How long would it take them to get here? I didn't have much time.

We all stood like figures in an oil painting.

Now what?

'One at a time, I want all of you to take out your guns and place them on the table. Dave, you start.'

I watched as Dave withdrew a gun from beneath his jacket.

'You, the one with the red hair. What was your name again? Scott? Your turn.'

He reached round to pull the gun from the waistband at the back of his trousers. I would've thought keeping a gun there was a good way to blow your buttocks off, but what did I know?

'Now you, Trevor.'

Trevor took a gun out of his jacket and put it on the desk.

'Trevor, you'd better get lost,' I said. 'Unless you want to stay here and wait for McAuley to realize that you're the one who works for the Dowds, not Byron.'

'What the hell . . . ?' McAuley gasped.

'Oh, didn't I say?' I said. 'Byron didn't work for the Dowds. That money was put in his bank account by Owen Dowd to make you think otherwise. But when I worked at TFTM, I saw Trevor coming out of Gideon Dowd's office. And Gideon's brother Owen told me that one of your men was passing on information. So it has to be him.'

Trevor looked from me to McAuley like he didn't know what to do.

'Are you staying or going?' I asked impatiently.

Trevor took off like his shoes were on fire. Honour amongst thieves.

Three against one. Plus the two outside. Much better. I could breathe easy now!

I glanced down at Byron. There was a small pool of blood around his neck and head. One bullet and Byron's life was over. One thrust of a knife and Rebecca was gone. Life was too precious to be so fragile. Or maybe life was precious because it was so fragile.

'All of you.' I waved them out from around the table. 'Walk over to the door, please.'

McAuley stayed his men with one gesture of his hand. 'Suppose we stay where we are?' he said. 'Suppose I don't think you've got the balls to shoot anyone?'

He reached for one of the guns on the table. I aimed and squeezed the trigger in the space of less than a second. The gun McAuley had been reaching for shot off the table, propelled by the bullet from my gun. Splinters of wood flew off in all directions. McAuley and his mob flinched away from the ricocheting debris.

'Suppose the next bullet goes straight through your heart?' I told McAuley. I might not have shot a gun at living targets before, but that didn't mean I didn't know how to shoot. My dad had seen to that. 'Now all of you – move.'

I swept the rest of the gun hardware onto the floor with my arm. I certainly didn't need one of McAuley's men getting any bright ideas. If we all headed out of the warehouse, then I could get a signal, phone the police and we'd wait for them to arrive. And maybe, just maybe I might make it out of this in one piece. Scott and Dave led the way, followed by McAuley, with me following behind all three of them. The moment Scott and Dave were through the office door, they sprinted off in opposite directions. There was no way I could stop them. I ran in front of McAuley and slammed the door shut before he could pull the same stunt. Never taking my eyes off McAuley, I locked the door behind me.

McAuley's men were somewhere in the warehouse, just waiting to pounce once I left the office. They couldn't get in. We couldn't get out.

Now what?

'Half a million pounds to the one who kills Tobey Durbridge!' McAuley shouted out.

Bastard! What a time to raise his voice.

The slamming against the office door started almost at once.

'Sit down on the ground,' I ordered McAuley, my gun in his face.

He did as I said, a look of intense satisfaction on his face.

'You're dead, Durbridge. Deal with it. And when I get out of here, I'm going to take care of your girlfriend too.'

'You already took care of Rebecca,' I said bitterly.

'The Dowds needed to be taught a lesson.'

'Rebecca had nothing to do with her family's business,' I told him. 'She was innocent—'

'She was a Dowd,' McAuley dismissed. 'I had hoped to swap her for my merchandise, but you refused to play ball, so I had to opt for plan B – which was fine with me. And you made it so easy to get to Rebecca. Thank you, Tobey. I couldn't have done it without you.'

My index finger stroked over the gun trigger. Shooting McAuley would be a public service.

'But we both know Rebecca wasn't your girlfriend,' McAuley continued.

At my puzzled look, his smile broadened. 'No, I'm talking about Callie Rose Hadley. I was aiming at you that day at the Wasteland when she got in the way instead. But next time . . .'

I raised my fist and brought it down against McAuley's face. I forgot I was still holding his gun. Blood started gushing from his nose almost immediately. McAuley cried out in pain. The pounding on the office door grew more frantic. It didn't matter whether McAuley's minions were trying to save him or earn the reward money he'd promised, I'd be just as dead. I looked down at the gun I was holding. The Glock 23 felt heavy and seductively comfortable in my hand. The pearl stock, warmed by my body heat, fitted snugly against my palm. I now held McAuley's custom-made semiautomatic.

A real, honest-to-God gun in my hand.

A proper killing machine.

Or was that me?

'You're dead, Durbridge – and there's nothing you can do about it.'

seventy

I pulled Eisner's bag of white powder out of my trouser pocket and dangled it in front of McAuley's face.

'You know what this is?' It was a question that didn't need answering. Of course McAuley knew what I was holding. This stuff paid for his white suit and the blood all over it. It paid for the drug houses he had all over Meadowview, and for Ross Resnick's life and my sister's pain. McAuley revelled in the stuff I held in my hands. The harder life got in Meadowview, the more profit there was to be made. Simple economics.

McAuley's eyes narrowed. He spat blood out of his mouth and wiped the sleeve of his jacket across his nose before speaking.

'You want your cut?' he asked. 'Is that what this is all about? You want to go into business for yourself?'

I said nothing. McAuley took my silence to mean that I was listening to him.

'You're a smart guy, Tobey. I could use someone like you working for me. I could show you what it's all about.

In five years you'd be rich beyond your wildest dreams.' McAuley's voice flowed like warm honey. 'And whether you like it or not, you need me. Rebecca died after a meeting with you. What d'you think the Dowds are going to make of that? I'm the only one who can protect you.'

He really thought he had me. I walked around him, my gun still pointed at his head. The banging on his door was getting more insistent. I had about a minute, if that, before the door gave way. McAuley tried to twist his body to follow my movements. My gun against his temple soon persuaded him not to. But he wouldn't stop talking.

'You and me, Tobey, we live in the real world. We know the way things really work. Those that don't know, don't want to know. It's too much for them to take in. Life in Meadowview doesn't happen to them, so it doesn't happen at all. But we know different, don't we?'

Standing behind McAuley, I pulled the top of the small plastic bag apart. The top of the bag gaped open like a transparent mouth.

'It's that knowledge that has made me rich,' McAuley continued. 'And it will make you even richer than me, 'cause you're a smart guy, Tobey.'

'You don't get it, do you, Mr McAuley?' I said. 'This was never about money. This was about you. Why d'you think I did all this? I know you tried to kill me and Callie got hurt instead. All I cared about was bringing you down.'

'Then why didn't you just go to the police?'

'The police were my last resort. I didn't know how many of them were in your pocket. Besides, it's not exactly the Meadowview way, is it?'

'Seems to me that wouldn't've stopped you.'

'You're right. If there was no other way to get you then I would've taken my chances with the police.'

'Don't you see, Tobey,' said McAuley, 'you and I are the same. We go after what we want and we're ruthless about getting it.'

'In your dreams, McAuley. I'm nothing like you.'

'No?' He smiled. 'Look at yourself. Tell me that gun in your hand doesn't make you feel powerful. Tell me this situation isn't giving you the adrenalin rush of your life. Tell me otherwise and I won't believe you.'

I didn't want to hear any more. I couldn't think straight with his words dripping like poison into my ears. Time to shut him up.

'Open your mouth,' I ordered.

McAuley tilted back his head. 'What?'

'You heard,' I said. 'Open up.'

He slowly did as I'd asked. I tipped the whole bag of white powder into his mouth. He writhed on the ground, kicking frantically as he tried to spit it out, but I clamped my hand over his lips, forcing him to swallow.

'This stuff means so much to you?' I hissed. 'Choke on it.'

His eyes raged against mine, but I couldn't hear or feel a thing. I kept my hand against his mouth and my gun against his head. He was the one who'd tried to shoot me down in cold blood, only he'd hit Callie instead. He was the one who'd decided I was a danger to him because I'd unknowingly delivered Ross Resnick's finger to his wife Louise and the police had become involved. If he'd just left me alone, none of this would be happening.

The door was beginning to splinter. It was all over.

Outside the door there was a loud unexpected bang. Then another. And another. Gunshots. Each shot was loud as the devil's shout and reverberated right through me. Did McAuley's men have guns salted away throughout the warehouse? Maybe they'd got tired of banging on the door and were shooting out the lock. Another gunshot, louder than before ... closer than before. I pressed my gun against McAuley's head, my finger on the trigger. He was coughing and retching. He could dish it out to anyone who wanted it and could pay, but he sure couldn't take it. The door burst open. I was ready. When I went down, so would McAuley.

Standing in the doorway was ... Dan.

He had the P99 in his hand and two dead men at his feet.

'Get out of here, Tobey,' he said grimly. 'The police will be here any minute. The guards outside must've woken up by now.'

'Dan ...' I stared at him. 'I thought ...'

'I know what you thought. Go, before I change my mind.'

'But I can't just leave ...'

'Yes, you can. You need to go,' Dan ordered.

'McAuley's got more men on their way.'

'The police will get here first.'

'Dan, I don't understand. What made you change your mind?' I couldn't help asking.

'I'm damned if I know,' he said. 'I owe you. You owe me. Everything is screwed up. Tobey, there are times, like now, when I hate your guts.'

'Then why?'

'The McAuleys of this world can't always win. Not all the time,' said Dan. 'And you and me, we were friends once.'

'We were friends,' I agreed. 'Once.'

Dan walked over to McAuley, watching with contempt as he vomited all over his suit, white powder smeared around his lips and frothing in his mouth.

'Dan, you don't have to stay here. Come with me,' I said.

He shook his head, adding with a defeated smile, 'Tobey, haven't you figured out by now, this is my proper place. But don't worry about me. McAuley and I have some business to take care of. Then it's every man for himself.'

I wanted to argue with him, but it would've been futile. I looked from Dan to McAuley, who was still retching. I didn't know if McAuley had brought it all up and I didn't care any more. I just wanted to be away from here. Away from all of them, including Dan. They made me heartsick. I went to walk past Dan, but he put out a hand to bar my way.

'Give me McAuley's gun,' he said.

We regarded each other. Laying the gun in Dan's open hand, I carried on walking. Would I feel the bullet tear into my back or hear the gun go off – which would be first? I looked straight ahead as I left the room. I could see nothing but Callie's warm, brown eyes smiling at me. I held onto her image. If Dan was going to kill me, then at least I'd die with her on my mind, at least I'd die happy.

I got McAuley for you, Callie, I thought with a grim smile. I got him.

Just as I'd promised her and myself when I'd cradled her in my arms at the Wasteland.

All this because of packages and deliveries and Ross Resnick and money. Thanks to my greedy impatience, I'd let myself get caught up in it. And thanks to my naïvety, so had Callie Rose. And because of me, Rebecca . . .

Rebecca.

Forgive me . . .

Who was I talking to? What was I hoping for? I was seeking absolution in a warehouse filled with blood. I blinked as I walked out of the building and into the moonlight. I was still standing. But only just. Behind me a single gunshot sounded. I flinched instinctively. The sound had come from inside the warehouse, from McAuley's office. Without turning round, I carried on walking away just as fast as I could. In the distance, I heard sirens approaching. I ran for cover, ducking out of sight behind some bins and staying there until the police cars had passed by.

I walked all the way home, my head down, my gaze turned inwards. I turned into my street, my whole body aching. But I didn't stop outside my house. Instead I went up to Callie's, intent on seeing her again. But I didn't knock and I didn't ring her bell. I just stood, staring at the closed door.

I did it for you, Callie.

But in doing so, I'd lost myself. I wasn't the same person as before and I couldn't bear to watch Callie turn away from the person I'd become. And she would turn away, maybe sooner, maybe later, but it would happen.

Slowly I trudged up the path to my house and went indoors.

The
Reckoning

seventy-one

'Tobey, Callie's here,' Mum called out from downstairs.

Five days had passed since McAuley had been shot. And my friend Dan Jeavons was wanted for his murder, as well as the murders of two other men who worked for McAuley. But Dan was still on the run and the police hadn't tracked him down. Yet. The DCI in charge of the case insisted that it was not a question of *if* Dan got caught but *when*. And all I could do was hope that Dan kept his head down and never stopped moving. And all I could do was wish he would stop running and give himself up, just to find some peace.

If it wasn't for him . . .

Dan and me. We were friends. Once.

Gideon Dowd and DCI Reid had both been arrested and charged on several different counts. I'd thought DCI Reid would be done for gross misconduct and kicked off the police force and that would be the end of that, but not so. The authorities wanted her skin, not to mention all her internal organs in a pickle jar. The deputy commissioner, no less, was at pains to assure the public that DCI Reid, if found guilty of the charges levelled against her, would be going to prison. The police were obviously on a roll. They'd even got Vanessa Dowd on a charge of tax evasion – not that she cared. She was still openly grieving over the death of her daughter Rebecca. The fatal stabbing had been all over the newspapers and the TV. Everyone seemed to be judging Rebecca and the circumstances of her death by the infamy of the rest of her family. She didn't deserve that. The press were still trying to establish a link between her death and the death of Alex McAuley as everyone knew about the enmity between the two factions. There was even speculation that Dan had been working for the Dowds.

My name hadn't been mentioned anywhere.

So Alex McAuley was out of the picture. And Owen Dowd now occupied the whole frame. Two days ago, I received a banker's cheque for a lot of money. Owen hadn't sent me a personal cheque – that'd be too easy to trace – but he'd sent me the money just as he had said he would. It arrived in an ordinary envelope with a first class stamp. And if the cheque had gone astray? Well, Owen had plenty more where that came from. Just touching the slip of paper made me feel unclean. I folded up the cheque just as small as I could, but I couldn't make it disappear. I went for a long walk to try and clear my head, dropping the cheque into the first charity collection box I came across. But I still felt contaminated.

Owen Dowd . . .

Not the outcome I would've hoped for as far as he was concerned. None of this was what I'd hoped for. I read a story once about a king who was greedy enough to wish that everything he touched turned to gold. Well, thanks to my desire for money and then revenge, everything I'd touched had turned to crap. I wasn't about to touch anyone I cared about ever again. Dan was right about me. So was Sephy. And Lucas. Everyone saw me more clearly than I saw myself.

I swung my legs off my bed to head downstairs. Too late. My door opened and Callie walked in. Her hair was loose, falling like a dark cloud around her face and shoulders and covering the scar on her temple. But in time, her scar would heal. She'd lost weight, but she was still the most beautiful thing I'd ever seen. She was wearing a white dress and white sandals and my insides started hiccupping at the sight of her. I remembered the last time Callie had been in my room. That'd been the first, last and only time in my entire life I'd been truly one hundred per cent happy. But that was another lifetime ago. And now I was broken inside.

Callie walked towards me and I froze. She reached out, her fingers brushing against the now permanent scar on my cheek, courtesy of McAuley. Her touch made my skin tingle.

'Your eye is a bit puffy and yellow,' she said softly. 'Does it hurt?'

I pulled away from her. 'I'll live.'

Callie's hand dropped to her side. 'Who did that to you?' she asked, indicating my face.

'Callie, I haven't got time to talk to you now. I was just on my way out.'

'Can I come?'

'No,' I said, pulling on my trainers. 'I have a date.'

'With who?'

'Misty.'

'I see,' said Callie. She studied my carpet as if she'd never seen it before.

'Why did you want to see me?' I prompted as I stood up. I had to get her out of my room. Seeing her like this was doing my head in.

'I came to tell you that Mum has invited you to come with us tomorrow to Bharadia and Hammond.'

'To who and what?' I frowned.

'Bharadia and Hammond. They're Nana Jasmine's solicitors,' Callie explained. 'We're going to hear Nana's will being read. Mum says you can share our car. We're leaving at two tomorrow afternoon.'

'Why do I need to be there?'

'You're mentioned in Nana's will,' said Callie.

I frowned at her. 'Why?'

She shrugged. 'No idea.'

Silence.

'Tobey, I was sorry to hear about what happened to your friend, Rebecca.'

I shrugged.

'Are the police any closer to finding out who did it?'

I shook my head. 'They'll never find out who's responsible.'

'You mustn't give up hope,' said Callie.

Hope? What was that? Every day was like standing at the gateway to hell. The knife McAuley had used on Rebecca hadn't been found on his body, so he'd obviously disposed of it before he got to his warehouse. They would never find it now. Rebecca's death would remain an unsolved mystery, at least officially.

'Callie, have you remembered anything about the day . . . the day you got shot?' I asked.

Callie shook her head. I waited for her to say more, but

she was silent. So she probably still didn't remember the night before the shooting either. She didn't remember the two of us together. I smiled bitterly. I didn't even have that to silently, secretly share with her. The memory was mine and mine alone.

'Tell me something,' I began. 'If you found out who shot you, what would you do?'

Callie flinched at my question, her gaze sharp. 'Tobey, d'you know who it was?'

I shrugged. 'It's just a hypothetical question.'

'Then my hypothetical answer is – I don't know,' Callie replied. 'I'd probably tell the police and get them arrested and sent to prison.'

'And if they were above the law?'

'No one is above the law.' Callie frowned.

I looked at her pityingly.

'OK, then. No one should be above the law.'

'What should be and what actually is are two completely different things,' I said with derision. 'The Equal Rights bill should've been made law decades ago, not a week ago. We shouldn't've had to wait for a bent copper in a gang-leader's pocket to be found out before the police started cracking down on the gangs taking over Meadowview.'

'Well, the law is man-made so of course it's going to be fallible,' said Callie. 'But there is such a thing as justice. Justice isn't the same as the law.'

'So what would you do to make sure you got justice, if you knew the person who'd shot you was above the law?' I persisted.

Callie shrugged. At my impatient look, she exclaimed,

'I really don't know, Tobey. I'd want revenge, of course I would. I'm human. But the desire for revenge is like hatred or anger, it eats away at you. And I should know.'

'And what if it was your mum or Meggie who got shot?' I asked.

Why was I doing this? Maybe I just needed to hear her say that what I'd done was not correct, but it was right, that it wasn't lawful, but it was justice and she would've done the same.

'I honestly don't know, Tobey,' Callie sighed. 'Why?'

I shrugged. 'I was only wondering, that's all. It doesn't matter.'

I tried to step past her, but she moved to stand in my way.

'Tobey, you and Misty? Is it serious?'

'Very,' I instantly replied.

'I see.'

This time she let me pass. I opened my bedroom door for her to leave first. As she walked past me, I inhaled deeply but discreetly. Callie didn't smell of my perfume any more.

'I'll see you tomorrow at two,' I confirmed.

Callie headed back downstairs with me following behind. I stretched out my hand towards the back of her head. Was her hair as soft as I remembered? I forced my hand back to my side.

'Oh, before I forget, I think this belongs to you,' Callie dug into one of the pockets on her dress and held out the letter I'd sent to her, the one with all the information about McAuley's shipments. 'Am I right? Is this yours?'

I nodded, wondering what she had made of the information on the sheets of paper. Had she read it? Did she believe I worked for McAuley? I wasn't about to ask.

'I'm afraid I opened it as it was addressed to me, but I stopped reading when I realized what it was,' she told me. 'I thought maybe it was sent to me for safe-keeping?'

I didn't answer.

'I take it you don't want me to hold onto it?'

'No. I'll take it,' I replied.

'Tobey, what happened when I was in hospital?'

'The Earth went round the sun. The tides ebbed and flowed. Life carried on,' I replied evenly.

Callie lowered her gaze momentarily. 'I'd better get back.'

'See you, Callie.'

'Bye, Tobey.'

Callie headed back to her house. I set off in the opposite direction. A conversation I'd had with my sister a while ago kept playing in my head. Jess told me that I'd never understand her until I experienced what all miserable, lonely, unhappy people shared. Only now had I finally figured out what she meant. Failure. I couldn't bear to look at myself in the mirror any more. I was someone I no longer recognized. I thought I could take my revenge on McAuley and emerge unscathed at the end of it. I had failed.

I thought about the stuff I'd poured down McAuley's throat and the gun I'd held against his temple. In that moment, I'd wanted so badly to hurt him. No, that's not true. I'd wanted to *kill* him. And if it had been anyone else but Dan who'd entered the office, by now I'd be a murderer. Who was I kidding? Rebecca was dead because of me, as was Byron. McAuley should've been dead because of me. The drugs I'd made him swallow would've done the job sooner rather than later. Dan had merely put him out of his misery.

Five people dead because of me. Rebecca. Byron. McAuley. The two guards Dan had shot . . .

I *was* a murderer. Now I truly knew who and what I was. No one should ever find out for certain exactly what they're capable of. It left you with no place to hide.

I walked around the block, then headed back home.

seventy-two

Mr Bharadia's conference room was truly impressive. The oval mahogany table was solid wood, not just mahogany veneer. At least I think it was, I'm no expert. I glanced under the table. The legs were carved like birds' claws on a stand. The ten chairs around the table all matched each other and had the same design on the front legs. The back legs were plain. The backs of each chair were also intricately carved . . .

Tobey, what're you doing?

I mentally shook my head. I knew exactly what I was up to. I was trying to take in everything in the room so that I wouldn't have to think about the one thing I was desperate to avoid. Callie Rose. She sat next to me, watching me with puzzled eyes. She was still trying to figure out what was wrong.

We all sat, waiting for Mr Bharadia to make an appearance. Minerva and Sephy were discussing Sephy's forthcoming wedding to Nathan, talking about the best places to buy a wedding dress. I wished Callie would join in their conversation. That way I wouldn't have to speak to her. Deciding to make myself scarce until the solicitor put in an appearance, I tried to stand up, but Callie's hand on my arm stopped me.

'Tobey, we need to talk,' she said softly.

Which was just what I was afraid of.

'How come I've hardly seen you since I've been home?' Callie's voice was barely above a whisper as she tried to keep the conversation strictly between us. Unlike Misty, she didn't believe in making a scene.

'I've been busy.'

'Too busy to even come round and say hello?'

'I've been busy.'

Callie looked at me, hurt clouding her eyes. 'Have I done something to upset you?'

''Course not.'

'Then why won't you even look at me?'

I turned to glare at her, my expression pure biting frost. She flinched. 'Tobey, what have I done? Why am I getting the treatment?'

'Godsake, Callie. Can we just get through the will reading without all this drama?'

'Tobey . . .'

'Callie, leave me alone. For God's sake, just leave me alone.'

The whole room went quiet. I jumped up and left the room before I did something incredibly stupid – like holding Callie and telling her the truth. I hid out in the men's loos until after the meeting was scheduled to start. It was the only way I could make sure that Callie and I didn't enter into the same conversation again. I went into the meeting room, grimly pleased to see that the solicitor had arrived and everyone else was waiting for me.

I sat down again, drawing my chair away from Callie as I did so. Callie kept looking at me, and I kept pretending I didn't see her. The solicitor started spouting some legalese which had me zoning out in seconds. I didn't even know what I was doing here. So Jasmine Hadley had mentioned me in her will. So what? She was probably using this opportunity to warn Callie off or something. This was a complete waste of time.

'Mr Bharadia, could you skip over all the legal jargon, please?' said Sephy, interrupting the solicitor's flow. 'I'm sure everyone here would rather just get to it.'

Apart from a slight tightening of his lips, Mr Bharadia's expression didn't change. He was too much of a professional for that. 'Very well, Miss Hadley. I'll get to the details of the will as you've requested.'

'How long before Mum died did she draw up this will?' asked Callie's aunt Minerva.

'Er, three . . . just a moment.' Mr Bharadia checked the top of the will and another document in the pile of papers before him. 'Yes, three weeks.'

The solicitor was obviously the kind of man who didn't yawn without confirming its date and validity first.

'Three weeks?' Minerva said slowly. 'So when she drafted this, she knew her cancer was terminal?'

Mr Bharadia frowned. 'I believe so.'

Terminal? I didn't know Jasmine Hadley's cancer had come back and was terminal.

'Minerva, what difference does it make?' Sephy asked her sister.

'I just wondered, that's all,' Minerva replied.

The solicitor turned to Minerva first and told her that she and her husband had been left a substantial six-figure sum and that half that sum again had been left in trust for their son Taj, which he would obtain when he was twenty-five years old. Minerva's husband was already a very rich man, but now they were richer. Taj was a lucky boy. How lovely to grow up knowing you had all that money waiting for you. I couldn't even begin to imagine what that would be like. Well, actually I could imagine. I could dream, just like everyone else. Minerva nodded at the solicitor, her face sombre.

Mr Bharadia turned to Meggie. 'Mrs Hadley wrote this letter one week before her death. She asked that it be read out to you before I tell you how much you've been left.'

Meggie nodded, but didn't speak.

Dear Meggie,

You and I were friends a long time ago, and giving up your friendship was one of the biggest mistakes of my life. I made a mistake and then lived in denial for years, blaming you instead of looking in the mirror for the real author of my misery. I really feel

that we'd started to get back to the
relationship we had when our children
were young - as were we. I hope so. Please
know that I think of you as probably the
truest friend I ever had. No amount of money
will ever make up for all the pain and
suffering you've been forced to endure in your
life. No amount of money will ever bring
back what you lost, but I hope that the gift
I leave you will at least ensure that the rest
of your days are spent in some comfort.
Your friend, always,
Jasmine

Mr Bharadia stopped reading the letter and turned back to the will. When he announced how much money Meggie had been left, a collective gasp sounded through the room. She'd been bequeathed the same amount as Minerva. It was six figures and one hell of a lot. Enough to buy a new house outside Meadowview and still have enough to live life as she pleased. I regarded Meggie, but her expression didn't change. Was it more or less than she'd hoped for? Maybe she'd got past the stage of hoping for anything at all.

Mr Bharadia turned to Sephy. '*To my daughter, Sephy, I leave my two houses, all their contents and all attached lands to do with as she sees fit. I truly hope that Sephy will use this legacy to make her life easier — something she has never been particularly good at in the past.*'

Sephy smiled faintly at the last comment.

I knew for a fact that Jasmine's house by the beach was

worth a whole roomful of currency just by itself. I didn't know about her second home, but whatever it was worth, Sephy was a very rich woman.

'Sephy, will you be moving into Jasmine's house now?' asked Meggie quietly.

Sephy regarded Meggie, then smiled. 'Not without you,' she replied. 'I'm not living anywhere without you.'

The relief on Meggie's face was very evident. She looked far happier about that than about the money she'd been left.

The solicitor turned to Sarah Pike, Jasmine Hadley's personal secretary for years and the only other non-family member present. '*To my loyal personal assistant, Sarah Pike, I leave the sum of two hundred and fifty thousand pounds plus my black WMW which she has always admired.*' Sarah allowed herself a big smile, followed by a small sigh.

Well, apart from Callie and myself, everyone in the room had been taken care of. Had Callie's nana left her anything? None of us had to wait long to find out. Mr Bharadia turned to Callie. '*To my darling granddaughter, Callie Rose Hadley, I leave all my stocks, shares, bonds and other equity. The portfolio will be professionally maintained for her until she marries or reaches the age of twenty-five, whichever comes sooner. My fervent hope is that she will not let this money spoil her and will use it to do some good, but the choice is hers.*' Mr Bharadia looked around the table. All eyes were on him, but no one spoke. 'Oh, I beg your pardon!' He started flicking through the papers before him, whilst muttering to himself. 'Ah! Here it is. As of the close of the stock market yesterday, the portfolio is worth . . . two million. That's it. Two million pounds, give or take the odd thousand.'

What was the odd thousand between friends? I stared at Callie. Two million . . . Callie was super rich. She turned to me, shock written large on her face.

'Congratulations,' I said softly.

Someone had taken an acetylene torch to my insides. Callie was rich. I wasn't. And that was the end of that. I hung my head, trying to come to terms with the fact that I was going to lose the one person I cared most about in this world. What was I thinking? I'd lost her long before today, and ironically money had had nothing to do with it.

'*To Tobey Durbridge, I say this,*' Mr Bharadia continued.

My head shot up. Jasmine Hadley had left me a message?

'*Tobey, I know you'll think me an interfering old woman, but age brings certain busybody benefits. In fact, that's about the only positive thing that age does bring. I've decided to stick my nose into your life for my own selfish reasons. Call it my way of atoning for past mistakes if you will. Years ago I had the chance to help someone like you, and to my shame I stood back and did nothing. I'm determined not to let that happen again. Tobey, I want you to finish school and go to university. I want you to make something of your life. Never take no for an answer. Never let doors slammed in your face stop you from moving forward. Grasp life and every opportunity presented to you with both hands. I've watched you over the years and I know how much my granddaughter means to you. So I'll make you a deal. I've set up a savings*' *account in your name. You will be allowed to withdraw up to twenty-five thousand pounds each year whilst you are at school and university. On satisfactory completion of your education, any monies left in the savings account will be yours to save or spend as you wish.'*

I stared at Mr Bharadia, convinced his monotone voice had put me to sleep and I was now dreaming.

'Would you like to know the total amount in the savings account?' asked the solicitor.

I nodded, still stunned. Mr Bharadia flicked through some papers underneath the will he was reading. 'Let's see. Three hundred thousand pounds, plus interest.'

'Mum left Tobey three hundred thousand . . . ?' Minerva couldn't believe it. She wasn't the only one.

'Plus interest,' Mr Bharadia added.

Jasmine Hadley had left me all that money? All the things I'd been through in the last few weeks, all the things I'd done . . . And I had that kind of money waiting for me all this time.

'I don't want it. Any of it,' I said furiously. 'Give it to Callie. Split it between the lot of you. I don't want a penny.'

'Don't be silly, Tobey. That's your money,' said Callie. 'Nana Jasmine wanted you to have it.'

'Not interested. Excuse me.' I got up and headed for the door before anyone could stop me.

Once outside, I kept going. I headed out of the office and along the corridor towards the lift. I pressed the button.

'Tobey . . . Tobey, wait.' Callie came running after me.

Where the hell was the frickin' lift?

'Tobey, what's wrong?' Callie asked, laying her hand on my arm. The warmth of her hand singed my skin.

I drew away from her. 'You should get back in there,' I said.

'Not without you.'

'You belong in there with your family.'

'You're my family too.'

I couldn't take much more. The lift was taking for ever to arrive.

'Callie, go back where you belong,' I told her, heading for the stairs without looking back.

Even though we were fifteen storeys up, I just wanted to run down the stairs and out of the building and to keep going. I wanted to run and run until I left myself somewhere far behind.

'Tobey, wait,' Callie called out, coming down the stairs after me.

'Godsake, Callie. Can't you take a hint? I don't want you with me.'

'I don't believe you.'

I grabbed hold of her arms and pulled her hard towards me, her face only centimetres away from mine. 'I've got what I wanted from you and your family,' I said, adding viciously, 'You were an OK lay and your grandmother has left me a great deal of money. I don't need you or anyone else any more. So do me a favour and get lost. Or better still, run back to your mum and aunt and get them to contest the will.'

I released her and she stumbled backwards, rubbing at her arms where my fingers had bitten into her flesh. Her eyes were shimmering with tears, but none of them fell. I forced myself to look straight at her so she'd get the message. I clenched my fists, despising myself for hurting her. Just despising myself. And even though my insides were churning, even though my throat was so swollen I could hardly breathe and my heart was being squeezed by a merciless hand, I was careful to make sure that none of that showed on my face.

Callie took a halting step towards me, then another. My whole body froze with a wary stillness. What was she doing?

'You're trying to make me hate you,' she said softly. 'But it won't work, Tobey. I think you hate yourself enough for both of us.'

'Just go away, Callie.'

'D'you really mean that?'

'Yes.'

'Would you like me to go away for good?'

'*Yes!*' I shouted. I started down the stairs again.

'D'you wish I'd been killed?' Callie called after me. 'Is that what you're trying to say?'

Her words tripped me up so badly, I had to grab hold of the banister to stop myself from pitching forward. The breath caught in my throat. I couldn't move. My brain kept telling my feet to keep going. Go down the stairs, one step at a time. Run. But all signals seemed to stop at my heart. I heard Callie descending the stairs behind me. She moved to the step above mine so she could look directly into my face.

'And if you really hate me so much, then why did you come to see me almost every day in the hospital – even if it was only for a few minutes?'

'How did you know that?' I whispered.

'You just confirmed what Mum told me,' said Callie.

I didn't answer. I watched her, unable to take my eyes off her face.

'Tobey, you may be my mender of broken things, but now it's my turn.'

'Callie Rose, you don't know who I am any more,' I whispered. 'You don't know the things I've done since you got shot.'

'So tell me,' said Callie.

'You'll hate me.'

'Never happen.'

But I couldn't take that chance. Maybe one day, but not today. I started to shake my head.

'Tobey, just tell me this,' said Callie. 'All the things you think I'll loathe you for, you did them for me, didn't you?'

I didn't reply. I sat down on the hard, cold concrete stair, too tired to even stand any more. Callie sat beside me, just as close as she could get.

'How was your date last night?' she asked.

'Fine.'

'Liar. You walked round the block and went back home.'

'How d'you know that?' I asked, stunned.

'I was in Mum's bedroom. I was looking up at the nearest star and wishing. And when I looked down you were just going back inside your house,' said Callie. 'So I got my wish.'

I closed my eyes. It didn't make any difference. I had to make her see that. I forced myself to look at her, bracing myself for her reaction to what I was about to say.

'Callie, because of me five people are dead, Dan is facing the rest of his life on the run or in prison, and you almost died.'

'But I didn't.' Callie took my face in her hands, her expression now sombre. But she hadn't looked away. Not once. 'Tobey, I didn't die. I'm right next to you. And as for the rest, we'll face that together.'

'No way. I'm in Hell and I'm not dragging you down with me. I have to do this alone.'

'No, you don't—'

'Five people, Callie Rose. Five people are dead because of my actions.' I pulled away from her. 'How do I get past that? How do I even try?'

'Tobey, look at me.'

But I wouldn't. I couldn't.

'Because of me, Nana Jasmine and Uncle Jude died,' said Callie softly. 'D'you hate me for that?'

My head snapped up. I shook my head. I could no more hate Callie than I could sprout wings and fly. Callie and I regarded each other, sharing something deeper and wider than the silence around us. She leaned forward to kiss me. Her lips were warm on mine, but I didn't respond.

'If you tell me to go away, I will,' she said, pulling back slightly. 'If you really don't want me any more, I'll leave. But if you do dump me, I'll just spend the rest of my life wishing that I hadn't come out of my coma.'

Callie's words ripped straight through me.

'Don't say that,' I said furiously. 'Don't ever say that again.'

'It's the truth. I couldn't bear to think that we'll never be together again,' she said, adding with a faint teasing note to her voice, 'Besides, you're my sexbot, no one else's. I saw you first.'

I stared at her. 'You remember? The two of us together, you remember?'

'I remembered the day after I woke up out of my coma. I still don't remember the day of the shooting. My doctor said that may never come back,' said Callie. 'But I remember the night before. I remember every detail. I remember you.'

There was a time when that was all I longed for.

'It's not enough. Not any more.' I started to turn away, but Callie's hand pulled my face back towards hers.

'Tobey, tell me the truth. D'you want me to go?'

Slowly, I shook my head.

'Why not?' asked Callie gently.

Somehow my hand found its way to her face. My fingers stroked against her cheek.

'Because I love you,' I whispered at last.

Everything else I'd known or believed in lay in ruins at my feet. Except for that. That was the only thing that hadn't changed. Callie hugged me, her arms tight around me like she'd never let me go.

She said softly, 'You and me, Tobey, against the world.'

My head on her shoulder, I did something I hadn't done in years and years. The one thing I thought I'd never do again.

I cried.

Epilogue

HEATHCROFT HIGH SCHOOL NEWSLETTER

Congratulations to the following students who have been accepted into university to read the subjects listed:

Student	Subject
Omar Ade	History
Solomon Ajuki	Medicine
Ella Cheshie	Medicine
Alex Donaldson	Modern Languages
Tobias Durbridge	Law
Jennifer Dyer	Geography
Samantha Eccles	Sports Therapy
Connor Freeman	English
Callie Rose Hadley	Law
Rachelle Holloway	Modern Languages
Misty Jackman	Popular Music
Bliss Lwammi	Communications Technology
David McVitie	Marketing
Gennipher Mardela	Maths & Economics
Maxine Mbunte	Physics

. . . *continued on page 4*

Other News

Our school is particularly proud to announce the opening of the Meadowview Shelter, set up and partially funded by one of our students, Tobey Durbridge. The shelter will provide support, help and information for those who seek drug and/or alcohol addiction rehabilitation.